THE KNIGHT
AND THE MONSTERS

Two monsters lumbered from the side-tunnels, reaching for me with their grotesque carrion-hooks.

The ghost horse faltered, turning his head back to look at me. More monsters were converging. "Run!" I cried at him as I poked the point of my sword over my shoulder to stab the face of the monster holding me. Hot ichor sprayed against my neck, and I knew I had scored. "Get out of here, Pook, before they catch you, too!"

The ghost horse took off, and I laid about me valiantly with the sword, hacking off arms and legs and ears as they came within reach. But as I had known, the monsters were too much for me. One scored on my head with a hammy fist, knocking me silly, and another took a huge bite at my face. I felt his tusks sinking into my cheeks.

Then I lost consciousness, just before they killed me.

By Piers Anthony
Published by Ballantine Books:

THE MAGIC OF XANTH

THE APPRENTICE ADEPT

INCARNATIONS OF IMMORTALITY

CREWEL
LYE
A Caustic Yarn

Piers Anthony

A Del Rey Book

BALLANTINE BOOKS ● NEW YORK

All rights reserved under International and Pan-American Copyright Conventions. Published in the United States by Ballantine Books, a division of Random House, Inc., New York, and simultaneously in Canada by Random House of Canada Limited, Toronto.

Library of Congress Catalog Card Number: 84-90936

ISBN 0-345-31309-7

Manufactured in the United States of America

First Edition: January 1985

Contents

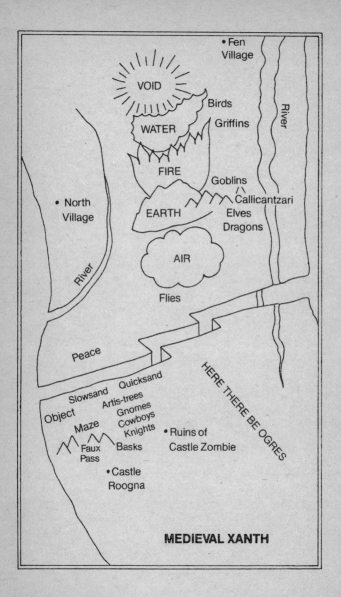

MEDIEVAL XANTH

Chapter 1. Ghost Quest

Ivy was restricted, for no reason at all, to Castle Roogna, and of course it was overwhelmingly boring. Her mother Irene had recently gotten quite fat in the tummy, but kept right on eating and pretending it was wonderful and didn't seem to have much time for Ivy any more. To make things worse, her father King Dor had ordered a baby brother for her. Ivy did not need or want a baby brother. How could they have been so thoughtless as to order something like that without consulting the one most concerned? What good was a baby, anyway—especially a boy?

But now the infernal thing had arrived, and Irene had evidently celebrated by using a thinning spell, because she was suddenly back to normal weight, but she still had next to no time for Ivy. To heck and darnation with all cabbage leaves! Even drear Mundania, she decided, could not be worse than this.

For a time, she played with the items sent by her pun-pal, Rapunzel, who had very long hair and was similarly confined to her castle. Ivy was still too young to read and write, so they exchanged small objects, and that usually worked well enough. But there was only so much a person could do with puncils and hot-cross puns, and Ivy soon tired of them.

She found herself watching the magic tapestry in her room for hours on end and more hours sidewise; the idiot cloth had become her amusement of last resort. Its moving pictures showed everything that had ever happened in the Land of Xanth. But the pictures were fuzzy, and she wasn't much interested in history, anyway. It was so much

1

more fun in the jungle, playing with clouds and tanglers and gourds!

As the tapestry played over a sequence several hundred years in the past, Ivy became aware of company. One of the castle ghosts was in the room. In fact, it was watching the tapestry.

Ghosts did not bother Ivy, of course; in fact, it tended to be the other way around. Ghosts avoided her because trouble seemed to follow only half a footstep behind her, and the haunts of Castle Roogna, like others of their kind, were basically settled creatures. So the presence of this one surprised Ivy, yet hardly alarmed her. She peered at it, but the outlines were fuzzy, and she could not make out which one it was. So she asked, "Who are you?"

"Jordan," the ghost replied faintly. It was hard for ghosts to speak with any volume, because their volume was mostly vapor, but they could do it when they concentrated.

Oh, yes. Jordan was the one who had helped Mare Imbri save Castle Roogna from the Horseman oodles of time ago, before she arrived on the scene. "What are you doing?"

"Watching my history." The ghost became clearer as she concentrated on it, shifting from amorphous cloud shape to humped sheet shape, which was an improvement.

Ivy suffered a flicker of interest. "*Your* history? That's Xanth history, silly!"

"I lived in Xanth four hundred years ago," Jordan said, becoming a vague human form.

"Was it as dull as it is now?"

"No, it was exciting!" the ghost said with greater animation than before. "It was a terrific adventure—I think."

"You think?" Ivy wanted to nail this down, because if there was anything interesting in Castle Roogna, she wanted to find it.

"Well, I died from it."

Oh. "I'm about to die from boredom," Ivy asserted.

"Oh, no," Jordan protested. "You're a Sorceress. You will grow up to be King of Xanth."

This was nothing new, but Ivy's interest increased. Now Jordan was a fully formed man, partly white, partly translucent, fairly large, young, and handsome. A white lock of hair fell down partway over his right eye, which was also white. Most ghosts were white; Ivy wasn't sure why. "How did you die?"

Jordan shook his head. "I can't quite seem to remember. I've been dead a long time."

"But that's easy to remember!" Ivy exclaimed. "Dying is a big deal, like getting born."

"Do you remember getting born?"

"Of course not. Animals get born. *I* was found under a cabbage leaf. I should have kicked over the cabbage behind me, because now they've found Dolph under it and they're making him my baby brother." She pouted, as the memory rankled. "If I'd been smart, I'd have sneaked out at night and thrown all the cabbages into the moat before Dolph arrived. It's probably all his fault I'm grounded."

"Yes, boys are a lot of trouble," the ghost agreed. "Almost as much trouble as girls."

"What?"

The ghost drifted away from her, realizing that he had said something provocative and unwarranted. Everybody knew that boys were much worse than girls. But Ivy decided to forgive him his transgression, because even ghostly company was better than none. "Tell me the adventure of your life."

"Well, I don't quite remember that, either. I know it was exciting, and that there were monsters and magicians and swords and sorcery and beautiful women, but the details have fogged out."

"Then how do you know your life is playing on the tapestry now?" Ivy asked alertly.

"I recognize bits of my life when I see them played. Fighting a dragon, kissing a woman—it begins to come back. I know I was there."

"Fighting a dragon?" Ivy asked. "Not the Gap Dragon?"

"I think I avoided that one," Jordan said. "It's alive today, isn't it? So I couldn't have slain it."

"Good." Because the Gap Dragon had become Ivy's friend, she didn't want anything bad to have happened to him, even four hundred years ago. The Gap was now being patrolled by Stacey Steamer, the female of his kind. Eventually Stanley would grow up and return to the Gap, but that was long ago in the future and she didn't worry about it. "Who'd you kiss?"

The ghost concentrated. "Several beautiful women, I think, but the last was most. There was a cruel lie, and I died. So I hate her. But I found a better woman after I died, so maybe it's all right after all."

This was getting downright fascinating! "How can you find a woman after you're dead?"

"A dead woman, naturally. A ghost, like me."

Ivy had always known the ghosts of Castle Roogna, but hadn't thought to question them about their lives. "What happened to her?"

"She's still here, of course. She's Renee."

"Oh, Renee! I hear her singing sometimes. Faint, sad songs."

"Yes, she is often sad. But she's a wonderful person. If I were alive again, I'd marry her."

"Silly, ghosts can't live again!" Ivy chided him.

"What about Millie?"

Millie the Ghost had been a resident of Castle Roogna for eight centuries, until restored to life. She had married the Zombie Master and now had twin teen-aged children, Hiatus and Lacuna, who on occasion baby-sat for Ivy.

"That was prehistoric," Ivy said shortly. "Back when Good Magician Humfrey was still practicing as an old man. He helped bring her back to life. Everybody knows that. But Magician Humfrey isn't animating ghosts any more, and nobody else knows how. How can *you* live again?"

"Well, my talent is healing," Jordan said. "So if my bones were found and brought together, maybe—"

"Where are your bones?"

"I've forgotten, if I ever knew," the ghost confessed, abashed.

So Jordan represented a mystery. Ivy was now fully intrigued. "This cruel lie—what was it?"

Jordan spread his hands. "I don't remember that, either. I thought if I watched it replayed on the tapestry, maybe—"

"Why not," Ivy agreed. They focused on the tapestry. It showed a towering wall of rock, the face of an almost vertical cliff. Down this cliff a huge snail was crawling—and a man clung to the snail's shell.

"Oh, yes, the snail," Jordan said. "That's me, riding it."

Ivy had never thought of snail-riding, but of course she had never encountered a snail big enough. "Where are you going?"

"I don't remember, but it was somewhere I had to get to."

"Why are you riding it, instead of walking there yourself? That snail's pretty slow."

"I don't remember that, either. But I think I had no choice. Maybe if we could see more detail—"

They peered closely, and the picture enhanced itself somewhat, as things did when Ivy paid attention to them. They made out a shadow, as of some monstrous bird, but they could not tell where the cliff was or how extensive. The progress of the giant snail was tediously slow; it was evident they would have to wait for an hour to see significant progress. That was the problem with the tapestry; it ran scenes through at regular speed. It was possible to reset it, but that tended to jump the picture to some quite different scene, and the original one could be lost for days. So it was necessary simply to let it play through at its own rate if a person wanted to see how a particular scene ended. This was no good for a bored child.

But Ivy's curiosity, once fairly aroused, did not accept denial. "We must find out," she declared. "I want to know all about that snail—and your life, and especially about the cruel lie." She put her hands on her hips, in the manner her mother did, to show the severity of her resolve.

"I'm sure I could remember, if the pictures were clearer," Jordan said.

Ivy contemplated the tapestry. "It's gotten sort of grubby over the centuries," she said. "And I guess my using it to wipe off my hands before dinner doesn't help much, either." Adults always had these pointless rules about clean hands for eating, so Ivy knew it really wasn't her fault, but now she wished she had wiped her hands somewhere else. "Maybe if we can clean it off, it will have better pictures."

They tried. Ivy fetched a bucket and water, but found she couldn't scrub the tapestry clean. The pictures were permanently dull, even when wet. "We need something better to clean it," she said, frustrated.

They tested everything they could think of, but nothing helped. Ivy was getting dangerously close to annoyance, which was another mood she had inherited from her mother. But she was determined to find a way. "Good Magician Humfrey would know, 'cept he's pretty young now," she said. "Still, he's probably better than nothing."

But how was she to get to the Good Magician's castle when she wasn't allowed out of Castle Roogna? Certainly her folks wouldn't take her there right now! Not when they were so confoundedly absorbed with the idiotic new baby. But she just couldn't wait till she was ungrounded; that would be forever or three more days, whichever was longer.

Fortunately, Jordan had a notion. "There's an old night mare shoe in the cellar," he said. "With that you could get in and out of the gourd."

Ivy clapped her hands, delighted. The gourd had turned out to be a pretty interesting place, but the problem of getting out of it made her cautious. She hadn't realized that it was the horse shoes that enabled the night mares to do it, but of course that made sense. One of the mares must have lost a shoe when trying to flee an awakening sleeper, because night mares were never supposed to be seen by awake folk. "Show me!"

Jordan guided her down to the cellar crevice where the shoe lay, and Ivy pulled it out. The thing was made of old rusty metal and was bent in the shape of a U; no wonder the mare had left it behind. "Ooo, ick!" Ivy exclaimed, shaking the gook off it. "How does it work?"

"You have to go into a gourd," Jordan said. "Then you travel through the gourd world until you come to one that's near your destination, and—"

"I know that, dummy! I mean how do I get *in*?"

"The mare shoe should make the rind pervious, so—"

"Where's a gourd?" Ivy was edgy and impatient because she was getting nervous about this business, so she was rushing things before she could make the mistake of thinking about the matter sensibly.

"There's one growing at the castle wall," Jordan said. "It's not supposed to be there, but it's hidden, so no living person has spotted it yet."

"Take me to it," Ivy ordered. She had to go somewhere fast, for her knees were threatening to knock. The gourd world was, after all, the place of bad dreams, and she suspected there were more hideous things in there than the night mares ever let ordinary people see.

Jordan took her to it. It was just outside a large crevice at ground level. She reached through, caught hold of the vine, and hauled the gourd in. "But don't look at the peephole!" the ghost warned.

"I know." Ivy had learned about peepholes recently; it seemed her mother had been perturbed to learn that Grandpa Trent had been into one and somehow had thought it was Ivy's fault. Possibly the grounding had something to do with that. "Now how does—?" She extended the bent shoe toward the gourd.

"Wait!" Jordan cautioned, in the manner adults had. "I think you need a map, to—"

The shoe touched the surface of the gourd—and sank in. Ivy, expecting resistance, lost her balance and fell forward. Her arm passed in and the rest of her did too, though the gourd was much smaller than she was. Suddenly she was inside and falling.

She started to scream, but before she could work it up properly, she landed on something soft. It was a huge marshmallow. So she filed the scream away for later reference, got up, and looked about. This wasn't nearly as bad as she had feared.

She was in a candy garden. Lollipops grew from the ground, and the weeds were licorice. She started to pick a pop, then hesitated; she was inside the gourd. If she ate anything, would she be able to leave? She wasn't sure; the gourd had funny rules. So she exerted supreme control well beyond the call of little-girl duty and left the candy alone. She had a feeling she would regret this the rest of her life, but she couldn't take the chance.

The night mares traveled through Xanth by going in one gourd and out another; there was always a gourd close by a sleeper who needed a bad dream. She had gone in at Castle Roogna; she needed to come out at the Good Magician's castle. But where was it?

Jordan was right; she needed a map—and she didn't have one. Well, she would just have to find her own way.

She walked down the hard chocolate path, past all the delicious-looking and -smelling confections, her mouth watering painfully, until she came to a house made of wood. She knocked on the door, but there was no answer except a faint chittering. So she turned the knob, opened the door, and stepped inside.

The door swung closed behind her. Suddenly the chittering became loud. Things rustled over her feet. As her eyes adjusted to the interior gloom, she discovered that the room was filled with insects. "Ooo, ugh!" she exclaimed with girlish distaste. "This is a bug-house!"

Indeed it was. Bugs of every description crawled on the floor, the walls, the ceiling, and the door behind her. Others fluttered in the air. One bug-eyed monster buzzed up to her, waving its purple antennae.

Ivy used the scream she had saved. She tried to use the mare shoe to fend off the bug, but the shoe missed and struck the wall instead. Shoe and hand sank through the wall, and Ivy stumbled after, stepping through as a ghost might.

She blinked in bright sunlight. She stood on a beach, just outside a gourd. Across the water she saw a large island, and near the island was a raft with a centaur standing on it. That must be Centaur Isle, down at the south of Xanth. She had come a long way!

But that wasn't where she was going. So she nerved herself and touched the mare shoe to the gourd. She was getting the hang of this. She fell right into the bug-house again.

Hastily she opened the door and plunged outside. She remained in the gourd, since she hadn't used the shoe this time. But now the garden was not candy; it had changed radically for the worse. Awful spinach grew all about, along with turnips and radishes and onions and other terrible stuff, the kind that existed only to nauseate children at mealtimes. There were even—horrors!—cabbages. She held her nose and hurried along the garden path until it came to a lake of placid, brownish fluid.

What could this be? Surely not anything worse than mashed squash! She touched her finger to it and tasted a drop, her curiosity leading her unerringly into mischief.

Instantly she spat it out. This was the worst yet! It was castor oil—the stuff used to lubricate rolling castors, the bane of all children.

She looked about. How could she get out of the gourd for another peek at real-life Xanth? She might be close to Humfrey's castle, and didn't want to pass it by. But with no walls to touch—

Then she had a notion. Carefully she touched the mare shoe to the surface of the stinking oil lake. It sank through, drawing her along with it. She held her nose and her breath, closed her eyes tightly, and passed painlessly through the surface to come to rest on firm ground. She opened her eyes and found herself standing in front of a gourd in sight of the Good Magician's castle. She had nerved herself to take the most obnoxious route, which naturally was the proper one, and she was there!

Well, almost. There was the little matter of getting in. She was standing outside the moat; there was no drawbridge, and the walls looked most forbidding.

First she had to cross the moat. She looked around. Under a spreading tree she found several small stones. "Stepping stones!" she exclaimed, recognizing the type.

She picked them up, but they were hard to hold all together, so she reached for a big green leaf to wrap them in. But lo, it was not a leaf; it was the wing of a giant luna moth. The creature was motionless, and just dangled when she picked it up; she realized reluctantly that it was dead. A tear squeezed from her eye; she hated to see pretty things die.

She found some blanket moss, set the stones, moth, and mare shoe on it, and carefully drew up the corners of the blanket so she could carry it as a bundle. She saw herself as a fairly resourceful child, so of course she was. Then she walked to the moat, held the bundle in one arm, and used her free hand to cast the first stone.

The stepping stone plopped onto the surface, bobbled, expanded somewhat, and settled firmly, the top of it just above the water. She tossed a second one a little farther out, and it settled similarly on the surface. When she had a somewhat irregular line of several—for stepping stones never settled regularly, no matter how accurately they were placed—she stepped carefully on the first. It gave slightly but supported her weight; that was, after all, its nature, enhanced by her talent. Incorrectly placed, a stepping stone could become a stumbling block, but she had set these down properly.

She stepped on the second, and the third, then tossed out a couple more. This was nervous business, especially when she stepped across deep water, but she had enough stones and she made it all the way across with one to spare. That was excellent management, if she did say so herself.

Now she was on a narrow bank between the moat and the castle wall. On one side, the bank narrowed until there was no space between the wall and the water, so she couldn't go there. On the other side, it curved around the castle. She was sure there was a door somewhere, so she started walking.

She passed an alcove that was absolutely dark; no light penetrated its depths at all. That was interesting, but not very; she moved on. Then she rounded a corner and encountered blinding brightness. She shaded her tender eyes, but the light squeezed through the crevices between her fingers and pierced her eyelids anyway. It was just too bright!

She retreated around the corner, and the day returned to normal, with only a dull red spot that played tag with her peripheral vision. How could she pass that region? If the door she wanted was there, she would be unable to see it. She might even blunder into the moat and get her feet all wet; that would be awkward to explain to her mother! Irene might have no time for Ivy when Ivy wanted attention, but she would appear like magic the moment those little feet and shoes got wet; that was the way mothers were. Also, Ivy wasn't sure just how fast her sight might recover, after too great an exposure to that light; how awful it would be to be blind! If she came home blind, they would feed her nothing but—screaming horrors!— carrots, because they had a magic yellow ingredient that was good for vision. There was no question about it: she had to find a different way.

"Come on, Ivy," she chided herself. "You're smart enough to figure out how to get through a little light!" Whereupon she became smart enough; confidence was wonderful stuff, especially when abetted by magic.

Ivy returned to the dark alcove and reached inside. Sure enough, there was a dark lantern. She brought it out, and its darkness spread all around her, converting day to night. Fortunately, she was able to see a little dim light ahead, around the corner, and she headed for that.

As she rounded the corner, the effulgence surrounded her—and was met by the darkness radiating from the dark lamp. The two struggled and canceled out, and an approximation of normal daylight returned. A small globe of darkness remained about the lantern itself, into which her arm disappeared, while the bright lantern remained too bright to gaze upon. But in between were the shades ranging from night to day. If Ivy had been of a more philosophical bent, she might have realized that life itself was like that, with the impossible extremes of good and bad at either side and many gradients between, through which normal folk navigated with indifferent success. But she was as yet too young for such a thought, so she shoved it aside and proceeded through the shades of gray until she rounded another corner. Then the dark lamp became too dark, blotting out everything; she set it in an empty alcove and went on.

But a new threat materialized. A small winged cat screeched and circled above her. When she tried to take a step, the cat circled lower, claws extended. This was too little to be a cat-bird; it was a kitty-hawk, and it would not let her pass.

She looked in her blanket bag, where there was one stone, the dead moth, and the mare shoe. She might throw the stone at the creature, but she doubted she could score; the throwing arm of a five-year-old girl wasn't strong. So she left that stone unturned. She needed another way.

As she pondered, the kitty-hawk circled lower. Ivy was right at the edge of its attack range and the creature hesitated. Probably it didn't want to get too close to the brilliance around the corner, as that would blind the kitty-hawk as readily as it blinded her. So this was a safe place to pause.

Ivy watched the creature, noting the separate components of its body. The hawk-wings were of the bird kingdom, with brown feathers, and there was a feathered tail to match; the head and legs were of the cat kingdom, with white teeth and claws. She wondered which kingdom was dominant. Did the creature lay eggs or give live birth? Animals had more direct and crude ways of reproducing themselves than people did; maybe cabbages didn't grow for animals. She blushed to be thinking such naughty thoughts, but still, she was curious. She knew that some creatures birthed and others hatched, or maybe it was the other way around, and people arrived under cabbage leaves, and then there was the matter of the storks—

Ivy frowned, because that reminded her of Baby Brother Dolph again. Too bad the stork *hadn't* brought him, because then there would have been a chance of dropping the bundle into a nest of cockatrices, or maybe onto a bad-tempered needle-cactus. She could almost see the needles flying out, striking the little cockatrices, who naturally glared balefully about, turning everything around them to sludge. Or was it stone? Anyway, the little bird-brained lizards were getting stabbed by flying stone needles, and it served them right.

Ivy caught a flicker of something just off the edge of her vision. It looked like a swishing horse's tail. The day mare! Imbri had brought her the nice, violent day-dream, but now the mare had to gallop off to her next delivery.

There was a yowl. Ivy looked up. The kitty-hawk had come quite close to her and was having some kind of problem. The parts of it had intensified, the cat-head and feet becoming more feline and the bird-wings and tail more avian. Now they were fighting for dominance. The head was reaching around to bite at the wings, and the wings were pounding on the head.

Ivy watched closely, so of course the intensification of separate qualities continued. The fight got worse. Feathers and tufts of fur flew out. Finally the kitty-hawk spun out of control, crashed into the moat, and was gone. This was one experiment of nature that didn't seem to have worked out. The sharpening of its facets, as it had approached Ivy and her violent day-dream, had caused the creature to fragment and destroy itself.

Ivy walked on, glad to be past the kitty-hawk but sad how that had happened. She was still looking for the door into the castle. She came to a small plot that contained a single headstone. It was in the shape of the head of an old man, with sparse stone-gray hair and white whiskers. It looked almost alive, and became more so as she contemplated it; its stony gaze was fixed on her. Slowly one mineral eye closed in a wink.

"You *are* alive!" she exclaimed, startled.

"No, snippet, I'm just cold stone," it said. "I take the form of the head of whoever is buried near me. That is my nature; I'm a headstone."

"You mean you look like—" she began, glancing at the oblong of dirt in front of it.

"Exactly, peanut. Like the loudmouthed old man who is buried here." Actually, he sounded to Ivy like a loud-mouthed golem, but maybe all loudmouths were similar.

"That's interesting," Ivy said. This headstone didn't seem like much of a threat.

"Last year I was planted near a lovely, dead, young woman; you should have seen me then! My surface was like polished alabaster, and my shape was beautiful."

"That's nice," Ivy said, losing interest. "I've got to go now."

"Ah, but if you try to pass me, I'll yell, and you'll get the brush-off," the headstone warned.

"Oh, pooh!" she said. "You can't do anything, rockhead!" She walked on defiantly.

"Intruder alert!" the headstone yelled loudly. "Undisciplined child! Probably a real brat! Give her the brush-off!"

From around the castle flew the most awesomely terrible object Ivy could imagine: a huge hairbrush. She scooted back the way she had come, covering her behind. That headstone hadn't been bluffing!

Ivy backed up against the wall so that her tender posterior wouldn't be exposed. What was she to do now? She couldn't face *that*—or turn her back on it, either.

The brush hovered a moment. Then, spying no naughty posterior, it flew back the way it had come. Ivy relaxed; she had escaped this time.

But she knew with sick certainty that the moment she passed the headstone again, it would cry another warning and that horrendous brush would return. She was stuck. She was a fairly self-assured little girl, but that brush—! She had to figure out a way to be rid of it!

Then she had another notion, for her mind was filled with notions, some of them almost as cute as she was. Suppose she nullified the headstone instead? If she could just stop that loudmouth from blabbing, somehow silencing it—

She looked in her bag again. Maybe she could get creative. Stone, mare shoe, dead moth. Nothing here to—

Then a creative bulb lit up, for an instant flashing as brightly as the brightside effulgence she had so recently negotiated with the dark lamp. Yes, there was a way, maybe!

She marched up to the headstone. "Hi, rockbrain!" she said boldly.

The stone eye eyed her stonily. "You again, twerp? If you try to pass this point, I'll see that you get the brush-off for sure. You won't be able to sit down without blistering the chair!"

"I've got something for you," she said, taking out the dead luna moth. "Let me just scrape out some dirt beside you here—" She dug a little hole.

"That doesn't look like much," the headstone said. "If you dig too deep, you may encounter something you don't like, sweetie-pie."

"I just want to bury *this* closer to you than *that*," Ivy said and dropped the dead moth in the hole. Then she swept the dirt over and patted it firm.

She stood and watched. If what the headstone had told her was true—

It was. The headstone began to change. The human features weathered into anonymity and assumed a greenish cast. Then a new form took shape. It was the head of a luna moth, with furry antennae and lovely color.

"That's very pretty," Ivy said and walked on by.

The stone-moth's antennae waved frantically, but there was no sound, for moths did not make sounds in the human range. The giant brush was not roused, and Ivy passed the dread region without hindrance. She had navigated the final hurdle, thanks to her creativity. She had used a dead moth in a way no one had thought of before.

She walked around to the castle door and pushed it open. A young and pretty woman came to meet her. "Why, hello, Ivy—you surprised me. Why didn't you use the carpet to fly in, as you usually do?"

Ivy didn't care to explain about being grounded; Zora was very nice, but no adult could be completely trusted in a matter like that. "This is business, Zora", she explained. "I have to see Good Magician Humfrey."

Zora shrugged. She was a zombie, but it was almost impossible to tell, for no flesh fell from her. She had been baby-sitting the Good Magician for two years because it was her talent to make people age faster. She was married, but when she turned on her talent, other people became nervous, fearing they were aging, too. Ivy didn't understand why anyone should object to getting older; maybe they had all forgotten what it was like to be a child. But it seemed they did fear age, and the older they were, the more they feared it. So Zora's husband Xavier tended to absent himself when Zora turned on.

Ivy understood the practical aspects of all this, if not the emotional ones, and wasn't worried. She often visited the Good Magician herself, enhancing Zora's talent with her own, so that Humfrey aged at several times the normal rate. It would not be long, as such things went, before he was an adult again; meanwhile, he seemed to be enjoying his second childhood.

Zora escorted her to Humfrey's playroom. The Good Magician was now about Ivy's size, which meant he had averaged about three years for one, for he was small for his age. "Hi, Ivy!" he said. "Come to put some more years on me?"

"No, this is a business call," Ivy repeated. Humfrey she had to trust, even if she didn't want to. He knew everything anyway, or seemed to, that being his talent. Physically, he was now a child, so perhaps would not be inclined to betray her to the grown-ups. "I'm grounded for no reason and had to sneak out."

Humfrey smiled in a too-knowing way. "No reason, as you define it, being the leading of your grandfather in a merry chase through tangler, jungle, and gourd, all because you didn't stay on course or heed his warnings, and causing the Night Stallion to shoot fire from his nostrils when he saw the damage to his haunted house set?"

"That's what I said," Ivy agreed uncomfortably. "No reason at all. So let's make this quick, before I get in trouble for even less reason if they discover I'm gone. I need an Answer."

"That will be one year's service," he informed her. "In advance."

"Well, I've already added more than that to your life by enhancing Zora when she ages you, so we're even. And if I do it much more, you'll owe me another Answer."

Humfrey stared at her belligerently. "What kind of logic is that, woman?"

"Female logic, of course," she informed him. "Want to make something of it?" Ivy already had a fair notion how to handle men, even those who could not readily be charmed.

"Um, no," Humfrey said. "Some distant day you're going to be King of Xanth, may the Demon have mercy on that day."

"I already know that, dummy, so watch your step." She had learned about firmness from her mother, just as she had learned about pedestals from her father. It would never do to let any man get the upper hand. As Irene had muttered ominously, there was no telling where he might put it.

"Okay, okay, where's your Question?" Humfrey asked grumpily.

"I need something to clean up the magic tapestry so Jordan the Ghost can remember."

Another person might have had difficulty grasping this, but Humfrey, young as he was, was the Magician of Information. He had had over a century of experience before being accidentally youthened back to babyhood, along with Stanley Steamer; now his power was returning, as was his irascible nature.

Humfrey pondered a moment, then brightened. "The Big Book should have it," he exclaimed. Ivy knew that some people claimed there was no such thing as a Big Book of Answers for all Questions, but those people had never seen Humfrey's study. The Good Magician went over to a table where a huge tome rested, and he scrambled up on the high stool to reach it. He turned the ancient pages. "Good thing I've learned to read again," he grumped as he pored over the fine print. "Tables...tadpoles... tailspins...talismen...tangle trees...tapestry! Nature of, History of, Present Location of, Abuse of—aha! Cleaning of!"

"That's it!" Ivy exclaimed.

"Quiet, woman, while I'm researching," he snapped.

Ivy opened her mouth to retort suitably, but decided

to restrain herself until Humfrey produced the Answer. Timing was important when dealing with men, as her mother had said. Anyway, it was no insult to be called "woman." She was glad he hadn't paused to read the entry under "Abuse of" because that very well might mention the wiping-off or laying-on of hands on its surface, which would be awkward to explain.

"Use crewel lye," he read. "Recipe as follows: half a tumbler of—"

"Wait, I can't remember a whole recipe!" Ivy protested. "I have trouble remembering the recipe for hard-boiling an egg! I need a written copy—and no big words." Ivy was learning to read, but preferred words like "Fun" and "Joy" to ones like "Delinquent" or "Punishment."

Humfrey blew air through his cheeks, exactly as he would when a century or so older. "Then fetch me that copy-cat."

Ivy looked where he pointed. In a corner sat a creature like a contracted caterpillar, with only four legs, one tail, and several long whiskers. It looked rounded, furry, and soft, but evinced an attitude of independence and aloofness.

She went and tried to pick up the creature, but it sort of slid through her hands and remained on its soft pillar. She tried to haul it up by the tail, but its eyes glowed in yellow slits, claws sprang out from its paws, and it yowled, so she desisted. It certainly was a strange animal!

Then Ivy tried another system. She walked in front of it. "Here, copy, copy, copy, copy!" she called. And the copy-cat came, walking exactly the way Ivy was walking.

When they reached the table, she pointed to its surface. "Jump, copy!" She jumped herself, to show how it was done, and the copy-cat jumped. But it jumped just the way she did, up and down on the floor.

So Ivy scrambled up on the table herself, to the Good Magician's annoyance. "Up!" she called, and the copy-cat scrambled up beside her.

"Don't stand on the pages!" Humfrey cried, grabbing the copy-cat and plunking it down on the page. "Copy that copy, cat."

The cat sat on the crewel lye recipe. It purred. In a moment it opened its mouth and extruded its tongue, which was a sheet of paper.

Humfrey tore off the paper—an act that startled Ivy—and handed it to her. "There's your copy. Now go away."

Naturally, Ivy got ready to argue, but realized that she *wanted* to go away, now that she had what she wanted, so she kept silent. Sometimes the directives of men had to be obeyed, when they chanced to be correct, annoying as that was. She scrambled down off the table and left the little Good Magician to his reading. He had become entirely distracted by the text before him, which happened to be taxidermy, while the copy-cat continued to extrude copies of the crewel lye recipe. A copy fell down before him, obscuring his text, at which he stared at the cat speculatively. "Very interesting techniques here," Humfrey murmured. "I wonder—" but at that point the cat hastily jumped clear of the text, not having the same interest in studying, or in being a subject for, taxidermy that Humfrey had.

The Gorgon greeted Ivy as she departed. The Gorgon was an elegant, tall, veiled woman with snake hair, the Good Magician's wife and the mother of Hugo, Ivy's friend. "Won't you stay for a cookie, dear?" she asked.

Ivy started to decline, but the Gorgon produced the biggest, loveliest, most aromatic punwheel cookie imaginable, and Ivy was overwhelmed. She realized that the Gorgon was probably lonely for living female company, so it would be only proper to visit for a while. She decided to stay for one cookie.

In due time, Ivy returned to Castle Roogna with the recipe, retracing her route through the gourd. No one had missed her except the ghosts—which, of course, was part of her problem. All anyone paid attention to these days was the confounded baby. She'd like to drop him into the peephole of a gourd, without the mare shoe!

But now she could clean the tapestry and get Jordan's complete story. All she had to do was use the recipe to make the cleaner. Fortunately, the ghosts knew where all the supplies were. Ivy got a pot and some lye and some

fat and stuff and cooked them together according to instructions. The lye was strong stuff that tried to burn her
little hands, but the recipe told her how to be careful.
Jordan's friend Renee Ghost helped Ivy to read the more
difficult parts of the instructions, so that she made no
mistakes. She had to say several spells along the way, to
tune the lye into the crewel, but finally she had a bottle
of the elixir.

She got a sponge, soaked it with her lye mix, and wiped
it across the surface of the tapestry. The result was star-
tling. There was a swath of much brighter and clearer
images. The stuff was working!

Ivy went carefully over the entire tapestry until it fairly
shone. The moving pictures looked so real she almost
believed she could walk into them. "Oh, yes!" Jordan
exclaimed. "I can see every detail! The memories are
flooding back!"

"Now tell me your story," Ivy ordered him.

She settled back before the tapestry, watching, while
Jordan concentrated on the beginning of his story. With
Ivy's help, because the ghost could not make the tapestry
respond by himself, he got the correct sequence of pictures to form. Then, as the pictures showed the action,
Jordan narrated the story as he remembered it. He skipped
over the dull parts, such as sleeping, and lingered on the
good parts, such as fighting monsters and kissing fair
maidens and encountering strange magic. It was a genuine
tale of Swords and Sorceries and Goods and Evils and
Treacheries, and Ivy was entranced. She loved tales with
guts. She watched and heard the caustic yarn as if she
were there herself. She thrilled to the Thud and Blunder
of it and suffered fervently with the revelation of the Unkind Untruth.

Chapter 2. Pooka

I believe it really started when I came of age. It was the fashion in those days for a young man to prove himself by indulging in some fantastic exploit; then he could marry and settle down, having earned his fame.

I had a wonderful girlfriend, Elsie, who could turn water into fine wine just by touching it with her little finger, and she was pretty and sensible, and she wanted to get married and start a family right away. I just wasn't ready for that yet; it sounded so dull. I wanted adventure!

This was getting very difficult. Elsie really wanted me to stay, and she didn't care about heroic tradition, and she was certainly attractive. We were having some awkward scenes. I promised her that, after I had my adventure and became a hero, I would return to her, but this was really a lie, because we both knew I would never get tired of adventure. She promised me that, after we started a family, she would let me go out and travel in Xanth and maybe slay a dragon or two, but we both knew that was also a lie, for a family never lets go of a man. I wanted to sow my wild oats first; that way I would be sure of them.

Elsie really wasn't very keen on wild oats; I'm not sure why. So finally we made a deal: Elsie would have one night to show me how nice tame oats could be and demonstrate the advantages of family living, to persuade me to stay. If she couldn't, then I would travel. It seemed fair enough.

Little did I know what kind of night she planned! I was really pretty naive in those days and knew a lot less about a lot of things than I thought I did. I supposed she was going to feed me good food and treat me well and talk to me convincingly about the advantages of the settled life. Instead she—well, I'm not sure I should say much about this to—in fact, I think we'd better just skim the pictures on past that night and—No? But I could get in trouble with your folks if I said too much about—well, all right, I'll describe just a little of it.

Elsie met me wearing a gown that—well, I had known she was pretty, but hadn't quite realized how pretty she could be when she really tried. I found myself staring at— at the way she breathed. And the way she sat. Then she took me inside her, uh, bedroom, and I followed her and found myself staring at the way she walked. Then she— this is really pretty dull, so maybe we should skip this scene—No? Um, well, she showed me how to send a message to the stork, and I agreed that this was all the adventure I ever needed, and we finally fell asleep.

But in the morning I remembered about the other type of adventure, exploring strange places and fighting strange creatures, and I knew I had to try that first. Elsie was still asleep, half smiling, and I felt really terrible as I dressed and buckled on my sword. But I didn't even kiss her; I just sneaked out of the house like a grounded child and started walking south, toward the center of Xanth, where the real action was supposed to be.

Guilt followed me like a lowering cloud, because my promise during the evening had turned out to be another cruel lie, and I almost turned back again. But the lure of the adventurous wilds drew me on and it was stronger than my guilt.

Somehow I didn't feel very bold or heroic at the moment. I felt more like a coward, for I had not had the courage to wake Elsie and tell her honestly, "I'm going, gal, sorry about that." She would have—well, women can be very difficult about that sort of thing. And once I was fairly on my way, I lacked the courage to return and apologize. Some heroes aren't very courageous or heroic inside.

But now I was committed and I had to look forward instead of back. Already I had learned a lesson of life:

that the sweetest, saddest thing is what-might-have-been. I suspected I was doing wrong and would pay some hideous price for it, but still I kept doing it, ashamed to confess that wrong.

The wilds of Xanth were wilder in those days than they are today, I think, and many strange creatures and magics existed that no longer exist today. The plants had not yet learned the proper respect for man, and the dragons came even to our village of Fen to gobble people. That was why we had a warrior tradition; we needed bold young men to fend off stray monsters. We were near the northeast border of Xanth, beside what was later to become known as the Ogre Fen, but at that time the ogres were far away, still migrating clumsily northward. My boots tended to bog down in the interminable reaches of the fen, and I soon realized that it was a long way to the heart of Xanth, where the fabulous Castle Roogna stood. It would take me forever or so to get there by foot, and I found I really didn't like walking. I needed a ride.

That was a problem. There weren't any centaurs in our isolated region of Xanth, and dragons did not make good steeds—they tended to conspire to carry their passengers inside their bodies instead of outside—and I was afraid to fly with a flying creature; never could be quite sure where one of those might drop you off. I knew there were sea-horses in the sea, but I was trekking inland. There was a man in Fen Village who made hobby-horses, but I hadn't thought to check with him before starting off. In any event, his horses didn't really carry people, they just seemed to. What was I to do?

I knew what: I had to toughen my legs so I could walk all day without getting so fatigued that I lost the pleasure in the adventure. So far, adventure wasn't really much fun. There was a lot to be said for staying home and starting a family. I almost turned about—but again found I could not. To turn back then, I would have to admit my error—that I had been wrong to leave Elsie. That was more difficult to do than fighting a dragon. If I had not been wrong, I think I could have turned back; but since I *was* wrong, I could not do it.

I think now, after four hundred years as a ghost to reflect on philosophical matters—ghosts are better with intangibles than they are with tangibles, because they are intangible themselves—that women are more practical than are men, and the reason that women have most of the sex appeal is to enable them to lure men away from the foolishness they are otherwise prone to seek. Certainly my adventure, when considered as a whole, was a consummate exercise in folly, and would have been even if it hadn't cost me my life. I could have had night after night with Elsie; instead I courted—and won—disaster. If vanity be the name of woman, folly is the name of man!

So I walked on—and fate came to me, undeserving as I was. At first it didn't seem good, but that is often the way of things. The bad seems good, like a pleasant path leading to the tentacles and maw of a tangle tree, and the good seems bad, like the pooka.

It was dusk, and I had scrounged up some sugar sand and tapped a beer-barrel tree for beer, the true barbarian beverage. My head was spinning pleasantly, detaching my mind from my tired feet, when I heard the sinister rattling of a chain. Now, I was young and foolish and a coward about personal relations, but very little of the physical world scared me. Yet this rattle did—and that brought me alert. If that sound sent a cold shiver along my spine, it had to be because it was *meant* to—and that meant magic. Therefore I was intrigued, for strange magic was part of what I sought. I had the sword; I needed the sorcery.

I quickly got up, drew my sword, and stalked the rattle. I heard it again, farther away, so I hurried to catch up. But still it was distant, leading me through the wildest and most desolate landscape. The trees were silhouetted by fuzzy moonlight and looked like gnarled giants frozen in place. But one was not frozen; when I brushed against it, its tentacles grabbed for me, and I realized that I had blundered into the clutches of a tangler, one of the most fearsome vegetables of Xanth. So I slashed about me with my blade, severing the tentacles, and the tree quickly let me go. My sword was not magic, precisely, but it was good and sharp, and I wielded it well; I really did not fear a tangle tree, either. To a barbarian, cold steel is the answer to most problems and, you know, it's a pretty effective answer. I suppose I might have felt otherwise if my magic talent had been different; I actually could afford quite a bit of foolishness.

After that, I realized that the rattling chain was only leading me into mischief. I was playing its game. But I remained intrigued by it; the sound had become a challenge, a minor adventure in itself. So I decided to get smart and make it play *my* game.

I returned to my camping spot. Sure enough, the rattle followed me, coming closer. But on the way I foraged in the darkness for some rustleweeds and centipede grass, and I set them at my place under a chocolate-smelling cocoa-nut shell. Naturally they rustled and scrambled faintly, so that it sounded as if a person were lying there somewhat restlessly, as he would if disturbed by a rattling chain. Then I sneaked silently away—I was good at that sort of thing—and circled widely around behind the chain rattle.

Sure enough, I fooled it. Barbarians are very cunning about such things. I watched as it approached my campsite, wondering why I no longer spooked. Spooks don't like to be ignored! It came over a ridge and I saw it in silhouette against the moonlight—and it was a night mare. No, not a mare, I realized after a moment, for several reasons. The mares did not tease sleepers with distant sounds; they came right in to deliver their bad dreams, then trotted on to the next. They did not have time to fool around, for there were many dreams to deliver. Besides which, I wasn't asleep. And this was no mare; it was a colt. Maybe a stallion. A shaggy, wild thing hung with chains; that was how it rattled. It was, in fact, a pooka—a ghost horse.

A horse. My barbarian brain began to percolate. I could use that horse! But how could I catch it? I was sure that it was at least halfway solid, because its chains rattled, so they were solid, and it had to be solid enough to carry them. But it could simply outrun me—which was one reason I wanted it. Not only would travel be easier with a horse, but would be faster, and I would be able to carry more. Besides, the challenge interested me; as far as I knew, no one had ever captured a pooka before. So this was exactly the sort of adventure I sought. Think of the amazement if I rode back into Fen Village on a ghost horse!

But I was very tired now; contrary to carefully fostered myth, barbarians do get tired on occasion. It would be better to get a night's rest and commence the pursuit in the morning. On the other hand, the creature could be long gone by then, so I didn't dare wait.

I sighed. It would have to be now. Fortunately, I was a robust young man, so my fatigue was an inconvenience, not a crippling thing. I organized for the chase.

First I used my sword to cut some supple long vines to serve as rope for a lariat, since I wanted to capture, not kill, this creature; that was a more difficult matter. I wasn't sure it was possible to kill a ghost horse, but I didn't want to take the chance. Naturally I had practiced with ropes in the course of my preparations for herodom and had a pretty good touch; it is one of the basic uncivilized skills. Then I started off.

Of course the pooka realized almost immediately that I was pursuing him; ghost horses are quite alert about such things. With a rattle of chains, he took off. I could not come close to matching his pace, but I could see his hoofprints in the moonlight, and the continual clink of the chains enabled me to follow him more readily by ear.

I plodded on, giving short shrift to whatever got in my way. I didn't like traveling by night, for the only class of menaces that is worse than that of the day-wilderness is that of the night-wilderness. But maybe the night-horrors realized that I was tired and irritable and not to be trifled with, for none attacked me. Maybe I was just lucky. Some fools have phenomenal luck, and of course they need it.

So I kept the clink of the chains just within audible range, for the pooka had not expected me to persist in the pursuit and kept pausing to forage. That confirmed that it was solid; true ghosts didn't have to eat. At that

point, in my mind, the pooka changed from "it" to "he."
It is a ghost; *he* is a living creature. I don't claim that this
was deep thinking on my part; it was just the way I saw
things.

I realized that the pooka had teased me simply because
I was there; it had been a chance encounter. Now I was
overreacting, and the ghost horse was uncertain. He didn't
know that I intended to capture him. He would stand for
a while in silence, thinking I would lose him without the
rattle; but I always walked directly toward the last chain
sound I had heard, using my unerring primitive sense of
direction. Inevitably he would move again. He couldn't
walk or run without those chains sounding off; that was
his curse. If this had not been the case, I never would
have been able to track him, either by night or by day.
At least, not so readily.

Morning dawned, and the pooka had led me generally
southwest. At that point, as the sun got ready to heave
itself up into the sky, he found a hidden thicket and froze.
I couldn't hear him and I couldn't see him, and the brush
was so thick I knew I would make so much noise searching
it that the pooka might escape, his chain clinks drowned
out. So I waited, and it became a siege. I knew he was
near, but had to make him move. And of course he was
determined not to move, having tired of this game.

I made good use of the wait. I snoozed. I really needed
that sleep!

But I woke instantly at the clink of the chain. The
pooka was trying to sneak out! He thought I was one of
the civilized sleepers who wallow so deep in dreams they
can't break free for six hours at a time. Not me! I knew
when I planned to go adventuring that I could never afford
to tune out the wilderness, so I had learned to wake the
moment anything threatened and to sleep again the moment the threat was gone. Wild creatures sleep that way,
and I was pretty wild myself. So that single little clink of
a link alerted me, and I unkinked my legs and set off in
renewed pursuit.

Now the pooka bolted. I followed, feeling better, though
I really hadn't had enough sleep. I had held the trail through

the night and gotten just as much rest as the pooka had. I grabbed edible berries from bushes as I walked, feeding myself; there again I had an advantage, for the pooka had to pause to graze and could not do that while running. He was probably getting really hungry now. I realized, now that I thought about it, that anything solid enough to carry heavy chains had to take in energy-food.

I passed a region where the bushes had twice as many berries, for each was double. I was about to pop the first twin-berries into my mouth when I hesitated. I had, of course, familiarized myself with many natural things, so that I could safely forage in the wilderness, but these were strange. Something nagged; Something about twin-berries, paired berries, double-berries—

I froze. Berry-berries! They were poisonous, causing weakness, paralysis, and wasting away. But the effects were slow, so that a person could eat a lot of them before being affected—and that would be too late. Of course my magic talent would protect me from serious damage, but while it was acting, the pooka could have gotten away. Better not to get into trouble to begin with!

However, I had a cunning primitive thought. I might be able to use those berry-berries for my own advantage sometime. So I harvested a number and put them in my bag. I noticed there were no B's buzzing around the plants that still had flowers; perhaps that had helped alert me. B's stayed strictly away from berry-berries, so that the berries could even be used as a B repellent.

Then I plowed on after the pooka, who obviously had had the sense not to nibble on these berries. Had he led me through here deliberately? I wasn't sure. Animals aren't supposed to be too smart—but then neither are barbarian swordsmen. Prejudices can be deceiving.

I came to hoofprints leading clearly to a line—and beyond that line was nothing. Not a cliff, not a wall, just—nothing.

Now, I always did get a little nervous about things I didn't understand, such as marriage and family, and I certainly didn't understand this. Was it magic? I had heard of magic mirrors that a person could step into and be in the reverse land beyond, and I knew better than to look into the peephole of a hypnogourd. But it looked as if the pooka had crossed this line and disappeared, so it seemed I would have to follow if I wanted to catch him. Then again, those berry-berries—exactly how cunning was this creature?

I decided to double-check. A little caution seldom hurts anyone. Another myth about barbarians is that they charge straight ahead heedlessly into danger; in truth it is the ignorant civilized man, blundering in the jungle, who does that. No barbarian ever walked blithely into a tangle tree! Well, yes, I *did* do that at night, but that was a special situation, and I had my sword ready.

I retraced the suspiciously clear hoofprints—and discovered another set diverging behind some bushes. This occurred on turf, where the traces wouldn't have been visible to the average person, but of course I had a keen wilderness eye. The pooka had walked up to the line, stopped, then carefully backtracked, setting each hoof in its own print, so as to make it seem he had crossed.

That was warning enough for me. I would not cross that line! Later I learned how smart my decision was; the line was the boundary of the Void, from which no creature returned. The pooka had led me to a pretty trap indeed!

This, however, showed how clever an animal he was. Now, more than ever, I wanted him for my steed. I followed the new trail and soon spooked the ghost horse back into motion. He had been standing in another thicket, watching me approach. The devil!

Now I was twice as determined to capture him. I pursued him with such determination that I hardly felt my fatigue. When he paused, so that I could neither hear nor see him, in some location where the trail was confused, I paused too, napping; when he moved again, I moved. I could tell he was getting nervous—and ravenous.

He was now fleeing southeast. This took me through a pleasant region filled with birds of every size and description. Some of them were pretty big; in fact, I saw a roc-bird circling overhead, but I wasn't too nervous because I knew I was too small to interest it. The pooka was another matter, though; I saw the roc swoop down and realized with horror that it was going for the ghost horse.

Quickly I unslung my bow and charged forward. I crested a ridge just in time to see the big bird lifting the pooka in its claws. But the chains added to the weight of the horse, off-balancing the bird, and it hesitated. Quickly I loosed a shaft. It sped directly to the bird's feathered rump. Of course, my arrow was no more than a little thorn to a creature that size. But the thorn must have lodged in a tender spot, because the bird let out an indignant, O-shaped squawk and dropped the pooka.

The pooka galloped away with a loud rattle and scooted past a tangle tree where the roc couldn't follow. The big bird screamed in fury—and oriented on me. Have you ever seen an angry roc? You never want to! The thing launched itself toward me, and its wings spread so wide they blotted out the light of the sun. I raised my sword, but I knew it was hopeless; this creature was simply too *big* for me to fight.

The talons came down, grasping for me—but they were so huge and spread so wide that they missed me; I passed right through their mesh. Perceiving this, the roc grabbed again, this time plunging its claws into the ground around me. They hooked into dirt, rock, turf, and a medium-sized tree and swept all up together, with me in the center.

I laid desperately about me with my sword as the bird took off. I struck at the nearest talon, which was as thick as my thigh, and severed it with a single mighty-thewed blow. Blood spurted out of the artery in its center, and the ground that talon had supported crumbled. Blood soaked the divot, further weakening the structure. The scooped-up tree fell through, and I tumbled through with it. We plunged in a messy mass to the ground from the height of a standing tree.

It was a bad fall, made worse by the gory dirt. I was knocked half silly, and my condition was not improved when several fair-sized rocks landed on me, crushing my legs. I don't know how other heroes manage to escape injury when caught in horrendous situations; certainly I had no such charm. I did the sensible thing—I lost consciousness.

I recovered an hour later, my crushed leg healed. Oh, didn't I mention this? My magic talent is healing myself. If I am cut, it will seal up immediately if small, and in minutes if large. If I lose a finger, it regrows. If I lose a foot, it takes about an hour to regenerate. If I am killed by an arrow through the heart, I will recover in a day. Longer, if no one pulls out the arrow. So my crushed leg was a job for an hour, and I was as fit as ever. Maybe fitter, because the restored leg wasn't tired, the way the other one was.

Evidently the big bird had left me for dead. That was a natural mistake. Similar confusions had happened before. I was, in fact, practically indestructible in any permanent sense. That was one reason I liked adventure. I had good magic for a hero.

So now I resumed the pursuit. The ghost horse hadn't gone far. Thinking me out of it, he was grazing nearby. Yes, he was hungry!

I yelled and bore down on him. He looked up, startled—and reacted as if he'd seen someone risen from the dead. Terrified, he took off, leaving half a munch of grass to drop to the ground behind. One might think a ghost horse would not be afraid of other ghosts, but that's not so; even ghosts fear what they don't understand, and the average ghost is a pretty timid creature. I ought to know! And, of course, a pooka isn't a complete ghost, because of that solidity; it's sort of in a halfway state, much the way a zombie is halfway between life and death. If the pooka ever slipped his chains, he'd fade into full spirit status. But the chains hold him to life, so he must graze and do most of the other things living creatures do, however inconvenient some of them may be. There are a number of things like that in Xanth, neither this nor that, but partaking of some of this and other of that.

The chase was on again. The pooka fled southeast— and led me into griffin country. I could tell by the old spoor, the claw marks on the trunks of trees, and the griffin manure. I kept alert, for griffins can be aggressive

creatures. I figured I could handle one griffin, but sometimes they traveled in prides, and that could be trouble.
The roc had left me because I was too small a morsel to
bother with, and it would have gotten dirt on its beak just
scooping up my body. But griffins would eat me, and I
wasn't sure how easy it would be for me to recover if
that happened. Maybe if one of them ate most of me, I'd
be able to collect myself together again—but I didn't care
to risk it. For one thing, injuries hurt me just the same
as they do other folk, until they heal; why endure all that
pain if I didn't have to? So I was careful. Maybe barbarians were supposed to laugh at scars as if they never felt
a wound, but the humor of that escaped me.

The pooka, hungry and tired, was less careful. He
charged right through a griffin-retreat, where there was a
big nest in a low-branching tree. A griffiness was on the
nest, incubating an egg or something—I'm not quite clear
on that aspect, as griffins are fussy creatures with royal
lineages and don't tolerate much snooping—and she let
out an awful squawk at this intrusion. The male griffin
had been snoozing on a branch up higher in the tree, his
wings folded while his claws gripped the bark. Startled,
he jumped right off the branch and plunged like a rock,
or maybe I mean a roc, before he spread his wings and
pulled out of the dive. He wasn't one bit pleased. I suspect I wouldn't be, either, waking up like that, with a
woman screaming at me about some creature violating
her privacy. Maybe that's another reason I was wary of
marriage; like the boundary to the Void, it's apt to be a
one-way trip into who-knows-what.

It took only a moment for the male griffin to catch on
that the pooka had started this. He wheeled in the air and
swooped after the ghost horse, who had recovered sense
enough to gallop out of there at top speed. I followed as
fast as I could.

The pooka was fast, despite the chains, when he ran
full-out; but so was the griffin in flight, and he wasn't
carrying any extra weight. I think, if the pooka had been
fresh or had better running turf, he could have escaped.
But the ground was getting marshy here, and there were

many trees, so the terrain hampered the ghost horse somewhat. The griffin was able to swoop efficiently around the
trees, so he gained.

The griffin pulled up above the pooka and pounced—
and I was too far away to do anything. I could only run
after them, and watch. Even if I had been within arrow
range, I'm not sure I would have used my bow, because,
if I killed the griffin, it would have left the griffiness alone
on her nest, unable to forage without leaving her egg or
whatever, and I really didn't like to do that. Meeting a
griffin in battle is one thing; messing up nesting arrangements is another. Yes, I know this sounds foolish, but
you can't live in the wilderness long without developing
a solid respect for the creatures there. These griffins had
not been looking for trouble; the pooka had started it
because I was chasing him, which really made the whole
thing my fault. I can kill creatures when I'm right, but
not when I'm wrong. So I was really pretty well helpless,
regardless.

The griffin landed on the pooka's back, and his beak
pecked down—and struck one of the chains. Ouch! The
griffin, dazed by the pain, tried to fly up and couldn't,
because one of his claws was caught in another chain.

The pooka bucked, trying to throw off the griffin; the
griffin wanted to go, but could not. Then the pooka charged
under an overhanging branch, and that scraped the griffin
off, the hard way. He fluttered, turning over in the air,
and bounced on his back on the ground. Little stars and
planets of discomfort radiated out from him as he bounced.
He scrambled upright and took to the air again, unsteadily, trailing lingering squiggles of confusion and dismay.
He had forgotten about the pooka, who did not linger to
remind him. The griffin lurched back toward the nest-
tree, radiating evanescent wattles of sweat. One hardly
ever sees a griffin sweat! I ran on after the ghost horse.

The marsh grew marshier, as such things tend to do,
and my boots squished in it. I didn't like this, but had to
keep after the pooka. The ghost horse didn't like it, either.
He veered south, heading for higher ground, but it became
apparent that the mountains visible to the south were too

far away to do much good for some time. So he turned west, and I followed, and we slogged up toward a bright wall. Evidently this region was outside the pooka's normal range; he wasn't quite certain where he was going.

The closer we got to the wall to the west, the brighter it became—and the worse the land got. Now it was a virtual bog—and triangular colored fins appeared in it, traveling at high speed. A green one came near me and rose up out of the muck; I saw that it was a big fish with a mouthful of teeth. The fish leaped at me, teethfirst, so I whipped out my trusty sword and stabbed the creature in the snout.

"Ooo, ouch!" the fish cried, plopping back into the muck. "You didn't have to do that! All I wanted was to loan you something."

I didn't trust talking fish. "What did you expect in return?"

"Only an arm and a leg," it replied.

"Well, I'm not interested. leave me alone, or—"

"That's what I'm trying to do! Leave you a loan. I'm a loan shark."

"I don't care if you're a lone shark or a hundred sharks, I don't want to see your green back near me! Take off, or I'll lop off your fin."

The thought of losing its finback discouraged the fish, and it swam rapidly away.

But the pooka was having more trouble. Three of the fins, red, blue, and yellow, were circling him hungrily, and he was mudded down in the bog. He slogged through the slough toward the west wall. But now I could see that it was a wall of fire. That was no good!

I forged toward him, waving my sword to scare away the fish. "Move off," I cried at them, "Or I'll saw your bucks in half." The fish hesitated, not wanting to experience this sawbuck. But the pooka saw my waving weapon and was scared away himself. He plunged for the firewall.

"No, wait!" I cried. "I'm trying to help you!"

But he continued, more afraid of me than of either the fins or the firewall, and soon he reached the latter. Now the heat stopped him. He couldn't pass that fire, but the fish hemmed him in behind. The red and blue fins were spiraling closer; the yellow, more fearful, circled farther out.

The pooka wrenched a forefoot out of the bog and struck at the red fin, but the effort mired the other three legs deeper. He was in real trouble! I shoved toward him, and now he couldn't flee me. But I wasn't sure how I could save him, let alone capture him.

The blue shark forged in at the pooka's side and tried to take a bite; its teeth crunched on chains. I saw little sparks fly up as enamel met metal; that must have hurt! The fish retreated, but did not depart.

Now at last I got there. The pooka was afraid of me, but so badly mired he couldn't move. "Look, Pook," I said. "All I want is to ride you. When I get where I'm going, I'll let you go. It's not a fate worse than death! And death is what you'll get here. If you don't drown, the sharks will skin you alive. Wouldn't you rather travel with me?"

The pooka just looked at me as if I were halfway tetched. I'm not sure he understood me. Animals vary in Xanth; some are smarter than people, but most are not. Maybe my voice reassured him, that and the fact that I wasn't trying to kill him. Maybe he was just so mired he couldn't budge.

The red fin launched itself at me. I chopped at it with my blade, severing the fin from the body exactly as I had warned the greenback I would, and this redneck swam raggedly away. Now the water was red, too!

But the blood attracted more fins. From all over the bog they converged, the colored light reflecting in what someone in a less precarious situation might have considered pretty. "Pook, we're in trouble!" I said. I slogged right up against him. He tried to flinch away from me, but could not. I climbed on his back, and my weight shoved him deeper into the muck. Then the first fin arrived; I lashed at it with my sword and cut it off the fish. Immediately six other sharks pounced on the wounded one and tore it to pieces. An arm and a leg? These monsters were out for anything they could get!

Another came at us, and I served it likewise—and so did its companions. And a third. Supported as I was, I could reach a full circle with my sword. Not one fin got close enough to bite before being severed. Soon the muck around us was a morass of gore.

After a time, so many sharks had been eaten that the remaining ones were gorged. The circle of fins widened and fell apart; they were no longer interested in us. As I have said, brute force and swordplay may not be the answer to every problem, but there are times when they are good enough.

The pooka was now up to his shoulders in muck. Before long the stuff would reach his head, and he would drown in dirty blood. I had to do something!

"Look, Pook," I told him. "I'm on your side. I want to help you. I saved you from the fins. I helped you escape the roc and the griffin before. Now I've got to get you out of here—but I don't know how. So I'll try to find a way. You just hang on here. I'll be back as soon as I can; keep your chin up." I dismounted and stood in the muck beside him.

Well, could I pull his feet out, one by one? I reached down along one hind leg, gripped it as deep as I could, and hauled. It did not come up; I sank down. That was no good.

I looked at the firewall. It was not as hot as I had first thought, and I could see vague shapes through it. Was it thin? I decided to find out.

I took a deep breath, closed my eyes, ducked under the bloodwater, and pushed toward the firewall. When I hoped I had gone far enough, I came up—and found myself in a burned-out forest. The firewall was behind me, and evidently the fire had recently left this spot. But, strangely, green shoots were already appearing on the charred trees. They were burned but not dead.

To the west, the muck soon dehydrated into a baked flat, dried out by the fire. The pooka would be able to walk here—if he could get across the firewall. Well, I had done it; he could use the same device, ducking under the water. If he could unmuck enough to move.

He would need help. I contemplated the smoldering, sprouting trunks and had a notion. I could *haul* him under!

I ducked under the firewall again and came up in the bloodbath. There was the pooka, unchanged, except a little deeper mired. He was keeping his chin up; he had to, to keep his nose clear of the bloodstream that surrounded him.

"I need a chain," I said. I put my hands on one of the chains that wrapped him and tugged at it. The thing was tied in, with no free end. I wondered who had fastened these chains on him and why, but this was not the time for idle speculation. Many things in Xanth don't have sensible explanations anyway; they just *are*.

"I'll have to do this the hard way," I said. "Steady, now." I stretched out a loop of chain so that it projected into the water beside him, then hefted my sword, lifting it above my head with both hands and bringing it down ferociously.

The pooka neighed with terror, but was unable to flinch away. Then the blade caught the loop of chain and sliced through it. I had a good sword; it had been dipped in dragon's blood, and so the blade was magically hard and sharp and could cut through almost anything.

I took one of the severed ends, passed it down around the muck-buried barrel of the ghost horse, and drew it up on the other side. I kept working, unraveling the chain until I had what I needed. Then I made sure the rest was securely anchored about the barrel and forelimbs of the animal, so it could not slip free.

"Now, Pook, I'm going to haul you under the firewall," I said. "To get you out of this mess. But you'll have to help. When you feel the pull, try to walk with it; you should be able to, with that help. When you reach the firewall, get your body as close to it as possible, duck your head down under it so you won't get burned, and I'll haul you across. Got that?"

The pooka did not react. I couldn't tell whether he understood. Well, no help for it; I had to do it. If this worked, I would save the ghost horse; if not—

I slogged back to the firewall, hauling the chain. I dived

under. On the other side, I picked a suitable scorched tree and strung the chain over a low, horizontal branch. Then I hauled on the end.

There was resistance, of course. That muck didn't want to let go of its prey. I hauled harder, hanging my whole weight on it. Gradually there was give; slowly the chain moved. I took a new grip and hauled some more, and more came. Now it got easier; the pooka was helping. Heave by heave and step by step, I hauled the animal toward the firewall, though I could not see him on the other side. If he failed to duck his head at the critical moment—

Then the taut chain dipped into the muck, and I knew the ghost horse was following my orders. I increased my effort, and in a moment his head appeared on my side.

After that, it was easier. I got the pooka past the firewall and into the shallow muck and finally onto the baked mud. I removed the chain from the tree and rewrapped it about the animal; he needed that chain to remain in existence, as far as I knew. But I did not let go of it.

When I finished, I mounted him. "Willing or not, you're giving me a ride," I informed him.

The poor thing was so bedraggled and tired he didn't say neigh. I had my steed at last—or so I thought.

Chapter 3. Callicantzari

I rode Pook to a region where the trees had grown back considerably and I prepared to spend the night. "I'm going to let you go," I told him. "But you can see how the firewall surrounds this region. You can't get out without my help. So there's no point in running from me; you

might as well just relax and graze." I dismounted—and
the ghost horse took off at a gallop.

I sighed. I had hoped—but of course I was just a backwoods lunk, not understanding the true motives of people
or creatures, however much I tried. I foraged for some
fruit for my meal—it was amazing how fast these trees
progressed after being burned!—then settled down to
sleep. I didn't worry about predators here; they wouldn't
pass through the firewall.

Smoke roused me. Night remained—but the horizon
was bright. Fire was sweeping across the plain!

I cast about, knowing I was in trouble. Secure against
animate menaces, I had overlooked the inanimate. The
fire had me halfway surrounded and was moving faster
than I could run. The green grass and foliage had turned
brown; apparently the accelerated cycle of growth did not
stop with maturity, but continued through the season. Fall
had come to this region—and with it the fire, to clean
away the husks and set things up for the spring in the
morning. Maybe I could bury myself in the ground until
it passed. But the turf was hard; it would take hours to
dig myself in properly, and all I had were minutes.

I heard a rattle. There was the pooka, running terrified
before the flame. "Get over here!" I yelled. "I'll guide
you out!" Naturally he paid no attention, but I cut across
to herd him toward the advancing flame, where there was
a cul-de-sac, then used my rope to snag him. I hauled him
to me and climbed onto his back and gripped the chain.
I had my steed again—just in time.

It wasn't comfortable, sitting on the chains. When the
ghost horse had been in the muck, I had not felt the chains
as much, but now I did. But I had no choice; the fire
provided no time for comfort. I steered the horse by kicking the side I wanted him to move away from. We galloped
for the closing gap in the ring of fire, my posterior bounc-
ing intemperately on the hard chains.

We reached the gap—and discovered that beyond it
was only another closing ring. No escape here! Now what
was I to do? I had promised to find a way out.

But I saw that part of the new ring was, in fact, the

outer firewall. That was the boundary; no fire beyond
that. We could dive under it, and—

There was no water or muck here to use to get under
the fire. There was also no time. The burn was avidly
pursuing us.

"We've got to go through!" I cried. "Close your eyes
and hold your breath!" And I whammed the end of the
rope against the horse's flank, causing him to leap wildly
forward.

In midair we sailed through that firewall. I felt the band
of heat flash past my body, singeing my whiskers and
clothing; then we were through. We had had the advantage of firm turf and high velocity this time; that had made
it possible. But I was not eager to return to the realm of
fire, if I had any choice in the matter.

We were on a plain before the southern mountain range
we had been unable to reach before. I was pleased; south
was the way I wanted to go, and I preferred mountains
to either bog or burn. I think Pook did, too.

We moved on toward the mountains as the sun came
up, then paused for breakfast. I let Pook graze, but this
time I did not dismount, knowing he would bolt. I simply
pulled down a dainty feminine fruit from an overhanging
branch and bit into it. I was surprised; it was not fruit but
meat—evidently a miss-steak, grown there by error.
Sometimes spells got befuddled. It made a good, solid
meal, however, though I would have preferred to cook
it.

In due course, we walked south again—and encountered goblin traces. Pook snorted nervously and I groaned;
we both knew that goblins were trouble. But we weren't
about to go back the way we had come. So we continued
south, much more warily.

It did us no good. A party of goblins spotted us. The
chase was on.

With goblins, you see, you didn't parley. Not in those
days, anyway; maybe goblins have moderated over the
centuries. You fought, or you ran, or you got tromped;
that was the extent of your options. Since there were
about ten of them, armed with sticks and stones to break

our bones, and only one of me and one ghost horse, plus my good sword—well, I was young and foolish, but not *that* foolish. I was no dragon, to chomp goblins by the dozen, or ogre, to hurl them to the moon. So I took the sensible option—I ran.

Pook, of course, was right with me. Under me, technically. Chains and all. He galloped. Ghost horses don't like getting eaten by goblins, either.

The goblins gave chase. They were afoot and they had stubbly little legs, big feet, and gross, ugly heads, but they moved along pretty well. Also, one of them sounded a blast on a horn, summoning the other goblins. It was a stink horn, and it made a foul-smelling noise, the kind that instantly attracted that kind of creature. So, though we handily outran that bunch, we did not get free of goblins.

They poured like hot lava out of the mountain. Today I understand there are not great numbers of goblins resident on the surface, though it may be a different story in the dank, deep caverns; but in my day there were more. They surrounded us in a putrid mass, grabbing at my legs, yelling obscenely. Goblins are about as obscene as any creature except the harpies.

Naturally I slashed with my sword, cutting off their hands or anything else that came within range. Fingers, noses, scalps, and other items flew out from our contacts; oh, you should have heard those goblins yell! But there were always more glaring faces, more hands, more sticks and stones. It is never a pleasant business, fighting off goblins, because they just keep coming thicker than before.

We tried to veer right, away from the goblin mountain, but encountered the firewall. It blazed up brightly, ready for us this time, as if daring us to try to get through it alive. So we had to veer left—and discovered that we really hadn't cleared the bog yet; an arm of it came down almost to the mountain, and a leg of it extended north of the mountain. That was no good either; the loan sharks were waiting in it to take *my* arm and leg. So we charged straight for the mountain—where most of the goblins were.

Pook bowled them over in his galloping fright, but I knew we would soon be buried in goblins.

We plowed straight ahead, because we didn't dare turn or stop. That was directly toward the mountain, which loomed ever larger as we drew nigh. The goblins surrounded it like a warty blanket. As we got close, I saw that parts of it were terraced, with narrow winding paths following the contours, and this gave me a notion.

I nudged Pook to the side, where a lance-tree grew. I severed a lance with a passing sweep of my sword. Then we looped back and slowed momentarily—the ghost horse, afraid of the massed goblins, was now obeying my every hint with marvelous alacrity, since I seemed to know what I was doing—so I could flip up the lance with the point of my sword and catch it with my free hand. I have pretty good coordination with weapons; it's another barbarian specialty. Then we resumed speed, and I sheathed my sword and used both hands to hold the lance firm. It was a good long one, with the point extending well ahead of Pook's head.

Now we reached the base of the mountain. I guided my steed to the nearest convenient path, and we swerved onto it, churning out divots of turf as Pook's hooves made the turn. The lance swept about, knocking goblins off the path; they tumbled heads over feets down the slope. Their heads were big and hard as rocks and dented the mountain slope where they struck, but their feet were soft; when the feet struck, the goblins let out angry yells. Gobs of goblins were crowding around the mountain, and the bowling ones knocked over the standing ones like eight-, nine-, or ten-pins.

We charged east along the path, the point of the lance leading, and the goblins ahead dived out of the way. They couldn't get at us as long as we kept moving. I began to relax; my impromptu ploy was working, and we were escaping this pesthole. All we needed was to follow this path right out of the goblin territory.

It turned out to be a trifle more complicated than that. The path curved wondrously, as if seeking to confuse us; it included a hairpin curve and a few nasty jags and jigs and it branched and intersected other paths as the convolutions of the mountain permitted. There were small goblin caves along the way, each with its messy little front yard strewn with fruit peels, animal bones, and other garbage. The goblins in these poked sticks out to try to trip us and threw rocks from their cover. Fortunately, neither their timing nor their aim was very good, and we escaped injury. But it was nervous business being bombarded from passing caves.

More enterprising goblins rolled rocks down the intersecting paths; most of these were small enough to be mere nuisances, so that Pook could hurdle them, but some were large enough to be threats. We were also conscious of the sheer malignance of the massed goblins; there was not one of them who wouldn't rejoice at our misfortune, simply because we were strangers. The goblins were the ultimate bigots of Xanth, hating all creatures who were not like themselves and not feeling too positive about themselves, either. I had heard that goblin females were different, but all I saw here were males. No doubt the females were smart enough not to indulge in this sort of quarrel.

Then the path slid down the curving mountain, as if tired, and into the crevice between it and the next mountain. Too late, I saw that this was a dead end; the path did not go up the next slope. Instead it led directly into a large cave whose depths were dark, ominous, and dreadful. No good ever comes of caves like that!

The goblins were massed and charging behind us, some carrying crude wooden shields, and several operated together to support a lance like mine. We could not turn about and go back that way. We would be trying to charge uphill against a prepared enemy formation. Neither could we turn aside; the slopes of the crevice were too steep for us to navigate. Glancing up, I saw goblins making ready to roll a boulder down on us; already it was nudging over the brink. They were leering with anticipation of the squash it would make of us.

I had no choice—I guided Pook directly into the menacing tunnel. He didn't like this and I didn't like it, but it was the only route left. Behind, I heard the malignant rumble of the boulder coming down; then there was a sinister shudder as it crashed into the tunnel, lodging there with gruesome finality and blocking the entrance. Some debris shook loose from the ceiling to shower down around us, but the passage didn't collapse. That was a relief; I knew that if the tunnel had survived this long, it was probably pretty stable, but doubts are easy to come by in the deep dark.

We halted, but knew before we checked that we were trapped. Even if we managed to push or pry out the boulder, we would encounter an army of vicious goblins beyond it, eager to hurt us with sticks, stones, and names. Once again we had no choice but to go forward. I have always had a distinct dislike of such unchoices; they generally led to mischief; and even if they didn't, I still preferred to get into trouble in my own fashion rather than the forced-path way.

It was good and gloomy in that cave. Light seeped in around the ragged edges of the boulder; but in the deeper reaches, it was foreboding indeed. Pook was a ghost horse; he could see pretty well, since ghosts normally did their work at night, but I had trouble.

"Pook," I said, "we're just going to have to follow this cave into the mountain fastness. It must go somewhere, because the path led right to it, and maybe the other end will let us out the other side of the hill." But I felt a chill of nervousness coursing along my spine and hovering in that one region it is impossible ever quite to scratch, because I knew that not all paths that led in to things led out again. The path to a tangle tree was a good example. But there was no point in negative thinking at the moment. "So I'm going to have to trust you to follow it through and not drop us into some deep fissure. I know you don't like having me ride you, but we're in this together, and maybe we can get out together. Once we're safely out, we can worry about who gets to ride whom where."

Pook made no response, but I hoped he understood the situation. I aimed him for the black hole ahead and nudged him with my heels. He moved forward at a walk, his hooves sounding sharply on the stone. In fact, there were little echoes—and I realized that my ears could serve in lieu of eyes, to some extent. Barbarians have keen hearing, though it can't compare with that of most animals. The echoes told me that the walls were close beside us, but not ahead of us.

The tunnel trended down, as such things tend to do. I didn't like that; I wanted to travel up and out of the mountain. But one must go where one's road leads, even when it's a distressing road.

After what seemed like an interminable time, I began to see a little. There were small fungi growing in cracks in the wall, casting a magic pastel glow. As we progressed, water dripped, and the air got cooler and damper; the fungi grew larger and brighter, until it was possible for me to make out most of the passage. Some fungi were yellow and some green or blue; in fact, they were all the colors of the rainbow, though faint. It was really rather pretty.

The tunnel expanded, becoming a series of galleries, each lined with the rainbow fungi. This was fine—but now there were branching passages, and I didn't know which ones to follow. Life is simpler when you don't have many choices, even if you don't like the route you're stuck on. So I didn't choose; I let Pook have his head, and we proceeded more or less straight ahead.

Then Pook paused to sniff the air. I could see his head only in silhouette, where it blocked the faint illumination of the fungi, but I knew his nostrils were flaring. He smelled something!

Then I smelled it, too—a fetid odor, the stench of some large and thoroughly unpleasant creature. We were not alone.

"We'd better try to avoid that thing," I murmured to Pook. "It stinks a little like goblin, but worse." I still had my lance, but wasn't sure how useful it would be in the confines of the cave. I might run the point directly into a dead-end wall and jar myself right off my mount.

We backed out of this chamber as quietly as we could and tried an alternate one, but the smell only got stronger. Then I realized that we weren't approaching the monster; the monster was approaching us. It had heard our footfalls, our hoof-falls, and was coming to investigate. "Let's get out of here!" I said urgently, yielding, with a certain relief, to panic. Oh, I know—barbarian warriors aren't supposed to experience such emotion. Barbarian warriors don't belong in deep, dark caves with stinking monsters, either.

Pook picked up speed, moving as fast as he dared along the passage. It wasn't fast enough; still the silent stink intensified. We were deep in monster territory and not getting out. Maybe the goblins had been herding us here all along, knowing what would happen to any creature who fearfully braved these dank depths.

Suddenly the monster loomed before us. It was a gross manlike thing, with horrible distorted features. The worst monsters are always manlike; I've never been quite clear why this is so, but it definitely *is* so. Fur covered this thing's face; from the fur, a grotesque and bulbous nose poked out, and under the fur, two great, ugly eye-slits peered, as from behind a dirty veil; at the bottom of the face, several twisted tusks projected. There must have been a mouth somewhere. The creature seemed to be male—the worst specimens of anything are always male, except for harpies. His arms were hairy extremities on which the muscles seemed to be attached backward, and his torso had several bones in the wrong places. In some ways he was like an unusually large and grotesque goblin, but in other ways he was worse—his breath, for one thing; his exhalations surrounded him like a putrid cloud. Pook and I were gagging.

Later I learned that this was one of the callicantzari, a race of monsters who lived mostly underground and undermined the roots of important trees, such as the Tree of Seeds on Mount Parnassus or the tree that supported the sky—the trees without which Xanth as we know it would cease to exist. Imagine a land without all the myriad and wonderful species of trees that stem from those magic seeds, or a land without any sky. How could we function without the sun and moon and stars and clouds safely out of the way? But it seemed that these monsters didn't worry about that; they just wanted to bring down the trees. Maybe that's one of the differences between monsters and human beings—the monsters don't care what happens next.

The callicantzari have tunnels going to every significant mountain and labor diligently to bring down those

trees, but when they get close to the surface and its un-
accustomed freedom, they rush out and run around, ter-
rorizing people and animals and dancing wildly, maddened
by the sight of the stars until morning comes. Even the
goblins can't stand them and will attack immediately if
they show up in goblin territory. That explains why the
callicantzari hadn't used our tunnel to escape. When they
get out elsewhere, and the sun rises, they flee its light in
terror. The shock always takes them some time to recover
from, and by the time they resume their normal equilibrium, such as it is, the trees have regrown their roots,
and the job has to be started over. Thus the callicantzari
are never successful, which perhaps is just as well. Generally, because of their repeated failures, they are in a
foul mood, and their breath suggests that mood. So they
really have quite a history, and are not just ordinary monsters. But at the moment, all I knew was that Pook and
I were in more trouble.

We slowed, to avoid the monster—but then another
appeared behind us, and we heard the tramping of others
in neighboring caverns. If there is one thing worse than
one monster, it is two monsters—and worse yet is a whole
slew of them. We were surrounded!

"Got to bull through and hope we win clear," I told
Pook. "Before we both suffocate from the stench. You
gallop, and I'll fend them off."

He galloped, and I aimed the lance at the monster
before us. The calli was too stupid to move, so that my
point caught him on the nose. The shock drove the lance
through his head and knocked it out of my grasp. We
charged on by the falling monster, who smelled even worse
wounded than whole.

But another appeared before us. I whipped out my
trusty sword, though I hated to soil my clean blade on ilk
like this, and struck at his ugly neck. Like the other, he
didn't move, and my blade decapitated him. Ugh, it was
gory! Barbarians are supposed to glory in blood, but this
was ugly, smelly, gunky blood that contained very little
glory.

Still there were more! Two lumbered from side tunnels,

reaching for me with their grotesque carrion-hooks. I cut the arms off the one on the right, but the one on the left got me in a gruesome hug and hauled me off my steed. Yes, I know that sort of mishap is not supposed to happen to heroes. The truth is, it happens, but the Barbarian Publicity Department censors it out.

Pook faltered, turning his head back to look at me. More monsters were converging. "Run!" I cried at him as I poked the point of my sword over my shoulder to stab the face of the monster holding me. Hot ichor sprayed against my neck, and I knew I had scored. "Get out of here, Pook, before they catch you, too!"

The ghost horse took off, and I laid about me valiantly with the sword, hacking off arms and legs and ears as they came within reach. But as I had known, the monsters were too much for me. One scored on my head with a hammy fist, knocking me silly, and another took a huge bite at my face. I felt his tusks sinking into my cheeks; then I lost consciousness.

Naturally I wasn't aware what happened next, but now I see it in the pictures of the tapestry, and my understanding of the situation helps fill it in. Satisfied that I was dead, the callis hauled me down to their main depot, where their cows and cubs lurked. There they clumsily used my own fair sword to cut my body open so they could gut me with their dirty claws. They yanked out all my innards and gobbled them down as delicacies, quarreling over the scraps. Then they jammed me in a big pot of cold water, to cook the tougher parts, and set about fetching wood for a fire. This took some time, for they had not planned ahead, and there wasn't much wood to be found in the deep caves. But after some hours, they scraped up enough, garnered from the roots of the trees they had been trying to destroy. Now at last they were ready to cook.

Meanwhile, some of them checked through my tattered clothing to see if there was anything interesting there. They chomped on the buttons and laces and ripped the cloth, liking the ripping sound. They found the bag of berry-berries I had saved, then fought again among themselves to see who could gobble the greatest number down. Well, I daresay they felt the effect in due course; it was almost worth dying to think of the effect those debilitating berries would have on those monsters.

There was another problem: the callicantzari were afraid of fire. It seemed its brightness, reminiscent of that of the sun, hurt their eyes. If you ask me what sense it makes to crave cooked food when you're afraid of fire, I can't answer; I suppose monsters wouldn't be monsters if they were sensible. If I had known about this before, I would have arranged to bring a torch with me into their caverns, so they would not have dared approach me. But barbarian heroes aren't necessarily all-knowing, either.

Not one of the monsters wanted to light and tend the fire. This problem hung them up another hour. At last they drew lots for the one who would do the deed—but then he had no spell to start the fire. They had to look for another hour to locate the spell—by which time it was their night, which happened to correspond with ours, though I don't know how they knew. Maybe the glowing fungi dimmed a little. So they left the feast until morning and snored. Their snores were absolutely awful sounds, like sawfish sawing down rock maple trees.

Meanwhile, Pook was galloping along the passages, searching for a way out. The monsters weren't chasing him, because they already had me for their meal and weren't very enterprising folk. Pook finally did blunder to an exit, went out, sniffed the air—and turned back. He had smelled something that made him pause, so he didn't want to brave it alone.

The ghost horse, now sure of the way, came back to the central caverns and, near morning, sniffed out where I remained in the pot. He nuzzled the top of my head, waking me.

You see, I had had about ten hours to heal, and this was enough. I hadn't really been killed; I had been knocked out, my face bitten off, and my guts eviscerated. By this time I had grown back my face and guts and healed the wounds. It took longer than it had to mend my crushed leg—the roc incident—because regrowing is more com-

plicated than merely healing existing anatomy. I remained
a little weak from loss of flesh, since my healing does not
create matter from nothing; it draws on the remaining
resources of my body. But I could function; I had been
a strapping young man before this started and now was
merely less strapping. Tissue from my big muscles had
been co-opted to replace my guts. "Knock over the pot,"
I told Pook.

He did so—this was the first solid evidence that he
understood my words completely—and I floated out with
the spilled water. The callis were such solid sleepers that
neither the clang nor the water sloshing by aroused them.
Indeed, the noise could hardly be distinguished over their
horrendous snoring, and the water was no more volu-
minous than their droolings.

I climbed unsteadily to my feet and got on Pook's back,
pausing only to recover my good sword. My bow had
been lost by the callicantzari; maybe they had used it as
part of the wood for the upcoming cooking-fire. I wouldn't
put such an outrage past such creatures! I still wore my
boots; they hadn't thought to take them off me before
putting me in the pot.

Then we were off, coursing upward through the passages, leaving the thick noise and stink behind. At last
we emerged into the wonderful bright morning on the
southeast slope of the mountain. Oh, what relief it was!
If I had to die, I much preferred to perish in the open
wilderness, rather than in the dank, closed caverns.

Chapter 4. Elf Elm

We found a fresh stream and a copse of pie trees, and I drank and ate and foraged for suitable replacement clothing from shoe-trees—my boots were sloshingly soaked, so I needed temporary footwear while they dried—trouser-trees, and shirt-trees, to replace what I had lost, while Pook grazed. I didn't try to hold or confine him; I lacked the strength, and anyway I didn't feel I had a right, since he had come back for me on his own. Maybe he wasn't tame, but he had chosen to be my companion for a while. I wondered why. I saw that he did not stray at all far from me, and I doubted this was from sudden affection. I hoped I wasn't being overly cynical—but then I knew I had brought him a lot of trouble, and barbarians aren't noted for comprehension of the nuances of interpersonal behavior.

It wasn't long before I found out. Pook lifted his head, rattled his chains, and moved toward me.

"You *want* me to ride you?" I asked, bemused. "You're not taking off alone into the wilds of the wilderness, knowing that I presently lack the strength or inclination to chase you down again?" Actually, I was stuffed with pies, which made me sluggish rather than weak, but this was also the first use of my new face and digestive tract. Startups are always awkward, and it takes a few hours to get the bugs out; there was a lot of gas, and I felt a little green. But every time I burped, another bug flew out, and I knew they would all be gone in a few more hours. There was no question that I was underweight, though; my thews were pitiful. In a few days I would be as good as new, more or less literally, but I needed lots of rest and food in the interim. I was no Magician; my magic talent had to be tempered with moderation.

I really appreciated Pook's offer, whatever its motive. It was easier to ride than to walk, until my leg muscles filled out. So I harvested some cushions from the surrounding bushes, fashioned them into a saddle seat that would prevent the chains from pinching my rear, and mounted. We began making our way south at a cautious pace.

And the elves arrived.

Oho! *That* was why Pook needed me. Elves generally leave human folk alone and aren't often seen, but they are funny in some ways. They can be deadly fighters, though they respect property rights. If they found Pook alone, they would run him down and tame him for their own use, making him a work horse. They could do that, because there were a number of them, they had little magic lariats, and they knew the terrain; they were experienced group hunters. But if they thought I owned him, they would let him be—at least until they had dealt with me. I was his buffer against the elves.

"Smart move, Pook!" I murmured with a certain rueful appreciation. There was an aspect of this that worried me. Elves usually, as I said, don't mess with human folk, because there is a standing covenant between our two species. It's a kind of mutual nonaggression pact. Since human and elven interests seldom intersect, it is easiest to respect one another's interests. It certainly saves trouble. But both humans and elves had uses for a creature like Pook. If the elves really wanted the ghost horse, they might choose to quarrel. It wasn't good to quarrel with elves in elven territory. They weren't always as small as they looked.

At least now I knew that Pook had a fair brain in that equine head. He couldn't talk—but of course, talking is not necessarily a sign of intelligence. He had made his problem mine. Unfortunately, I was in no fit condition to do battle at the moment.

This was a party of six elves. They were armed with assorted weapons and they wore green tunics. They were proportioned and dressed like human beings—oh, sure, human beings do wear tunics on occasion—but stood only a quarter my height. I met them with respect, for I knew that, at the best of times, they were far better as friends than as enemies, and this was an indifferent or middling-poor time. I cast about in my uncivilized mind for the proper form of address. Was it Sire? No, sir.

"What be your business in Elven demesnes, Man?" their leader demanded.

"Just passing through, sir," I replied carefully.

"How did you get past the goblins?"

"They drove us into the mountain, sir, and the monsters there left me for dead, and my pooka rescued me."

The elf eyed me suspiciously. "You tamed a ghost horse?"

"Well, partway, perhaps. It's hard to tame such a creature completely."

The elf considered, eyed Pook, and shrugged, satisfied. "You seek no quarrel with us, Man?"

"None, sir. I'm just a barbarian warrior in search of honest adventure."

"Honest adventure, eh?" He considered me again, and I wasn't clear what thoughts were percolating through his mind. "Would you agree that there are other kinds of adventure than battling callicantzari?"

That was when I learned the identity of the mountain monsters. "I certainly hope so, sir!"

"Then you will be our guest tonight."

Amazed, I had to stifle a gape. I had hoped only to be allowed to pass without quarrel. "That's very nice of you, sir."

"What's your name, Man?"

"Jordan, sir."

"I am Oleander Elf, of the tribe of Flower Elves. These are—" He indicated his companions in turn. "—Cactus, Dogwood, Knotweed, Bloodroot, and Arrowhead." Indeed, I saw that they were armed in the manner of their names. Cactus had a dagger made of a large cactus thorn, Arrowhead had a little bow and quiver of arrows, Knotweed had knotted rope, Bloodroot had a red bag of

fluid that might be blood-poison, and Dogwood had a
wooden spear tipped with a large canine tooth. Only
Oleander carried no visible weapon—but he was the
leader, and I suspected he had something, perhaps a fighting spell. There were no goblins on this side of the mountain, and this was surely because of these elves. Elves
did not seem as fierce and were certainly not as numerous
as goblins, yet they kept the goblins clear. That spoke for
itself. Like many people, I wondered what their secret
was, since, as far as I knew, goblins respected nothing
but brute force.

Oleander led Pook and me along a winding path to a
hidden glen. I was glad to go with them, for this was a
signal honor, and elves were creatures of integrity; as their
guest, I would be absolutely safe. But I remained mystified as to why they should extend this honor to a wan-
dering barbarian. It could not be purely for delight in my
company; barbarians do not make very good company.

The journey took over an hour, for the little folk did
not travel as fast as a man, though they stepped out
sprightly enough. I did not mind, since I was riding and
also recovering from my recent injuries. The nourishment
from all those pies I had stuffed in my new face and gut
was working its way though the rest of my body, and my
thews were strengthening.

The elven camp was around and in an elf elm, of course;
everyone knows elves will reside nowhere else. When
danger threatened, the women and children retreated to
the heights, while the warriors ringed the base of the tree.
At the moment, most of them were down, for they were
setting up for their midday meal. The smells were good,
but I was still digesting pies and wasn't really hungry.
That was just as well, for their portions were small.

We sat on the ground, and the elven maidens served
leaves filled with stew. The leaves were cleverly worked
into bowls, so that the stew did not leak. I accepted mine,
curious what was in the stew but hesitant to ask. There
seemed to be chunks of vegetables, nuts, fruits, and meats
in it, and I suspected that the meat was from mice and

grasshoppers. It tasted good, anyway, and was just enough to top off what I had eaten before.

Then Oleander brought an elf maiden to meet me. "This is Bluebell, who wishes to ask a favor of you, Man," he said somewhat brusquely and departed. I wondered at that anew; had I given some sort of offense? I had certainly tried to be a good guest, but one never can be certain with nonhuman cultures, though the elves were about as human as such cultures got. If it were not for the distinction of size, I would hardly know the difference.

"A favor?" I asked. "I will be happy to help in any way I can, but I don't know much about elves—"

Bluebell smiled. She was a lovely little creature, perfectly proportioned, like a doll in her green dress. "I will tell you about elves, Jordan-Man," she said. "But first I must do you a favor, so it's even. What would you like?"

"I am quite satisfied to accept the elven hospitality," I replied cautiously. I glanced across to where Pook was grazing. Few animals got to touch grass as lush as that which the elves cultivated around their elms. "And so is my horse. That is favor enough."

"No, you will repay that by telling us your story tonight," she said. "I mean, a favor from me personally."

What was she getting at? "Your charming company is enough," I said. "Please tell me what you wish me to—"

"Not yet," she demurred. She jumped up to perch on my bent knee, dangling her pretty legs in the way girls had. "I must do you my favor first."

I shook my head. "As I said, I'm just a backwoods man, unfamiliar with elven ways. I don't want to give offense by making mistakes, and I have already antagonized Oleander in some way. So you will have to explain to me exactly what—"

She emulated my motion, but the effect differed: when she shook her head, her lovely elf-gray hair tumbled about fetchingly. "Don't worry about him! He's just perturbed because he wanted Cowslip to get your favor, but I won the toss. Cowslip's his cousin, and she's all right if you like that type." Bluebell indicated an elf maid nearby. I looked and saw a stunning example of the type; I did indeed like it.

"I will do a favor for each of you, to keep the peace," I said magnanimously. "But I need to know what—"

She laughed merrily. "Only for me, Man; that's the rule. I've got the spell. I won it and I won't share it."

I was more perplexed than ever. "What spell?"

She glanced at me sidelong. "You are delightful! I will show you in due course. Now—name your favor."

I sighed silently. Evidently she preferred to play her game with me, in the fashion of maidens everywhere, and I felt every bit as ignorant as I was supposed to be. "Well, I'm an adventurer, but I don't quite know where I'm going. That is, I'm headed for Castle Roogna, the Man capital, but there are a lot of barriers along the way, like the goblin mountain, that I would have avoided if I'd known. If I had a good map—"

"A map!" she exclaimed. "Of course! You shall have it!" She bounced off my knee and ran to the tree, her hair flinging out behind her. Doll she might be, but she was a woman-doll!

Soon she was back, hauling a scroll about as big as herself. Breathlessly she unrolled it for me on the greensward, pertly sitting on the top end while I spread my fingers to hold down the bottom end. "This is Xanth," she panted prettily. "Here we are, in the center, with the goblins, griffins, and birds to the north and the dragons to the south. To the east, beyond the river, is the big ocean, and to the west are the five terrible Elements— Air, Earth, Fire, Water, and the Void. They aren't nice places; you don't want to go there. In fact, nowhere is as nice as right here."

I perused the map with interest. "I came from up here, in the fen. I ran into the—"

"Oh, no, don't tell your story yet," she protested. "Save it for the whole tribe. Where are you going from here, specifically?"

"Well, I thought south. I don't want to pass through the Elements I see here, and I doubt I'd care for the Region of the Flies below it, so if I go south and then loop around to the west below—um, I don't see Castle Roogna on this map."

She cocked her head and wiggled her toes, considering. "I have heard the name, faintly. We elves don't concern ourselves overmuch with human business. But all the other details should be right. I think your castle is south of the—the—I don't quite remember what, but south of it. Maybe here." She pointed to the bottom section of the map, marked HERE THERE BE OGRES, and shuddered.

Ogres! Naturally I knew of those huge, awful creatures, but never had I seen one. "That's the sort of adventure I'm looking for!" I exclaimed. "When I recover my strength."

She glanced at me with feminine concern. "You are ill?"

"No, not exactly. I was severely wounded by—" I broke off as she began to protest. "I know—save it for the tribe! Anyway, I'll recover fully in a few days, so that's all right. It's mainly a matter of regrowing my lost muscle tissue. I'll be in fit condition by the time I encounter the ogres. Then I'll go to Castle Roogna and see what adventure awaits me there. This map will help me get there faster. Thank you, Bluebell."

"So you accept my favor," she said, pleased.

"Certainly I do," I agreed. "Now what do you want from me?"

She gazed at me with eerie intensity. "I think you wouldn't understand yet," she said. "But when you are ready, I'll tell you."

I shrugged. "Just so it's before I depart your charming elf elm realm."

"It will be, Jordan-Man," she assured me.

Then the elves cleared away the remnants of the meal and faced the tree in a great circle. The King elf stood beside the trunk, clapping his hands for silence. "That's Crown-of-Thorns," Bluebell whispered to me. She was now perched on my shoulder, dangling her legs down into my right shirt pocket. She was so light I hardly felt her, and her grasp on my right ear, to steady herself, was like a caress.

King Crown-of-Thorns spoke, and a well-spoken King was he. "I welcome the traveling Barbarian Man who visits us this day," he said formally. "I invite him to exchange entertainments with us. First we shall show him ours."

And from the towering foliage of the elf elm descended ten elven damsels, suspended by threads, pirouetting in the air. They came to rest just above the ground, then began to swing like pendulum bobs, their motions slow because of the length of their threads. They bounced in unison, spreading arms and legs as they swung around the tree. Then they swung in differing directions, forming patterns that changed before my eyes could quite grasp them, generating fleeting impressions of stunning beauty. In and out they wove, now together, now apart, now linking hands, now spinning separately. It was a unified dance, lovely in its parts and in its whole, and I was duly enchanted.

Then the damsels dropped to the ground, and a dozen male elves approached the tree. These were young, healthy specimens, muscular and coordinated—the equivalent of barbarians. Their dance was on the ground, and it incorporated feats of strength. They spread out in a wide circle about the elm. Each lifted a sizable stone, held it a moment, then dropped it.

Then they moved into a tighter circle, where larger stones had been set. Each lifted one of these with no more apparent difficulty than he had lifted the smaller one, to my surprise. Once again they contracted the circle, where lay yet larger stones, and each picked up one of these. I wondered whether the larger stones were of lighter substance, to make this possible. Pumice, for example—magic stone spewn up from the depths, some of it so light it would float on water. That would explain what I observed here.

King Crown-of-Thorns spied my perplexity. "You doubt, honored Man?" he declaimed. "We will show you the magic of our tree! Fetch us the largest log you can carry!"

"Go ahead," Bluebell urged in my ear, her breath tickling it. "Your present strength is enough for that, isn't it?"

"For a small log," I agreed. I got up and searched nearby, and there, conveniently laid out, were several logs of assorted sizes. I hefted one and found it too light; my strength had already recovered somewhat. I tried another, and it sufficed; it was all I could handle in my present condition. I got it up on my shoulder, displacing Bluebell, who scampered nimbly onto my head and clung to my hair, and I staggered toward the elm. Despite my effort, I was aware of Bluebell clinging to my head, her feet now on my left shoulder, her torso plastered across my left ear, and her maidenly bosom squeezed against my hair.

"This will do," the King said, indicating a spot on the ground some distance from the tree. With relief I set down the log, letting one end thunk solidly to the ground, then easing the rest of it down. No elf would move that!

But the elves intended to try! As I backed off, the twelve approached the log. They set themselves about it and got their little hands under it and heaved together. It wobbled but didn't lift. I was not surprised; since each elf was a quarter of my height, depth, and breadth, that meant each was about one-sixty-fourth my mass; that was why Bluebell was so slight on my shoulder. I could have supported her whole weight readily with my littlest finger. So each elf might be able to heft one-sixty-fourth what I could, and all twelve together—well, I'm not that apt at math in my head, but it seemed reasonable that all twelve elves acting in concert could lift only a fifth as much as I could, maybe less. Of course, I did not have my full strength back, and they had many little hands and had to lift the log only marginally off the ground. Still, chances were it was three times as heavy as they could manage.

The elves gathered at one end and lifted and shoved. The ground was uneven, and this end was slightly raised, so they were able to pivot the log about its center support without lifting it. They got it parallel to the elm. Then they all pushed, and slowly it rolled toward the tree. Well, they were using their minds now, and leverage helped.

That was the way to do it. The velocity of the roll increased as it went.

Then they stopped. They ranged themselves on either side of the log and heaved—and this time they actually got it up! Amazed, I watched as they carried it to the region where the first small rocks had been dropped. There they set it down, and six elves walked away. The remaining six tackled the log—and lifted it.

"There's something funny here!" I exclaimed. "Twelve couldn't lift it before, and now—"

"There's more, Jordan-Man" Bluebell murmured ticklishly into my ear.

I watched. The elves carried the log to the second ring of stones. There they set it down, and three of them departed. The remaining three got at each end and the middle of the log.

"Now I'm *sure* they can't—" I began.

The log came up. I gaped. They were doing it!

Bluebell tweaked my ear. "We Elves have magic you Men wot not," she whispered. Then, I swear, she kissed the rim of my ear. I'm not sure which startled me more— the log-lifting or the miniature kiss. What was going on here?

The three carried the log to the third ring of stones and paused. Then the two at the ends let go and walked away— and the lone elf in the center carried the log the rest of the way to the trunk of the elm.

I couldn't let this impossibility pass. I got up and strode to the tree. "I want to check that log!" I said. It was in my mind that they had found a way to make things lighter near the tree.

The elf set it down. I reached down and picked it up— barely. The thing was every bit as heavy as it had been. How had he—?

Then I felt something odd. I was rising!

I looked down—and discovered that the elf was picking me up by my shoes. His tiny hands gripped each of my heels, and I was in the air, still holding the log.

I began to wobble, as much from surprise as from unbalance, and he set me down. Then I put down the log and stood dazed. I had succeeded only in further confusing myself. The elves around the tree were smiling merrily.

"It is the tree, Jordan," Bluebell told me. "We elves grow stronger as we approach it. That's why we always camp near an elf elm."

"You mean—?" But already I saw that it was true. The stones—as the elves' strength increased, they had lifted larger stones. It had been no trick, just a demonstration. At the base of the tree, the strength of an elf became practically infinite. "Females too?"

"Want me to pick you up?" she asked. "I can do it—here beside the elm."

"You—do elves keep getting weaker, away from the tree?"

"Yes, but it's on a declining curve. We change rapidly near the tree, slowly away from it. As long as we don't range out too far, we're all right."

"And if a monster attacks you—"

"We retreat as far as we need, toward the elm," she agreed. "We protect the elms, and they protect us. The magic doesn't affect anyone who isn't of elven stock. So our retreats are almost impregnable; an elven child could heave a monster away. But we don't go out of our way to bother other folk."

That explained why elves weren't seen much around the fen where I had been reared. There were no elf elms in that vicinity.

"Now it is your turn," she said. "You must tell your story, for we elves are very curious about the other species and regions of Xanth. I hope it is a good tale."

I shrugged. "I can embellish it if you wish."

"No, we prefer the truth."

So I settled down by the tree and narrated my story, much as I have been doing here, and they listened attentively and asked intelligent questions. They really were interested, and I saw a scribe-elf making notes. It seemed to me that what I had to tell was actually—if you'll excuse the expression—pretty mundane stuff, since I had slain no dragons and encountered no phenomenal sorceries, but they really were interested and, at the end, satisfied. The odd thing was that they seemed most taken with the portions they knew most about, rather than those that were beyond their experience.

Bluebell had said they wanted to hear the truth, so that was what I gave them, unexciting as it might be, and they liked that. Later I realized that this was only in part entertainment for them; they were also judging me, and on the basis of my story they judged me to be an honest man, though they asked some very penetrating questions about my talent for healing.

Finally, perceiving that they doubted, I suggested that they cut off my fingers and watch them regrow. They recoiled, I think, not so much from horror at the notion of deliberate injury as from not wishing to seem to cast aspersion on my integrity. So I simply rubbed my forearm along the blade of my sword, cutting the skin so that blood flowed, then held up my arm so that they could see how rapidly it healed. They protested strenuously that such a demonstration was not necessary, but in their very protestation I concluded that it was. As I said, I am not expert in the judging of other cultures, so maybe I have misinterpreted whatever significance existed.

Now it was growing late in the day. The elves served some sort of fragrant grog in leaf mugs; mine was tiny, of course, but I drank it—and the stuff burned down my throat and filled my belly with fire and sent my head floating somewhere above my body. Potent stuff!

"It is time for the favor," Bluebell informed me.

"Favor?" I asked, confused. "Oh. Yes. Tell me."

"This way," she said, leading me back to the tree. I walked somewhat unsteadily, feeling the grog. That is to say, groggy.

I stopped at the base of the trunk, but she proceeded to climb the elm. "I can't go up there!" I protested, eying the virtually vertical ascent. The tree was large, having had time to grow during the centuries the elves had protected it; two human men would barely be able to reach around it. There were no low branches; it was a great column rising to the mass of foliage far above.

"Yes, you can, Jordan," she told me. "The grog gives you the power."

Dubiously, I tried it. I put my hands to the bark—and they clung as if cemented. I brought up a foot, and it adhered similarly. When I lifted one hand, it came free, so I could take hold higher. Like a fly, I could walk the wall! This, of course explained how flies did it; they sneaked sips of elven grog.

So I followed her up, though the height was dizzying. If the magic failed, I knew I would fall and be killed— but I wasn't worried for three reasons. First, I did not believe the elves meant me any harm, so the grog-spell should hold. Second, if I did fall, my body would heal the breaks within a day, so death would be only temporary. Third, the pleasant stupor the grog has put me in made all this a matter of indifference; I simply didn't care. It seemed almost natural to be following a doll-sized elf lass up a huge tree.

At last we reached the first bifurcation of branches and entered the foliage. Bluebell led me up through it until we came to a great tangle of mistletoe in the highest reach. The points of the missiles and toes scratched me, but I healed in seconds. Bluebell entered this mass, and I followed, discovering a way through; and lo! inside it was a great globed nest, with pillows and a comfortable floor. The fading light of day filtered in through the levels in diffused fashion, pleasantly illuminating leaves and vines of many colors.

I lay against the resilient and fragrant leaf wall. "This is lovely," I said. "Now what is the favor I owe you? Do you need some heavy object carried down to the ground, or lifted up from the ground?" Though, with their super-strength, it hardly seemed the elves would need my help there.

She smiled as if finding something funny. Girls of any species can be like that. "You need lift no object too heavy to manage, Jordan," she said.

"Well, I'm ready to serve. Name it."

"It is the service that only you can give," she said. "Your most precious possession."

Dismay sliced through my daze, abolishing it. "You want my sword?"

She looked at me, astonished, then tumbled over in laughter. I had to laugh too, for it seemed it was not my weapon she was after; and indeed, I realized that a creature her size and sex would have no way to handle it.

I pondered, and sobered again, realizing what an elf would want of a man like me. "My horse!"

Bluebell managed not to laugh this time, but obviously she was feeling merry. She came to sit on my knee, as she had done below. "Now how could I get a ghost horse up here?" she asked, and then the laughter bubbled up and overflowed again. Elves certainly are merry folk!

"Well, I know elves need transportation and hauling, away from the tree," I said. "A creature like Pook doesn't lose strength—" But I saw she was just about to fall off my knee with mirth, and of course I was relieved to know that this had not been a ploy to demand Pook. He really would have felt I had betrayed him, and certainly I had not intended to do that. "But—what *do* you want, elven maid? I'm out of precious possessions."

I don't know why she was so overbubbling with laughter. "You can not guess, Jordan-Man?"

"I'm only a barbarian warrior, not too smart," I reminded her somewhat tersely.

"But honest and strong and nice," she said.

"And not good at riddles," I added, annoyed.

She unbuttoned her green tunic, slipped out of it, and sat again on my elevated knee. She was a lovely miniature woman in every respect. "Now can you guess, Jordan-Man?"

"You want me to fetch new clothing for you?"

This time she doubled up and rolled about with the force of her laughter, in the process showing a good deal more than she ought and landing in a pretty heap in my lap. "Oh, barbarian, you still have something to learn about elves—or about women," she said when she had recovered some of her breath.

"I know about women," I replied somewhat stiffly, remembering Elsie. "I never claimed to be expert on elves.

I knew of you Little Folk mainly by hearsay, until I met you today. You seem very like human beings, except for your size and your magic."

"There you utter truth indeed!" But still she seemed to be bursting with some horrendously humorous secret. "You don't know the nature of an Accommodation-Spell?"

I shook my head. "No."

"Oh, this is fun!" she exclaimed, peering up at me and kicking her legs about. "I knew barbarians only by hearsay, too. You're much more fun than I expected."

"Thank you," I said awkwardly.

"For your information, Man, the Accommodation-Spell was fashioned by one of the Magicians of your kind. I think his name is Yin-Yang. He packages spells of all types and peddles them to anyone who is interested."

"I never heard of him."

"I think he lives down near Castle Roogna."

"Castle Roogna!" I exclaimed. "That's where I'm going!"

"So you said. After completing my favor."

"Yes. If you'd only tell me what—"

She tired of teasing me. "Jordan, you force me to be direct. I want your help to summon the stork," she said, or words to that effect. "I want a baby—a halfling, able to be among men and elves."

I gaped at her. "That's impossible!" I protested. "The size—it—I—I've got to get out of here!"

"The favor!" she cried. "You promised!"

"But—"

"Here, I'll invoke the spell," she said. She made a gesture with her hands. There was a flash, and then a funny wrenching sensation.

When my equilibrium re-established itself, I discovered that the bower had expanded enormously. It was now twice as big in diameter as it had been and eight times the volume. Length-volume judgments come readily to a person who may have to carry home the mass of the animal he puts an arrow through; he quickly learns that twice the height means a good deal more than twice the weight. The cushion I sat on was now more like a small bed.

"How do you like me now, Jordan?" Bluebell asked.

I turned my head to look at her—and gaped again. She was my size—or as close as a woman need be. She was phenomenal; the attributes that had been cute when she was small were now voluptuous. "I—what happened?"

She laughed yet again. "It's the spell," she explained. "It accommodated us. You are now an eighth your former mass, and I am eight times mine, so we're the same."

I looked at the bower again and the cushion. Yes; every dimension had doubled, which meant that my own dimensions had halved. I was half as tall, half as wide, and half as deep, while she had doubled every dimension. It certainly made a difference!

"But the baby," I protested. "If—"

"When," she corrected me.

"When the, uh, the stork brings—what size will *it* be?"

"My size, of course, so I can take proper care of him," she said. "Until he leaves the tree. Then—who knows? Some halflings can change size."

"I certainly never expected this!" I said.

"So I gathered," she said. "Well, let's not waste time. I know you want to get on with your more interesting adventures, where there be ogres and such."

There is no point in describing in tedious detail what followed. I'll just say that elven maidens are fully as adept in summoning storks as are human maidens, and I was glad to do my part. When I had done it, I got ready to leave the bower, but Bluebell held me back. "Not yet," she said.

Oh? Well, the Accommodation-Spell hadn't dissipated yet, so there was no point in my leaving the bower then; I would be too small to do much adventuring.

We ate, for the bower was stocked with giant fruits and nuts and bags of beverage. I suppose they were normal size; I was the one who had changed. Anyway, we feasted. There was a privy region for other natural functions. Then I napped for perhaps an hour and felt much improved when I woke.

It seemed she wanted to signal the stork again, so we did that. When that was done, again I thought it was time to depart, but again she restrained me. So we had another meal, and another sleep, all very nice, and I woke yet further restored. It turned out that she wished to generate a third message to the stork—or maybe she figured that three storks were better than one—and she was so lovely and persistent that I could do no less than cooperate.

"Now it is complete," she said. "The stork will come."

"You're sure?" I asked. "Maybe it would be better to send a few more messages."

She laughed, as she did so readily. "You are truly delightful, Jordan-Man, but I have held you too long already. I have felt the stork's acknowledgment; the baby will be delivered in due course."

That was the funny thing about the stork: it insisted on a delay before delivery. Maybe this was to give the prospective mother time to change her mind, or learn how to pin diapers. But I knew Bluebell's mind was set; she wanted that halfling.

So she dismissed me, and I had to depart. Such is the life of an adventurer. "It's certainly been fun," I told her, "and I'll remember it always."

She kissed me, one last time. "You're sweet." Then she waved her arms, reversing the spell, and in a moment we were back to our original sizes.

We drank another draught of grog and left the bower, climbing through the foliage and on down the massive trunk of the elm. The other elves of the tribe were awaiting us at the base.

"We have cared for your horse these three days, Barbarian," King Crown-of-Thorns told me.

"Three days?" I said incredulously.

"Aye, Man! Did you not know?"

"It seemed like three hours!"

"Now we must see to the augur," the King said. He led us to an old woman elf who sat at a shaped stone and had a sparkling ball before her.

Bluebell stopped before the old woman. "The fate of my baby," she said.

The woman picked up the ball and flung it at Bluebell. The ball expanded to englobe her for a moment, then contracted and returned to its place on the stone.

The woman peered into its sparkles, which now seemed to have a different pattern. "A son," she said. "He will leave you when he matures and go seek a wife among the human kind. He will never achieve notoriety, but his descendants may."

"Thank you," Bluebell said, sounding disappointed. Evidently she had hoped for more.

Aware of this, the woman peered more closely, tracing down a particular sparkle. "Let me see—there is one, far down the line, centuries hence—yes, she will consort with human Kings of Xanth."

"Oh!" Bluebell exclaimed, brightening.

Then the old elfess threw the globe at me. Surprised, I stepped back, but it expanded to my size and englobed me. For an instant I was dazzled by the sparkles; then they were gone, and the globe was back on the stone.

The elfess' little face turned grim as she contemplated the sparkles. "Let's pass on this one," she muttered.

"No, I want to know," I said. "If I am to be ancestor to the consort of Kings, what it says about me should be known."

The elfess grimaced. "You will be doomed by a cruel lie," she told me. "Yet it is not the end. After your flesh has rotted, you will find true love."

"Uh, thank you," I said, no more thrilled than Bluebell had been at first. I didn't really believe in fortune-telling, but I didn't really disbelieve, either.

Then the gathering dissipated. The King bade me farewell, ironic as that might seem after the prophecy, and Bluebell climbed up to give me a parting kiss.

I went to Pook, who had been happily grazing for three days on the rich elf-sward and was fit and fat. He had not tried to leave, for that would have implied that he was not my true steed, and the elves might have become awkwardly suspicious. So he had stayed, and when the elven children had begged him for rides "in the name of the Barbarian Man," he had obliged. I knew he was not yet tame, merely smart enough to play the role he had to. Just as I had been, up in the bower of the elf elm.

I mounted and rode away, pausing at the fringe of the glade to wave to the assembled elves. They waved back. Then, somewhat sadly, I moved on.

Chapter 5. Bundle of Joy

I rode through the pleasant elf-kept forest, feeling better as the poignancy of parting passed. I had indeed spent three days with the elves. My body had completed its process of healing, and I was at full strength again. Maybe that had been one reason Bluebell held me so long—to send me out into the jungle fully ready, rather than partly ready. If so, she had done me a favor beyond my realization at the time. Surely the other elves would not have let me stay, once she finished with me; they were businesslike folk at heart. But if I ever encountered another such tribe, I would be sure to pay my respects; I liked their mode of entertaining travelers.

The map showed that I was approaching dragon country. But I couldn't skirt it to the west; the Elements of Earth and Air were there, marked unfit for occupancy. The map was accurate about the northern regions I had already traversed, and I believed it about the southern ones. That left the eastern side, and I decided to go that route. How nice to have forewarning about the dragons! Naturally barbarians boast of slaying dragons, but the closer a barbarian actually gets to a dragon, the less inclined he feels toward combat. I found myself in absolutely no hurry now. So I veered Pook east.

We traveled for a day without event. Things were quiet in the elven region; there weren't even any tangle trees. It occurred to me that in some respects the elven society was superior to the human one; it certainly wasn't this pleasant or safe in the vicinity of Fen Village.

But as we left the elven region, the terrain became rougher, and we came up against the river the map showed as originating in the south and flowing north, parallel to the more distant coast. I considered crossing it, but there were flashes of color in the water's depths, and Pook balked. He remembered the sharks in the bog, and I couldn't blame him. So we turned south, into dragon country after all.

Then Pook sniffed, winding something. He wasn't afraid, just nervous, so I let him go toward it. It turned out to be a patch of blood on the forest floor, a scratchy trail, and a few feathers.

"Some bird came down to drink from the river," I conjectured. "And some predator attacked it. Bird got away, but injured. Happens all the time in the wilderness."

But still Pook sniffed, perplexed. "There's more?" I asked. "Want to track down the bird? I warn you, it won't be pretty." I knew that few horses, ghost or otherwise, had much taste for blood.

Pook sniffed out the trail, and I let him. He had a better nose than I had thought. Why was he so interested in this?

Then we came in sight of the bird. It was a white stork with a broken wing—and it had a bundle.

I doubletook, astonished. This stork was making a delivery! That bundle contained a baby!

Could Bluebell—? No. As I said, there was always a delay of several months before the baby was delivered. The bureaucratic lapse differed, and tended to be longest for human beings; evidently storks didn't like human people as well as they liked mouse people or gremlin folk or whatever. Certainly the wait was more than a day for elves. Besides, the bundle was way too big to hold an elfling.

The stork looked at me. His eyes were glazed with pain. "Friend or foe?" he asked.

"You talk?" I asked stupidly. It was difficult to believe that such a long, hard beak could form human syllables. But it was also not easy to believe that those backward-bending knees could enable it to walk. If we disbelieved everything that was hard, we wouldn't believe in Xanth at all.

"I talk," he agreed. "I don't fly, at the moment. I suffered a mishap." He craned his head about on his marvelously supple neck to eye his torn wing, from which blood still dripped. "Are you planning to help or hinder?"

"Uh, to help, I guess," I said awkwardly. I hadn't known that storks conversed with people like this. If they spoke our language, why did we have to make such intricate signals when ordering babies? It should be easier just to send a letter. No—immediately I relized that illiterates like me would never be able to order offspring, then; so there had to be a nonverbal or nonwritten signal. Anyway, I had never met a stork before; evidently their line of business required human communication at times, so they were trained for it. "But I don't know exactly what I can do. I'm not apt at healing others."

"There's a healing spring south of the—I forget what, but that's where it is," the stork said. I realized that the bird's brain was suffering some fuzziness. "I could fly there quickly—I know right where it is—if I could fly. But that confounded little dragon caught me unawares. I pecked it on the snout and it ran home to its mother, but alas, my wing was already gone. So I'll just have to hoof it, so to speak."

I studied the bundle. "That looks pretty heavy," I remarked. "Are you sure you can carry it, in your condition?"

"I must deliver!" the stork said, folding his good wing across his breast and gazing reverently upward.

"Uh, yes. Maybe we can give you a ride."

The stork looked at Pook. "That would be appreciated. But it's a fair bit, by foot. And it's to ogre country."

"That's where we're going," I said. "Let me give you a hand with that." I reached for the bundle.

There was a growl, and a hairy hand came out and grasped my wrist with appalling strength. Startled, I jerked my hand away—and the thing came right out of the bundle, hanging onto my wrist. It was a hairy mass of glower and growl.

"That's no baby!" I cried, shocked.

"Yes, it is," the stork said tiredly. "A baby ogre. Technically, an ogret. I told you where I was taking it."

"So you did," I agreed. Barbarians are not too bright about some things; I had missed the obvious connection. Of course ogres had babies, too, just as did humans and elves. Hardly as *nice* as humans and elves, but a similar principle. "Now how do I get this little monster off my wrist?" The matter was getting urgent, because the ogret was chinning himself up, one-handed, and was angling to bite off my hand.

"Knock him on the head until he lets go," the stork advised.

"But he's a *baby*!"

"That's how ogres show affection."

"Oh." Live and learn. I rapped the baby on his stony skull with my free knuckle, bruising my hand, and he let go and dropped back into the bag.

"We'd better deliver him before he gets hungry," the stork said.

Excellent notion! I loaded stork and bundle on Pook, then mounted. The ogret grabbed onto a link of chain and started chewing on it. The three of us were crowded, but Pook could handle it. Apparently he had some sympathy with the plight of the stork. Pook was a pretty decent animal, really.

The ghost horse started out at a brisk pace. I knew why; there was an incoming smell of dragon on the wind. How long would it take for the dragonlet to bring its mother back here?

"It's really not far to—to—" the stork remarked, but seemed to forget what he was going to say. It was as if his blood were draining right out of his memory.

There was a sound. I felt a shiver; that was a dragon snort, off to the right. I was in no mood at the moment to take on a dragon! I urged Pook to faster speed, but he needed no urging; he fairly flew across the land. I looked back over my shoulder to check on stork and ogret; the stork had his feet hooked firmly into a chain, so was secure, but the ogret had chewed almost through the link he was working on. "Stop that!" I snapped at him, and he growled and continued chewing. The trouble with juveniles these days is that they have no discipline!

The dragon heard us, of course, and moved to intercept us. Dragons have phenomenal ears that tune in on whatever interests them; what interests them most is prey, and just about any living creature is prey to a dragon. I had heard folk tales about single men fighting and slaying single dragons, but the closer I came to that sort of activity, the less I believed it. The fact is, the smallest grown dragon is generally more than a match for the largest man, unless that man has magic. I did have magic, of course, but I wasn't sure how much good it would do me in the belly of a dragon. I suppose in time my bones would reconstitute from the dragon droppings, and I would recover, but I didn't care to try that out. Certainly there would be some discomfort and awkwardness. Who wants to wake in the middle of a pile of dragon manure?

Pook was making excellent time. We were leaving the dragon behind. But then another popped up ahead, and I knew we were in trouble. In fact, I was coming to resent the myth that barbarian warriors love to fight dragons; it seemed that the dragons were the first to believe it, being eager for the fray. There is a distinction between adventure and folly that even the average barbarian is aware of.

We veered to the left, to the bank of the river. The river was smaller here than it had been downstream, but when we sought to cross it, a water dragon lifted its head and hissed. No escape there!

"Hang on—I've got to fight!" I warned. Supposedly, barbarians fight just for the fun of it; that's a half-truth.

We enjoy combat when we expect to win. With dragons, the odds are inclement.

I guided Pook with my legs. He was very responsive, knowing that once again his half-life was on the line as much as my whole life was. I anchored my left hand on a chain and lifted my good sword with my right. The dragon behind me was a fire-breather, so we stayed clear of it; the one in front was a smoker. That would be no fun, but was a better risk than fire. They say that where there's smoke there's fire, but that's not generally true among dragons. They also say that more people die from smoke inhalation than from direct burns, but I didn't trust that. So we charged the smoker snout-on.

The dragon opened his mouth, inhaling. Naturally he didn't stay stuffed with smoke all the time, any more than a man holds his breath all the time. The smoke is generated in the belly at need, a bit like gas in the human belly, and it takes a moment to work up the proper pressure and richness. I did not allow the dragon that time; I came up so fast that I arrived just as the first puff of smoke started out. I didn't bother with anything fancy; I simply rammed the point of my sword up his right nostril. Since I was hanging onto Pook, and Pook was charging forward, that thrust packed a lot of wallop.

The sword shoved its full length up the dragon's nose, and my gloved hand followed it, and also my arm up to the elbow. It was an excellent shot; I knew the point had skewered the creature's tiny brain. That wasn't a mortal wound, of course, but it did cause the monster some discomfort. Dragons don't really like having swords rammed up their noses, and they can get quite perturbed about having their brains skewered. For one thing, it causes their coordination to suffer somewhat, and that's inconvenient when one is engaged in mortal combat.

I braced my body against the dragon's warm snoot and hauled out my sword. A gout of blood followed it, dousing me in gore. But the dragon's head of smoke was already under way, and now this shoved the gore clear and blasted out to surround us. I held my breath, of course, and trusted the others were doing the same; it's a natural and sensible reflex. I urged Pook away from there. He obeyed with alacrity, and in a moment we emerged from the smoke ball. The dragon was thrashing and choking, as the blood and smoke mixed in his nostril to form smog. Blood and smoke are relatively harmless separately, but smog can be deadly. The hole in the monster's brain was bothering it, too, so it wasn't handling its pipes as well as otherwise. Thus the smoker was preoccupied for the moment, and we didn't need to worry about him.

But now the fire-breather caught up. "Go for the tail!" I told Pook. I meant the tail of the smoker, which might shield us from some of the blast of the fire-breather's breath. But the ghost horse misunderstood and galloped for the wrong tail.

Naturally the dragon's head whipped about, a jet of fire chasing us in an apparent curve. We hurdled the tail just as the fire caught up—and the dragon toasted its own tail. Now, dragons have insulated pipes for the fire, but their flesh lacks that protection. You should have heard the roar it made!

"South!" I cried.

Pook oriented south and shot forward like an arrow. The two hurting dragons bumped into each other and got tangled in their own coils. By the time they realized we were gone, we were too far gone for them to catch us. I'd like to claim that this was my consummate skill in maneuvering, but it was simple garden-variety luck, and I wouldn't care to try it again.

But we weren't home free yet. A flying dragon had been attracted by the commotion and was cruising overhead. It had not descended while it looked as if the big land-bound dragons would eat us, but now it looped about and zeroed in. I saw its body huffing up fire and knew we had to get out of the way in a hurry. We couldn't outrun that!

"River!" I cried. Pook angled for the river, trusting my judgment, and his hooves struck the water as the first jet of fire slanted down. The fire missed, generating a huge hiss of steam as it hit the water. Water never did much like fire, and the sentiment was mutual.

The water dragon humped up. It elevated its head and roared at the flier, angry at this poaching in its preserve. When the flier didn't sheer off fast enough, the water dragon pursed its lips and squirted a column of water up, scoring on one wing. *Now* the flier changed course, spinning out of control; the blast of water had dislocated one wing.

"I know how that feels," the stork remarked as the dragon tumbled into the water.

We got back on land and galloped south again, having escaped all four dragons. No doubt I would boast to my grandchildren of this exploit—but I never wanted to run that particular gantlet again!

Then a second flier appeared and drew a bead on us. This was the land of dragons, all right!

"Trees!" I yelled.

Pook headed for a copse of trees ahead. I hoped their trunks and foliage would help shield us from the flame. But then the horse braked to a halt.

"What are you doing?" I cried. Then I saw why.

The copse perched on the edge of a monstrous fissure in the ground. It was a sheer cliff leading down beyond vision; we couldn't go there! "What's that?" I asked incredulously.

"Now I remember!" the stork said. "It's the Gap Chasm! Can't think why I forgot about it before. I've flown over it hundreds of times."

"It's not on the map!" I muttered. What a thing to leave off!

Then the flying dragon caught up. Its jet flame seared down. Pook leaped out of the way—but the fringe of the fire touched us.

It fried my right arm and heated the hilt of my sword stove-hot. The stork's feathers caught fire. The ogret growled as his bag smoldered.

Pook leaped again, and the chains on his body slipped around his barrel, and we were dumped hard on the ground. My face smacked into a rock, and the whole Land of Xanth seemed to whirl about me. I saw my sword fling free—right over the brink of the chasm. Then I lost consciousness. I do that when I get knocked hard enough, embarrassing as it is.

When I woke, I could tell by the slant of the shadow that only a little time had passed. My talent was already healing me; after all, it was only a burn and a fall. But I wasn't able to move yet; maybe my neck had been broken, paralyzing me, and that hadn't healed yet. So I lay there with my head on the ground, absolutely still, and saw what I could see.

Nearby was the bundle of joy, with a short length of chain dangling from it. The little monster had chewed right through the link! Beyond was the bashed body of the stork. The fire had burned away the feathers and cooked the rest; the stork was dead. There was no sign of Pook; he had his freedom at last, if he had managed to escape the dragon. Well, I couldn't blame him for that; I had not done too good a job of protecting us from evil.

Then I saw a shadow. The dragon was returning! That was good for Pook, for it meant he had found cover and hidden from the monster. But it was bad for me. I willed my neck to heal, but nerves can't be rushed, and bone is slower yet; I still couldn't move anything below my head. And anyway, my sword was gone. How could I fight off a fire-breathing flying dragon bare-handed?

The dragon spiraled down and glided to a landing. It was ready to feed. It hobbled along the ground, weak on its feet in the fashion of its subtype, and snapped up the body of the stork. Two chomps, and the bird was gone.

The dragon hobbled another pace and reached for the bundle of joy. Suddenly the bag burst open, the ogret's hairy arm came out, and it swung the length of chain in an arc that smacked the links smartly across the dragon's nose. Little stars flew up, and a comet whirled away; it had been a hard strike.

The dragon blinked. Then it hissed. It pumped its bellows, preparing for another blast of fire to cook this arrogant morsel.

Just as the flame was ready, the ogret's ugly head popped out of the bag. Few things in Xanth are as ugly as an ogre's puss, and the sudden appearance of such a grotesquerie can be a shock. *"Growr!"* he growled in the dragon's face. If there is one thing worse than an ogre's puss, it's his growl.

The dragon was so startled he swallowed his fire. In fact, it backfired. There was a sort of internal rushing sound, and flame shot out of the dragon's tail. The monster straightened, its system reamed out, then curled and thrashed about as the heat of the fire cooked its own flesh. It rolled across the ground—and tumbled over the cliff.

Now at last my neck healed. The paralysis left me, and I sat up. My right arm remained inoperative, but was also improving. "You do have your points, ogre baby," I said. For it was a fact that the ogret had just saved me from getting toasted and consumed.

There was the sound of hooves. Pook was returning.

"What's this?" I asked as I stood. "Are you tame now?"

Pook snorted indignantly and swished his tail. He glanced back over his mane.

I looked. More dragons were coming. They had us surrounded!

"I should have known," I said, flexing my recovering arm. "You figure I can get you out of this?"

Pook nodded. He had confidence in me. Maybe he had given me more credit for dealing with the flying dragon than I deserved.

I considered, briefly. "Well, we can't go back the way we came. And my sword's down in the—what did the stork call it? The Gap Chasm."

The ogret growled. "Oh, yes," I said. "You need to be delivered, and the stork can't do it. I guess I do owe you a favor." That reminded me of Bluebell Elf, and the favors I had exchanged with her. My map was gone, burned, but I no longer needed it; anyway, the Gap had not been on it. I thought again how odd it was that the map should be in error about so gross a feature of landscape, when the elves were generally so meticulous about accuracy. And the stork had been unable to remember it, until actually seeing it. Maybe there was magic involved.

I peered down the cliff. It was impassable. I looked east, along it—and saw the river. It flowed up the cliff face, over the lip, and on to the north, where I knew it broadened out into a refuge for water dragons. It hadn't occurred to me that a river could flow up a wall, but, of course, there was a lot of Xanth I hadn't seen before. I have heard it said that travel broadens the mind; it certainly was doing so for me! "Maybe there," I murmured.

I loaded the bundle of joy on the ghost horse, and the hairy hand latched onto another length of chain. I knew the strength of that hand; he would be secure.

I mounted and guided Pook east to the river. Again I flexed my right arm; it was just about better now. I don't know how I'd survive without my healing talent!

We reached the river before the dragons did. The water at the lip was too shallow for the water dragon, fortunately. We could cross it—but so could the land dragons. No real escape there.

How about down into the chasm?

"We'll wade upstream," I told Pook, putting more confidence into my voice than I felt. I headed him for the water at the brink. His ears went flat back and he balked. So I dismounted and led him. I stood at the lip, then stepped over. My body tilted around at a ninety-degree angle, and I found myself standing on the face of the cliff, knee-deep in water. It was working!

After a moment, with the dragons closing in, Pook followed. His forehooves passed the corner, and he straddled the lip as if it were the top of a pyramid, his belly almost scraping. Then he got his hind legs across and stood with me, his head pointing down into the Gap. "See," I said. "It has to be level for the water to flow without falling. Rivers have ways of navigating that we can only emulate. As long as we wade, we won't fall." I certainly hoped that was true!

But Pook remained uncertain, so I continued to lead him. We waded upstream, downcliff. A dragon poked its head over the corner, but lacked the courage to follow. After a moment, the dragon fired a jet of flame, but the perspective confused it and the jet missed. We proceeded out of range. Fortunately, no more flying dragons appeared; maybe this region was awkward for their flying.

The water was cold. The chill of it soon soaked through my boots and into my feet. "We'd better get to the bottom of this," I remarked, looking down into the Gap. But the bottom was still a long way ahead.

I moved to the edge of the water channel, hoping the effect extended beyond the water. But I was cautious. I scooped up a handful of water and hurled it to the side, out of the channel.

The moment the water left the region of the channel, it made a right-angle turn and took off forward, accelerating toward the base of the cliff. I couldn't hear the splat as it struck, but I knew I did not want to go that route myself.

Nevertheless, my toes were becoming numb, and I could see that Pook wasn't comfortable, either. No one likes to get cold feet! At this rate, our toes would freeze before we could get out of the water. I had to do something!

I bent to peer into the water. Now I saw small fish swimming in it. I scooped one up—and cold stabbed through my hand. That was one cold fish!

"I wish I had a hotfoot," I said. "Or a hot dog. That would drive away the cold fish." But wishes wouldn't do me much good. I needed something more tangible and immediate. My feet were freezing!

I glanced back again at Pook. He was shivering. My eye fell on the bundle of joy. A notion bulbflashed in my skull so brightly that I suspect some light leaked out of my ears.

I went to Pook's side, selected a chain, and yanked it upward. Naturally it descended on the other side, as all the chains went around and around his barrel. The ogret went down with it, for he was chewing on it and refused to let go. I suppose teething is rough for babies. I continued to haul until the ogret hung upside down below Pook's belly. He didn't let go, for no one had knocked him on the head. But when his head dipped into the frigid water, he was annoyed, for no ogre likes to be coolheaded. He roared.

The force of the roar sent froth shooting through the

river. The cold fish scattered in terror, and the water warmed. I hauled down on the chain, and ogret came up on the other side, until he was upright again, still chewing on the link. We proceeded onward.

After a while, the cold fish came back, so I repeated the performance and drove them away again. By the third time they collected, we had reached the foot of the cliff and were able to step out on upright land. That was a relief!

Now we were in the Gap Chasm. The river crossed its base and went up the far wall. Came down it, that is. No doubt we could walk up that the same way we had walked down, but I thought I'd explore for an alternate route. I didn't like having to dunk the ogret all the time, and didn't want to be caught with cold feet halfway up if that trick didn't work.

So I got on Pook, and we traveled west along the floor of the chasm. I spied my trusty sword lying near the river, beside the body of the flying dragon the ogret had backfired. I recovered my blade, welcoming it like an old friend, washed it in the river, and watched bemusedly as the bloodstained water flowed around the corner and up the wall. Fascinating! Then I dried the sword on the hot hide of the flying dragon and returned to Pook.

It was pleasant here, with green grass, bushes, and patterns of racks and dragon tracks—

Dragon tracks?

I examined them more closely. Yes, these were the spoor of a big dragon, one who evidently hunted here. That made me a trifle nervous; I had already had enough experience with dragons to last me the rest of my life— a life that would not necessarily be long, if I encountered one more dragon.

I was nervous with reason. Now Pook's ears perked, and I heard it too: *whomp-whomp-whomp!* That was the whomp of a low-slung, heavy-set dragon!

The sound was coming from the east, so we galloped west. Soon I looked back and saw it—a horrendously toothed monster of the steam variety. Whomping wasn't the most efficient way to travel, but with a creature this size, it was fast enough.

Pook put on a little more speed, and we stayed comfortably ahead of the dragon. That was one big advantage to having a horse! But I saw that the chasm was narrowing, and this made me nervous; suppose it dead-ended? That was one hefty steamer back there; I didn't think I could slay it. It would take a full-grown ogre to fight that thing!

An ogre. I glanced back at the bundle of joy. No, that was a baby ogre, formidable enough for his age, but only a tiny fraction of the ugliness and power of a grown one. Some qualities of ugliness take a lifetime to achieve. We'd simply have to escape this dragon—which would be easy enough if the Gap remained wide, and impossible if the Gap became too narrow. I didn't really care to gamble that the chasm would favor us.

I looked at the cliffs on either side. No hope there! We needed a channel, a level path cut into the steep slope that a horse could navigate. One trouble about this was that anything a horse could travel, a dragon of this configuration could also travel. Still, if we followed the path and stayed ahead until we got out of the chasm—

This was the stuff of daydreams. There was no path cut into the side.

The floor of the chasm became corrugated. There were ridges in it, as if the walls had squeezed together and wrinkled the base. These ridges gradually rose up until they were as high as Pook. I didn't like this; we were being channelized, and I preferred room to dodge the dragon. If one of these little channels should dead-end, it would slow us in scrambling out, and the dragon would gain on us.

Pook sniffed. "You smell something?" I asked. "If it's a way out, I'm for it!"

He came to an intersection of channels and swung left. The walls of this channel rose up higher, up to my riding head height. Then, abruptly, the channel ended.

Pook's hooves skidded, churning up turf, but he couldn't stop in time. We spun halfway around and crashed into the end. Dirt shook down as we righted ourselves, and the ogret growled.

Then I saw a tunnel slanting back. It hadn't been visible from the other side, as the entrance was narrow. And I heard the approaching whomp of the dragon. "Get in there!" I cried.

Pook squeezed in as the dragon whomped by. I was afraid the dragon would turn and pursue us, so I urged the ghost horse on into the darkness. As my eyes adjusted, I was able to see because wan rays of light leaked in through cracks. This tunnel was close to the surface, but never quite emerging. Where did it go?

It twisted in wormlike fashion to the right and then began to rise. Surely we would break out of the ridge any moment now! But we didn't.

Then I saw a larger crack and paused to peer through it. There was the chasm—slightly below us! We were in the wall!

We continued on up. The tunnel meandered up and down and around, and sometimes formed large spirals in the earth, but generally trended upward. I hoped it was a way to the surface. It smelled dank, and there were spider webs in the cracks, so it seemed long disused, but it had to go somewhere. Wherever that was, that was where we were going.

It took a long time, but our hope ascended as the tunnel did, and we got there. The tunnel finally debouched into a lesser crevice, one running at right angles to the Gap Chasm but intersecting it well above the base, so that we could not have entered here without using the worm tunnel. We followed this one south until it lost interest and surfaced and we returned at last to the ordinary ground of Xanth. This was the heart of what the lost map claimed was ogre country—which was right where I wanted to be.

Now all I had to do was deliver the bundle of joy to its expecting family and proceed to Castle Roogna. I found I had lost any interest I might have had in challenging a mature ogre to heroic combat. If a baby ogre was this horrendous, I had better stay away from a grown one!

But also, I no longer saw ogres as bestial monsters; because of the ogret, I realized that they had personalities and families just as real people did. It's hard to condemn any creature whose glare and growl has stopped a dragon from consuming you.

But where was the ogret's family? Ogre country was a broad, vast region; there could be many ogre tribes, and many families within each tribe. How could I know which one was the right one? Without that information, how could I deliver this bundle of joy?

It was evening now, and I was hungry after the day's adventure. So I foraged for food, finding some fruits for the ogret. I didn't know what babies ate, but suspected this one would eat anything. After all, if he teethed on chains...

My assumption seemed to be correct. I offered him a banana, and he grabbed it in one hairy mitt, squished it in the center so that the pulp shot out at either end, and jammed the remaining skin into his maw. He took an apple, squeezed it so hard juice spurted, and gulped down the skin and seeds with evident gusto. This sort of eating was messy, but, of course, babies are messy eaters. I gave him a milkweed pod, afraid that he would just squish the milk all over himself, but this one he chose to swallow whole. Finally I gave him a pomegranate, and he really liked that; he knocked the granate on his head, cracking the stone open, then picked out the red, juicy seeds, threw them away, swallowed the stone, and burped up a seed he had overlooked. He was really sort of cute in his horrendous fashion.

Taking care of a baby, it turned out, was no problem at all. My only concern was changing the diaper, but it seemed the ogret hadn't existed long enough to process food all the way through yet, so the diaper remained clean. That was just as well, since I wasn't sure I had the strength to take it away from him for cleaning.

I didn't worry about Pook, either. He could go off now if he wished to, since I had gotten most of the way to Castle Roogna and he no longer needed me to save him from being taken over by elves or eaten by dragons or whatever. We could get along without each other.

I leaned back against an acorn tree. "What am I going to do with you, ogre baby?" I asked rhetorically as I held out a fruit-punch. Naturally the ogret punched it. Juice exploded, and the baby crammed the husk into his big mouth. He spat a seed at me that just missed my head and embedded itself in the tree trunk behind me and growled contentedly. The shudder of the seed-shock traveled up the trunk and caused the branches of the tree to shake, dislodging a corn, which thunked into the ground before the ogret. He picked it up and chewed on it.

I saw a sparkle on him. What could it be? I reached for it, but he grabbed for my hand, so I had to let it be. But it was something he wore. What would an undelivered baby wear?

What else except an address tag? I had to see that! But the ogret wasn't going to turn it over voluntarily.

I fetched another fruit-punch and shoved it at his big mouth. While he punched and chomped on that, I took advantage of his distraction to grab the tag.

It was blank. Of course, I couldn't read, anyway, and wouldn't if I could—barbarians take justified pride in being illiterate—but that was a separate problem. How was I to get an address from this?

I turned it over—and it flashed. One side was bright, the other dull. When I turned it again, the brightside dulled and the dullside brightened. When I held it flat, both sides dulled. It was as if the thing were a mirror that reflected light only when properly oriented—except there was no source of light that accounted for the flash, just jungle.

But a magic mirror would use another type of light source.

I smiled. Now I knew in what direction the ogret's parents were. The flash pointed the way.

I cut off a length of vine and tied it to the ogret's bag in such a way as to keep the baby inside while allowing him to look and reach out. Then I passed the vine over a sturdy branch and hauled the bundle of joy up about halfway; that kept the baby off the ground, which was no

safe place at night even for a tyke as horrendous as this,
and prevented him from going anywhere while I slept. As
an afterthought, I sliced off a section of ironwood and
passed it up. The hairy hand snatched it from my grasp,
and the teeth happily gnawed on its end. It was a decent
pacifier that should keep the ogret halfway quiet.

I climbed the tree, found a suitable niche, and settled
down to sleep. Pook continued to graze below; he wasn't
concerned about the spooks of the darkness, being a ghost
horse himself. In fact, the rattle of his chains probably
frightened away other spooks.

It was a quiet night, and I woke refreshed. Naturally
Pook was gone—but to my surprise, he returned when
he heard me stirring. "You mean you're tame now?" I
asked him, as I had before. He snorted derisively, as
before, but did not depart.

I found some rock candy and several more milkweed
pods for the ogret, and he chomped them up violently
and spat seeds at flying bugs, scoring an impressive number of times. I wondered whether the night had soiled his
diaper, but it seemed all right. Maybe it was a magic one,
self-cleaning. The storks seemed to have deliveries down
to a science, if that's not a meaningless term in Xanth.
That is, they are impossibly well organized. In real life,
of course, things are never scientific, and it's foolish to
believe that they can be. Only in a place like Mundania
would anyone try to hold such a view.

I loaded the bundle of joy back on Pook, not bothering
to untie the vine-rope, and mounted. Naturally, the ogret
found another section of chain to chew on. Babies are
always putting things in their mouth. But it kept him quiet.
In ogre country, silence is a special blessing.

We headed in the direction indicated by the tag-flash,
which was roughly southeast. We galloped through forest
and plain, over hill and valley, past cliff and cave, monster
and river. We passed curse-burrs, ant-lions, drifting magic-
dust, a colony of fauns and nymphs, harpies, and a mouth-
organ tree that tootled a low note of warning at us. It was
a pretty dull trip.

We made excellent time, for Pook liked to run, and in

the afternoon we reached the region of the ogres. I could tell, because some trees were twisted into knots, others were broken off at the base, and small ironwoods had been bitten off at ground level; ogres liked to play with things. I had heard somewhere that the ogres were migrating north, but this seemed pretty far south to me; maybe they were slow movers. Well, they could take three centuries to move north if they wanted to; no one was going to tell an ogre what to do! Just so long as they never got too near to Fen Village.

I checked the ogret's tag for reorientation. It was glowing like a little fire; we were very close. But now a problem occurred to me. How was I to hand over the bundle of joy without getting myself clobbered? I didn't want to defend myself with my sword; what good was it to deliver a baby to a dead mother? But I didn't want to be pulped and eaten by the ogres, either.

I located the family domicile, which was a pile of trees torn up by the roots and shaped into a crude nest. Ogres never did things carefully when brute power sufficed. I saw the ogress; she was almost twice my height and so ugly that her puss made spots of gook dance before my eyeballs. It was like a cross between the rump of a sick sphinx and a squashed ant-lion. I could hardly look at her, let alone go near her!

I worked up a notion. I suspended the bundle of joy by the vine and swung it around in an arc. The ogret chortled; he liked swinging through the air almost as much as he liked chomping chain. Then I nudged Pook forward.

We came to the ogress. She was ripping a small tangle tree from the ground and chewing on its flailing tentacles. Expectant females were known to have odd tastes!

"Here it comes!" I cried and charged toward her, whirling the ogret. I passed her just out of reach, which was a scary thing, because ogres have phenomenally long reaches. The swinging bundle of joy whomped into her belly, knocking her onto her back, her feet in the air, the bundle atop her. The ogret's head popped out, and he growled so horrendously that the remaining tentacles of the tangler she held straightened out stiffly in sheer terror.

The ogress let out an equally horrendous screech of joy and clutched the ogret to her. Mother and son—what awful music they made together! I galloped away, unmolested. The delivery had been made!

Of course the male ogre spied me. He did not appear to be completely pleased about the delivery, or maybe he had simply decided that Pook and I would make an excellent repast. He lumbered after us, making surprising speed because of the length of his stride. He was even uglier than the ogress and ogret put together, incredible as that sounds. Small birds, startled by our passage, flew up, glimpsed his gross puss, and fell from the air stunned. Bugs died in clouds where he passed. Trees quaked, their leaves turning yellow around the edges. In the sky a cloud looked down, saw him, and puffed into vapor. We zoomed on; we didn't want to look at him, either.

When the ogre saw he couldn't catch us, he paused to rip a boulder out of the ground and hurl it. I saw it coming and had Pook dodge behind a great rock maple tree for shelter. The boulder struck the tree and knocked off its top. We sprang out of there as rocks and sand showered around, for the maple had been shattered. What a brute that ogre was! If this was his reaction to the happy occasion of becoming a father, I'd hate to be near when he was angry! I was sure the ogret would have a happy home life.

We managed to lose ourselves in an intricate pattern of geometrees, and the ogre gave up the pursuit. He wasn't very smart, for ogres are as stupid as they are strong, and that is the standard against which all other strength and stupidity is measured. He gave up the chase and went back to glower at the bundle of joy.

I hoped that when a stork set out to find Bluebell Elf, it would be able to deliver its bundle with less trouble than this one had been! Certainly I no longer thought that the storks had an easy job. In fact, it is all too easy to believe others have easy times when you don't know anything about their problems.

We walked back the way we had come, roughly northwest, for I understood that Castle Roogna was somewhere in that region. At this slower pace the journey took a couple of days, and I fought off a few minor threats along the way—griffins, carnivorous plants, giant serpents, hostile centaurs, that sort of thing, purely routine—and I was beginning to get bored when at last the dusky towers of Castle Roogna hove into view.

I had arrived!

Chapter 6. Hero's Challenge

Actually, Castle Roogna wasn't the easiest place to approach. It was surrounded by a spreading orchard, and the trees were unusual. I thought it was coincidence or bad maintenance when I found the approach path blocked by a massive branch. I guided Pook around it—only to discover that it interlocked with the extended low branch of another tree. So I guided Pook around the other way, to circle the first tree—and there was another branch tying into another tree. They were too low for Pook to pass under, yet too fluffed out with brush for him to leap over.

I paused and scratched my head. We could get by, of course. But I marveled that the path to the castle could have become so overgrown. Had no one passed this way in the last fifty years? Surely the road to the capital would be kept up! Did this mean the castle was deserted? In Fen Village we had not had direct news from Castle Roogna in a long time, but we assumed this was because we were a minor backwoods hamlet. Now I wondered about the frontwoods region; could it have gone out of business?

Now that I thought of it, I realized I had encountered no men on my long journey here. Goblins, elves, ogres, yes— but these were only distantly related to men. Well, perhaps not *too* distantly related, in the case of the elves; Bluebell had been most womanlike, divinely feminine, when the adaptation-spell was in force. But where were the regular men and women? I had understood there were human villages scattered all around Xanth. Where were they?

Well, I would just have to get into Castle Roogna and find out. I dismounted, drew my sword, and walked to the center of the path. I picked my spot and used my weapon like an axe, hacking into the wood.

I swear, that whole tree shuddered at my first blow. There was a rain of twigs and leaves, and a groan as if wind were making the trunk shift.

I hacked again, at an angle, so that a wedge of bark and wood flew out. The tree shuddered again, and reddish sap oozed from the cut.

Pook neighed warning. I leaped back—and a solid branch crashed down where I had been standing, the kind they call a widowmaker. It was just as well I had avoided it, since I wasn't married so couldn't leave a widow. Apparently I had shaken the tree hard enough to dislodge some deadwood. Apt name for it! I kicked it out of the way and made ready to hack again.

But now, oddly, the branch was lower. In fact, it touched the ground. It would be easy for Pook to step over it. I considered hacking the rest of the way through it, anyway, to clear the path, but dusk was drawing nigh in the creepy way it had, and I wasn't sure what I would find ahead. Best not to expend more time here now. So I remounted Pook, and we stepped across and proceeded onward.

As we passed under the looming height of another tree, a great rock maple like the one the ogre had shattered, Pook leaped ahead. Behind us, a rock crashed. No ogre was present; the tree itself had bombed us!

I looked ahead. The trees beside the path stood close and threatening, and I didn't trust them. The things of the vegetable kingdom can be just as bad as those of the animal kingdom when they take a notion to be.

I decided to use Standard Barbarian Approach Number One: the direct threat of mayhem. I drew my sword again.

"Listen, you trees!" I yelled. "Whichever one of you drops anything on me will get its branches lopped off or its trunk girdled!"

There was no response. Holding the sword ready and glaring about me like an ogre, I guided Pook forward. His ears were turning this way and that, alert for the sounds of treachery. But nothing happened, and soon we were clear of this region. It seemed that my warning had sufficed; I had cowed the trees. Don't tell *me* that violence is the refuge of incompetence! It's the only language some things understand. Of course, I *am* a barbarian warrior, so there may be a modicum of self-interest in that statement.

Now the orchard opened out, and Castle Roogna came into view from fairly close range in the light of the setting sun. I was ready to behold and marvel at its glories.

I stifled my disappointment. Castle Roogna was no glowing edifice; it was a mildewed, rundown structure whose gardens were overrun by weeds and whose moat was a mass of brown goo. This was the capital of Xanth? It was more like a witch-hag's den, or the fabled past residence of the Zombie Master, who had lost his love and turned himself into a zombie four hundred years before. What was wrong?

I rode up to the moat. The water was low, but closer inspection showed that there was not much goo, just brackish stuff. The moat monster was asleep. "Hey, wake up, soursnoot!" I called indignantly to it. "Sleep on your own time!"

The thing opened an eye, flicked its tail, and went back to its slumber. How lax could castle security get?

Disgusted, I crossed the drawbridge, which was down and unattended. The castle was the largest human-constructed edifice I had seen, imposing despite its rundown state, but I was saddened to see the authority of man at such reduced level. I had expected to come to the center of a flourishing empire; instead, it was little more than my home village.

A woman appeared at the interior gate. She was middle-aged and dumpy, and her apron was dirty. "Welcome, Hero!" she exclaimed. "Do come in!"

"How do you know I'm a hero?" I demanded, not completely flattered. Oh, I like flattery as well as the next barbarian, but this seemed gratuitous and possibly insincere. Also, flattery is much easier to accept from young, pretty women than from old, dumpy ones.

"The prophecy," she explained.

"What prophecy?" I asked, somewhat aggrieved because I remembered the one made by the old elfess that I was to be doomed by a cruel lie. I don't really like such prophecies, so this was one I preferred not to be reminded of.

"King Gromden will have to tell you that. Come on in; we have supper waiting."

I shrugged and dismounted. It was strange that the trees had tried to prevent my approach to the castle, while people welcomed it. I remained on guard. But the prospect of a good meal was tempting. "What about my horse?" I knew Pook would be interested in the same kind of protection he had had among the elves; he was helping me in the wilderness, and I was helping him in civilization.

"We have a nice stall for him, with magic grain," the woman said.

Pook's ears perked up. He whinnied. He knew a good thing when he heard it.

Obligingly, the woman led us to a stall set in the wall. Sure enough, there was a pan of grain there, and it looked delicious even to me. Pook went to it and started eating, and I saw that when he took a mouthful, the level in the pan did not drop. It was magic, all right, and evidently the grain was good.

"You'll be all right?" I asked him. "Remember, we don't really know these people." But he ignored me; he was happy. I wondered if he had not gotten too tame. It was not good for an animal—or a barbarian—to be too trusting of strangers, especially civilized strangers. Civilized people did not share the simple values of barbarians and could be very devious.

"That's pretty concentrated stuff," I warned him. "If

you eat too much, you could get sick—" He snorted, sending oats flying; he knew what he was doing and didn't appreciate my meddling. I suppose I wouldn't have appreciated his cautions on women, sword-fighting, and such, either. We human beings can be awfully arrogant in little unconscious ways.

I followed the woman into the human region of the castle. This was in better repair. The floor was clean, and there were attractive tapestries on the walls. We came to the banquet hall, and there a sumptuous repast was laid out.

A man stood at the head of the table. He was old and bald and fat, with straggly white whiskers and sunken eyes. He wore a fancy robe and crown, so I realized he was the King of Xanth. Naturally I greeted him with the respect due his rank. "Hello, King," I said.

"Hello, Hero," he replied, batting an eye.

"Um, King, I don't know about this hero business."

"It is the prophecy," he explained. "In our time of need, a young, well-formed man of primitive lineage is to appear, riding a pooka he has tamed. You are evidently that man. Now sit down and eat, before it gets cold."

"Uh, sure," I agreed, disconcerted. That prophecy did seem to have me nailed down pretty well, except that Pook claimed he wasn't really tame. I suppose it's a matter of perspective. But if that prophecy was on target, what about the elven one? I didn't like that thought, so I flushed it from my mind.

I sat down, and the woman served us both. It seemed to be dragon steak and fruit salad, with foaming brew from a beer-barrel tree. Standard fare, except for the dragon meat; I wondered how they had come by that. But on occasion dragons suffered mishaps, and men were able to snatch the bodies before some other creature did. I was good and hungry, so I went to it.

"You're really supposed to wait till King Gromden starts," the woman murmured in my ear as she poured the beer.

I paused, mouth full. "Mf mmf?" I asked.

"Quite all right," the King said quickly, taking a mouthful himself.

So we ate, and it was an excellent meal. The King didn't eat much, so I polished off most of it, tucking a spare dragon steak in my pocket for future consumption. Then we settled back to talk. "You may not know it, King, but I'm just a barbarian warrior," I said, burping vigorously and wiping my mouth on the tablecloth.

"That is surprising," he remarked gravely.

"What's this hero business? I mean, so there's a prophecy, but what do you need a hero for?"

"It would seem that we have a problem," Gromden said. "We do need a hero, and evidently you are it."

"Well, it's true I'm looking for adventure, King. What can I do for you?"

"You can undertake the Hero's Challenge."

"Sure, King. Just tell me where to go and what to do." I yawned, as it had been a long day.

"Tomorrow," Gromden decided. "You are obviously tired from your journey."

"Suits me, King," I agreed politely.

And so the maid woman showed me to an upstairs room, complete with a fine big bed, mirror, and chamber pot. I'd never had a room with such modern sanitary facilities before! Soon I flopped on the bed and slept, snoring roundly. I know I snored, because I heard the echoes off the walls. I really preferred the forest, but I'm adaptable; I can make do with civilized fixings when I have to.

In the morning I woke to a peremptory knocking. I bounced off the bed, set my hand on my sword, and went to the door.

It was only the serving woman. "Something has come up," she said hastily. "I won't be able to fix your breakfast, but you can forage in the orchard."

"That's fine," I said. "What's come up?"

"Well—" She looked pained. "His Majesty is indisposed."

"Oh. You mean the old boy doesn't want to talk today? Well, I guess I can wait."

She didn't answer. She just turned quickly away. Women can be funny that way.

I used the chamber pot and dumped it out the window, then went down and out to the orchard. Pook was already there, grazing. He looked satisfied; that load of grain had done him good. "How come you haven't run away?" I asked him. "You've been sticking with me when you don't have to, and you even served as part of the prophecy. Are you sure you're not tame?"

He snorted derisively, as he always did, and continued to graze. It occurred to me that even ghost horses might get lonely, or maybe tired of rattling chains at night. While he was with me, he had company and was admitted to the territories of elves and men, where there was good eating. Maybe it made sense to be tame, or to seem to be.

I found plenty of ripe fruits on the trees and soon fashioned myself a sandwich from slices of breadfruit and cheesefruit. I saw snapdragon bushes, and so the mystery of the dragon steaks was abated; it wasn't real dragon meat. I didn't mind; it tasted the same, as far as I knew. I could see that this had once been a well-kept grove, but now it was clogged by weeds. There just didn't seem to be much doing here at Castle Roogna. I remained disappointed, though I hoped the King had a good adventure for me.

When I went back inside, I decided to check on the old boy. I found King Gromden's door with a crown painted on it, so I pounded on that. There was no answer, so I pushed it open and went in. "You here, King?" I called politely. I didn't want anyone to think I was just barging in.

There was a muffled sound from the bed, so I went there. King Gromden was lying on his back and he didn't look well at all. "Hey!" I exclaimed. "You're really sick, King!"

His eyes ground open. "Astute observation," he whispered.

"Hey, look, Grom, I'm sorry," I said. "I didn't know.

The wench just said you weren't talking. Is it something you ate? Can I help?"

"I am old," he confessed, as if that weren't obvious. "I won't live out the year. Perhaps not the month. My wife and child deserted me years ago. You can help by undertaking the challenge."

"Sure, King," I said. "I told you I would yesterday. What is it?"

"It is—" He paused for a labored breath. Last the year or the month? I wasn't sure he'd last the hour! He had seemed okay the night before, but I guess these things come and go when you're old. "It is the challenge for the succession."

"The what?"

"The succession. When I die, there must be a new King. The best Magician in the land. But there's a problem I lack the strength to resolve—"

He faded out. "Yes, King?" I prompted, prodding him with a thumb. "You say you have to do something before you croak?"

"So there must be a contest," he whispered. "A contest of magic, and—"

I waited, but he seemed to have lost consciousness. Too bad; I really wondered what he had been trying to tell me. A contest of magic sounded pretty interesting, but I didn't see how I fitted in. I was, after all, just a barbarian; I didn't know much about strong magic.

I went back to my room. There was the maid, looking flushed. "Where have you been?" she asked severely. "I've been looking all over for you."

"I was talking to the old boy," I said.

"You bothered the King?" she demanded as if shocked. Women get shocked by the littlest things. "He's ill!"

"He sure is," I agreed. "You should have told me. Don't you have a pill or spell for him?"

"It's past that stage," she snapped. "Now you go downstairs; Magician Yin is here to see you in the audience chamber."

"Who?"

"Magician Yin. You'll see Magician Yang tomorrow; they refuse to come together. They're very competitive."

I shrugged amiably. "Sure, I'll talk to anyone. I hope the old boy feels better soon. Maybe he's constipated; if you give him some prune juice—" But she was already bustling away. I suppose she was one of those people who didn't take kindly to good advice.

So I went downstairs and found Magician Yin. I remembered that the elves had said someone with a name like that made the canned spells that could be so handy. He turned out to be a medium-sized, medium-aged man in white who really didn't look like much. Naturally I told him so; barbarians believe in straight talk.

He smiled, for some reason reminding me of the way the King had reacted to some of my comments. I just don't understand the attitudes of civilized folk, I suppose; it's as if they are piped in to some other kind of awareness that passes me by. Women are like that, too.

"Let me show you what I do," Yin said. He reached into a bag he carried and brought out a small globe. He handed it to me. "Set it somewhere and invoke it," he said.

"Oh, you mean it's a spell," I said.

"Yes, I make spells."

I set it on the table. "I invoke you, spell," I said.

Instantly the globe glowed. The light from it brightened the whole room. "Say, that's pretty good," I said, turning my eyes away from its brightness. "How long does it burn?"

"Until nullified," he said.

"You mean till I tell it to quit?"

"No, you can not un-invoke my spells; they are permanent. It requires a counterspell to nullify it—one equal and opposite. Some of my spells do lose strength as time passes, though; it depends on their nature and complexity."

"Okay, let's have a darkness spell," I said.

"I don't make negative spells," Yin said.

"Oh? Who does?"

"My twin brother, Magician Yang."

"You mean there are two of you?" Now that Yin-Yang reference was clarifying.

"Equal and opposite."

"Say!" I exclaimed, catching on. "You and he—the contest? To see who's best?"

"Correct," Yin agreed. "One of us must be King after Gromden expires. The strongest Magician. But we haven't been able to determine which of us that is."

"But how do I fit in?"

"Obviously Yang and I can't just throw spells at each other; they'd simply nullify one another and it would be even. We need to discover whose magic is more effective in practice. So we need a third party to use the spells for some practical purpose. Then we can ascertain whose spells are best."

"A third party," I said. "That must be me!"

"Correct," Yin agreed. "You will go on a quest, using my magic to assist you and to facilitate your mission, while Yang's magic opposes you. If you succeed, I will win and be designated the next King of Xanth; if you fail—"

"Um, what happens to me if I fail?" I asked.

"Well, it is simply a matter of fetching an object. If you don't bring it back, then Yang wins and becomes the next King. But I'm sure my spells will enable you to succeed."

"I guess so," I agreed uncertainly. Equal and opposite—it seemed to me the spells would still cancel one another out, leaving no advantage for either side. But I was the first to concede that a barbarian is not the one to comprehend the nuances of magical interplay. "How do I get the spells?"

"This bag is for you," he said. "Our agreement is that I provide seven spells to assist you. Yang will set the opposite seven spells to oppose you. Mine you can carry with you; his will intercept you without warning. You merely have to nullify his evil spells with my good ones and complete the mission."

"Seems simple enough," I said, disappointed. I had hoped for news of some dark tower defended by monsters with a fair damsel to rescue and magic to blow up the monsters and scale the tower wall. Ah, well; a mundanish adventure is still an adventure, I suppose.

"It should be," he agreed, with a certain subtle civilized nuance of the type I have already remarked on.

I looked into the bag of spells. It was filled with objects: a little white shield, a figure of a monster, a skull, a stone, a doll, a tangled length of vine, and a magic compass. "But these are toys!" I protested.

Yin laughed. "Hardly! They are inert representations. When you invoke them, they become full-sized and potent."

I lifted out the little skull. "I don't need a full-sized skull!"

"Allow me to explain. Because all Yang's spells and mine are equal and opposite, they have similar forms in many cases. King Gromden decided on the seven spell-sets that would be used in this contest; he wanted to allow a fair trial of magic, without endangering bystanders. Thus we are permitted no deadly explosive spells, or basilisk spells, or noxious contagious-disease spells. The seven are fairly straightforward, and you should not have trouble understanding them. His negative spells are black; my positive ones are white. So when you encounter his black skull, you must invoke my white skull. The black skull brings death; the white one brings just the opposite, life. They don't complete their effects instantly; you will have a minute or so to invoke the life-spell when you feel the death-spell taking hold."

"Oh." I reached into the bag for another spell. "Maybe you better explain them all for me so I know exactly what to do in my minute, each time." I brought out the little white shield. "What about this?"

"The white shield counters the black sword. A sword, of course, is negative; it exists for one purpose only, to cut and kill. A shield exists to preserve limb and life, and this shield, when invoked, will preserve yours."

It certainly made sense. I looked forward to seeing that magic black sword; that was the kind of sword and sorcery I understood. Maybe I'd take it on with my own sword before I invoked the shield, just to see how good it really was. I brought out the twisted vine. "This?"

"That is a representation of an eye-queue vine; note the eyeballs braided into it." I had thought those were beads, but now I saw that the tiny dots were pupils. "In nature, the eye-queue dispenses temporary or even illusory intelligence; the victim thinks he is far smarter than he is. But my vine is real; put that on your head and you will become far smarter than you are now, and the effect will last for several days, slowly fading. Most spells don't work well on the brain; that's why it can't be a permanent enhancement. But you don't want to use it before you encounter the black idiocy vine Yang has crafted, for you want it at full potency to counter his. The two are even at the start, but if you use mine two days before his strikes you, you will be somewhat duller than you are now, for several days, because the negative one will be fresher."

"I see the point!" I agreed. "I'm just a backwoods barbarian, none too smart to begin with; I can't afford to be any worse than I am."

"Precisely," Yin acknowledged politely.

I brought out the compass. "Now I've heard of these magic gimmicks," I said. "Their little arrows always point north. But I already know where north is, and if I don't, I can find it by garden-variety backwoods magic, such as the moss that grows on the north sides of trees. Why do I need this?"

"This compass doesn't necessarily point north," he explained. "It points to the object you need to find and bring back to Castle Roogna. This spell you must invoke first, so you will know where to go."

"And Yang's compass will point the wrong way?" I asked. "I'll simply ignore it."

"Yang's compass will make *this* one point the wrong way," he clarified.

"Well, I'll just remember the direction, then. I have a good sense of direction, once I get my bearings; all barbarians do."

"Unfortunately, the object may move about, so you can not track it without the compass until you know its nature. Also, it is not merely the compass needle that points; it acts on your mind, so that you know in which direction to go. The black compass will prevent you from knowing where to go, even if you don't look at it."

"Oh," I said, getting slightly confused. "Then if the two compasses cancel each other, how do I find the object?"

"You must try to avoid the black compass until you find the object. After that, the black compass can't hurt you."

"How can I do that? If I know where Yang's spells are, I'll avoid them all!"

"Unfortunately, again, you can't; they will be placed in your path so that you will intercept them all in turn."

"I'll change my route!"

"No, your route has been divined by magic; Yang will place the spells in your way. But nothing can be totally predetermined. If you are alert, you will be able to spot them and nullify them with mine before they cause you unredeemable mischief. I am trusting you to do that." He smiled thinly.

"Well, I'll certainly try," I agreed. "Will his spells be out in the open?"

"Yes and no. He will place them in such a way as to try to confuse you, so that you are likely to overlook them until you come into range. Your mere presence will invoke them. So you must be alert at all times. The key here is not avoidance, since you can not avoid them, except perhaps the black compass, but your readiness to nullify them promptly. If you spy a black spell from a distance, you can approach it deliberately with the white counterspell in hand. So your state of readiness will be critical."

"I will be ready. Barbarians are always alert to their surroundings." I was getting to like this challenge, after all.

I drew out the monster figurine. "This?"

"Yang's spell will summon a horrendous monster, one that will surely destroy you if not dealt with promptly. My spell will banish that monster, so you won't have to fight it at all."

"Oh," I said, disappointed. "I like fighting monsters."

"I assure you, you won't like this one," he said. "It's the tarasque."

"Never heard of it," I said disdainfully.

"Just keep an eye out for the black spell, and keep this white one handy. Don't use it on any routine monster."

I brought forth another spell, the doll. "This?"

"That particular set is one of the most insidious. Yang's spell will exchange your identity with that of the person or creature nearest you at the moment it is invoked. It won't hurt either of you specifically, but I doubt you'd be pleased if it wasn't nullified. For example, if the nearest creature is a fruit fly, you would find yourself in the body of the fruit fly, and it would have your man's body. My spell will restore both of you to your original bodies—provided you make sure they are adjacent when you invoke it."

"Um, yes, I wouldn't want to be a fruit fly," I agreed. I fished out the last spell, the stone. "And this falls on my head?"

"Not exactly. The black stone spell will cause you to become stone; the white one will return the stone to flesh. Both have a substantial overkill factor."

"Huh?"

"This one is powerful enough to turn several barbarians and their horses to stone, if allowed to run unchallenged. So the other can convert a large amount of stone to flesh."

"How does it know the difference between natural stone and converted stone?" I asked. "Is the type of stone different?"

"The spell merely acts on the closest stone to it. Since you will be invoking it as you are turning to stone, that will be you. Only you can invoke the white spells; that is a necessary safeguard."

I pictured a mimic-bird flying by, squawking, "Invoke! Invoke!" and bringing to life my entire bag of spells at once. I nodded; it was indeed a necessary safeguard. They had worked out the details of this challenge pretty well.

I took a deep breath. "So if I just keep this bag of spells handy, I'll be able to counter each of Yang's spells and complete the mission. That seems straightforward enough."

"Well, there are always unexpected details of situation," he said, "and also complications of terrain."

"I'm a barbarian. I'm used to handling terrain."

"And on the return trip you will be burdened with the object. That may distract you. You must be especially careful once you have the object, for the difficulty of the challenge may increase exponentially then."

"There is that," I agreed, wondering what "exponential" meant. I assumed it was just a highbrow Magician term for "a lot." "Just what is this object I'm supposed to fetch?"

Yin looked moderately embarrassed. "I'm afraid I am not permitted to tell you that. King Gromden decided that some things should be held as surprises to make the contest more, er, sporting. I have informed you of the nature of the spells and counterspells, giving you a certain advantage; some unknowns are necessary to counterbalance that. Perhaps Yang will tell you more. However—" His face darkened. "You must not believe everything Yang tells you. I am a Good Magician; he is an Evil Magician. Therefore I must always use my magic positively and speak the truth. He uses his magic negatively, and . . ." He let the words fade out.

"You mean he always lies? Then I'll just believe the opposite of what he says."

Yin looked further embarrassed. "It is not quite as simple as that. Truth is not necessarily the opposite of Untruth. For example, you could ask a liar what direction the nearest pillow-bush was, and he would tell you it was east when actually it was south; if you went the opposite way, you would go west and still be deceived."

"Well, at least I'd know one direction it wasn't—east. That would be some help."

"Not necessarily so. Yang does not lie, precisely; he seeks to deceive. If he can best deceive by indirection, or even by telling the truth in a way you will doubt, he will do that. Thus the bush might indeed be east—the one direction you would not go after asking him."

I began to appreciate the ramifications. The civilized folk had evidently developed lying into a sophisticated art! We barbarians were straightforward liars, when we lied at all.

"I really would prefer that you not talk to Yang at all," Yin said. "But the rules of this contest give us equal access. So all I can do is warn you not to trust him, either to speak the truth or to lie, for he will surely mislead you to his advantage. He is insidiously clever."

I shrugged. "Thanks for the warning, Magician. I'll be careful."

He smiled. "Do be that. And farewell, Hero; I hope to see you again at the conclusion of the mission."

"Sure thing, Yin." I left him and took the bag of spells to my room.

The rest of the day was frankly dull. The serving woman fixed me a decent lunch and hurried off to attend to the sick King. I amused myself by exploring the castle, which was big and empty. In one upstairs room was the magic tapestry, showing scenes of Xanth during the last four hundred years. There had been a long succession of kings, some of them pretty good. I rather liked King Roogna, who had supervised the construction of the castle; he had used centaur labor, and Evil Magician Murphy had tried to interfere, but a barbarian had arrived to help King Roogna. Trust a barbarian to show up in the nick of time, when the civilized folk couldn't manage! I was of that heroic mold myself, as I may have mentioned.

But somehow it seemed that the power of man had faded in Xanth, slowly over the centuries, and the once far-reaching activities of the castle had contracted, until today old King Gromden was about all that remained. Gromden meant well and was a good man, but people lacked confidence in him. Maybe it was that there just weren't enough human folk left in Xanth to hold back the jungle.

The woman appeared. "The King asks for you," she said disapprovingly.

I went to Gromden's room. He was sitting up in bed, evidently somewhat recovered, though he did not look at all spry. "Feeling better, King?" I asked brightly. "Maybe the prune juice helped?"

"My malady comes and goes," he said, "and each siege is to a new nadir. It derives as much from the soul as from the flesh. How I wish my wife and daughter were here! But—" He shrugged with deep regret. "A man can pay a lifetime for a moment's folly."

"That's for sure, King!" I agreed. "I remember when I found this tangle-seed and thought I'd plant it in our garden—"

"I summoned you in this period of my lucidity, because it may not last long. I have something important to tell you that I fear you will not believe."

"I'm just a barbarian, King," I reminded him. "I can believe almost anything."

He smiled tiredly. "That is surely why the prophecy named you for this mission; you have no preconceptions. But I fear you are being deceived unnecessarily, so simple fairness requires me to set some things straight."

"Sure, King." I nodded. "What's crooked?"

"This contest between Yin and Yang is not precisely what it seems. It is not really a trial to determine which Magician shall assume the throne of Xanth after me, but rather which one shall serve the other."

"Isn't that the same thing?" I asked. "The one who loses doesn't get to be King, so—"

"No, not the same," he asserted. "And that object you are supposed to fetch has certain qualities that will greatly complicate your task. This is no simple matter, Barbarian! Yin and Yang don't realize that I know any of this, but—"

"How *do* you know it, King?" I asked.

He smiled again. "I see that you, like they, question my remaining mental acuity. Indeed, I found the truth difficult to believe myself. Perhaps it will be more convincing if I demonstrate how I ascertained my information."

"I guess so," I conceded doubtfully. The old boy did seem a little confused. But that was what happened to sick people sometimes.

"If you would be so kind—fetch me an object from the grounds."

"Sure King," I agreed amicably. Might as well humor him. I turned my back, left the room, went down and out, and looked about. What would be suitable? A fruit? Maybe a prune? A stick of wood? No sense going to a lot of trouble, since he'd probably be asleep when I returned.

I spied a chip of stone, fallen from the castle wall. That should do. I picked it up and went back inside.

King Gromden remained awake. I handed him the chip. He held it before him, staring at it. "This is a fragment of stone from the outer wall of this castle," he said. "It was quarried by centaurs and hauled to this site four hundred years ago."

"What do you know," I remarked. It really didn't take any magic talent to know that; *all* the castle rocks were quarried and hauled in at that time. If that wasn't common knowledge, the magic tapestry showed it to anyone willing to watch, as I had been.

"The centaur who hauled this particular stone had a speckled hide and gray tail," he continued. "He struck one hoof against a root and issued a bad word, for which he was duly reprimanded by his superior on the crew."

"Sure," I agreed noncommittally, convinced he was making this up.

"Later, before the castle was finished, the goblins and harpies attacked," he continued. "A harpy hen laid an egg that detonated close by, cracking the block, but the mortar held it in place. Then the goblins stormed the castle, and their dead piled up against the wall; the eyeball of one was wedged against this chip, somewhat to the chip's disgust."

I chuckled obligingly. I'll say this for the old boy: he could spin a yarn! Maybe not as fancy as the yarns of the tapestry, but still good enough.

"Then the goblin bodies were melted down, and some of the stain soaked into the chip. And it endured that way for centuries, until recently a bird brushed it, and the chip was finally dislodged and fell to the ground. There is a spell on this castle to keep it in repair, but age and neglect may have weakened that spell. You picked up the chip between the wall and the moat, near a yellow flower."

"Hey, I did!" I exclaimed, remembering. "How'd you know that, King?" For there had been no window covering that region; he could not have peered out and seen me.

He smiled. "It is my talent, the magic of Magician caliber that made me eligible to assume the throne. I can hold any object and see and hear its history. That is how I discovered the deception of Yin and Yang. A button fell from Yin's clothing; I picked it up and read it to determine whose it was, and found that it was his, but also—"

I glanced at him. He was looking worse; the effort of sitting up and talking was bad for him. "I'd better let you rest now, King," I said.

"But I must warn you," he protested weakly. "It is important for you to complete this mission, for Yin—"

He coughed and spat up some phlegm, and his words were choked off. I didn't want him to pass out while trying to talk to me, so I beat a hasty retreat. Barbarians don't really understand illness. "You sleep it off, King," I said at the door. "I'll talk to you again tomorrow."

It certainly was dull here at the castle. I was eager to get going on the challenge; at least that promised to be halfway interesting.

Next day Magician Yang showed up. He wore black cloak and looked forbidding, but his features were just like Yin's. "I can see you are twin brothers," I said observantly.

"Naturally," he agreed, unsmiling. "We two represent the Good and Evil aspects of magic. Let's get on with this. Where are the spells?"

"Huh?" I replied, perhaps not displaying my full intelligence, such as it was.

"Yin's spells, yokel. I need to check them so I know which ones to match."

"Oh." I had somehow thought he knew which spells, since the King had specified them in advance. Evidently I had misunderstood. I went to my room and brought down the bag.

Yang grabbed it and opened it and peered in. "The usual garbage," he said. "Yin never was one for much imagination."

"I think King Gromden selected the—"

"Him too. Dullards, all! No wonder Xanth is sliding to the depths in a basket case." He reached in and hauled out the eye-queue vine. "I can match this idiot-string readily."

"Well, sure, since your spells are equal and opposite."

"And this airhead," he said, bringing up the white skull, then dropping it back into the bag with a clunk. "And this freak." Now he had the white monster figurine. "And the old magic shield gig, yet! Yin's got no spunk at all!"

"Well, as I said, the King—"

"And as I said, him too! Now this one had possibilities," he said, bringing up the doll. "You ever been in someone else's body, bumpkin?"

"No, not exactly that way—"

"And the stone-age ploy," he continued, holding the white stone. He peered at me. "Take my advice, would-be hero; save yourself a lot of grief. Take a dive!"

"A what?"

"Just go out there and don't come back. Vanish from the scene."

I had trouble grasping this. "But the mission—"

"The mission is to determine whether Yin or Yang should be the next King. If you fail to bring back the object, that determination will be made. Yang will be King."

"But—not even to try—"

"Well, you have two ways to go, ignoramus. You can go out there and get yourself killed, or you can go out there and take it easy and survive. Either way, the result of the contest will be the same—but your own situation will differ. You have to consider your personal stake in this."

"I couldn't—I said I'd make an honest try, and—"

"You fool!" he cried indignantly. "Don't you know the contest is rigged? You *can't* bring back the object! The whole deal is a cruel lie, set up to appease the masses."

Masses? I wondered where they were. "But King Gromden said—"

"That old fool is in his dotage, simpleton, and sick to boot! Look how Castle Roogna has deteriorated under his administration. We don't need more scandal in the castle. It's past time for a strong hand to take the reins and restore the throne to its proper glory."

There was some sense to that. "But Magician Yin could—he has similar magic—"

"Yin is constrained by his foolish notions of ethics. He places the means before the ends. No person can accomplish anything if he worries more about how he does it than what he is doing. That's why Yin is doomed to lose this contest."

I have never regarded myself as a clever man, and I saw right away I was outclassed here. I couldn't argue with someone as smart and ruthless as Yang. Still, I had stupid doubts. "I don't know—"

"Of course you don't, rube," Yang agreed. "So I will tell you. When I am King, I will reward you handsomely. Do you like nymphs? I will give you a barrel of nymph spells, each nymph good for a day and willing to do anything you say. Do you like food? I will arrange a feast every night. Creature comforts? The most comfortable creatures shall be yours."

"—whether I should accept the mission," I continued doggedly, "if I'm not even going to try. If I didn't know better, I'd suspect you were trying to bribe me to—"

"The light dawns at last, oaf! What is your price?"

"Besides, it sounds like a good adventure, and that's what I really came here for." I certainly didn't much like Yang!

"What kind of adventure is it to get your head bitten off by a monster? Dead men can't enjoy life!"

Actually, for me there was life after death; evidently he didn't know that. In his arrogance he hadn't bothered to check out my talent. I decided not to mention it. "Yin said you would try to deceive me."

Yang laughed loudly. "How do you know *he's* not

lying, hick? Naturally he doesn't want you to listen to *me*!"

He had a point. Now I didn't know whom to believe. "I guess I'd just better go ahead with the mission, and do my best, and see how it turns out."

"Fool!" Yang dropped the bag of spells on the floor and stalked out.

I wished I could get some good advice, but there was no one with any sense around here except maybe the King, and he hadn't heard this conversation and might not believe it. Then I remembered his talent. He could evoke the dialogue or whatever from a button on my clothing; then he would believe!

I went to his room, but he was asleep, and I didn't want to wake him. He might go into another coughing fit. Well, what could he have said, anyway, except for me to do the mission as planned. Actually, he might already know about Yang's dishonesty, for he had been trying to tell me something the day before. Now, maybe, I knew the nature of his warning: that Yang would try not merely to deceive me, but also to corrupt me. Fortunately, I was not clever enough to be corrupted.

Chapter 7. Mountain of Flesh

I set out the next morning ready for action, with the bag of spells tied to Pook. I had my good sword and a knife I had picked up at the castle. The woman had also found a good sturdy replacement bow and a quiver of arrows in the armory. I had plucked some cherries and pineapples from the trees of the orchard, as well as some edible fruit to consume along the way. I wore light body armor consisting of leather strips magically pickled and hardened. There was a lot of good stuff at Castle Roogna; too bad there were not more people to enjoy it.

I was at last starting my adventure! This buoyed my spirits, despite the aspects that puzzled me, and I feared that it would not be as exciting as I hoped. All I knew of the object I had to fetch was that it was vaguely northwest of Castle Roogna, but that was enough to get me started. I could invoke my finder-spell anytime, but preferred to wait until I had passed the loser-spell I knew was in my path. Then I could nullify the black spell completely, hoping enough of the white one was left over to enable me to pinpoint the object when I reached its general area.

Was it possible that all the evil spells were in a straight line to the object? In that case, I would be better off meandering somewhat, so as to avoid most of them. Then I could invoke the white compass when I was close and nail the object quickly. After that, it wouldn't matter what the black compass did; it would be too late. So my not using the white spell was like saving my last arrow until well within range of the target—plain common sense.

Except that Yin had assured me that I could not avoid the black spells; they would be set in my predetermined path. If I meandered, they would be set along that meander. I found this difficult to accept. After all, I could keep changing my course randomly. But magic has strange aspects that are beyond the comprehension of louts like me. I'd just have to see what happened.

The band of aggressive trees tried to give me a hard time, as they had done before; I wondered why they didn't like me, since I was here to do some good for Castle Roogna and have a nice adventure. Maybe they, like Yang, figured I'd fail. But in that case, their obstruction just made it more likely that I would fail. At least they should be glad to see me going; they could oppose me again on the way back in, if it were just me they didn't like. This made no sense. But what can you expect of blockheads? So I just made my little statement and held my sword aloft, and Pook charged through. The branches trembled with rage, but did not strike. Sometimes force is the only feasible alternative, especially for those who possess it.

We trotted along, making good time, and soon came to a range of mountains. I pondered whether to go around them, but I didn't know their extent and was afraid I would have to go far out of my way and perhaps lose track of my general direction. So I took the simple barbarian course—over the top.

Naturally, the obvious course is not necessarily the easiest one, as the firebird discovered when he tried to romance his reflection in the water and got his flame doused. But it was in the middling-rear of my mind that no one would have expected me to be dumb enough to go right over the top, so maybe there would be no evil spells there. This was really a test case—whether I could do the unexpected and mess up the predetermined path. If I couldn't be smart, I could at least be cunning.

The slope got steeper as we went, until Pook was puffing, and I had to dismount to ease his burden. At one point I had to unloop one of his chains and throw it around a tree trunk above us, so I could pull on it and help heave him up. Actually, those chains were one reason he was struggling; they added a fair amount of weight to his climb. But we persevered and got so high by dusk that the Land of Xanth spread out below us, its lakes and jungles a lovely patchwork. One lake turned brighter and larger as I looked at it, trying to impress me; the inanimate can be just as vain about its appearance as any animate creature.

Unfortunately, I could not see what was ahead of us, to the northwest, because the remainder of the mountain blocked that off. But I knew we'd see it once we crested. That should be as good as a map; maybe I'd even see the object, whatever it was. But would I recognize it?

The mountain went up and up. It certainly hadn't looked this big from below! The thing seemed to be drawing itself up, trying to outlast us, making this its own special contest.

Well, next time I'd go around and risk the bad spells! But having started this course, I wasn't about to quit now. As I may have remarked, barbarians can be oinkheaded on occasion, and I was typical of the breed.

The air grew cool, then cold; we were entering the

snow region. Sure enough, a flock of snow-birds wheeled
in the sky, coming to investigate us. I didn't know much
about snow-birds, but didn't trust them, and neither did
Pook. We moved faster, seeking to avoid them, but they
came over and buzzed us. White powder drifted down
from their wings. Then they were off and out of sight.

"No trouble after all," I said, relieved. "Let's find a
spot to camp for the night. I'll have to make a fire so we
won't freeze."

But Pook laid back his ears and plowed on up the cold
slope. "Hey, what's the matter?" I demanded. "We've
got to stop before the ground gets frozen and there's no
brush for a fire. See if you can sniff out a level section,
or maybe even a small cave."

Still he traveled, not slowing or searching at all. I began
to get annoyed. "Now look, Pook, I'm tired and I want
to rest, and you're not that fresh either—"

Then I noticed that snow was falling. But there was
no cloud; the snowflakes were forming in the air. As I
watched, they expanded, becoming wonderfully large and
intricate disks, each one different from all its companions.
I caught one by its rim, and it was the span of my spread
hand, with six spokes radiating out from a hexagonal center, each branching and rebranching into finer networks,
until the rim was another finely wrought hexagon. I marveled at the beauty and symmetry of it, when it melted
in my hand and fell apart. I was unhappy at the loss of
such a wonderful artifact; to stifle the unbarbarian tear
coming to my eye, I grabbed another snowflake and concentrated on it. This one was like the finest doily ever
crafted, in all ways absolutely delightful. But in a moment
it, too, dissolved and was lost.

Now the snowflakes became more ornate. They were
no longer disks; they were prisms, reflecting and diffract-
ing the slanting sunbeams so that rainbow hues radiated
out in spokes of their own, forming larger hexagons of
colored light that filled the air before me. The light-flakes
became so solid I thought I could climb upward by grasping their interlocking spokes, but my hands merely changed
colors when I reached, finding nothing.

Ahead was a crevice in the mountain, too wide to leap across, its depths too deep and awful to contemplate. But the snowflakes multiplied and interlocked to form a bridge across it, and I guided Pook there.

He came to the brink and balked. I kicked his sides, urging him forward. "It's a perfect bridge," I told him.

"It's a hallucination, you fool!" he told me.

"How can you be sure of that?" I argued.

"This is all a form of illusion," he insisted.

"Give me some proof, mule-head!"

"It has to be illusion, because in real life I can't talk human speech," he said.

I pondered that, considered it, and cogitated a bit on it. "Could be," I opined at last. "But what's the cause?"

"That snow the snow-birds dropped on us, of course. That's why I tried to get out of it. The stuff spaces out your mind and makes you see and hear things that just aren't there."

"You mean there aren't any big snowflakes, and you're not talking to me now?"

"That is precisely what I mean, lunkhead. The only big flake around here is you. Now sit tight while I get us out of it." He picked his way on up the mountain. "Real snow cancels out the mind-bending snow. The cold freezes it, I think. No matter what you see, don't get off my back."

"Why doesn't it zonk out your mind, too?"

"Don't be silly, barbarian. I'm just an animal."

I decided he knew better than I did. "Actually, it's sort of fun," I said.

Pook just snorted and plowed on.

Now the flakes converted to snow-fairies, dancing on the breeze. They leaped, they twirled, they pirouetted most prettily. One of them beckoned to me and she reminded me of Bluebell and the dancing elven maidens; I started to dismount, but Pook gave a shake that jolted my memory, aggravatingly, and I desisted.

Slowly the colorful images faded, and the mountain slope was revealed in its grim reality, all rock and scrub and patches of genuine snow. I looked below, at the crevice, and saw there was no bridge across it. I would have plunged into it, to my doom or great discomfort, had not Pook cautioned me about the illusion spawned by the snow-dust. The next snow-bird I saw would get an arrow through its body!

Suddenly I recalled the elf crone's prophecy: that I would be doomed by a cruel lie. That snowflake bridge had been a lie, all right! Thanks to Pook's horse sense, I had avoided that doom.

I glanced at Pook. "Thanks, ghost horse," I said "You saved me from my own folly back there. You were more sensible than I."

Pook twitched an ear affirmatively and kept climbing.

"But since you can't talk—how did you warn me? I mean, if I just imagined you spoke to me in human words—"

The horse continued moving.

I sighed. "Well, I don't quite know how much of what is real, but I'm sure you saved me, Pook. So I guess I can call you tame now."

Pook snorted, insulted.

"Sorry," I apologized. "But if you're not tame, then why do you stay with me?"

The horse merely shrugged, rattling a chain.

Then I had about as bright a notion as a barbarian was capable of at that hour of the day. "Pook, if I may not call you tame—may I call you friend?"

He nickered affirmatively. I had finally caught on!

When Pook was satisfied that we were secure from hallucination, he stopped. We found an indentation, not really a cave, but enough to shelter us from the cutting wind, and I gathered straggles of half-buried brush and made a little fire. Pook was able to find dry grass and lichen under the snow for his supper, while I consumed my rations. It didn't seem like much of a meal for him, but I suppose he was used to that sort of thing.

The fire sank to embers and we settled for the night. Pook lay down, and I curled up next to him, glad for the heat of his body. I didn't worry about watching for enemies; what man or monster would climb way up here, past the snow-birds and snow-dreams, just to bother a lone man and a horse? Anyway, I slept lightly, and so did Pook. We would be all right.

I believe I have remarked before on the weakness of barbarian reasoning. This was demonstrated again this night. A sound would have roused us both, but there was no sound—not until it was almost too late.

Pook became aware of it first; his nose was more alert than mine. He didn't move; he puffed a nostrilful of warm air in my ear. I woke, wondering what he was up to— and felt the chill slithering across my ankle.

I knew instantly what it was: a snowsnake. How utterly stupid of me to forget about them! They were snow-white and snow-cold and lived in snow; it was difficult to see or hear them in their habitat. But they were poisonous and they liked fresh meat.

We were in trouble. I lay there, feigning sleep the way Pook was, assessing the situation. One bite would prove fatal for me, and probably three bites for Pook. I would recover in due course, assuming the feeding snakes left enough of me to be reconstituted, but Pook wouldn't. So I had to prevent him from getting bitten.

First I needed to know how many snakes there were and exactly where they were. Then I needed to eliminate them. First I had to deal with the ones who were most ready to strike, then the others.

I cracked open an eye. That didn't help; it was too dark to see. So I listened and felt. That didn't help either; they were silent, and once the one passed my leg, I had no way to track it. But I knew the snakes wouldn't wait long before striking; they would be eager to feed. They would pick their targets, and—

Very well; we would have to shoot for double or nothing. "Roll!" I cried suddenly.

Pook was ready. He rolled while I leaped up, grabbing for my sword. I heard a hiss; Pook had squished a snake under his crunching chains.

I jumped for the leftover fire, sweeping my sword point through it. Embers and coals flew about, brightening angrily as they felt the cold air. One struck a snake; I heard the hiss of anguish and I chopped at the sound. There was a violent thrashing in the dark; I had scored.

Now the snakes were all carelessly active, frightened by the glowing coals among them. Probably they would have moved on us earlier if that fire hadn't been there; they had waited till it was low and then been cautious. Not cautious enough! I struck at every hiss I heard, and my reflexes were barbarian-swift, and my blade sliced through reptilian flesh. In a moment or so, I had cut up everything that made a sound.

I returned to the fire and tossed on fresh brush. In a moment it blazed up, and I saw what I had wrought. There were four dead snakes—one squished, three cut to pieces. Each was about man-length, too small to be much opposition by day, but big enough to do a lot of damage by night, especially considering the poison. If any of them survived, they had fled.

Pook returned. He had rolled downward and bounced to his feet. He did not seem to have been bitten; his chains had protected him, and, once he rolled free, all the snakes had been in my area.

We had won through unscathed, but neither of us was inclined to lie down again. Even the slightest scathe by one of those snakes would have been a whole lot of trouble. I stoked the fire, and Pook stood near it, almost astride it, and I mounted him. Thus only his four feet were vulnerable, and they were close to the fire. But I held a cherry in my hand, just in case; if anything approached, it would get bombed. We spent the rest of the night like that, sleeping on guard. And the snowsnakes did not return.

In the cold morning we ate again and resumed our journey. The pieces of snowsnake near the fire had melted, of course; there was nothing left of them. It really hadn't been much of an adventure, just an inconvenience; I would rather have had undisturbed sleep. Maybe I just didn't have the right attitude.

Another cutting wind came up; that kind of wind seemed to like the upper reaches. I wrapped my cloak tightly about me for warmth and kept my gloved hands in toward

my belly. Mainly, I depended on Pook for heat; I couldn't
have made this trek without him.

By noon we reached the crest. Not the peak; there was
no point in going right over that, as we weren't interested
in height, just in getting past. We headed for the lowest
notch in the ridge that ran from peak to peak in this range.
Wind cut through it with extra effort, stirring up powdered
snow; I was reminded of the snow-birds' snow and shuddered, but I knew it wasn't that. I would be glad when
we got down to good old-fashioned garden-variety tangle
trees and hypnogourds again!

But as we passed through the pass, I saw something
lying in the snow, black against white. I got down and
picked it up. It was a black compass, just like the white
one I had in my bag of spells. It flashed.

Suddenly I felt dizzy. "Where am I going?" I asked
plaintively. "What am I looking for?"

But in a moment I remembered. "I'm looking for an
object to settle a claim for the new King of Xanth. But I
have absolutely no idea where it is. The loser-spell has
nullified my sense of location."

And then I said: "Now's the time to invoke the finder-
spell so I can restore my sense of location. Or whatever.
That way I'll know where I'm going."

Pook did not protest, so I decided that made sense.
That black compass had really reamed out my mind, leaving me fundamentally uncertain. I don't like having my
mind messed with.

I dug in the bag and brought out the white compass.
"Invoke!" I quavered at it.

Something strange happened. The snow on which I
stood began to melt. Well, no, not exactly melt, but it
was turning slushy. No, not exactly that, either. The
ground beneath the snow was softening.

How could that be? I scraped away the snow and saw
that it was bare rock below and that the rock had become
pale pink flesh. Was this mountain in fact a monster creature? It couldn't be; I knew the nature of mountains, and
this was definitely a mountain. Yet the rock below me
had become flesh.

The flesh spread rapidly outward. I saw the snow sinking in an expanding ripple, marking the progress of the transformation. The whole mountain was turning to living flesh!

Pook neighed nervously. He was balancing on the spongy surface uncomfortably and wanted to get off it. But I retreated cautiously from the fringe of the conversion, wanting to understand this phenomenon to whatever extent my primitive barbarian mind was able, so I wouldn't fall into some trap of magic. Why should the mountain turn to flesh just when I was invoking unrelated magic?

I looked down at the white compass I had invoked, only to discover that both it and the black one had disappeared, expended. But I still had no idea where the object was. Then I reached into the spell-bag and pulled out the white stone. Wasn't *that* the spell that was supposed to turn stone back to flesh? Then why had it happened with the compass?

I wasn't bright, but I wasn't completely dull, either. "Yang!" I exclaimed. "He switched the spells!"

Pook neighed again. He was right; we had to get off this mountain of blubber! "I don't know where we're going, but maybe you do!" I cried. "Go for it!" I jumped onto his back and hung on.

He started off down the mountain's north slope. His hooves skidded as the snow made the flesh beneath slippery. I saw that the transformation had now reached to the peak, and it was quivering like jelly. Indeed, the whole mountain was quivering, as its solid bedrock turned soft. Magician Yin had not been kidding about overkill on the spells; this one was strong enough to convert a hundred men and horses to—that is, to reconvert—well, anyway, it was one hideously powerful piece of magic. And it was being wasted, doing me no good at all.

Pook's hooves slid as the slope steepened; he was having real trouble keeping his footing, what with the heaving of the mountain itself. "Just sit down and slide," I suggested. "It's probably safer and faster."

He tried it. We slid down, on cold posteriors, and it

was indeed faster—but maybe not safer. We soon got up
formidable speed, and there was still a long way to go.

If Yin's spell was strong enough to convert a mountain
to flesh, how strong was Yang's spell, the one that turned
flesh to stone? They were equal and opposite, weren't
they? What would happen when I triggered the Evil
Magician's spell—and had nothing to counter it? Would
it turn me to stone—and Pook, and everything near us?
My talent was good, but I couldn't handle that! If we were
doomed to encounter the black stone, that meant we were
doomed indeed—by the cruel lie Yang had made of this
contest!

Yang had suggested that I give up this quest, letting
him win. That seemed like good advice, in retrospect!
Wouldn't it be better to abort the mission now and at least
salvage my life?

But as I said, the oinkheadedness of barbarians is legendary, and justly so. Even though it now seemed pointless, I was determined to push on. I had agreed to
undertake this mission and I always did what I said I
would do if I could, even if it made no sense at the time.
And who could tell; maybe my talent would heal me from
being stoned. Of course, that might take a few years . . .

We slid to the snow line. The flesh had not reached
here yet, and the mountain below remained stable. Pook
got to his feet, swished his tail about to dislodge the snow
sticking to his rear, and moved on down, not eager to
have the rock turn mushy under his hooves again. Horses
don't go for that mushy stuff. Actually, I wasn't sure that
would happen; there had to be some limit to the effect,
or all of Xanth would become flesh.

Indeed, the mountain seemed to stabilize above the
snow line. If the conversion was continuing, it had slowed;
there was just too much rock in the mountain for the magic
to digest, if that was the proper word.

Once we were safely below the region of flesh, we
paused to eat and graze. Our slip-sliding had taken some
time and more energy, and we were tired and hungry.
Horses, I had discovered, had to eat a lot! I had somehow
supposed that a man with a steed could travel long dis-

tances at high speed; now I knew it wasn't so. But, of course, Pook had become more to me than mere transportation. Much more. Maybe his companionship was more important than his average velocity.

So we took time to fill our bellies in our separate fashions, foraging for grass and leaves and fruits, and scouted around for a suitable campsite. We were below the level of the snowsnakes, but what about the snow-birds? I didn't want to have my mind zonked out again by their snow job.

However, a completely different threat materialized. We had ignored the mountain of flesh because we were beyond its range, we thought. That turned out to be overly optimistic.

The ground shuddered. At first I thought it was an earthquake—a magical tremor that was very unsettling to experience, resembling as it did the heavy tread of an ogre, but not too dangerous in the open. But then I realized that it emanated from the mountain of flesh above us. The stuff was shaking with increasing violence, as if trying to get free.

Of course it wanted to be free! Here it was, abruptly waking as a huge mass of living tissue—with no eyes or ears or nose, no way to discover where it was or what it was doing there. So it was doing the only thing it could— bashing its way out. If I were blindfolded and deaf and tied down, I'd struggle too!

Snow crashed down beyond the snow line, heading for us. The shaking flesh had started an avalanche! There wasn't enough snow to do real harm, but I did not feel easy. Sure enough, pretty soon the rocks on the fringe of the flesh-zone were shaken loose and they started rolling down. *Those* could harm us!

"I think maybe this is not our best place to camp," I told Pook.

He agreed. I mounted, and we started on down.

But now it was getting dark, and the struggles of the mountain increased. The violence was such that the welkin was jarred, and an early-showing star was jostled out of its socket. It fell nearby, tracing a fiery path across the sky, and set the dry brush aflame. More trouble!

The mountain heaved again and shook the firmament. Other stars fell, starting other fires; they really weren't very well anchored when they first came out. Soon there were sizable conflagrations, and we smelled the smoke. But we couldn't hurry, because the footing was treacherous in the gloom, and we had to be alert for more rolling stones.

The mountain peak belched. A mass of gas burst out, soiling the sky. Several stars coughed, and a comet sneezed so hard its tail flew off. Bad business!

We traveled as well as we could, but it was nervous business, with fires blazing on either side, boulders rolling down from above, and clouds of the mountain's stomach gas hovering in the night sky. The scene was very like my private picture of hell, and I was not eager to remain there long.

The conversion of stone to flesh had not melted the snow; apparently it was cold flesh. But the fires raging up the slope were now heating the upper reaches, and water was beginning to flow from the fringe of snow.

We came to a cul-de-sac. Ahead was a section so steep as to be clifflike, while the fires closed off the escape to the sides. We did not want to retreat back up the mountain, but did not want to stay in place, either. The ground was still shuddering with the motions of the tortured flesh, threatening to dislodge us from our perch. Behind, we heard the increasing sibilance of rushing water. We could soon be washed on down the cliff, becoming part of the waterfall!

There is something about personal hazard that sharpens my native cunning. "Diversion!" I exclaimed. Pook cocked an ear at me questioningly, perhaps fearing I was losing what little wit I possessed. "I'll show you!"

I dismounted and scrambled to the side, near the fire. I used my boot to scuff a channel in the ground, and my sword to cut through the brush in the way. Quickly I extended the channel upward at a slant, forming a bank on its lower side. I took advantage of whatever natural declivities there were, so that my channel curved but was reasonably deep. Pook was perplexed, but helped me excavate through a small ridge by bashing it with a hoof.

Naturally we struck a buried boulder, too big either to circle or to pry out. Now was the time for my reserve equipment! There was very little time for excavating around the boulder, so I poked a hole with the point of my sword and dropped in a cherry bomb. The explosion blew out a much bigger hole. Then I tossed in a pineapple and dived clear.

This explosion blew the top off the boulder. It crunched into a tree in the fire-zone; lucky for us it hadn't gone the other way! Now my channel was complete; all I had to do was touch it up where the explosion had messed it up.

Just in time! The trickle of water was becoming a river, and now this coursed down my sluice. I stood by to free any clogs that developed. Soon there was a torrent, and the water deepened the channel itself and sought to overflow it; hastily I shored up my embankment. I wasn't perfectly successful, but most of the water did stay on course. This meant that only a little of it swirled around our feet and poured on over the cliff, and most flowed down into the rising blaze. We had saved ourselves from being washed away and had diverted the water to the more useful employment of fighting the nearest fire.

There was a continuous angry hiss as the water intruded on the fire's domain, and a cloud of steam puffed up. My new channel ended at the fire's edge, so there the water spread out, coursing over a much broader area. Soon the fire was gone from there, and a swath of blackened but unburning terrain appeared, leading down the mountain.

"And this is our route down!" I said, pleased with the success of my strategy. I mounted Pook, and he stepped into the channel, walking carefully to prevent the moving water from interfering with his footing.

Thus we made it off the mountain. It wasn't easy or comfortable, but the farther from the mountain of flesh we got, the less severe the effects were. Finally, near dawn, we felt secure enough to rest. We doubted any wild

creatures would be bothering us; they were all terrified
by the strange events of this night, and most had fled the
scene.

As I settled down to sleep beside a nice, solid boulder,
I pondered the significance of what had happened. So
Yang had switched the spells; he must have done that
while handling them in my presence. Of course he had
known what they were; he had pretended ignorance so
as to have a pretext to touch each one. He had distracted
me with talk of the futility of my mission so that I would
not catch on to the real nature of his skulduggery. His
attempt to bribe me had not been serious; why bribe me
when he already had the situation in hand? He had indeed
deceived me, obliquely. Not for nothing had he remarked
on my bumpkinishness! He had proved it.

He had, ironically, spoken the truth when he said he
was convinced that I would fail. He had ensured that by
cheating. Yin and the King thought this was a straightforward spell-vs.-spell contest set in the field; Yang knew
it was an ignorant barbarian trotting blithely into disaster.
Yin's spells were now just about as dangerous to me as
Yang's!

Maybe the King *had* caught on, and had been about
to warn me not to let Magician Yang touch those spells.
I had been too quick to dismiss his effort. Talk of blundering fools! I had just done the cause of Barbarian Public
Relations a singular disservice, by being precisely as oaf-
ish as charged.

How could I hope to complete this quest when I had
no idea where the object was or what it was? I had climbed
the mountain, back when I had some notion; was it because the object was up there? Should I go back to the
fleshy peak? I could not be sure, but since I hadn't seen
anything up there except snow, I concluded that wasn't
it. Could the thing be on one of the other peaks of this
range, and I had been about to check them all until I
found it? Again I couldn't be sure. The black compass
had somehow nullified my brain in this respect, so that I
could not even decide where to search. The only confi-

dence I had was that whatever I decided to do would be
wrong, because of that hostile magic.

Somewhere among my remaining white spells was the
true finder compass. But which one was it? If I invoked
one and guessed wrong, not only would I be wasting another spell that I would certainly need later but I could
be getting myself into immediate trouble, as I had done
atop the mountain.

I had supposed this adventure was going to be slightly
tame for my taste. Abruptly it had become slightly too
challenging. Elsie had tried to warn me that there could
be days like this; naturally I hadn't listened. A barbarian
who thinks he can interact on an equal basis with Magicians
is a fool, indeed!

Well, Pook had been farther from the black compass
than I had been, so wasn't affected as much. Perhaps he,
being equine, had not been touched at all. I would just
have to trust his horse sense to get me where I was going.
I suspected that Evil Magician Yang had not realized that
I would have a sensible friend along.

With that modestly renewed sense of comfort, I slept.

Chapter 8. Tarasque

In the middle of the day, the heat forced us awake.
Pook had been grazing in his sleep; that's a talent his kind
has that I was coming to envy. I foraged for bread sticks,
picking them off a stale bread tree; they were better than
nothing. Then we went on.

We were in hilly country now, but there were no more
mountains, for which I was duly grateful. I had climbed
the mountain in part to avoid the predestined route and
the evil spells on it; obviously this had been ineffective,

so there was no point in bothering with such efforts henceforth. Pook proceeded northwest, which I was sure was the wrong direction, but I didn't argue. I hoped he had some inkling where the object was, though I despaired of either finding it or bringing it back to Castle Roogna. How could I, with my own spells loaded against me? Magician Yang had really fixed me, but that ol' barbarian oink-headedness prevented me from quitting. If there's one thing worse than blundering, it is admitting the blunder.

As evening dawned—well, you know what I mean—we spied a region of caves and considered using one of them for the night. Barbarians, of course, are not far removed from cavemen. But in the shadows we heard myriad clicking sounds and saw little pincers lifted in eager anticipation of our flesh. Nickelpedes! No, these were smaller, but twice as fierce; they were dimepedes. They had ten little legs, and silvery pincers that could readily gouge out serrated disks of flesh. They couldn't do much to Pook's hooves, but all they had to do was scuttle to the flesh above and begin work. Certainly we were not about to lie down there!

So we found a little lake with a littler island and leaped across to that. The dimepedes could not swim—in fact, they sank in water like so many bits of metal—so we knew they would not bother us in the night. And since they would be foraging in this region under cover of darkness—they could not tolerate the full light of day, because that showed up the dirt on them—no other creature would be in this vicinity. We had an ideal nocturnal retreat.

But as darkness closed, the fish came to the surface of the lake, and they were strange ones. One had little gauzy wings, so that she could fly just above the surface, and a little halo of light formed above her head. "What are you?" I asked, not expecting an answer, for few fish talk.

"She's an angelfish, man-visitor," a voice at the shore said. There was a fat-faced fish there, and it seemed that one could talk. "She will dance for you, if you wish. Angelfish are very nice creatures."

"Well, sure," I agreed, seeing no harm in it. Some

civilized folk think there is nothing good in the wilderness, but we uncivilized folk know that there are fewer threats to man among wild creatures than there are among our own violent kind.

The angelfish stood on her tail just over the water, buzzed her wings, and did a pirouette. Then she leaped and circled and splashed lightly against the lake; the light from her halo was enough to make her reflection visible in the still water, so that there seemed to be two of her. One was upright, above the surface, and the other was inverted, below. It was a pretty effect.

Then another fish appeared, his motions sending ripples that broke up the reflection of the first, spoiling the effect. He hoisted himself up; he lacked wings, but somehow was able to walk the surface. He was reddish and had little horns, and his tail curved back behind him as he stood, ending in a barb.

"And there's the devilfish," the fat announcer said. "He always shows up to spoil things."

Indeed it was so, for the angelfish made a little bubbly scream and fled, the devilfish chasing her with an evil leer on his gills. But she could not leave the region of the water, and the lake was small, so they went round and round in circles.

Suddenly I jumped. Something had cut my foot, which was near the water. I looked—and saw a cuttlefish, its tentacles like knives, brandishing those little blades at my tender toes. I had taken off my boots to air my stinking feet—barbarian feet can be pretty bad when confined, and when the stench gets so thick it squishes, it's time to let it out—so now they were vulnerable. "Get away from me, you creep!" I snapped, grabbing a boot and flailing with it.

The fish dived below the surface. My boot struck the fringe of water—and stuck. Now, I knew boots could get pretty gunky, but they had never stuck to water before! I yanked—and found that something had clamped onto the boot's toe. It had giant dull pincers—and when I hauled harder, the whole thing came up, and I saw it was

nothing but pincers, broad serrated things. "What's this?"
I demanded.

"A shellfish, of course," the other fish replied.

"How do I get it off my boot?"

"Well, it's afraid of starfish—"

I looked into the dark sky. There was a star in the
shape of a fish, but it was out of reach. Some starfish
shine brightly in the water, while others hover in the night
sky; I suppose there is enough water up there for them.
But my animal cunning was operating. "Let go, shellfish,
or I'll fetch down that starfish," I threatened.

Immediately the shellfish dropped off my boot and sank
back in the water. I had bluffed it.

"You should have eaten it instead," the other fish said.
"And the cuttlefish too."

"They wouldn't have liked that," I said.

"Who cares what *they* like? They don't count! Nobody
counts but Number One!"

My brow creased. "What kind of fish are you?"

"I thought you'd never ask! I am a sel-fish, of course."

"Sell fish? What do you sell?"

"Instant gratification—that's the selfish way. Don't
worry about the welfare of others!"

"Don't listen to him!" the angelfish called, pausing in
her flight. Then she screamed, for in that moment of her
distraction the devilfish had caught up with her. He
wrapped his fins about her quivering body and bore her
down despite her struggles. The two disappeared under
the surface, and only her little halo remained floating on
the water.

"He always wanted to catch an angel like her," the sel-
fish said smugly. "She won't be needing that halo any
more—not after he's through compromising her."

I was angry about the fate of the pretty angelfish.
"Something's fishy about your attitude," I said. I fished
the halo out of the water, but it disintegrated in my hand.
Halos were not for such as I.

"You're a fool," the sel-fish said witheringly and swam
away.

"I surely am," I said under my breath. People like me

were always getting victimized by clever, unscrupulous people like Magician Yang, just as the angelfish was ravished by the devilfish. Yet somehow I didn't care to trade places with the obvious winners. I couldn't make much sense of my own attitude; it was simply the way I was. Just an ignorant barbarian.

I slept, discontented.

Next day we left the island and set off again. We came to a kind of gateway in the forest, formed by two large trees linking branches above. I didn't like this; it reminded me of the trees guarding Castle Roogna, the ones that didn't like me. But there was so much thorny bush around that the portal appeared to be the only practical way to go. Pook didn't like it any better than I did, but also saw no better way; it seemed that was the direction we were supposed to be going in, by his reckoning.

So we went. Pook nudged through the gate, and I kept my hand on my sword. Nothing happened. But Pook sniffed the air nervously, winding something unpleasant, and I experienced a feeling of claustrophobia. This was definitely ugly territory!

Yet the sun shone pleasantly, there were playful little breezes, the footing was good, and there did not seem to be any bad animals in this region, so we moved along well. I did notice that the trees interlinked, forming veritable walls of foliage, but these were intermittent, so that we had no trouble passing through the spaces. Both of us remained nervous about the confinement, but all we needed to do was trot along until we got out of the region. Certainly it was better than climbing a snow-topped mountain.

Then there was a buzzing. I didn't like the sound of that, and Pook switched his tail nervously. Horses tend to dislike buzzing things generally, but some buzzes are worse than others, and this was bad buzzing. The sound loomed louder, and then the source manifested—a swarm of huge flies.

I muttered a repeller-spell. Some people claimed spoken spells didn't work in Xanth, but in my opinion those

folk hadn't given them a fair trial. I used spells to make
fire, put myself to sleep, abolish warts, adjust my eyes
to sudden changes of light, ease pain, and the like; that
sort of magic generally worked for me. Of course, it helped
to have two magic stones to strike together for the first
spark for the fire and to relax properly before using the
sleep-spell; the magic took weeks or months to work on
the warts and several seconds on the eyes; and there was
only so much that incidental magic could do for pain. But
weak magic was better than none at all, I always said,
knocking on wood. Sometimes, when I was very tired and
really needed to sleep, the sleep-spell zonked me out instantly, and that was a blessing. One simply had to understand the natural limitations of magic; then it worked just
fine. Once in a while one encountered a bum spell, one
that simply did not perform as advertised; then it was
simply a matter of reporting it to the Barbarian Better
Business Bureau, so that no one else would be deceived
into using that spell.

Anyway, I used the fly-spook-spell, but that swarm
came right on at us. Then I saw that these were not ordinary flies; they were dragonflies, resistive to such little
magic. Normally dragonflies did not deign to bother people, but buzzed about their own business, preying on other
bugs and keeping company with real dragons. On occasion, a dragonfly would adopt someone's garden, keeping
it clear of bugs. But these ones were different; they were
wild, not tame, and they were out after us.

Pook broke into a gallop, but the dragonflies were faster
than we were and quickly overhauled us. I flailed my arms
and Pook swished his tail violently, but to no avail. The
flies came at us head-on, jetting fire, and veered away
only at the last instant. Thus their fire continued on at its
target. One of those little scorches scored on my bare
forearm; it hurt!

This seemed ludicrous, but I drew my sword and sliced
the air with it, swiftly. I cut a fly in half and winged
another; the first fell with smoke trailing from its fuselage,
and the second plunged out of control because of the loss
of its wing, crashed into the ground, and exploded. A

mushroom cloud of smoke roiled up from the site of the impact.

That made the others pause for a moment. Then they formed into a wedge and charged us together. I put up the flat of my blade to deflect their massed firepower, and their flame reflected back at them, scorching several. You would think dragonflies would be immune to their own heat, but as with many creatures, they can't take what they give out. There were three more spins out of control and two more explosions. The third just fizzled, sending up a few sparks before melting down.

Now the flies withdrew into a huddle, consulting. I didn't like the look of this. If they charged us all at once, from all sides, Pook and I would get badly burned. But instead they retreated.

"What do you make of that?" I asked aloud. Pook twitched an ear, as mystified as I. Some of his hide was scorched, and he had surely expected worse to come. These flies had seemed more ornery than that and certainly no cowards; their abrupt departure was as ominous as their approach had been.

But there was nothing better to go on. "Maybe they ran low on fuel," I said. "The way that last one fizzed, maybe he lacked the oomph to blow." But I didn't really believe that.

Then Pook stepped over an object on the ground. There was a flash of something awful.

"The next evil spell!" I exclaimed with dismay. "We triggered it! The dragonflies knew it was lurking here!"

But what spell was it? Nothing seemed to have happened. So I leaned down to peer more closely at whatever it was, before it faded out. The dragonflies would not have veered away from an innocuous spell!

It was in the shape of a black monster.

I needed the monster-banishing-spell, and I had it in my bag—but did I dare invoke it? It was possible that not all the white spells had been garbled, but I decided not to risk it. For one thing, no monster had appeared. Maybe this particular spell had malfunctioned.

We heard a gleeful buzzing returning, and with it the *thunk-thunk* of the footfalls of some massive creature.

"Now I could be wrong, but that sounds like large trouble to me," I said.

Pook agreed. He took off at a gallop, leaving the ponderous noise behind. It's always best to avoid trouble, if possible, especially when it's bigger than you are. I know that sounds unbarbarian, but there are a number of myths about barbarians I've been trying to dispel. When the only safety is in flight, the sensible man flees.

But we came to a curve in the path, and the vegetation was too thickly intertwined to permit any ready egress; we had to follow that curve in a loop back. The pursuing thing made a shortcut and gained on us. We just didn't have time to hack through the meshed trees and brush; we had to keep moving. That was, of course, why that spell had been placed here; it was a very bad place for me. Fortunately, we had developed enough of a lead so that we were still well ahead of the creature. We took off down a new path and again left the *thunk-thunk-thunk* behind.

And again we encountered a curve. This was inconvenient, annoying, and perhaps dangerous, for it allowed the thing behind us to catch up once more. This time the snout of the thing showed around the curve before we left it behind. It had whiskers and a feline aspect.

As we left it behind this time, I wondered: What had a feline aspect and six legs? For that was the number it had; I could tell by the triple thunk. I was long accustomed to identifying animals by their traces and sounds. Two-legged creatures have an even beat when they run; four-legged have double beat, as the two forelegs and two hind legs strike. This was triple. I had not so long ago encountered a six-legged creature, I couldn't quite remember where, but it had been so low-slung as to whomp rather than run. This was different.

And another turn! This was awkward as anything! Now all of the pursuer came into view, and I recognized it at last—the tarasque. Of course—Yin had warned me of it. Of all the creatures I might have encountered here, this was the one I least preferred, now that I grasped its nature. The tarasque was technically a dragon, but not a normal one, for it possessed certain nonreptilian attributes. Its head was that of an ant-lion, it had six ursine legs—we don't have what the Mundanes call bears in Xanth, but we do have their legs—a big spiked carapace, and an ugly reptilian tail. All in all, an ugly customer.

Once more we outdistanced it. But still we were in the confines of this maze, and the tarasque seemed tireless. Some of these big ones are boosted by magic, unfair as that may seem to their prey. If we ever got out into open forest, we could outrun it permanently—but we were stuck in this mess of channels.

And, of course, that was the point. The evil spell had been placed to summon the monster as the final wedge of a careful trap. Naturally, the bumpkin had marched right into it.

It was now apparent that the evil spells were not simply strewn along my predetermined path in random fashion. They were set where they would do the most harm. The odds against me were even worse than I had imagined.

I had no choice. I would have to risk a defensive spell. Maybe it would turn out wrong, but at least it was a chance.

But which spell? The white compass had converted a stone mountain to flesh; would the monster-banishing-spell relate any better? But I didn't know what would be better than the correct spell. I just had to hope that not all the spells would turn out to be mixed up.

So I grabbed for the white monster figurine as we moved along. "Invoke!" I cried as I held it in my hand.

It flashed. But the triple pounding of the monster's paws continued unabated behind us. Whatever the spell had done, it wasn't monster banishment.

My awareness enlarged as the white object faded from my hand. I knew we were in a maze-warren that might have only one exit, so that the tarasque could run down unwary prey at his leisure. That way the monster's slowness did not matter. Just as I had worn down Pook when I stalked him and herded him into an inescapable situation, so the tarasque would wear us down. Flight would not accomplish anything except tiring us out, and that was no good. It would be better to stand and fight while we were strong.

"Pick a good place to ambush the monster," I told Pook. "We'll fight." He wiggled an ear in acknowledgment.

One thing about tripping the evil spell—it meant we were still on course for the object, since the spells had been placed along that course. In fact—another light bulb sprouted momentarily above my head, brightening the whole region but not, alas, blinding the tarasque—that course was predestined. Yang knew where to place his spells because he knew where I was going to go, according to the prophecy. There really should be a law against such prophecies, I thought darkly. But this was actually good news for me. Since my route was predestined, I did not even need the finder-spell; I would get to the object regardless. In fact, I couldn't avoid it.

That also explained why Yang had tried to bribe me to quit. If he really believed I would fail, he had no need of bribery. But if my route was predestined, then I would find the object—unless I deliberately gave up the mission. It was not failure that stalked me, but success—assuming I could handle the hazards along the way. Presumably, if I got permanently killed, that would be the same as giving up, and the remainder of my predestined route would be voided.

Now why was all this obvious to me now, when it had been obscure before? Was I thinking better? And the answer was yes, I was thinking quite a bit better. I was more intelligent than I had been. That meant that I had invoked Magician Yin's spell of intelligence. It had been intended to counteract Yang's lurking spell of idiocy, but now had simply increased my normal level. I was a barbarian genius!

The irony was that genius is wasted on a barbarian. It doesn't take brains to swing a sword, it takes muscle. No really smart man would *be* a barbarian. Another counterspell had been wasted.

Well, I was stuck with it. Could intelligence help me escape the monster? That was doubtful. Given a little time, I could devise a weapon from plucked foliage that would cause the tarasque to draw into his shell and be helpless—but I had no time. The smartest thing to do was to stay out of the monster's labyrinth; I would have realized that, had I invoked this spell before entering. So it wasn't much help to me at the moment. Nevertheless, being smart couldn't hurt.

Quickly I reviewed what I could recall about the tarasque. I had thought I had never heard of it, but I had merely forgotten. There turned out to be more information stored in the crannies of my brain than I had realized; bits and pieces of things I had heard elsewhere in my life and not remembered until this moment of heightened intelligence. The tarasque was a deadly monster, and not a stupid one. It preyed only on live, healthy creatures, so that it would not pick up any loathsome diseases or suffer indigestion. It avoided carrion and tainted meat. The classier predators were like that; griffins were notoriously finicky, for example.

There was my strategy of survival! I would try to kill the tarasque—but if I failed, I would pretend to be tainted. Then it would not eat me, and my talent in due course would restore me to full health. It was not the easiest way to get through, but it was feasible.

What, then, of Pook? *He* could not heal rapidly, or grow back lost limbs, or return from death. "Pook, if I lose, you take off immediately. You must escape while the tarasque is tending to me."

He neighed in negation. "No, I will heal," I assured him. "You need time to find your way out of the maze. I can give you that time."

He snorted, disliking this, obviously believing that I was exaggerating my healing propensity, but he assented.

Suddenly he veered into a side pocket. This was just large enough to give us fighting room while protecting our sides and rear. If we could hold off the monster, this was the place to do it.

"But first let's give the tarasque a chance to pass us by," I said. "We don't want to fight unless we have to."

In a moment the monster shot past our alcove, screeched to a halt, backed up, and stared in. I realized that I should have struck at its midsection before it got its head oriented, now that I saw it clearly; the head had tusklike teeth and orange-glaring eyes and was framed by a tawny mane. Overall, the tarasque was as big as Pook—but the horse was constructed for running, while the monster was constructed for combat. Its bear-paws attached to hugely muscled legs, and their claws were stout.

I drew my sword as I dismounted and stood before Pook, facing the tarasque "I don't suppose we can settle this amicably?" I inquired of the monster. I really didn't expect any affirmation, but I wouldn't want it said that I had fought without reason. There are forms to be followed, after all.

For answer, the monster roared. The sound made the trees confining us shudder, their leaves curling. What power! An ogre could hardly do much better than that! I'm a husky barbarian, of course, so I don't properly understand fear, but that sound provided me with an inkling. The wind from the monster's exhalation blew back my hair and tore at the interlocking branches of the trees. The odor of it was not exactly sweet, either.

"I feel obliged to advise you that I am a primitive warrior type, excellent with my weapons," I said. Too bad the monster's carapace was so sturdy; it would resist the blast of a pineapple. Otherwise I would have had an easy way out. "If you should choose to back off now, I will understand."

The tarasque took a step forward. Its three left legs moved together, then its three right legs. It opened its mouth marvelously wide, so that I could readily perceive exactly how horrendous its jaws were. Those teeth were like a forest of spikes, some narrowing to points, some splitting into multiple cutting ridges, some serrated like the surface of a saw. There were ledges and valleys and sculptured contours that I was sure meshed neatly with their opposite numbers when those jaws came together; hapless indeed the creature on whom those jaws closed!

I tried once more, for courtesy requires three attempts at peaceful settlement. "There is one special thing you should know about me—"

The tarasque pounced, mouth gaped wide, another roar forming in the tonsil region.

Ah, well, I had tried. Now I fought, free of any reservations. I'm actually pretty good in that sort of circumstance. I swung my blade about with the legendary skill for which barbarians are justly famed. It blurred in an arc that passed through the gaping mouth and severed the tongue, a tonsil, and the forming roar. That cut the bite short; the jaws clapped together as my sword exited, and spurting blood overlapped those finely chiseled, clean white teeth.

"I did try to warn you, turtle-shell," I said. "I am not your routine terrified, helpless prey; I am a swordsman. You will take severe injuries and perhaps die, if you persist in this quarrel."

The tarasque's eyes blazed. That was, of course, the point to my discussion: to enrage the creature beyond the edge of reason. It is Standard Barbarian Artifice Number Three, verbal aggravation of subject. Some weak swordsmen with strong tongues do very well on the adventure circuit, I understand.

The monster nudged forward, swiping at me with a massive forepaw. I ducked back, and the swipe missed and caught the trunk of the tree to my right, gouging out four channels of bark. The tree shuddered and groaned woodenly, and sap dripped from the wounds. That from channel number 4 smelled very good.

But I had concerns of my own. I poked my point at the monster's left eye. The tarasque ducked back alertly, avoiding the thrust. My first strike had caught it by surprise, but now it was wary. Having one's tongue cut off tends to facilitate caution. So I struck down at its black nose and lopped off two whiskers.

That made the creature angry! The loss of those whiskers disfigured its puss, and it seemed the monster was vain about its appearance. The severed tongue and tonsil didn't show, but those whiskers did! The tarasque let out a blood-flecked scream and pounced at me. Of course I ducked down and jabbed the point of my sword up, seeking to cut the exposed throat. The monster spun aside just barely in time, lost its balance, and crashed against the clawed tree.

My advantage! I squeezed out on the other side and made a powerful two-handed chop at its side. All I hit was its heavily armored carapace. My blade bounced off with no injury to the tarasque, but with a numbing shock to my hands and arms. Ouch! I wouldn't do that again.

Now I was outside my alcove and afoot; I had no protection to sides or rear. I would be lost in a moment if I didn't do something.

The tarasque was bringing its head about. I jumped forward, grabbed the nearest spike, and hauled myself up on the dragon's carapace. I doubted that the monster's head could reach the middle of its armored back. "Ho, halfwhisker!" I cried as I seated myself between spikes, bracing my boots against them. "What do you say now, stinksnoot?" Tastefully selected insults are naturally a key aspect of Artifice Number Three.

What the tarasque said was an unrepeatable roar of wrathy rage. It whipped its head about to snap at me, but couldn't reach me. I chopped at its furry ears with my sword, cutting off one of them. That made the monster angrier yet.

The tarasque tried to buck me off, but was too solid to accomplish much, and I was well braced. It tried to reach up a paw to swipe at me, but the six legs were designed for nether support of its solid mass, not for upward mobility, and this one never got close. It tried to bash my leg against a tree, but its own spikes extended well beyond my leg, so that all it did was poke a hole in the tree and get itself temporarily stuck in the wood. It tried to roll over, squashing me, but the spikes prevented it from rolling. Meanwhile, I constantly nicked those bits of flesh I could reach with the point of my sword, harrying the monster unmercifully.

Unfortunately, I could not do the tarasque serious harm from where I perched. Its carapace protected it from injury as effectively as it protected me from molestation. So we were hung up for the moment, locked in combat without being able to terminate it. Maybe this would become a kind of siege, with the one who lasted longest emerging the victor.

Alas, not so! The tarasque's long, serpentine tail whipped about and stung me on the back. *That* could touch me!

I tried to lop off the end of that tail, but it flicked in and out so fast I couldn't catch it. In fact, I didn't even dare turn my head, for fear the tail would twitch out an eye or two. My light body armor was getting cut up, and stripes were appearing on my flesh. I had to get out of range of that tail!

But to do that, I had to get off the carapace—and that would render me vulnerable again to the rest of the monster. Was there some other way?

Yes, there was. I squirmed around and crawled backward, passing one spike after another, moving toward the tail. Naturally the flashing tip tore up my back considerably, but I pressed on until I was able to turn partway, shield my face with my free forearm, and poke my sword down at the base of the tail where it emerged from the carapace. I sawed away at that exposed flesh, trying to sever it from the body. My leverage wasn't good, but my blade was sharp, and soon I penetrated the thick hide to the tender flesh beneath.

The tarasque screamed and leaped, prodded by the sudden pain. That motion was so abrupt and vigorous that I somersaulted from my perch and rolled on the ground. Now I was in trouble!

The tarasque blinked, taking a moment to realize that I had been dislodged. Then it got its reflexes back in order and pounced. I had hung onto my sword; now I brought it up and stabbed it at the monster's snout. The point sank into the tender cheek. The head jerked back, coming off the blade, and blood gouted out.

I scrambled to my feet and backed toward the alcove.

The enraged monster sprang at me again, this time swiping with a forepaw. I parried the paw, and the blade sliced into it, cutting off a claw and its supporting pad, but the shock of the swipe dashed the sword from my hand. I was disarmed!

Well, not quite, I still had my knife. I had left my bow and arrows and the bag of spells with Pook; they would not be useful in combat like this. But the knife seemed pitifully inadequate.

The tarasque figured it had me and pushed forward, mouth opening to take a juicy bite of barbarian. It's an established fact that barbarians taste better than civilized folk do, because they are healthier, with more lean red meat.

Well, monsters make mistakes, just as men do. I stabbed the knife blade into its black nose and twisted.

That smarted! The creature let out a feline screech that threatened to turn my fingernails green and jerked back with unbecoming haste. I hung onto the knife, wrenching it out just ahead of a gout of blood. For the moment, the tarasque was blinded by pain.

Naturally I followed up my advantage; I am not a warrior for nothing! I lunged again for the monster's throat, seeking the vulnerable vein. But the head pulled back quickly. This thing wasn't a predatory monster for nothing, either. I was a good deal more of a contest than the dragon had figured, but the odds remained in its favor, especially as it learned from its little misjudgments. I missed the throat and stumbled into the chest area.

Actually, this wasn't a bad place to be. The tarasque was accustomed to chasing and catching fleeing prey, not to scratching for it underfoot. Chickens scratch, not dragons! It tried to swipe at me with a forepaw, but lacked proper leverage that way, and I had no trouble avoiding the clumsy motion. Then, realizing that its right midpaw was pretty well pinned to the ground while the right forepaw was swiping, I squatted and plunged my blade through that portion that was against the ground, right above the big claws.

Hoo, what a fuss that monster made! It yanked up the

paw—but with two paws in the air at once, it lost its balance and sank down on that side. I had to scramble to avoid getting crushed under the descending carapace. This creature was armored all around its midsection, so that I could not get in a good belly-stab. Too bad; in this moment the region was wide open.

Aha! The legs weren't armored, just the body. Where the legs emerged from the carapace, they looked especially tender. There was room for motion around each leg so that it wouldn't bang into the carapace. The monster would not be able to chase down swift prey without free play for the legs. It all made sense—but it offered me my opportunity.

I dug my blade into that cavity between carapace and leg. I was rewarded by another roar of enraged anguish. I was really scoring on the monster now! Both Magician Yin and the tarasque itself had underestimated the barbarian powers of close combat, and perhaps I had done so, too. Maybe I could take this monster!

But I had overplayed my hand. The tarasque flopped all the way to the ground, and though I had to scramble out from beneath and did so with alacrity, my knife hand got pinned between the leg and the carapace, and I was caught. That's the one time when the leg does come up against the shell—when the creature lies down. My knife hand wasn't hurt, but I couldn't quite scramble free, and the mass of the monster whomped down on my left leg, crushing it. It was my turn to howl.

The tarasque got up and turned about to come at me headfirst. I tried to fend it off with one bare hand, but one fell swoop of its forepaws nearly ripped my arm from its socket. Then the monster pinned me to the ground with one paw and got ready to bite off my face.

"Pook! Get out of here!" I screamed, just before the slavering, blood-soaked mouth closed on my head. There was an instant of extreme discomfort as those tusks dug in—it really isn't much fun, getting your face bitten off—then darkness.

Pook galloped out of the alcove, his chains rattling. The monster glanced up. It wasn't finished with me—in fact, it had hardly started on me—but the horse's motion confused it. Maybe the sight of fleeing prey activated its chase circuit. But of course one morsel on the paw is worth two on the hoof, so the tarasque returned to the business at hand, so to speak. It chomped the rest of the way through my face.

Pook whirled, charged back, and delivered a two-hoofed kick to the monster's hind shell. The gross body was shoved forward, and the snoot plowed into the dirt beside my head.

That did it. The tarasque spat out my face, shook the dirt out of its eyes, and started off after the ghost horse. This was, of course, exactly what I didn't want, since Pook hadn't had enough time to get clear. But I was in no position to protest, being unconscious. In fact, only now do I see in the tapestry what happened, and how it was that Pook once again rescued me. I owe a lot to that horse!

The dragon limped, but was still able to get up respectable velocity. I had hurt it in tongue, cheek, nose, foot, and shoulder socket, but not enough to dim its fighting spirit. I had not, it seemed, slowed it enough to give Pook a decent chance.

However, Pook was a smart animal. He remembered the route out of the maze and followed it. He did lose time going around the curves; maybe he was guided by smell and sight as well as memory and did not dare to leave the exact trail we had made, lest he get lost and confused and be trapped by the tarasque. So it was close, but he was able to remain just ahead. Perhaps the fact that he was no longer carrying my weight, added to the injuries the monster had suffered, helped; what might have been a small but critical deficit in relative velocity became a small advantage. In due course, Pook found his way to the entrance.

But it was closed. Vines had strung themselves across it and interlaced and sprouted wicked thorns. Pook skidded to a halt, four hooves churning up turf. What was he to do now? He had no sword to cut through this mass.

The dragon puffed up behind him. The tarasque was

an oddball among dragons, possessing no fire, smoke, or steam; but when it ran, it puffed. Pook took one look to the side, realized that it was folly to remain in the maze to be chased down, and leaped into the vine-shrouded gate.

The thorns bit cruelly into his skin, but his chains protected him some, and he was able to scramble through just as the monster came up. The tarasque snapped at Pook's hind legs, and that was a tactical error, because those hooves shot back with a force of one horsepower and pasted it on the snoot. Then the ghost horse was through, outside the maze.

But the dragon didn't desist. It shook its sore snoot and roared at the vines—and they shriveled and fell away. The tarasque leaped at Pook, who whirled and galloped off.

Now the nature of the chase changed, for the terrain favored the horse. Pook began to draw ahead, but paused, as it were, in thought, and then deliberately slowed, allowing the monster to close the gap. Pook ran just ahead, always seeming about to be caught, luring the predator ever farther away from its maze. Pook was, of course, very good at this sort of thing, for this was how ghost horses earned their living—luring fools into bad regions, or scaring them away from good ones. I ought to know!

That gave me time to heal. Fortunately, I wasn't dead, just unconscious and face-chewed; in an hour or so, I could grow back my eyeballs and things and be as good as new. Instead of my using myself as bait to distract the monster so Pook could escape, Pook was distracting the monster so I could recover. I think that was really nice of him.

Pook led the tarasque to the region of caves we had passed—the ones with the dimepedes. What was he contemplating? He could not hide there, for the dimes would nickel him to death.

But it turned out he was more canny than that. Pook was a master of traps, as I had discovered when I first chased him down. He went and stood in a patch of sunlight before a deep-dark cave. The dimes avoided sun, so they did not show their silvery little snoots.

The tarasque came up. It was a solid creature, with its heavy carapace, and maybe its injuries were telling; it had slowed and was huffing loudly. But now it thought it had trapped the horse, and it charged.

Pook stepped aside, letting the monster burst into the cave. It disappeared into the darkness. There was a pause, then a roar that shook the hillside. The tarasque had discovered the dimepedes, or vice versa! Then the monster started to back out—but Pook braced himself and kicked with his hind hooves again at the rear of the carapace, using his horsepower to shove the monster back in.

It was a beautiful ploy—but alas, not enough. The tarasque weighed more than Pook did, its huge shell made it invulnerable to kicks, and it had strong reason to get out. It hunkered down and shoved, and Pook could not confine it. Soon it got its head clear, pawed away the clinging dimepedes, and rotated to face the horse.

Pook was no coward. He stepped close to the tarasque's face and spun about. His chains flung out and whipped across the dragon's head, knocking out a tooth or two, or maybe an eyeball. The monster was so surprised it pulled its head and forelegs back inside its shell—whereupon Pook kicked sand and dirt in after the head.

It seems monsters don't like having sand kicked in their snoots. The tarasque bellowed so hard that the sand was blown out of its neck hole and three leg holes. The carapace almost lifted off the ground, propelled by the blast. As roars go, that was a good one!

Now the baleful head came out of the shell, teeth gleaming furiously. And Pook scored on the nose with another kick. His hind hoof jammed the sore black nose right back into the dragon's sore head, so that the tarasque's face became concave instead of convex, and shoved the head back into the shell.

Pook was fighting the monster better than I had!

Then the horse sniffed, smelling something. Quickly he trotted to the side, where a ragweed bush grew. He snatched a rag between his teeth, ripped it off, held his breath, and trotted back to the tarasque, whose head was just emerging again from the carapace. Pook flung the rag onto the monster's nose and backed out of the way.

Now, ragweed was not a normal choice for cloth, because of a special and objectionable quality of the rags. No one wove ragweed into rugs or clothing, except perhaps as a practical joke, and not just because the rags were ugly. But in this case—

The tarasque sneezed. That was what ragweed did. It caused uncontrollable sneezing. Some creatures could sneeze for days after a single whiff; others could struggle to keep their heads attached. Once the monster got a good, deep whiff of the potent rag—

It was some sneeze. The blast from it blew the leaves off bushes and stirred up little dust devils, who uttered unkind syllables and fled. The dragon's whole body slid back a distance because of the recoil. The next sneeze slid it back some more, and the third put its tail well inside the cave. Half a dozen more sneezes had the tarasque all the way back in the cave.

Pook trotted over to the ragweed and harvested another rag. The sneeze-dust practically oozed from it, itching to do its nefarious job. Pook tossed it into the cave, then scrambled up the hill, found some debris, and kicked it down. He managed to start a minor avalanche that piled up junk before the cave, partially blocking it. That wouldn't stop the monster from powering out, of course, but it did tend to enclose the air and deflect the wind from the sneezes, so that the magic sneeze-dust from the rag remained mostly inside the cave. That meant the tarasque had to keep inhaling it, which in turn meant continued sneezing.

Pook cocked an ear, listening, as the hillside shook with the reverberations. I know what he heard: a number of little sneezes along with the big ones. The dimepedes were affected, too! They would be very angry, once they managed to stop—and there, deep within their cave, was the apparent instigator of it all, the tarasque. The dimepedes could not pinch through the carapace, but they were small enough to scuttle up inside the leg holes, head hole, and tail hole, and mad enough to do considerable damage to whatever flesh they found in there. The tarasque was too deep inside the cave to escape readily this time. There was about to be a reckoning.

Satisfied, Pook trotted back toward the maze. He had, to most intents and purposes, defeated the monster. Now he was returning to rescue me.

But I had problems of my own. I had been healing nicely—but then the dragonflies arrived to harass me. I was just regaining consciousness when they swarmed in and blasted me with dozens of little fiery jets. Singly, each blast was painful; together, they were devastating. My newly healing skin was blistered, my clothing burned off, my hair set on fire. My sight was lost again, and my sense of smell, and then two flies zoomed down to jet into my ears and deprive me of my hearing, too. They actually tore me up much worse than the tarasque had done, now that they had me helpless. Nothing is quite as cruel as a weakling with sudden power!

When Pook returned to pick me up, he found me lying under a cloud of dragonflies. He charged in, swishing his tail so violently that dozens of flies were knocked out of the air and sent spinning to the ground, where they detonated. The explosions were somewhat feeble, because the flies' fuel was almost exhausted. Now Pook was strong, the dragonflies weak; they had used up most of their reserves on me, cooking my flesh. They spooked and fled. There was no point in their remaining, anyway; they had already had their vengeance by destroying my body.

It seems Pook did not yet properly understand the full nature of my talent. Maybe he thought my recovery had been a fluke before, in the caves of the callicantzari. He did not realize how badly the tarasque had hurt me or how far I had recovered from that before the flies returned. Thus he did not understand that I would recover on my own, given a few hours. So he tried to help me.

He rolled me over with his nose, shoved me into the bushes fringing the maze passage, and wedged me up. I rolled off and flopped back on the ground. He tried again, and again I flopped limply. One seldom realizes how useful human hands are until one observes a horse trying to pick up a man with hooves. It is just about impossible.

My burned-off skin was now plastered with dirt, so that I looked like a zombie fried in bread crumbs. Anyone else would have sought a decent burial for the appalling remains. But Pook wouldn't give up. He found a better place, where a low branch touched the ground, and rolled me to that, then nosed me up on it, got his head under, and finally managed to hump me off the branch and onto his back.

My head and hands dangled on one side of his body and my feet on the other, but he was able to carry me. He took me out of the maze, then on around it, proceeding generally northwest. Probably he knew there was no help where we had been, so he was hoping there would be some where we hadn't been.

As the day waned, I healed partway and began to stir. Pook didn't realize the significance of that; he might not even have distinguished my motion from that of inert flopping.

At last he spied a cabin in a clearing in the jungle. He gave a nicker of relief and headed for it. There, perhaps, there would be human help for me.

Chapter 9. Threnody

I woke in a bed of fragrant ferns. I saw the interior of the cabin, neatly ordered, with shelves bearing spices and herbs. In a corner was a strange, large, hollow gourd with strings stretched lengthwise across it. And sitting in a wicker chair was a quite pretty young woman in a brown dress.

She saw me react and got up to approach me. "So you

are recovering," she said in a low voice. "I wasn't certain you would."

"Oh, I always did before," I said. My body ached, but I knew that would soon pass as the healing was completed.

"Your horse brought you in," she said. "You seem to have been pretty badly burned."

That was when I realized that the dragonflies had returned. The awareness had faded out, but now I remembered. "Yes."

"I don't get many visitors," the woman said. "So I may be rusty on the amenities. Let me just say that my name is Threnody. I live alone and like it, and we'll get along just fine if you keep your hands to yourself and depart as soon as you are able. Your horse is grazing outside."

So this was a woman who wanted to be left alone. Some were like that; I never did quite understand why. Well, I had never been one to force my attentions on anyone. Barbarians generally encountered enough willing women so that they had little taste for unwilling ones, and I don't care what the civilized folk claim to the contrary.

"I am Jordan the Adventurer, I heal very fast, and I have a mission to accomplish, so I'll be on my way soon enough," I said. "I thank you for taking care of me while I was unconscious; I must have been pretty dirty."

"You certainly were! I had to wash you all over. Sand was virtually embedded in your hide. I thought you were dead, but you weren't as far gone as it seemed. I put some ointments on your burns and let you rest. You must have blundered into a dragonfly nest." She eyed me appraisingly. "I must say, you do have a hardy constitution; you're quite a robust figure of a man."

"Yeah, I'm a genuine barbarian, mostly brawn, not too much brain," I said, smiling. Actually, I was pretty smart at the moment, because of the eye-queue spell I had accidentally invoked. "Fortunately, Pook is on hand to take care of me."

"Pook," she repeated. "Your horse? Does that mean—?"

"Yes, he is a pooka, a ghost horse. That's why he wears those chains."

"You tamed a ghost horse?" she asked, surprised.

"No. We're just friends."

She laughed. She was beautiful when she did that. "Well, he's loyal. He could have dumped you off anywhere and left you to die." She glanced toward the kitchen corner. "Are you well enough yet to eat?"

"Oh, yes, I'm hungry!"

"You *are* recovering swiftly! You look better already."

"Yes, I'm always hungry after a fatal injury," I agreed.

Again she laughed, taking this as humor. She poured some gruel from the pot on her hearth into a wooden bowl and brought it to me. The stuff was as dark and liquid as her hair, but it tasted good and seemed to be nutritious; I felt rapidly stronger.

"I have a trouser-tree growing in my yard," she said. "Never thought I'd need it, as I prefer dresses." She held up a pair of brown jeans. "These should fit you."

"Thank you," I said. I got out of the fern bed and into the jeans, and they did fit tolerably well.

"That's amazing," she remarked, watching. Evidently she wasn't one of those prudish civilized women, though in other respects she did seem civilized. "Your skin is almost whole again! You were so badly burned—"

I shrugged. "Guess it looked worse than it was." I could have explained about my talent, but it didn't seem necessary, since I was about to leave. Actually, I wasn't paying full attention to her, as my ensmartened brain was distracted by philosophical insights and intellectual exercises it hadn't been interested in before. Today I can only vaguely appreciate the mental convolutions I indulged in then, for now I am of only ordinary smartness. That is why I am not telling this story in the intelligent way I could have told it then.

Yet I think, in retrospect, that I must have made the error of overlooking the obvious in the course of my pursuit of the esoteric, for I really did not *act* very smart in Threnody's house. Some extremely smart people are sort of dull about practical details.

"I had no idea you'd be on your feet so soon," she said. "What is your mission?"

"Oh, nothing that would interest you," I replied off-handedly. "I have to go fetch an object and bring it back to Castle Roogna."

"Castle Roogna?" she repeated, interested in a peculiar kind of way. I should have noticed that, but didn't, then. "Is that still functioning?"

"Oh, sure. But old King Gromden is dying, and there's a problem about the succession. So I—"

"The King is dying?" she asked alertly.

"Yes. And these two Magicians, Yin and Yang, are vying for the throne, so—"

"Yin and Yang—but they—"

"Can't agree on anything," I finished. "Except on this magic contest, to see whose spells are stronger. So I—"

"I'm beginning to understand! You are working for them!"

"Yes, in a way. I've got to complete my mission so Yin will win, but Yang's spells are interfering. It's been pretty rough, but I think I'm getting close." I shrugged. "I won't bore you with the details. I'll be on my way now. Thanks for the gruel, girl."

"Wait," she said. "This object you have to fetch—do you know what it is?"

"No. I have Yin's finder-spell, but haven't used it yet. But I think the object is somewhere around here, because I'm predestined to—"

"Sit down, Jordan," she said. "Let me tell you a story that you may not have heard. I'll serve you some wine."

"Oh, sure. Thanks." I was always willing to be sociable.

Threnody mixed some fluids in a cup, which surprised me, for I had always thought wine came directly from wineskins grown by wine-lilies. She brought the cup to me, and I drank it while she talked. It was pungent stuff, with a bitter aftertaste but pretty good. Barbarians don't have much taste, anyway.

"King Gromden had a child, a daughter," Threnody said.

"Oh, sure. He told me."

"What else did he tell you about her?"

"Nothing much. Just that his wife and child had gone away and he missed them something awful." I burped; that wine was bubbling up inside me.

"There was a bit more to the story than that," Threnody said.

"Well, he's pretty lonely now." Then my intelligence had a flash. "Yang mentioned scandal; maybe that was—"

She was silent a moment, then resumed her story as if she had not been interrupted. "King Gromden's daughter was the apple of his eye, and indeed she was said to be very pretty. His wife grew jealous of the attention the child got and put a curse on her: if she remained at Castle Roogna, the castle would fall. This saddened the King very much, but he had to preserve the capital of Xanth at all costs, so he sent the girl away. Because he was angry with the Queen for putting on that curse, he sent her away, too. But before the Queen departed, she put a curse on him also. That was her talent, of course—curses. She came from cursefolk stock, deep in southern Xanth; some call those folk fiends. She caused him to forget the nature of the first curse.

"So ever after, the King sought his banished daughter, not realizing that he himself had banished her, and for good reason. He finally located her, but she remembered the curse and refused to return with him to Castle Roogna. He could not understand why, for when she told him of the curse, he immediately forgot. A good curse can't be circumvented just by a person's being told its nature; it operates until revoked, or until it just wears out, and the curses of the curse-fiends don't wear out.

"Since he could not grasp the truth and insisted on an answer, she had to tell him a lie instead, cruel as it was: that she preferred to live in the open wilderness instead of in a gloomy old castle. He kept trying to find ways to change her mind, but was never successful."

"That's very interesting," I said. "He never said anything to me about the curses."

"Naturally not. He remembers his daughter's absence,

though," Threnody said. "And he swore he would find a
way to bring her back and make her happy at Castle
Roogna. In fact, he hoped she would marry his successor,
the next King of Xanth, so his line would continue in
power. The throne of Xanth is not hereditary, as it goes
from Magician to Magician, but sometimes there is a lineage through the female side. His daughter wasn't a
Sorceress, of course, but that doesn't matter for wives."

"Well, I guess that didn't work out." I set down my
empty mug. "His successor will be Yin or Yang, and I
don't think either is much interested in marriage right
now."

"They are interested. The people would be more ready
to accept a Magician who married the prior King's daughter, and her magic power would help him reign, so she is
a moderately valuable property as well as being physically
attractive. Men tend to put too much stress on the latter
aspect."

"Um, yes," I agreed, contemplating Threnody's own
figure.

"In any event, they would not have a choice. The King
arranged it so that neither could become King unless he
married her."

My head was whirling pleasantly. That was strong wine!
"Maybe he'll spring that detail on the winner, once I bring
back the object," I said. "But it will be too bad, because
if her return to the castle means it will fall—"

"Yes, it is a cruel situation," she agreed. "That girl will
never return to Castle Roogna, because she loves her
father and loves Xanth, nothing else. She will do anything
to prevent her return, no matter who the next king is,
though it breaks her father's heart. She has no choice."

"Well, it's not my business," I said, standing. "I just
have to fetch the—"

I reeled, staggered, lost my balance, and fell against
the bed. Something was wrong!

Threnody came to me. "I'm sorry I had to poison you,
barbarian," she said. "But if you should succeed in your
mission, and Yin becomes King, he will do what King
Gromden wants, and marry Gromden's daughter and keep

her at Castle Roogna. I must prevent that, for when Castle Roogna falls, so does the human domination of Xanth."

"But—" I protested groggily.

"You see, barbarian innocent, *I* am King Gromden's daughter," she said. "I felt it only fair to let you understand why I had to kill you. Better that the life of one foolish adventurer be forfeit than that Castle Roogna should fall. It is nothing personal; you seem like a nice person, for a barbarian."

Then I passed out, and I suppose I died, for the poison had spread all through my system and it was potent stuff. Threnody dragged my body across the floor—she turned out to be pretty strong for a woman—and to a trapdoor in the back of the cabin and shoved me in.

I slid down a dark chute, then out into the light and into empty air. The chute opened into the forgotten Gap Chasm! I dropped a horrible distance and thunked head-first into the rock at the bottom. If the poison hadn't quite killed me, the fall certainly had!

Pook heard the distant thunk. His ears twitched. The edge of the chasm was curved here, and the chasm itself was narrow. Pook found a ledge that overlooked the depth and he peered down. His sharp eyes or nose spied my still remains below, and he gave a neigh of dismay. Maybe he felt responsible, for he was the one who had brought me to Threnody's cabin.

But he was a pretty smart animal, and maybe some of that intelligence spell had rubbed off on him, for he set about getting down to me without hurting himself. He trotted west along the brink of the Gap to where it intersected the sea, then jumped into the deep channel of water. He had a long way to fall and made an awful splash, but in a moment he bobbed to the surface, despite the weight of his chains, and swam into the chasm until the water thinned and he could walk on land. Evidently the Gap Dragon had business elsewhere, for there was no sign of him. After all, the Gap extends all the way across Xanth, as we now know, and no one creature can be everywhere at once. Still, it was a considerable act of courage on Pook's part, unless perhaps he had forgotten about the dragon. On the other hand, he had turned out to be pretty good at fighting dragons, so maybe he wasn't afraid. Or maybe he remembered, and was afraid, but was determined to go to me, anyway. It wasn't long before he trotted up to my remains.

I was not a pretty sight. My legs were broken, and my head had cracked open and spilled some of its contents out. Nothing important, just some gray matter that I suppose was stuffing or insulation. But it was messy, and there was a good deal of blood spread about. I was as dead as I had ever been. My sword was lying nearby, bent and chipped, too. That makes me sad to contemplate, for that sword had served me well and could not heal itself.

Pook used his hoof to scrape the pieces and gunk into a pile; he pushed the pile onto a big leaf and made as good a bundle as he could manage. There was dirt and garbage mixed in, of course, but that couldn't be helped.

Pook shoved the bag around, trying to figure out how to carry it, but could not. So he cast about for a decent burial spot, believing me to be finished. There was none. He decided to take me to the shore—but that was some distance away. What was he to do?

He managed to get the top of the bundle knotted together somewhat, then hooked one of his chains through it and the sword's guard and dragged them. The bundle bumped across the terrain, getting its contents thoroughly mixed. When Pook reached the small sandy beach where the chasm joined the ocean, he left the bag at the edge and set to work excavating a hole with his hooves. Obviously he intended to bury the remains. He was, after all, a ghost horse; he knew about death and burial.

But when the hole got deep, water seeped in. Disgusted, he moved farther from the sea and started a new hole. He didn't want my remains to get wet; maybe he thought I'd be uncomfortable if I rotted in the water. But the new hole, too, filled with water. He moved yet farther away—but here it was rocky, impossible to dig with hooves.

Pook pondered. Then he got smart again. What about

sea burial? He could weight the bag down with a big rock and sink it in the sea. Evidently he thought my remains wouldn't be as uncomfortable in *deep* water. But there were several problems. For one thing, he had no way to tie a rock to the bundle. Even if he had good vines, he couldn't tie knots in them. And he knew the big wrapping-leaf would soon disintegrate in the seawater, releasing its contents. As he peered out across the water, he saw a lurking sea monster, licking its chops. He knew I didn't like getting eaten by monsters. Good thing that monster hadn't been there when Pook had jumped into the sea!

Finally he shrugged and resumed dragging the bundle. He intended to get it to a suitable burial place, no matter how much effort it took.

He hauled and he hauled, finding paths up the steep slope to the higher ground. He was panting and sweating, but would not desist till nightfall made it too dark to continue without risking a misstep and a tumble back to the beach. Pook was used to night, but this was treacherous terrain, and the bundle was awkward to manage. So he parked it in a niche, then braced himself below it and slept on his feet. He was tired and hungry, but he refused to quit until he had done the burial properly. Pook was one faithful friend in death, as he was in life.

But in the night, the creatures of the nocturn emerged to forage. Unseen things slithered along the slope, and there were sounds of scuttling and scratching. Insects set up a persistent chirruping. Pook stirred himself to stomp anything that approached the bundle. A hatch opened a short distance below, and a goblin's head poked out. Pook nudged a stone to roll down and scare the goblin back into his hole. As he knew, goblins could be very bad in quantity, but this place was evidently out of the main goblin country. A solitary goblin could be dealt with more readily than a mob.

Then a smell developed. Pook sniffed and snorted, disliking it. For a moment he might have been afraid the stuff in the bag was decomposing. Then he heard crass flapping and realized it was a harpy. The ugly-faced avian crone loomed near, sensing her type of prey: namely, something helpless. But Pook squealed warning and reared up, milling his forehooves and clanking his chains, and she reconsidered. "I didn't know that carrion was yours, pooka!" she screeched. "Most nags don't eat meat. Next time, let a girl know, you blippety blip!" I doubt I am repeating the exact words she used, as they weren't nice words; they flattened Pook's ears against his head and caused the scuttlings in the vicinity to curl up and die.

In this manner the ghost horse guarded the bag during the night, and never was there a more loyal and forlorn service rendered. Pook thought he was protecting the remains for decent burial; actually, he was giving me time to heal. My talent had both poison and the fatal fall to nullify, and that was a considerable task. I doubt that I had ever before been killed quite so dead. But all my pieces were there, plus some dirt for good measure; I had been granted a day and a night without disturbance and I was indeed on the mend. As the light of morning peeped hesitantly over the brink and crept into the chasm, I stirred.

Pook had been horsenapping. The motion in the bag brought his ears straight up in shock. Had a predator sneaked inside to guzzle out the goodies? He investigated immediately, pulling the bag open.

I looked out at him. "Hi, Pook," I said. "Was it bad this time?"

He almost fell off the slope.

I stretched and climbed out of the leaf. I was weak but whole. It's rough, recovering from two deaths simultaneously! I would need to eat and rest to replenish the formidable energies expended in the reconstruction.

"Say, didn't I hear a harpy in the night?" I inquired. "You shouldn't have driven her off; you should have used her for stork fodder."

Then I paused, appalled, while Pook looked at me as if I had sprouted demon's horns. What was I saying? *Nobody* got that close to a harpy! How could I have spawned such a dirty thought?

Actually, it's clear now, though it was muddy then. Some of that dirt had gotten scooped up with my remains

and tied in the bag—that dirt had gotten caught in my
cracked head as it healed, and now I had a dirty mind.
Too bad—but, of course, it had been a very difficult feat
of healing.

After a moment, Pook recovered from his amazement
and disgust, decided it was really me back alive, and came
to nuzzle my hand. "Oh, didn't you understand about
me?" I asked him, realizing that he hadn't actually seen
me heal before, not all the way from death. He had always
been away, avoiding dragons or searching for an exit from
callicantzari caves or battling a tarasque. "My magic talent is to heal rapidly from wounds or whatever. If I lose
part of my body, I regrow it; if I am killed, I recover.
You must have collected everything together for me, so
I could recover most rapidly. Thank you, Pook; that was
very nice of you."

He just stood there, embarrassed. I petted him on the
neck. Horses have excellent necks for petting; chickens
don't. "I see you brought the bag of spells along also.
And my sword. That's good; those spells may be jumbled,
but I'll probably need them. I still have my mission to
complete." I looked around. "But how did we get here
on the slope? Last I remember, Threnody had given me
poison—but it shouldn't have taken me a day and a night
to recover from that." I glanced at my body. "And that
wouldn't account for the destruction of my clothing and
all the new flesh I have grown. I've just been through a
major healing."

Pook gestured with his head, indicating the chasm.
"You mean she dumped me down there?" I asked. "I must
have splattered like a broken egg!" He nodded agreement.
Now I understood just how much he had done for me,
and what it had meant when he gave me his friendship.
I knew I owed him a big one.

We climbed on up the slope, slowly, for I was weak
and he was tired. As I moved, I remembered what Threnody had said just before I died. She was King Gromden's
daughter, cursed to stay away from Castle Roogna lest it
fall, and afraid that Magician Yin would marry her and
make her return if he became King. I could see her con-

cern—but it seemed somewhat extreme for her to murder me so abruptly just for that. I had nothing to do with it, really. Well, not quite true; if I succeeded in my mission, then Yin would become King, and the heat would be on Threnody. But why couldn't she simply refuse to marry him, or refuse to return to Castle Roogna? She had said no to her father the King; she could say no to Magician Yin. She didn't have to kill me to prevent Yin from winning; she could have asked me not to mention her whereabouts, or she could have moved to some other, hidden place before I returned to the castle. Thus her action didn't seem to make sense, and that bothered me, for she was a most attractive woman. A woman I would have been happy to—

Then I wondered just how much sense my own thoughts were making. But I had an excuse—the dirt mixed up with the other gunk in my head. For all I knew, some rich, brown dirt was a good substitute for the useless gray stuff that had spilled; still, my head wasn't quite the way it had been. Of course, as I said, I didn't realize this at the time, for I hadn't seen myself splat in the Gap Chasm. Nevertheless, my mind did feel somewhat like an egg scrambled in sand. For one thing, I seemed to have lost most of the advantage of the intelligence spell, since no more complex philosophic thoughts churned about inside my skull. Maybe the eye-queue spell had compensated for the mixing my skull-innards had received, resulting in approximately normal intellect. Had I been really smart, I could have figured out exactly what made sense about Threnody and maybe saved myself an extraordinary amount of grief. But the eyeballs of the eye-queue must have been pointed every which way, so they couldn't quite focus on the obvious. I can't say, even now, how my thoughts ran then; I guess I hadn't properly appreciated the extent of my injuries, since I had been dead at the time. I really didn't want to believe that a woman as lovely as Threnody could have done as much damage to me as she had. I wasn't nearly as sensible as a barbarian should have been.

One thing was muddily clear, though. I should stay

away from Threnody, because she was either crazy or dangerous, possibly both. If Yin was going to marry her, that was his problem, not mine. He was a Magician; maybe he could handle her. I couldn't see why he would even want to marry a woman like that. Um, no; I *could* see. To gain King Gromden's sanction for the succession, and— The dirt in my mind smudged a picture for me of what she might look like without clothes and of what a man might do—well, never mind. I would just go about my business, fetch the object, bring it to Castle Roogna, and then get out of this region before the ship hit the fanny, so to speak. (I think that saying derives from the time someone accidentally sailed his ship into the posterior of a snoozing giant sea monster. That was not a smart thing to do.)

We made it to the top of the slope by midday, to our immense relief. There was a nice green plain loaded with tall grass and dotted with fruit and nut trees. Here we could relax and fill up, as we so desperately needed to.

I took three good steps toward the nearest tree—and tripped over another black spell. This one was in the shape of a stone. It flared up darkly.

I knew what that meant—and if I hadn't known, I could have guessed, for my foot was turning to black stone. Quickly I kicked the spell so hard it flew out over the edge of the plain and rolled down the embankment toward the sea. There wasn't much damage it could do there; most of the slope was already stone. It might be awkward for the goblin and harpy in the vicinity, and perhaps the sea monster, but that was all. It wouldn't catch Pook.

Then I grabbed for a counterspell, for now my other foot was calcifying, too. Evidently that moment of contact had been enough for the spell to get the measure of me; I hadn't stopped its progress merely by kicking it away. The stone-to-flesh spell had already been expended, but maybe I wasn't thinking clearly; the dirt fuzzing my brain could account for that, too. Mostly, I think, I was just too rushed to make any really smart decision. When one feels one's legs getting stoned, one doesn't pause too long for reflection.

I came up with the white doll. That was the bodies-exchange spell, to reverse the black spell of that type; I didn't need that now. But since the spells were all mixed up, I knew it would be something else. Maybe some other spell would help, crazy as that notion seems, now that I can consider it more objectively. "Invoke!" I cried.

The doll flashed—and suddenly I had a vision of an arrow pointing east.

An arrow? What could that be? Oh—this was the needle of the compass of the finder-spell for the object I was to fetch! Now I could find it, since this positive spell was fresher than the negative one I had encountered atop the mountain.

But that didn't do me a phenomenal lot of good at the moment, for my legs were still changing to stone, and my thighs too. Maybe getting rid of the black spell had weakened the effect, but I had gotten a good dose, and it looked as if I were going to become a statue. Now what should I do?

As I hesitated, my hands stiffened, and the hair on my head became brittle and heavy. My face glazed over. My breathing got labored, for stone is not very flexible. I felt myself falling, and felt the thunk as I struck the ground, hard. I hoped my stone body did not hurt the ground too much. Then I faded out, as my brains were stoned, too. This was my third death in the space of a day or two—not what I would call a very positive record.

Pook watched all this with alarm. He had hardly gotten me to safety when this happened! But he was smart enough to realize that if I could recover from getting smashed at the bottom of the chasm, I might recover from getting stoned, too. Pook's brains, after all, had not been scrambled. So he nosed me over, hooked a chain under my rigid arms, and dragged me to the shade of the tree I had been headed for. There he let me lie, while he grazed about the tree in a widening circle, keeping one eye on me and the other out for any stray monsters that might pass by.

Creatures did appear. One was a small feline on the

prowl for prey, but Pook stomped a forefoot and it fled, for it was a scaredy cat. A swarm of frisbees flew over, but they were only interested in flowers. They were shaped like little disks and they sort of glided down to a flower, then spun away to the next. A long, dark shape flapped in, its wings leathery, its body like a thin club; it was a baseball bat looking for a baseball. There was none here, as the bases generally held their balls in the evenings, so it flapped on past. Some june-bugs buzzed me; no, they were je-june bugs, comparatively dull and uninteresting. A bird flitted about the tree under which I lay, a brown thrasher, but there was nothing brown here to thrash, so it dropped a dropping on my nose, taking me for a statue, and flew off. Now I understood why sculptures objected to birds!

Dusk came, creeping guiltily across the plain. Pook stood near me, making sure nothing bothered me. The truth is, very little bothers stone figures, apart from hammers and earthquakes and the aforementioned attentions of birds. But the ghost horse remained as faithful as ever, trusting me to recover in due course.

His trust was rewarded, for gradually my talent fought the curse of stone and prevailed. My head returned to flesh in the night, and my torso, and I began to breathe again. It was a good thing that Evil Magician Yang hadn't known about my talent. He thought the stone-spell would finish me, and he was wrong. Had he suspected, he might have arranged to have my statue smashed into little pieces and scattered; I'm not at all sure I could have recovered from that. Certainly it would have taken a long time, and probably by then Yang would have been deemed the winner and crowned King.

As dawn dawned, I was able to sit up. Pook gave a neigh of pleasure; his faith had been justified! But I was far from well, for my legs and my left arm remained stone, and my skull felt sort of rocky. Usually my healing accelerated as it neared completion; this time it was stalling.

I realized that my talent had been severely strained. I had been savaged twice in the tarasque's maze, and killed twice by Threnody's poison and the fall into the chasm, and this was the fifth bad accident in two days or so. I had never been killed before faster than once a day, and usually not that frequently. Also, these had been pretty thorough killings, not simple to heal. So my talent had at last exhausted itself and was unable to complete the job on my body.

Well, I couldn't blame it. In a few hours or days, I was sure my magic would recover its strength and polish off the remaining stone; meanwhile, I would have to function on an as-was basis. In retrospect I conclude that my talent, having expended its last gasp getting me mostly restored, lost track of the job and assumed that I was supposed to be partly stone, for it did not rush to complete the job when it could have. Just as a man coming into a strange house does not realize if a chair is out of place, my reviving talent did not realize that the stone foot and hand were wrong. But this is only conjecture, long after the fact; I don't really understand magic.

Pook stood close, and I grabbed onto his chains and hauled myself to my feet. Then I reached up to harvest enough of the fruits and nuts growing on the tree to sustain me. After a while I managed to stand and walk by myself, though my feet remained stone. It was like walking on stilts; I could manage, but for traveling I needed the ghost horse.

Now the day was fairly on us, and the image of the arrow was in my mind. East—the direction of the object! I had to go there and find it!

We went east, following the fringe of the monstrous chasm. Odd, I thought, that no one had warned me of this natural hazard; it could hardly be overlooked! And what kind of an object would be hidden here? Well, the arrow was clear in my mind, showing only a little smudge along the shaft, doubtless from the dirt in my head, and I knew I would learn the answer soon. This was, after all, a good time to have invoked the finder-spell; the object was evidently close, so the spell tuned in strongly.

We approached Threnody's cabin, perched at the very brink of the chasm. Obviously the object was beyond it, so we turned south to give the cabin wide clearance. But the farther south we went, the more the arrow veered. It was pointing right at the cabin!

I tried not to believe it, but when we were east of the cabin, the arrow pointed west. There could be no doubt— the object was there.

I sighed. I would just have to go and get it. I knew Threnody would not be pleased; after all, she had already killed me twice to prevent me from getting the object. Now I would have to take it from under her nose. But I'd have to do it quickly and get away from there before she found some other way to kill me. I couldn't blame her for not wanting to have someone bring her back to Castle Roogna, but I did object to being killed, even if it wasn't too serious a matter.

We went to the house, and I dismounted and knocked on the door. I heard music inside, rather pretty; she was playing the stringed instrument I had seen before. When I knocked, the music halted, and in a moment Threnody opened the door. She stood aghast as she recognized me; her mouth fell open and her fair skin paled.

"Got something to pick up," I said gruffly. I would have been more curt with her, but she was so pretty I didn't feel as angry as I should have. This is one sort of foolishness that barbarians are prone to; they tend to believe, despite significant evidence to the contrary, that women are as beautiful inside as they are outside. I *knew* better; still, the way she had treated me seemed less objectionable than it might have. "I'll just take it and be gone in a moment; please stand clear."

She stepped out of my way, her eyes round and staring, and I brushed by her and rechecked the arrow.

It pointed back toward Threnody. "Okay, you have it," I said. "I guess you knew it all the time, but didn't tell me. Hand it over."

"You're dead!" she gasped.

"Not any more; I heal fast," I said gruffly. "Now give it to me."

"I—don't have anything." She still acted as if she had seen a ghost; maybe she thought the ghost was me.

"Look, woman—you killed me, so I don't think I owe

you anything. Give me that object, or I'll take it from you."

"I tell you I don't have it," she said, losing some of her pallor. "I don't even know what it is."

I had had enough. There are limits to what a barbarian will tolerate from even the prettiest of women, and perhaps some stone remained in my heart. I grabbed her and proceeded to search her, patting her body all over.

Threnody did not resist. I didn't find any object on her, but the arrow still pointed to her. "Maybe it's something you're wearing," I said. "Take off your clothing."

"I'll do nothing of the kind!" she exclaimed, recovering her indignity as she got accustomed to the idea of my being alive.

"Then I'll do it for you," I said and began unbuttoning her dress.

"You barbarian!" she cried.

"That's right," I agreed, pleased.

She saw I wasn't bluffing. "Oh, all right, I'll undress," she said. "I did undress you before, after all." She undid the rest of her brown dress and stepped out of it. She wore nothing underneath it. She took off her slippers, too, and stood completely bare. I picked up her clothing and set it in a pile on the bed, then stood between her and it. The arrow pointed directly at her.

I looked closely at her. There was a lot to look at, but there simply wasn't any object there. "Maybe you ate it," I said. "So it's inside you."

"Don't be ridiculous!" she snapped. "I don't want you cutting me open to verify it isn't there!"

I scratched my head. "I just can't figure it, unless—"

"Unless I am the object you seek," she concluded.

That, of course, was it. Suddenly it made sense. Why fetch an object to win the throne, then go after an unwilling woman to marry? How much simpler to fetch the woman herself!

And if she didn't want to come—might, in fact, even kill the one who tried to bring her—well, get an ignorant barbarian to do the job for you.

I had had a low regard for Magician Yang. Now,

abruptly, Magician Yin didn't seem phenomenally good to me, either.

Well, I was stuck for it, since I had agreed to undertake this mission. Maybe this was what King Gromden had been trying to warn me about. He hadn't known—because of the second curse—that Threnody's return to Castle Roogna would cause it to fall; he just wanted his daughter back, and married to his successor, so that his bloodline would remain in power. But he *had* known she didn't want to return and would resist any effort to bring her there with all the forces at her command.

I could see her point, even though I did not approve of her methods. If I knew that my return to Fen Village would cause it to be destroyed, I would resist that return as strongly as I could. Now I felt guilty about what I had to do—yet I *did* have to do it. It was not my place to decide on the larger rights and wrongs of the situation; I just had to complete the job I had agreed to do.

What a pile of mud this assignment was turning out to be!

Chapter 10. Demon Striation

Threnody didn't bother going for her clothes; she leaped for the door. I intercepted her, knowing she would be difficult to catch if she got away, as she was bound to be more familiar with this region than I was. She struck at my face with her small fist, but I fended her off with my left arm. "Ow!" she cried. "What are you made of, oaf?"

"Stone," I said. "My feet and left arm, anyway. I ran into a spell."

She relaxed. "Sounds like one of Yang's spells. You turned partway to stone?"

"More or less," I said, letting her go.

She bolted for the door again, this time getting out. But she ran smack into Pook, who had thought to backstop me. She bounced off his hide, and in a moment I caught her again. "I just have to take you back," I said. "I'm sorry, but I agreed to bring back the object and I will."

"I'm no object!" she protested, struggling in my arms, but this time I was smart enough not to release her.

"Sure you are," I said. "The object of my mission."

"You'll never take me alive!"

"Listen, you've already killed me," I told her, still distracted by her motions. If I hadn't already known that barbarians were often clumsy with women, I'd have suspected it now. "You should know that's no good."

"I'll kill you again!" she said, trying to bite at my shoulder. Unfortunately, she picked the wrong one and bruised her teeth on the stone.

"Well, I'd better get you dressed," I said. I knew it wasn't right for bare women to be out of the house; the flies would bite them.

I hauled her into the house, tossed her onto the bed, and held her down while I wrestled the brown dress onto her. It wasn't easy, because she was punching and kicking at me all the time, but finally I got the dress buttoned.

"You oaf!" she snorted. "It's backward!"

I had, of course, put the buttons in the front, where they belonged, but the fit did look a little awkward. "Does it matter?" I asked innocently.

"Get off me, you buffoon, and I'll do it right."

I let her go and stepped back. She stood, unbuttoned the dress—now I saw that I hadn't aligned the buttons properly, so that the buttons ran off the top while the holes ran off the bottom—and took it off. She turned it about—and suddenly leaped for me, the dress stretched between her hands. She wrapped it about my throat and twisted it in back, choking me.

But some of the stone remained in my neck, too, and

the choke was not tight. I struggled for a moment, then let myself relax, feigning unconsciousness. She choked me a while longer, making sure, then let go. "What am I going to do with you?" she muttered rhetorically, supposing me to be beyond hearing. "You're basically a decent guy, but if I let you live—"

I grabbed her about the legs and hauled her down again. "You forgot your dress," I said and spanked her smartly on her bouncy bottom.

She made a sound as of water dousing an angry fire. "You're impossible!"

"I'm barbarian," I corrected her. "Now if you don't get into that dress, I'll wrap a sheet around you and take you that way."

"This dress is ruined!" she protested. "It's all twisted up!"

Because she had used it to choke me. "Well, untwist it."

"I'll get another," she decided. "And you'd better put something on, too. You look like a zombie."

I realized it was true. Clothes don't heal the way I do. My shirt was a tatter, and my trousers might as well not have bothered. A few dangling leather strips were all that remained of my leather armor.

"You can have this dress," she said, jamming it at me.

Well, it was better than nothing. I would use it until we passed the trouser-tree in her garden. I put it on. I couldn't button the top because my shoulders were too broad, and the bottom hung halfway to my knees, but it did provide some cover.

"Backward, again," she remarked.

I did not reply. Apparently a dress was backward no matter which way a man put it on.

Threnody got a gray dress from her closet and donned it and her slippers. She stood before a mirror and brushed out her hair. She had lustrous black tresses, matching her midnight eyes. I had been partial to fair women, but now I realized that the dusky ones could be every bit as appealing, physically. "All right, I'm ready," she informed me.

I took her left arm, to lead her outside—and with her right hand she struck at me. She had picked up a knife! The blade dug into my stone arm, harmlessly, its edge chipping. "Oh, I give up!" she cried in disgust. "I forgot about that!"

I realized that I could not trust her for a moment. I saw some clothesline vine hanging on a hook. I took it down.

"Oh, no, you don't!" she cried, making another break for the door. But she wasn't very strong, despite being strong for a woman, and I held her and got her hands tied behind her. I picked up several scratches and a bite in the process, but I had expected that. She was a hellkitten! And the dirty truth was, that was every bit as appealing to me as the milk-and-honey type of woman.

Then I took her out and set her on the ghost horse and tied her dainty feet to the chains. Pook seemed disgusted at having to carry her, but he understood. I couldn't trust her on her own two feet.

It was too bad, I reflected, that women weren't more like horses. Horses were so much more reasonable.

"My lute!" she exclaimed. "I need my lute!"

"Your what?"

"My lute, bumpkin! My musical instrument. So I can play and sing."

But I distrusted her motive. She certainly didn't plan to play music at Castle Roogna, since she believed it would fall when she got there. She wasn't going to play for me, since she was fighting me. "Forget it," I said.

Her mouth closed in a hard line. She was really angry about this—more so, it seemed, than about getting captured and tied. Women are funny creatures.

"Where is your trouser-tree?" I asked, looking around.

"Forget it!" she snapped.

Ah, well, I should have known. I would simply have to use the dress.

We started off toward Castle Roogna. I didn't want to go through the tarasque's maze or over the flesh mountain, so I went east instead, along the brink of the chasm, hoping to cut south beyond the range of mountains I had encountered before. Progress was slow, because I had to walk and keep a constant eye on Threnody as well as on the landscape. Traveling in Xanth is not much of a picnic, anyway, and was less so now. My heavy stone feet thunked into the ground like ogres' pads. I had learned to walk, but it remained clumsy.

Threnody, evidently getting bored with riding, started talking. "How did you survive the poison and the fall?" she asked, as if this were a routine matter of curiosity. Perhaps it was for her.

I saw no harm in explaining, since I intended to give her no chance to kill me again. She listened attentively. "So you can not die," she concluded. "Not to stay."

"Well, it hasn't happened yet," I said. Was she mellowing? I didn't trust it. I had had experience with gentle, straightforward, loving women, but never before with a treacherous vixen like this. Maybe she was just trying to figure out how to kill me permanently. So, despite my halfway desire to believe her, I remained cautious.

"Demons can't die either," she said.

"That's because they're not alive to begin with," I said.

"Oh, no, they're alive—it's merely a different sort of life. They have feelings and interests, just as human folk do."

"Only the evil feelings," I said. "They don't have love and conscience and integrity."

"Do barbarians?" she asked as if nettled.

"Certainly. We're primitives, closer to nature than civilized folk are. We care about nature and magic and friendship."

"Do you have any friends?"

"Pook's my friend!"

"A ghost horse!" she sneered.

Pook's ears laid back again, and he made a motion as if to buck her off, but controlled himself. He certainly didn't like this woman!

"As I said," I said, "we barbarians are close to nature. Pook's a fine animal, and I'm proud to be his friend." I noted as I spoke that now Pook's ears were blushing.

"What about love?"

"I love my father and mother—"

She rolled her eyes. "Imbecile! I mean man-woman love! Have you ever truly loved a woman—or do you merely use a woman and go your way?"

I pondered. Elsie had been nice, and I liked her—but if I had really loved her, I would not have left her. As for Bluebell Elf—there never had been more to that than the favor I had promised. So the barbarian virtue of integrity forced me to yield the point, grudgingly. "No, I guess it's just a passing thing, so far."

"In that you do not differ from a demon," she said, smugly establishing that point.

"But I *could* love," I said. "A demon can't."

"True. But what's the big difference between a person who can't love and one who *doesn't* love?"

"Listen, I'm no demon!" I protested hotly. "What are you getting at?"

"You are taking me against my will to a castle that will be destroyed by my presence," she said. "Do you call that an act of conscience?"

This was uncomfortable, because I had already experienced a nudge of guilt about it. "I undertook to perform a mission," I replied, disgruntled. "My conscience says I must do what I agreed to do, whatever it is."

"Even when you know it's wrong?"

Now I understood what she was doing. She was trying to talk me out of it. But some of the intelligence from the eye-queue spell remained, despite being filtered through dirt and stone, and I was able to answer her. "How can you talk to me of right and wrong? You treacherously killed me twice over!"

"Well, I told you I was sorry!" she snapped. "I didn't like it, but I had to do it."

"Well, I don't like doing this," I retorted, "but I have to do it."

"*Touché*," she murmured. Or something like that. There's only one human language in Xanth, but this sounded like another. She was silent for a bit, then started in again. "You had a normal human barbarian upbringing?"

"Sure. And then I went adventuring."

"And this is your adventure."

"Right. Fighting monsters and spells—good old-fashioned sword and sorcery."

"And kidnapping helpless maidens for a fate worse than death?"

She certainly had a way with a barb! But I could barb back, thanks to that dirt in my mind. "Bringing a murderess in to be married."

She mulled that over for a while. Finally she said, "It's true I tried to kill you, and you have a right to be perturbed about that. But I knew your mission could cause great harm to Xanth, so I had to stop it. I still have to stop it, any way I can. If I can't kill you, maybe I can reason with you."

Something about that seemed backward to me, but it did seem better to have her talking than to be coldly silent. "Reason away," I said. "Barbarians aren't very smart about things like logic."

"If I employ methods you disapprove of, it's because I am not a barbarian," she said. "In fact, I'm not precisely human."

I glanced at her. She was tied to the horse, probably not in the most comfortable position, but she was a beautiful figure of a woman. Barbarians have an excellent eye for that sort of thing. "You look pretty good to me."

"Thank you." She made a little curtsy. I don't know how, since she was astride the horse with her feet tied, but she did. Women can be remarkably talented in insignificant little ways. "But not all that looks good is good."

"Yeah, like the nice little paths leading up to a tangle tree," I agreed. It happened that there was a tangle tree in the distance, and we were avoiding its too-convenient path. Analogies are easy to come by in Xanth.

"There is something I didn't tell you about my ancestry."

"You're not the King's daughter?"

"I am his daughter—but the Queen was not my mother. That's why the Queen resented me so much and finally

cursed me. She hated me for what I represented and for
what I was."

"Not your mother?" I repeated blankly. "How is that
possible?"

"You simpleton, not all offspring derives from marriage! I am a bastard."

The word appalled me, coming as it did from so lovely
a creature. Of course I knew what it meant, but it shocked
me to think that *she* should know it, let alone describe
herself by means of it. "You—the King—?"

"The King was seduced by an unscrupulous temptress
who cared not a whit for him," Threnody said. "I was the
result. My mother conceived me purely as a challenge;
she had no interest in keeping me, only in embarrassing
her lover. And that she did—by turning me over to King
Gromden and proclaiming my origin."

"But—but that's inhuman!" I exclaimed.

"Naturally—considering the nature of my mother."

"No decent woman would—"

"But, you see, my mother was neither decent nor a
woman."

"But—" I skidded to a verbal halt, confused. "You're
obviously not a half-breed, like a centaur or harpy or
werewolf. You're human!"

"Half human."

"I don't understand!"

"My mother is a demoness."

A female demon! Still it did not explain everything.
"King Gromden wouldn't—not with a demoness—he's
a good man!"

Threnody smiled grimly. "So it would be nice to believe. But the fact is, human beings are sometimes naïve
and often vulnerable. I love my father and know he's a
good man. Therefore I have spent some time rationalizing
this matter of my birth. It is necessary to understand that
the Queen, my foster mother, was not the most attractive
of women and was no longer in her prime, while the King
was a virile man. He had married her for practical reasons,
to help unify the diverging subcultures of Xanth. She was
from a village in the south that had felt neglected, among

the so-called curse-fiends, who are actually human but live apart from others. They are said to be great actors. When he married one of their women, it cemented their loyalty to Castle Roogna and strengthened the throne. He really was trying to do what was best for Xanth! But she was barren and, in any event, not much interested in storks."

"I know about storks," I murmured.

"Then you know that they do not choose the couples to whom they deliver; they must wait for the couples to summon them. They merely fill those orders that have been properly entered. It is a peculiarity of their nature."

"Yes. And they always deliver to the woman, no matter how hard the man works for the baby. I don't think that's fair."

She laughed. "Many things in life and magic aren't fair, barbarian! So this meant that if the King wanted a baby, he had to make arrangements through some woman other than the Queen. I think that was in his mind when the dusky demoness came to him. Maybe there were other things in his mind, too—men can be quite superficial about such things—but I must believe that he really did want me."

"Of course he did!" I exclaimed. "And he wants you back home now! That must be why he agreed to this—"

"And I don't think he knew the nature of my mother. You see, a demon can assume any form. So she became the most beautiful woman anyone could imagine, midnight of hair and eye, perfect in every physical detail—"

"You favor her," I said.

"Be quiet, imbecile!" she said angrily. "My mother was a terrible creature! She had absolutely no conscience. Demons are soulless; they have no human values, just human passions. She wanted to make mischief for the human folk, and she knew the most telling way to do that was to compromise and humiliate the human King. So she assumed a ravishing form and came to him with a story about being outcast from her distant village and needing help and protection, and when she got him alone— oh, you don't know what lying is until you've seen a

demon do it! She—well, she got him to help summon the
stork, and the stork took the order for me, and when my
mother was assured of that, she laughed and changed into
the semblance of a Mundane monster called a crock-o-
dile so he would know what she was without any further
illusion, and then she became a puff of laughing gas and
faded out. The King was mortified when he realized he
had been with a demoness, but it was too late."

"Poor King Gromden," I agreed. Now I remembered
that there had been a passing mention of scandal at Castle
Roogna; that reference was coming clear.

"And when the stork delivered me, she had the other
part of her terrible fun—causing everyone in Castle
Roogna to know what the King had done. She brought
me openly to him in broad daylight, when the King and
all the people of the castle were at dinner, and set me
down before him, saying, 'Here is your bastard baby, O
adulterous King! Dare you deny it?' And the King, being
an honest man, whatever other weaknesses he may have
had, did not deny it, perhaps in part because he knew I
would fare ill indeed if he refused to accept me. In that
sense I was the cause of his loss of respect in Xanth. Then
my demon-mother vanished in another puff of smoke,
only her cruel laugh remaining. She had deceived the
King, ruined his reputation, and forever finished any decent relation he might have had with the Queen. After
that, the people associated with the castle began drifting
away, each one finding some important business elsewhere, and of course the King could not say nay. He had
been rendered impotent by the cruelest of lies. When the
Queen cursed me, there were fewer than a dozen people
remaining there."

"There are only a couple now," I said.

"Only the ultimately loyal," she said wryly. "People
resemble demons in some respects, but they react more
slowly and make excuses for their dereliction, while the
demons act swiftly and without apology. I wish I could
be with my father now and provide the support he needs.
But I can not; that curse prevents." She shook her head
as if clearing it of distress. "So now you see why I had

to go. I don't blame my foster mother the Queen. My presence was demoralizing the whole region, simply because of my origin; I was a constant reminder of the King's peccadillo. The King never held this against me, but the others did—at the same time as they condemned him for that error. They magnified it grotesquely—" Threnody paused to choke back her rising emotion. "I don't think much of the average human being."

"It's better among the barbarians," I said. "We would never—"

"It was getting difficult for the King to govern Xanth effectively. The Queen had no love for the King, but she did see the need for Xanth to be unified. She knew that could not be while I remained at Castle Roogna, and she knew the King would never send me away himself, so she arranged for me to take myself away. Her curse made it plain to me that I was destroying Xanth. I had been unable to see it until she made it literal. If I was going to destroy Xanth as the seat of effective government, why not bring the castle down, too, and complete the job? So she was right; she did what had to be done, and I don't hate her for it. I had been a child; I grew up in a few hours and I left Castle Roogna forever."

I felt the impact of her story, but I remained suspicious. "You said she was jealous of you."

"She was. I don't say she wasn't petty in some ways; that's part of what had alienated her from the King before my mother stepped in. I was beautiful, while she was not, and the King loved me and not her; that was grounds for resentment, though I had not intended any evil. She never made any attempt to relate to me, and so I had neither mother nor foster mother. She shares some of the blame. No one's hands are entirely clean in this. But she was right about me, and about the need to make me leave."

"Then why did she curse the King to forget why you left?"

Threnody shrugged. "I exaggerated. My father never understood why I left. He was absolutely blind to any negative thing about me. I was his favorite and only child, and he wanted me to inherit the throne after him. Of course that was impossible for several reasons, and I always knew that, but it shows how he felt. No curse was needed to make him forget. He simply refused, and still refuses, to believe that my presence is bad for Castle Roogna in any literal or figurative manner. He thinks of me as his darling little girl."

Some darling! But I knew how fathers could dote on their daughters; I would, if I had the chance. "Well, aren't you?"

"Damn it, I'm half demon!" she flared. "Have you any idea what that means?"

I shrugged. "That you're a crossbreed. That you have some human and some demon traits. Xanth has a lot of crossbreeds. I happen to know of an upcoming human/elven crossbreed—"

"You fool, it means I have no soul!" There was the anger of despair in her tone.

"I don't know much about souls," I said. "But I thought they came with human ancestry. Since your father is human—"

"A human parent means a soul is possible, not that it is guaranteed. I suppose the chances were even for me—but since the delivery was to the demoness, not the human man, I lost. I didn't get one." Her voice was flat and cold.

"How do you know?" I asked, genuinely curious. I had some concern for the son the stork would bring to Bluebell; would he have no soul?

"Do people with souls kill passing strangers?" she demanded.

I pondered, taken aback by the point. "I'm human," I said after a bit. "I'm ready to kill strangers if they attack me. I'm a barbarian warrior; I live by my sword. It depends on the circumstance. In war—"

"This isn't war! You came to me injured, and I poisoned you and dumped you into the Gap."

There was that. "But you said you were sorry."

"Big deal! I'm also sorry you returned to capture me."

"But demons have no conscience," I pointed out. "They're never sorry."

"You're wrong, ignoramus. They can be sorry—when

a plot turns out bad. Like my killing of you. It didn't work, so my effort was for nothing. I'm sorry you ever set foot on this misguided mission."

"But you said you were sorry before you knew I would recover," I persisted. "I remember hearing that, just before I died."

"I say a lot of things," she said irritably, but she seemed slightly mollified. "I also inherit the demon capacity for lying, the more cruelly the better. You can't afford to believe anything I say."

I found this confusing, but there had to be some truth in it. If a person tells you he's a truth-teller, he may be lying; but if he tells you he's a liar, he has to be telling the truth, ironically. Because a truth-teller could never call himself a liar; he could become a liar by that statement. A liar, in contrast, can't lie all the time, because that makes it too obvious; people start interpreting what he says the opposite way, so he becomes a truth-teller in reverse. It's confusing, but Magician Yin had helped clarify this matter for me. So I had to believe that Threnody could lie, and that therefore she spoke the truth when she warned me to be wary of anything she said. "Maybe so," I agreed. "But you could still have a soul. Some human beings are liars, like Magician Yang, and you're more human than demon."

"No, I'm not! I can't love!"

"Now that's a lie right there! What about your father? You said you love him."

"I lied!" she cried without conviction.

"I don't believe you. I think you're lying *now*. You do love him. Therefore you *can* love, and you do have a —"

"You're a fool to believe me!"

"Then why do you care what happens to the King, or to Castle Roogna? Why don't you just come along with me without protest, and watch the castle crumble, and laugh as it falls? What does any soulless one care about the welfare of Xanth?"

She looked at me with a peculiar mixture of relief and frustration, but did not answer my questions. I was satisfied; she might be a liar, but she was more human than demon. Her humanity, ironically, was proved by the manner in which she opposed me.

And what of *my* soul? If I believed her, I could not afford to deliver her to Castle Roogna. So I had to believe that she had lied about the curses and just didn't want to marry Yin. I couldn't blame her for wanting to make her own life instead of getting tied down to a family; I was that way myself. But that was no reason for me to abrogate my own mission.

I was, of course, a fool in several respects, but I didn't know that then.

We moved on, and gradually the terrain changed. The trees and brush thinned out, and the ground became sandy.

"You'll never get through here," Threnody said.

"Why not?"

"I know this region. This is slowsand."

"Seems ordinary to me," I said, undaunted.

"You'll see, barbarian," she said confidently.

The patches of sand became larger, until finally they linked and we had to walk through them, rather than remain on rock and turf. But as Pook and I stepped on the sand, we slowed. Our steps became measured, then dragging; we seemed unable to move at normal speed. "What's this?" I asked, surprised.

"I told you," Threnody said. "Slowsand."

Now I understood. "It slows us down!"

"To a crawl. We'll starve before we get through here."

Fortunately, this was only a thin barrier, with more hard land beyond. After a tedious trek, Pook and I made it out of the sand and resumed normal velocity. Now we stayed off the sand, however circuitous the route had to be. But this became difficult and finally impossible. The level region between the mountains and the chasm turned into a desert of slowsand. We had to go around it—but there was no way through the chasm to the north, so it had to be the slopes to the south.

We meandered that way, our progress slowed almost as much by the deviousness of the necessary route as by the sand itself. The last section before the slope had a strand of sand cutting us off; Pook hurdled it—and slowed in midair so that he seemed to be floating. He wasn't; he was merely in mid-jump. But it took about fifteen seconds for him to make it to the opposite bank. I jumped, too, with the same effect, so we were both crawling through the air. The slowsand affected creatures above it as well as on it.

"Won't do you much good," Threnody said smugly. "Farther along, there's quicksand."

Quicksand. Obviously that would speed us up as much as the slowsand slowed us down. "I'll risk it," I said gruffly.

"Suit yourself, idiot."

"Anything that happens to Pook and me happens to you, too," I pointed out.

"Since I'd rather die than betray my father by returning, that's all right."

We got well clear of the sand by ascending the gentle slope of the foot of the mountain range. But now dusk was looming. We stopped under a spreading chest-nut tree whose chests were loaded with nuts; no problem about food here. I unbound Threnody's feet so she could dismount. She reacted without gratitude. "How do you expect me to eat or whatever with my hands tied?"

"Whatever?" I asked.

"I'll do it behind the tree."

Oh. Embarrassed, I untied her hands. "But you must give me your word you won't try to escape."

"Sure," she said wryly, chafing her wrists. Then she went behind the tree, while I reached up to harvest a chest of nuts.

It turned out to be a fine selection: Q-nuts and P-nuts; green pistachios; blue, red, and hazel nuts; soft, yellow butter nuts; sandy beach nuts; even a small brown cocoanut; plus a few bolts for good measure; and even some washers. That was convenient; I used a washer to wash my grubby hands.

After a time, I realized that Threnody hadn't returned from her errand behind the tree. I hesitated to go and look, since I never really did understand how women managed these things and preferred not to inquire, so I

called, phrasing it discreetly: "Hey—did everything come
out all right?"

There was no answer. Suddenly nervous, I went and
looked.

Sure enough, Threnody was gone.

I had been a fool again. Well, I would just have to track
her down. I could follow the traces through the brush and
weeds of the slope, and if she had gone down into the
slowsand plain, I'd be able to see her, despite the en-
croaching darkness.

I found no traces. Perplexed, I hesitated. Could she
be so adept at hiding that she left no trail? Then my lingering intelligence provided me a notion; use my lingering
compass sense! I tuned it in—and the arrow pointed up
into the tree.

I smiled. That was a neat ploy—hide, and when I
dashed off in a fruitless search for her, she could come
down and proceed without pursuit. Whatever her half-
demon parentage might have cost her, it wasn't clever-
ness.

Well, two could play at that game. I finished my meal
of nuts, then climbed the tree myself. I settled on a comfortable lower branch and slept.

After an hour or so, she climbed quietly down. She
tried to pass me, but of course I woke and caught her leg.
"Going somewhere, woman?" I inquired.

"Damn!" she swore, trying to yank her leg free. But I
held on, sliding my hand up for a better grip. She was my
prisoner again.

"You told me you wouldn't try to escape," I chided
her.

"I also told you I was a liar," she reminded me. "It's
my demon heritage."

"Then I'll just have to tie you again," I said regretfully.

"How do you expect me to sleep if you tie me?" she
demanded.

I pondered. "Very well. I won't bind you hand and
foot; I'll tie you to me, so you can't go without me." I
brought her to the ground and used a cord to tie her right
wrist to my left one. I made the knots too tight to untie

readily; barbarians are good at that sort of thing. Since she had no knife, she wouldn't be able to free herself without alerting me.

"How do you know I won't strangle you in your sleep?" she asked as we lay there in the dark beneath the tree.

"I wouldn't stay dead, and if you start wrestling with me at night, I might forget that I'm saving you for marriage to Yin!" I replied.

"Barbarian!" she spat, and somehow it didn't sound like a compliment.

"Precisely." I thought that would shut her up. As I've said, barbarians don't really force themselves on unwilling women; that's just hype put out by the Barbarian Publicity Department. Image is very important to our kind, even when the reality falls short.

I hadn't shut her up, though. "If I have to," she said warningly, "I'll use my talent."

"Oh? What's your talent?" I asked, interested. Of course she had a talent; everyone did. But some talents were better than others. Some people were proud of their ability to make a dust mote bounce in the air. Maybe hers was better.

"Striation."

"What?"

"It derives from my heritage, lout. Demon-striation."

"Oh." I didn't care to admit that this still didn't make much sense to me, so I let it be. Only those who are not ignorant feel free to confess their ignorance. "Well, you do what you want, only let me sleep."

"I will," she agreed.

I slept, and there was no jerk on the line and no attempt to strangle. But when I checked automatically after an hour or so, I discovered that she was gone. The cord remained undisturbed, the loop that had been about her wrist now empty. Somehow she had slipped it.

I got up immediately, activating my finder-spell. It showed her nearby; apparently she had only freed herself in the past few minutes. "Going somewhere, King's daughter?" I inquired.

"Oh!" she cried, furious. "Why couldn't you stay asleep longer?"

I brought her back to the tree. "How did you slip the loop?" I asked. "It's too small for your hand to pass through, small and fine as your hand is."

"I told you, oaf: striation."

"Demon-striation," I agreed, realizing she was not about to tell me her secret. I hung onto her hand so she couldn't flee again, regretting that the contact was for this antagonistic reason instead of for a positive one. It was indeed a fine little hand; she was nicely formed in every part. "Since the cord's no good, I'll just have to hold you directly."

"I'll kick, scratch, and bite," she warned me.

"I'll heal."

"It will hurt, though, and you won't get much sleep."

"I'll make you a deal," I said. "You don't kick, scratch, and bite me, and I don't let the dirt in my mind tell me what to do with you."

"You—you *man!*" she exclaimed in a cute little fury. I guess she realized that I wasn't bluffing and that I halfway hoped she would abort the deal.

I wrapped my arms about her as she lay beside me and settled back for sleep. My stony left arm was hardly aware of her, but my right arm tingled from the contact with her soft body. She struggled a little, evidently considering the kick-scratch-bite-dirt route, then relaxed. She laid her head down next to mine, so that her black hair tickled my nose, and she slept.

As dawn crept reluctantly in, I woke—to find my arms empty. Threnody was gone again—and my arms had not been disturbed. How in Xanth had she managed that?

I tuned in on her with the arrow. She was threading her way past the slowsand, going home. I went down and caught her again, lassoing her from the edge of the sand so that I could move faster than she could. But I was more curious than angry. "I was holding you in my arms that time; how did you escape?"

"You can not hold me," she said.

Evidently not! There was something very odd about

her. But I put that from my mind for the moment. "Well, have some nuts and we'll get moving."

She had some nuts, and we got moving. This time I didn't tie her, but I watched her, and she did not try to escape. We moved on around the mountain slopes.

Then I spied a cloud looming from the east. It sparkled iridescently. I peered at it. "I don't trust that type." Actually, barbarians don't trust anything they don't understand; it's a necessary paranoia in the wilderness. That was the main reason I didn't trust Threnody.

"It's a technicolor hailstorm," she said. "They develop in this region; I think it's because of interactions between the slowsand and the quicksand, generating fierce convections. Better get under cover."

"Cover—from a hailstorm?" I asked derisively. "We'll ignore it."

"Suit yourself, moron."

I didn't like either the storm or her attitude, but there wasn't much to do but move on. We did so, and the storm loomed massively, seeming almost solid in the sky, spreading out until it blotted out much of the welkin. I heard a low, throbbing, sad melody; I looked, and discovered it was Threnody, singing. "What are you doing?" I demanded.

"I'm singing the dirge of our demise," she replied. "I'm good at that sort of thing; that's how I got my name. But I do better when I have my lute."

She was still angry about not being permitted to bring her musical instrument. Actually, it would have hampered her attempts to escape—which meant that I might have been better off to let her bring it. But I had a more immediate concern. "Demise? From a mere hailstorm?" I asked incredulously.

"Well, maybe you'll recover after it passes, since you can return from death. The rest of us won't."

I didn't like the sound of this, and I saw Pook's ears perking up with alarm. He was a ghost horse, but if the living aspect of him died, he would be just a ghost. And if Threnody died, my mission would be finished; I was

sure it would not count if I delivered a dead body to Castle
Roogna.

"Okay, I'll seek cover." I cast about and saw a small
stand of timber trees upslope. We moved to them. I used
my sword to chop the timbers and used the timbers to
construct a pointed edifice, then bound it tightly at the
top with cord and wedged its base into the ground below.
I think this type of construction is called a tee-wam; it's
useful in an emergency. I wrapped bark about it, tying it
in place. It was a crude structure, but sturdy. We crowded
into it, the three of us, just as the first hailstones struck.

"You're pretty good at this," Threnody remarked in-
differently.

"It's a barbarian skill," I said, foolishly flattered.

"Live and learn! I didn't know barbarians were good
at anything except kidnapping helpless damsels."

"That, too," I agreed.

A hailstone struck the shelter with a crash like that of
solid rock. I jumped. I peered out—and another stone
just missed my head, thunking into the ground so hard it
made a formidable dent. It was green and pitted.

I reached out and grabbed it before it rolled away.
"Hey—this is a real stone!" I cried.

"What did you expect?" she asked. "Colored ice?"

"Well, yes. Little light balls of ice."

"Maybe elsewhere. Here it hails real stones."

So it did. Another struck the shelter and rolled away.
I could see them falling all around, red and blue and or-
ange and brown. They were pretty—but any one of them
would have brained a person or animal. Maybe that was
why we had encountered no large animals in this region;
only the small ones could hide from this sort of storm.
Threnody had been right to urge shelter.

We could not travel while the storm raged, so we waited,
huddled together. Threnody was astride Pook, and I beside, my torso against her left leg. She resumed her song
of lamentation. Pook's ears were laid back; he didn't like
either her or the song. But I thought both were rather
pretty. That leg certainly was! I wished again that things
were more positive between us.

The storm raged for an hour. I snoozed on my feet, leaning against the leg. When the storm finally abated, I woke, finding myself leaning against Pook's side. I looked about. Threnody was gone again. "Hey—where is she?" I asked.

Pook had been snoozing too. He woke with a start. He sniffed the air, but was as baffled as I. It was amazing how she could depart without alerting us.

I used the arrow again. It was slowly fading as time passed, but was enough to do the job. It pointed west. Threnody was headed for home again.

We emerged from the shelter, which was now sadly battered by the stones, and hurried west around the slope. Soon we caught up to her. She hadn't gotten very far. She was moving very slowly, though she wasn't in the slowsand.

I charged up and caught her by the arm—and my hand passed through it. "You're a ghost!" I exclaimed, appalled. "You went out too soon and got clonked by a hailstone and now you're dead!"

"No, I'm just diffuse, lout," she said faintly.

I passed my hand through her body. Sure enough, there was some resistance, like that of thin water or thick fog. She was more substantial than a ghost, though not by much.

"You're pretty fresh, barbarian!" she informed me as my hand emerged from her chest.

I jerked my fingers back guiltily. "What happened to you?"

"It's my talent," she explained. "Striation. I'd have been long gone, if I hadn't encountered a headwind. It's hard to fight a wind in this state."

I saw that it was so. A gust of wind passed and almost blew her off her feet. She hardly weighed anything at all. "You can just thin out?"

"I told you I have demon parentage. Demons can turn to smoke and change size and shape."

"But if you can do that, why did you ever let me tie you?"

"I can't do it fast," she said bitterly. "It takes an hour

just to change one aspect—and you never gave me more than an hour to myself."

I almost felt guilty. "The loop of rope!" I exclaimed. "You diffused out of it!"

"Of course." She was slowly becoming more solid. "And I diffused enough so that the hailstones couldn't hurt me. But the storm stopped too soon, so you weren't confined, and this stupid headwind—"

I had started to wonder how I could hold her when she was smoky-diffuse, but now I realized that all it would take was a fan to blow her anywhere I wanted her to go. Her escape had been slow because of the air resistance, which was much more formidable for her than for those of us in the solid state.

"You say this is just one aspect? You can change other ways too?"

"Oh, you might as well know it all," she said with angry resignation. "You seem to have the blundering luck of ignorance. Demons can change form instantly; that's why my mother was able to fool King Gromden, who would never have touched her if he had known. Her natural appearance was horrendous, but she emulated the human form so well that nobody could tell the difference. But I'm only half demon, so I can't operate as well. I can only do one aspect at a time. If I want to be big or small, I have to take an hour for that. But then I'm either diffuse or concentrated—a smoky giant or a super-solid midget— until I change my density to match. That takes another hour. Because my mass hasn't changed, only my size. And if I want to be in the likeness of a normal mouse, it takes a third hour to get the shape right. If only you'd let me be for three hours!"

I was amazed. This creature was more of a handful than I had known. She might have changed into a dragon and devoured me—had I given her time.

"I can't see why Yin would want to marry you," I said.

"Of course he doesn't want to marry me!" she cried. "He's only doing it to provide continuity of a sort, so the human beings of Xanth will accept him readily as King and not hold it against him that he's filling Gromden's shoes. It's the same for Yang. They have only politics in mind. I don't want to marry either of them."

"But if your arrival was such a scandal, the people wouldn't want you to marry the new King," I objected.

"The common folk don't know my origin. It was strictly a palace scandal. No one tells the common folk anything."

I sighed. "I'm sorry about having to bring you in, Threnody. I really am. But a barbarian always keeps his word. Maybe you can escape, after I turn you in."

"Escape from a Magician?" she demanded bitterly. "I was able to avoid them in the forest; I threatened to throw myself into the Gap Chasm if either one of them came near. That's why I set up a chute right in my house. But I can't do that at Castle Roogna." I saw her vaporous tears as she spoke. "I'd rather die than marry one of them—but I won't have any choice, thanks to you, you unfeeling wretch."

I nodded glumly. I was a wretch, but I was not unfeeling. I felt awful.

We returned to the shelter, and within an hour Threnody was solid again. There was not enough time left in the day to warrant more travel, so we remained where we were. The nearby trees had been badly battered by the hailstones, but we were able to forage for fruits that had been knocked to the ground.

Now how was I to keep Threnody captive during the night? Her demon-striation talent meant I could not hold her physically.

Not physically—but how about emotionally? A small ruse might simplify things considerably. It was certainly worth a try.

I went out at dusk, circling our camp as if looking for something. I put my hand on my sword. "I wish I had my bow," I muttered nervously.

"What's the matter?" Threnody called. "You plan to put an arrow through me next time I escape?"

"Oh, I wouldn't want to worry you," I said, shading my eyes with my stone hand and peering into the gloom. "They probably won't attack in the night anyway."

"*What* won't attack?" she demanded.

"The traces aren't really fresh," I said. "Couple days old, at least, so they're probably gone. Do you smell anything fresher, Pook?"

Pook sniffed the air, then shook his head no. He was smart enough to play along.

"*What* are gone?" Threnody asked, annoyed by the mystery. I knew the feeling!

"The harpies, of course," I said.

"There are no harpies in these parts!"

"That's what I said. They seem to be confined to the cliffsides. This flock was probably just passing through, and won't be back."

She was silent. We settled down for the night. "You take the shelter," I said. "I'll sleep outside."

"Aren't you going to hold me?"

"It doesn't do any good," I pointed out. "You can slip any tie, any grasp. I guess you could have done it anytime when you were riding, but you didn't want me to see."

"True, barbarian. My talent's more effective when it's secret." She considered. "Still, you can hold me if you want to. It might give you earlier warning."

"No, I think I'd better remain outside," I said, glancing nervously about as if aware of a harpy. Then I put my right hand on the hilt of my sword and lay down.

"Suppose the harpies come, and you're asleep?" she asked.

"There are no harpies in these parts," I reminded her. But I unsheathed my sword.

She grimaced, then lay down in the shelter. Pook grazed on the slope. I slept; barbarians can nod off instantly and wake instantly, in the manner of other animals.

There was a rustle in the night, as of some winged nocturnal predator. I woke just long enough to identify it as a genuine bird, harmless to us, and slept again. But in a moment I felt a body beside me. "You'd better hold onto me," Threnody murmured. "I might try something foolish."

Uh-huh. It seemed my ploy was working. *Nobody* sleeps well when harpies are about. "Suit yourself, demon-spawn."

She nudged closer, warm and soft. "I'm truly sorry I killed you, Jordan."

Now she was calling me by my name. "You're also a liar."

She struck at me. "Damn you!"

A point for me. But her body was delectable, touching mine, and I wished for the umpteenth time that things were otherwise.

"This is a lie, too," she said after a moment. Her head came over mine, and she kissed me on the mouth, firmly and lingeringly.

The irony was, I *knew* it was a lie. Threnody cared nothing for me alive. She just wanted to lull me into complacency so she could escape. I'm pretty naïve about women, but there are limits to naïveté, and I do learn quickly enough from experience. Yet a part of me wanted to believe that a lovely creature like this, a King's daughter, demon or not, could really care for me.

"I guess I know how it was with King Gromden," I muttered when she released my lips.

She stiffened, then laughed ruefully. "I swore I'd never do to a man what my mother did to my father. I guess I lied about that, too." Then she put her face down against my shoulder, and it became wet there.

Could a soulless creature cry? I wondered. Probably *could*, I decided, but never *would*. Except to deceive. Still... "You okay?" I asked.

"Oh, I am a cursed creature!" she sobbed.

Literally true. I knew myself for a fool, but I couldn't help it. Sometimes a man just has to be a fool, if he's a man. I put my arms about her and held her close to me, not to prevent her from escaping, but because it was necessary to do.

She cried for a while, and then she slept, and after a while I did, too.

One other thing bothered me, though. I woke, thinking of it, and finally I murmured to the night sky: "There really aren't any harpies here."

"I know it," Threnody murmured back. I had thought she was asleep.

But in the morning she was still there. This night she had not tried to escape.

Chapter 11. Sword and Stone

We followed the slope as it curved around to the south and, when we had left the slowsand region behind, we returned to the level land. Normal animal life returned; I had to dispatch a griffin and a river monster that menaced us, but that was routine. In another day we should be at Castle Roogna.

"You know I don't want to go there," Threnody reminded me, her eyes very big and dark.

"I know."

"You know Castle Roogna will fall."

"I don't know. You could be lying."

"I could get very friendly, if you cared to delay the journey a while. It wouldn't seem like a lie to you at all."

"I know."

"I could even get to like you for real, if—"

"I don't know. You'll say anything to get your way."

"Let me show you how friendly I can be when I try."

"I'd be a fool." Of course I was a fool, for I was sorely tempted. She might be a completely selfish, lying demon-creature, but she was beautiful, and barbarians appreciate physical beauty more than they do mental beauty. So I fended off her advances, not because I feared her body, but because I feared what her body could do to my mind. But my resolve was weakening.

"I can still change form and escape you," she said.

"But without my arm and sword to protect you, you

would be vulnerable to the monsters of Xanth," I pointed
out. "That's why you are no longer trying to flee. There
may be no harpies here, but there are other creatures."
What little remained of the smart-spell had enabled me
to work it out. "When you change form, you may look
like some other creature, but you aren't. You can assume
the form of a bird, but you can't fly—not unless you
become so diffuse as to be as light as the air, and then
the wind will blow you away. It takes a lifetime to learn
to fly properly."

She shrugged, not denying it. "Actually, I can do some
of the things the animals I emulate do, but it is true that
flying is a very specialized discipline, and certainly I would
not be good at it; I'd probably blunder into the nearest
tree and be easy prey for any winged predator."

"And you probably haven't practiced it much, because
of the danger. You need skill as well as form. So your
talent is limited at the moment."

"When you threatened me with the harpies, I realized
that was true. There is always *something* in Xanth to prey
on the unwary or unprotected. You're a primitive man;
you have muscle and a sword and you like to fight. You
can handle strange territory and slay monsters inciden-
tally. But once you got me more than a day's journey
from my home—" She spread her hands. "I may have a
heart of stone, but the monsters don't care about that.
They'll eat my flesh in a moment—and I can't recover
the way you can."

"So I'm the sword and you're the stone," I said, conscious of the irony, since part of me really was stone now.

"Yes. If I had your body, I could go right home."

"You can assume my likeness," I said.

"I suppose I could," she agreed, tilting her head in
temporary reflection. "But I wouldn't have your skill with
the sword, or the power of your masculine muscles, or
your ability to heal so fast when wounded. So that's no
good."

"If I had your body, I'd be a lovely creature," I said.

"I'm not beautiful in my soul—if I have one at all."

I had no answer to that. Threnody was the first pretty

woman I had known who was demonstrably ugly in her
origin and nature—literally demon-strably—and I still
had difficulty reconciling that combination. I kept wanting
to believe she was as lovely inside as out and that her
evident intelligence translated to good personality. Sometimes I almost succeeded. Certainly she was not all evil,
even though she was far from all good. This just isn't the
kind of problem a barbarian is fit to cope with. Life is
simpler when the alternatives are flat good or flat evil,
clearly labeled. And correctly labeled!

At noon we came to a pleasant grove of ances-trees.
Each had a solid base that soon split into two major
branches, and these split into four, and thence to eight,
until at the fringe there were so many little branches that
the eye lost track. The bark was corrugated and thus
resembled printed words; sometimes I wished I could
read, so that I could contemplate my own family tree.

"I can read," Threnody said. "It's a skill required of
royal children. But I don't care to be reminded of my
demon branches."

We went on and came to a pattern of artis-trees, each
a many-splendored thing, with ornate multicolored leaves
and sculptured lines. We paused, awed by the sheer mag-
nificence of this display.

One tree was dead—but its skeletal form was impressive, each branch perfectly contoured, the whole a marvel
of symmetry. There was a hole in the base of its trunk,
and even this was beautifully arched, so that it resembled
a doorway to some sublime realm.

We walked toward it—and suddenly at my feet a small
black sword flashed. Quickly it expanded to full-sword
size, a thing of glistening, dark iron, suspending itself
menacingly before me. I had heedlessly blundered into
another of Yang's evil spells! When would I learn to watch
out more carefully for them?

My own sword was in my hand, for barbarian reflexes
are necessarily swift. "Get clear of me!" I cried to Pook
and Threnody. "This thing's dangerous!"

Indeed it was! The black sword slashed viciously at
me, and it was all I could do to parry the blade in time.

As it was, the power of its blow drove me back and shook my arm. Nothing was wielding that sword, but it felt as if there were an invisible giant behind it.

I had fended off its cut, but the black weapon recovered with horrible quickness and struck at me from the other side. I parried again, and again felt the shock of the collision. Sparks flew from the place where the two blades met, and mine was nicked. Of course, it was already battered and slightly bent from its fall into the—well, I didn't remember quite where, but it had fallen somewhere. Yet a blade that could so casually nick this one—

The evil sword whirled about in the air, danced over my head, and slashed at me from behind. I threw myself aside, avoiding it, but the moment it missed, it reoriented and came at me again. I fell to the ground, barely getting my blade around to block the thing. Never before had I been subjected to as savage an attack by a sword as this! I prided myself on my expertise with the sword; it was one of those things barbarians specialized in. My sword was the only reason I had no real fear of tangle trees or griffins—albeit a healthy respect for them; I could strike with it before such monsters could get me. Dragons were more difficult, because of their steam or fire and their scale armor, but of course dragons were the top of the predatory chain. So my sword was my strength. However, this was no beak or tentacle I faced; it was another sword. It struck and struck again, and a third time in as many seconds. Then, realizing it could not get me with a frontal or rear attack, it spun to the side and lunged.

I scrambled halfway to my feet, but had to dive clear again, rolling on the ground. The black sword sliced at my feet, missing no opportunity. I jerked them clear, and it struck the ground so hard where they had been it seemed the very land would cleave asunder. I fought my way back to my feet in time to parry the next strike.

I normally have plenty of muscle, speed, and coordination. I had died three to five times recently, but the past three days had enabled me to recover almost completely, except for my stone extremities. (Say—I should have let the sword strike my feet! How could it hurt them?)

So I fought very well—but already I knew I was over-matched. This magic sword had a ferocity beyond anything I had encountered before and showed no sign of tiring. One thing I had to say for Magician Yang: his spells were not anemic ones! I had to get away from this thing!

I tried, but it pursued me relentlessly. It wanted my blood, all my blood, and nothing but my blood. It whistled at my left side before I could get my own blade around; I lifted my left arm and it took the cut.

There was a clang, and the black sword bounced back, shaken. Of course—my left arm, too, remained stone. For the first time, I had occasion to bless the failure of my talent to tackle this detail; it was evident that the evil blade could not slice stone. One hears stories about swords that can do this, but I think this is merely more hype; stone is awfully tough stuff. This was pure barbarian luck: the lingering trace of the last evil spell was helping me fight this one.

The black sword shook itself as if confused, then charged back to the fray. It swept at my neck with a ferocity that threatened not only to sever my head from my body but send it flying to the moon. That would have been awkward for me; it is no easy thing to grow a whole new head. I blocked the swipe, barely. Then the sword dropped down again to my feet, and this time I didn't move them, so it clanged again against the stone.

My luck was holding—but I really needed the magic shield, because the black sword was not letting up and was getting more imaginative about spots to attack. I was tiring from this frenetic activity, and that sword wasn't. Sooner or later it would find or force an opening and get me in a vital spot.

"The spell!" I cried to Threnody. "Get the spell!"

"What spell?" she asked.

Oops—she didn't know about that complication, and might not care to help me if she did. After all, if I died, she was free to go home, and she could be long on the way before I recovered. On the other hand, she could not safely travel alone, so she might have to help me. What choice did I have? I ducked as the black sword whistled over my head. "*Any* spell! Pook has them!"

Threnody hesitated. I knew she was considering whether it was better to help me or let the black sword take me out. But Pook snorted warningly at her, and she decided to help. She went to him and opened the bag of spells he carried.

Meanwhile, the enemy blade pressed me harder than ever. It wove a perplexing pattern in the air and dazzled my eyes, so that it was increasingly more difficult to parry its sudden lunges. It looped around me, forcing me to turn constantly to protect my flank and rear. I was getting dizzy—and that, too, could be disastrous. I had to have some kind of cover for my back, or I would shortly be wiped out!

I spied the dead artis-tree, with its architecturally shaped hole in the trunk. That would do! I fended off the sword and retreated toward the tree. Soon I managed to wedge my back against it and nudge into the hole. The space was just my height, so was very convenient. The black sword could no longer attack me from behind.

The thing was furious. It chopped at the trunk of the tree, but the deadwood was hard as well as beautiful, and only small chips flew. This protection would last me for a good long time. I was careful not to back all the way into the hole, for that would restrict my motions and work to my disadvantage. I used the tree just enough to maximize my efficiency. Now I was holding my own, resting as the enemy sword wasted its energy on the wood.

All this had taken very little time, the seconds seeming like minutes, while Threnody was fetching the spell. It's hard to describe two separate actions at once, so I'm doing it one at a time, but they were happening together. Now Threnody drew out one of the white objects Magician Yin had given me. "Is this the right one?" she called. "It's a bit of vine with an eyeball tied in. Gruesome thing!"

The eye-queue spell—which had already been expended. So I was sure this one stood for some other spell—maybe the magic shield I needed. "It will do!" I called back. "Throw it here!" And another spark flew as blade met blade. It was a good thing my own sword was a sturdy one, albeit battered; now it had many nicks to go with its dents.

She came toward me, then threw the spell, in the underhanded female way. Her aim was good, however; the spell struck the tree and dropped directly before me. The black sword, sensing danger, sliced at the spell. "Invoke!" I cried.

I saw it glow, just before the black sword struck it. Then the strangest thing happened.

My consciousness seemed to leave my body and fly ghostlike through the air. Had I been abruptly slain by an unseen strike of the evil blade? Was my soul now flying to wherever it was fated to go? But this had never happened before when I died!

Then my awareness approached Threnody as she stood between me and Pook, prettily concerned. Suddenly it dived into her body and settled there.

I heard a hoarse scream. I saw myself drop my sword and hunch back into the dead tree. Immediately the enemy sword lunged, running its blade through my unprotected heart. My blood spouted from my chest as I fell forward, dead.

But the black sword was not finished. It lifted itself high, then struck down on my exposed neck, cutting off my head. The head rolled a few paces away and came to rest in a hollow, staring up with a slightly bemused expression.

Still the evil sword did not desist. It hacked at my right arm, cutting it off, then started on my left, up at the shoulder where it remained flesh. The thing meant to dismember me entirely!

I ran toward it, unable to watch this destruction of my body without acting.

Then I paused. How could I run toward it when I was already dead and decapitated?

I realized that, though my body was dead, my consciousness was not. It was now in Threnody's body. And her consciousness—must be in mine. Presently unconscious. For I had activated the spell of exchange. Well, of exchange-back; the one intended to counter Yang's exchange spell. Since we hadn't been exchanged, we couldn't be un-exchanged; the un-exchange constituted an exchange in itself. I had brought upon myself the very mischief I had hoped to avoid!

When we exchanged identities, Threnody had found herself in my male body, fighting the deadly sword—and she hadn't known how to defend herself. As with the notion of assuming the form of a bird and trying to fly without practice, she was unable to fight like a man simply because she had a man's body. Womanlike, she had screamed and cowered. Thus she had been instantly vulnerable, and the enemy weapon had seized its advantage and gotten her. It didn't realize it had killed the wrong person; how could it know?

Theoretically, I had a minute to reverse the spell before it took full hold. But how? Only by finding the black exchange spell could I do that—and then I would merely exchange myself into a dead and dismembered body! Also, that minute had already passed, as if time meant anything now. What a picklement this was!

When would that terrible enemy sword stop? It seemed determined to mince my entire body. I might have the use of another body now, but I still couldn't stand idly by and let it happen! Since my talent had been strained by overuse recently, I wasn't sure how much more it could take.

Or had my healing talent flown with my consciousness to Threnody's body? If that were so, then my body—and Threnody's consciousness—was dead, and I was stuck forever in her body. Would Yin be after me to marry him?

Thinking of it that way, I felt greater sympathy for Threnody's resistance to the idea of being taken to Castle Roogna for marriage.

No, I had to assume that our talents remained with our bodies, so that it was possible for my body to revive and take me back. I had to stop that sword from doing more damage!

Well, maybe I could bluff it. I resumed my run to it, leaned down, and grabbed the hilt. The sword paused in surprise. "Well done, excellent sword!" I cried in Threnody's voice. "You have acted courageously and saved me from a fate worse than death! Now you can rest."

The sword hesitated, then decided to accept this. I smiled winningly at it, knowing the power of a lovely female expression over masculine things. Threnody herself had used it on me, and I had been hard put to it to resist.

But I wasn't sure how long I could fool this dread instrument. If and when it caught on to my real identity, it would attack this body and dismember it, too, and then I would be truly finished. I had to put the evil weapon out of commission before it did catch on. But how?

By using Threnody's talent, of course! When she went diffuse, so did her clothing; otherwise she would have been naked when I caught her, and I was sure I would have remembered a thing like that. She had been clothed in her gray dress, which I now wore, which meant that things closely associated with her shared the effect. So I could go diffuse, and do the same to the sword I held, and—

And when I let it go, it might return to its original state and come after me with a deadly gleam on its surface. Better not to risk that. Going far away from it was not the answer, either; it could fly, and the other spells had shown dismaying longevity. It would catch me in time.

Well, what else could I do with it? Whatever it was, I didn't want to wait long—because until I nullified the sword, I couldn't do anything for my dead body. It bothered me, seeing that severed head staring up. Suppose a predatory animal came to gobble it down?

Ha—my elevated intelligence remained; in fact, it seemed a little enhanced, because there was no dirt in Threnody's brain to mess it up. Or was I using her brain? I surely wasn't using my own! Whatever, my thought was this: diffuse the sword, then put it into something that would hold it in place when it solidified.

Of course, first I had to see if Threnody's talent would work for me. I had never had a talent like hers before and I wasn't sure how to invoke it. Should I just will myself thin, or smoky, or what? Was there some key phrase to utter? Well, my own talent of healing didn't need any special attention; it merely operated at need. Maybe this did, too. So I would concentrate on being smoky, and see what happened.

"Let's take a nice little walk," I said to the black sword, still holding it in my delicate hand. It was surely too heavy for this slender arm to support for long, but it was self-sustaining and felt quite light. Maybe that was another masculine trait. I had to admit it was a handsome weapon, and there were no nicks in its blade. It was therefore superior to mine. But it was *not* mine, and I couldn't trust it. Especially not when my own body revived.

I wondered where this instrument had come from originally; surely Magician Yang had not forged it himself. He must have obtained the sword, then enchanted it. The same would be true of his other spells, and those of Yin. It was remarkable that the twin brothers had such similar talents; I had heard of twins before who had quite dissimilar talents.

I turned—and there was Pook. His ears were flat back, his teeth bared, his nostrils dilated, and his eyes were rimmed by white. His whole body was tense, and his chains rattled warningly. This was one hyper-nervous horse!

I realized what was wrong. He thought I was Threnody and that I had now armed myself with the terrible evil sword! "Pook!" I cried. "Let me explain!"

But then I realized that the sword was listening too. If I told Pook who I was, and convinced him, the sword would also know, and that would be disaster. Threnody's slender arms did not have the strength to hold this thing if it got violent. Maybe my own arms would not have been strong enough. It was one wicked weapon!

How could I let Pook know without giving myself away to the dread sword? Fortunately, the residual eye-queue spell enabled me to think of a way. Or maybe it was Threnody's brain, which was a good one.

"Stand aside, animal," I said to him. "This fine sword will strike down any creature who seeks to convey me to

Castle Roogna. It is quiescent now only because I am
free. You saw what it did to that ilk." I glanced back at
my horrendously hacked body.

Pook's ears went even flatter back. In a moment he
would attack me, overcome by grief and rage. He was an
animal, but he was loyal, and I was indeed proud to have
him as my friend.

"Whom do you suppose you are facing, animal?" I
demanded, looking him directly in a dilated eye. I held
the black sword in my right hand, near my body; slowly
I winked my left eye, which was out of sight of the sword.

The ghost horse blinked, startled, but his menace did
not abate. He knew what a liar Threnody was.

"Remember the nature of the spells you carry," I said.
I had described them to him in the course of our journey
to Threnody's house, since they might affect his welfare
as well as mine. "Remember which have been invoked
and which have not." That was as close as I dared hint,
for the sword might know about the other spells, too, and
I didn't know how smart it was. I dared not tell it too
much.

Still Pook did not react; the hint had not been enough.
I had mentioned the various types of spells to him, but
maybe he had forgotten the exchange spell. Indeed, who
would have believed how it had acted on this occasion?

"Remember your past experiences," I continued. "How
you were herded into the firewall by this dead ilk behind
me, who only wanted a free ride. How he cruelly rode
you into the territory of the goblins and the lair of the
callicantzari." Again I winked, and again Pook blinked.
Threnody had not been with us then, and I had not told
her; Pook had been with us and would have known if I
had gone into that with her. But now he was mystified,
not certain.

"And the elves," I said. "Remember how he dallied
three days with Bluebell, deserting you! What do you owe
him? And think of the stork, the dragons, and the baby
ogre; that barbarian made you wander all over Xanth, and
for what?" I fixed his eye again. "What was there ever
between you and this man? Whatever it was, let it remain

unchanged." I paused, knowing he knew the answer—friendship.

A third time I winked, covertly. "Whom do you suppose you are facing, friend?"

Slowly Pook's ears relaxed, and the white circles around his eyes disappeared. Now at last he had caught on. He would go along with what I planned, as he had done before.

"I have an errand elsewhere," I said briskly. I glanced back at my body. "You know what to do with this corpse, to whom you owe nothing. Now stand aside."

Pook moved aside. I walked on by him, the sword extended before me. I passed on through the grove of artis-trees, admiring each. Barbarians don't have much culture, but maybe Threnody's royal tastes were rubbing off on me, for each tree seemed to be a marvel of individual expression and form. No two were alike in color or structure or size, but each was a masterpiece of its type. Xanth could use more artis-trees!

While I walked, I concentrated on becoming less dense. It didn't seem to be working, but since it was my only hope, I had to keep trying. A shift of form or size or density took an hour, she had said, so I would try for an hour—or whatever it took.

And as I walked, concentrated, and hoped, I was aware of the nature of this body. It differed from mine. The proportions were funny; the legs seemed sort of short and fat in the thigh; the arms were short and so low on muscle as to seem like pipestems. The center of weight was lower, and the balance was strange, seeming bottom-heavy. With my free left hand I felt about, verifying that there was an unseemly volume of posterior, and the chest—it seemed unnatural, having all that flesh on my chest. It bounced when I walked too fast. In fact, I had extra flesh distributed all over; I felt ungainly.

There were other problems. My black hair flopped about my shoulders and tended to fall forward to obscure my vision if I didn't keep my chin up. There was something about the way I walked; my hipbones were set too far out, or something, so that my whole pelvis gyrated awkwardly when I took full-sized steps. The only way I could control it was to confine myself to mincing little steps that slowed forward progress.

Ah, well, doubtless it was worthwhile to have the opportunity to appreciate first-hand the liabilities of the female form. No wonder women tended to be jealous of men!

In the course of half an hour, to my immense relief, I verified that Threnody's talent was working; I was definitely lighter, and the resistance of the air seemed greater. Now I needed to find a suitable place to stash the sword.

In a tree? No, it might cut its way free. In a deep hole? No, someone might dig it out too soon. It had to be permanently bound.

Then I spied a sitting boulder at the edge of the artis-tree community. The rock was about half as tall as a man, and massive; it seemed to be solid marble.

I continued to walk until the transformation was complete, and the sword and I were as diffuse as fog, or more so, I kicked at a tree trunk, and my small foot passed through it with hardly perceptible resistance. I was ready!

I marched up to the rock, lifted the sword in both hands, shifted my grip so that it pointed straight down, and plunged it into the boulder. It sank in to the hilt. I removed my hands, stood back, and contemplated it with satisfaction. "Stay there, dread blade!" I said.

I shouldn't have said that. The sword heard me and evidently realized that something was amiss. It began to lift itself out of the boulder.

Quickly I grabbed the hilt and shoved the sword back. "Relax, relax!" I cried. "You have done so well, honored blade; now you must rest. You can't be a gay blade all the time." I batted my lovely eyelids at it.

The sword relaxed. But I didn't dare risk letting it go again, for if it pulled out of the boulder and flew away, I would never catch it. So I held on, soothing it with my gentle feminine touch—that, too, I had learned about when Threnody kissed me and held me the night before, despite the lie that touch implied—keeping it in place while we slowly solidified.

But it had some suspicion and started to wiggle; I was afraid of its brute force, so I pacified it by singing to it. My voice was lovely and sad; I didn't know the proper tune or words, so I just sang *la-la-la* with enormous feeling, and as long as I did that, the weapon was quiescent. No wonder women practiced subversive wiles on men; what else was effective?

I stood and sang for the full hour it took to restore body and sword to full solidity. Then at last I let go of the weapon—and it was embedded firmly in the boulder. Good enough! That blade would bother me no more.

I left the sword in the stone behind, retreating cautiously, watching to be quite certain that dread weapon did not abruptly free itself and resume its mischief. It remained in place. I wondered whether someday, in some other land, that blade on the boulder would turn up in some significant spot, and someone would learn how to—no, ridiculous! What use was a sword in a stone? No one in Xanth would fool around with anything like that.

I started back toward the site of my body's demise . . . and a shadow descended. Oops—that looked very much like a—in fact, it *was* a—

I reached for my sword, and of course my delicate hand slapped only soft flesh. The sword I had carried was in the stone; my own blade was with my body. I was unarmed.

The creature glided to a landing before me. It was a fair-sized griffin, a female, for her color was shoe-polish brown. In virtually every species of living creature, it is the male who is the creature of splendors with the brightest colors, the biggest muscles, the best proportions. There is one exception—the human species; there the female seems to have most of the splendors. I have never been certain what went wrong. Maybe some long-ago curse was put on man and on man-related creatures. Also, the females of other species are good hunters and fighters, while those of ours are not. In this more-decorative-than-functional body, I was suddenly aware of my extreme vulnerability. This griffiness was well equipped with beak and claws, while I—

It was too late to hide; the griffiness had landed because she had spied easy prey. I could not fight; I had neither sword nor muscle to wield it. I could not change form; that took too long. More than ever now, I appreciated the position of human women. No wonder Threnody had not wanted to travel home alone; she would have been dead in hours. Predators that never showed their mugs to me, knowing that armed barbarian warriors were not to be trifled with, would freely stalk an unarmed woman. What was I to do?

Well, Threnody had tried to use guile on me, and I had used it on the black sword. Now that I was in her position, it seemed like a natural course. I would have to trick this predator somehow. What were griffins concerned about?

Aha! They were notoriously clean creatures, the opposite of harpies. Griffins spent hours preening their feathers and stroking their fur and cleaning their claws. They never fed on carrion, but always killed fresh. They were like the rocs in that respect. No griffin or roc ever died from food poisoning. They were good enough hunters so that they could afford to be choosy.

I huffed myself up and issued a feeling groan. The advancing griffiness paused, cocking her bird-head. She had been approaching me slowly, knowing I could not escape; griffins were more efficient than dragons and never scrambled when they did not have to. When a dragon made a kill, it was apt to be messy, with blood and gobbets of flesh strewn across the landscape; when a griffin did it, there was hardly even a scream. She was hesitating, not from any nervousness, but to make quite sure there was nothing here that might soil her feathers.

"Oooh, it's so horrible!" I lamented. "If only I'd known those berries were contaminated!"

Griffins don't have visible ears; nevertheless, her head perked up. Contamination?

"Now I've got the Green-Spotted Gut Rot in my gizzard and I'm filling up with purple pus. Please slay me before I rupture!" I staggered directly toward her.

The griffiness backed off—but not too far. She had a keen eye for flesh, and mine did not look spoiled. In fact,

I was about as delectable a sample of female anatomy as could be found in Xanth, surely tasty in every portion. Had I had more time to prepare, I could have smeared green juiceberries on my tender skin, staining it impressively. That was the problem with extemporaneous efforts; the verisimilitude suffers.

But I improvised, discovering the genius of desperation. "Would you believe," I pleaded distraughtly, "that I am actually a man? My innards have been so mixed up that there's no telling what will squeeze out next! Look at this!" I used my hands to cup my well-endowed bosom. "My chest muscles are practically drooping off!"

The griffiness backed off another step, her beak curving uncertainly. I pursued her. "Oh, please—cut me open and let out the gook before it geysers out on its own!" I made as if to squeeze a breast.

The griffiness spun, spread her wings, and took off. She didn't want any gook on her! Maybe she wasn't entirely convinced, but she preferred not to take the chance.

I relaxed. That had been a close call! Surely no genuine woman would have used that particular ruse—and perhaps the griffiness had known that. I wondered how Threnody had managed to survive alone in her cabin so long. A threat to jump into the—the—somewhere to her death would not stop an animal predator. But I knew the answer—by guile and poison. She had dealt with me as she had handled any other threat, and I could no longer blame her. I would do the same in her place, wearing her body.

She had told me she was a liar—and she was; but of course, a weak creature with tasty flesh could not afford the fighting integrity of an armed barbarian warrior. Understanding this, could I fail to understand also her desire to avoid Castle Roogna and marriage to a Magician whose only real interest in her was to shore up his standing as King? If I were in her place—and it seemed I was, for the time being—I'd rather go with a man whose interest was in my—in her body. At least that was honest.

But I had more immediate concerns. I hurried back to

my own body. Over two hours had passed; anything could have happened!

Fortunately, it hadn't. Pook had gathered the remains together in another leaf bag and this time had managed not to include too much dirt. If any monsters had threatened, the ghost horse had stood them off.

"I got rid of the sword," I said. "But now we have a problem, friend. I'm in the wrong body."

Pook nodded, having figured that out for himself.

"I really can't do much in this body," I said. "It's weak and misshapen for barbaric purposes, and—" I shrugged. "I just prefer my own."

The ghost horse nodded again. He never had thought much of Threnody's body.

"Of course, it could have been worse," I said. "If you had been standing closer to me than she was, I would have switched identities with you."

Pook snorted, revolted by the notion. I laughed, though I can't say I was totally thrilled by his reaction.

I checked my own body. It was beginning to heal. Pook had rolled the head against the neck and the arms against the shoulders; these had reattached, and most of the spilled blood had soaked back in. My eyes were no longer staring; the lids had closed in halfway normal sleep. My body would be all right in a few more hours; decapitations weren't so bad when the head was not lost. If I had had to grow a new one, I'm not sure how my memories would have fared, as they are packed mainly in the head. Looking at my body this way, seeing it undergoing the process of healing, I really appreciated my talent. Never before had I stood there and watched it from another body.

But the afternoon was passing, and we needed a secure place for the night. "There are griffins in this region— and probably worse when it's dark," I said. "If I had my body, I could handle it; but in this poor thing, I'm in trouble." I glanced down at my present form. Oh, it was an excellent-looking form, but at the moment I didn't want to look at it, I wanted to use it.

Pook nodded again. Evidently he had sniffed monsters in the area.

"Of course, you can survive better alone," I said. "We're a burden to you, especially in this condition. So maybe you should go your own way now."

Pook stamped a forefoot in negation. He would not desert me in this hour of desperation. I was so grateful I almost cried, being caught unaware by the reactions of this body. I stopped myself just in time and gave him a maidenly hug of gratitude instead. He tolerated this stoically.

"Well, I've got to protect myself until I can change back," I said. "Maybe I can climb a tree and—" But I looked at my unconscious body and at my present thin arms, and I knew I could never get us both into a tree. My barbarian body was simply too massive for my feminine body to lift. That was a confounded inconvenience; why did barbarians have to be so big?

"Maybe I could take this sword and—" But again I knew it was useless; these slender arms could never wield that great blade effectively.

I uttered an unladylike syllable of frustration. My present mouth almost choked on such a gross word. Threnody might have been quite ready to kill a man in defense of her interests, but she was not a foul talker. So I grabbed a hank of my black hair and yanked on it, venting my displeasure. All my avenues seemed blocked!

Then I spied the hole in the dead artis-tree. "I can drag my body into that," I said. "And squeeze in myself. And you can stand guard outside. That should get us through the night. In the morning, my body should be mobile, and you can carry it to some safer place."

Pook nodded agreement. I gripped my body by the shoulders and hauled. It was a real effort, but I managed to heave it a little. I reminded myself that Threnody had managed to drag me to the brink of the—I couldn't remember where, but surely she had dragged me, so I should be able to do it, too, in her body. I braced again, hauled again, and moved it some more. Soon I was panting, my bosom heaving prettily, but I got my body to the tree.

When I peered into the arched hole, I saw something I hadn't noticed before: there was a stairway in there!

The steps led down into darkness beneath the ground. This wasn't a hole in a tree, it was an entrance to—

To what? I gazed, pondering. Steps usually meant people or some roughly similar species. They were small steps, but there was clearance for human height. Was it wise to go down there?

Pook looked around nervously, sniffing the air and rotating his ears to catch some sound that was beyond my perception. Whatever designed human beings really messed up on the ears; not only were ours less efficient than those of most animals, they weren't nearly as pretty. Pook's ears, for example, were superior to mine in just about any respect you'd care to consider.

"Something dangerous?" I asked, and he nodded affirmatively.

"Something we can't stand off?" Again the nod.

"Like a dragon?" Yes.

"Then we have no choice," I concluded. "You range free, maybe leading it away—that's your specialty!—and I'll haul the two of us down the stairs." It was obvious that Pook wouldn't fit in the nether passage.

I took another hold on my body, then paused. "Uh, Pook, in case this doesn't work out—"

But I couldn't finish the sentence, so I just gave him another maidenly hug about the neck and a sweet-lipped kiss on the ear and dropped only one or two tears on his hide. Then I hauled my lunky, unconscious body on into the hole and down the stairs, headfirst.

Going down was easier, because gravity helped. Gravity can be very useful magic sometimes. I paused to look back and saw Pook's silhouette above; then we rounded the curve, and the parting was complete.

Chapter 12. Gnobody Gnomes

I felt halfway naked without Pook, and it was much worse to feel naked in this body than in my own. I reminded myself firmly that Pook really was better off free in the forest, where he could outrun any threat. With luck, we would find the subterranean region empty and be able to rest and recover in private safety. Of course, there might be a problem about food, but we could emerge to forage in the morning. Without luck—well, what choice did we have? That evil spell-sword had really cut down our options. I had managed to use the wrong white spell to salvage something, at least.

I reached the foot of the stairway. Now we were in a rough passage that wound among the descending roots of the artis-trees. The roots were aesthetically shaped and arranged, just as were the branches above, and it was in consequence a rather scenic passage, nicely contoured, though it was formed of packed dirt.

Where should we go from here? If anything used this stair these days, I wanted to be clear of it. I had not noticed any cobwebs as I descended with my body, and that suggested that the stairs had been recently used. Maybe there was a room along the passage where my body could be hidden.

I left that body for a moment and explored. Yes, there were occasional chambers opening from the passage. They were just rounded places that perhaps had once been used to store things. I went back and resumed the haul on my body. What an awful job it was!

Then I became aware of another presence. It was gloomy here, and getting more so as the day waned above, reducing the light leaking down the stairway. But now there was yellower light at the far end of the passage. Someone was coming!

I tried to haul my inert body the rest of the way to the chamber, but I was tired and the body seemed heavier than ever, and there wasn't enough time. The light of a lantern rounded a corner and paused.

"What have we here?" a gruff voice growled.

Oh, no! I recognized that quality of speech. This was a gnome! The gnomes lived underground, and their profession was mining; they tunneled endlessly, ferreting out pretty stones, and they weren't partial to intruders. Sometimes they ate visitors; sometimes they did worse things. Especially to attractive young women. For some obscure reason, I was now far more acutely conscious of the problems of young women than I had been before. Gnomes weren't as bad as goblins, being slightly more civilized—yes, even I, a proud but ignorant barbarian, could appreciate some aspects of civilization!—but they were bad enough. Some idiots thought of gnomes as innocent little men, like the elves; I knew better. I didn't like this at all.

"My—my friend and I—he's injured and must have shelter," I said, hoping to rouse some element of sympathy in the gnome. It was a faint hope, but all I could muster at the moment.

It was promptly dashed. "You are intruders!" the gnome growled. I saw that he carried a wicked-looking pick in his other hand, the kind that could pry stone from bedrock. "I, Gnasty Gnomad of the Gnobody Gnomes, shall deal with you forthrightly!" Gnomes were very forthright folk; that was part of their problem. He lifted his deadly pick.

Had I been in my own body, with my trusty sword, I should hardly have been concerned. Gnasty stood only a third my normal height, was short-legged and short-armed, and the pick was relatively clumsy compared with the sword, however devastating it was against unarmed folk. But I was not in my body, and my sword remained above-ground. I could not effectively oppose the gnome physically, shamed as I am to admit it.

So I scrambled cunningly once more. "Wait, good gnome, sir!" I cried. "No need to kill us! We can be useful to you! We—" Oh, what could I offer, that I was willing to offer, in this body? Again the genius of desperation struck. "We can sing!"

"I care nothing for human hilarity," Gnasty said, touching his squat, dark cap dourly. But he paused.

"No hilarity!" I said. "Sad, very sad! Listen!" And I used Threnody's voice, as I had done to calm the black sword, ululating fervently. It sounded as if something gross had just expired.

Gnasty Gnomad considered. "Maybe so," he said, grudgingly impressed. "Then follow me." He turned about and tramped back down the passage.

I returned to the dragging of my body. "Oh, leave him!" the gnome snapped. "We'll cut him up for broth."

"No!" I cried. "He can sing too; we're a duet! Much better together!" I hoped that was true. My body's ability at singing was nil, as song is not a barbarian thing, but if Threnody animated it, her skill might compensate.

The gnome shrugged. "It better be true," he grumped.

I hauled, and somehow got my body moved along. Fortunately, it wasn't far; down the passage was a chamber hollowed from stone, with a ventilation shaft penetrating to the surface. It had a barred wooden door. When I struggled in there with my burden, the gnome slammed and locked the door.

"But we'll need food, water!" I cried. "In order to sing well!"

"In due course, chattel," Gnasty said and marched off.

Well, for the moment we were secure. Too secure, perhaps, since we were prisoners. But maybe that was better than nothing.

I checked my body carefully. The healing continued apace; the head and arm were now so firmly attached that only faint scar lines showed where the severings had been. What a marvelous talent I had!

Actually, Threnody had a marvelous talent, too. I felt

I should use it to rescue us from this fix. I could change into a snake and crawl out between the bars and up the stairs and out—

But my body could not follow. And I didn't want to leave it unattended. Suppose dimepedes or nickelpedes showed up, or the Gnobody Gnomes, while I was absent? So I just had to sit tight—at least until the healing was far enough along.

I settled down beside my body and slept.

By morning, my body had healed enough to return to consciousness, but still had some healing to do. I noticed that the legs were flesh again; my talent had cleared up that detail while it was at it. Good enough; I really didn't need stone feet, or even feet of clay.

However, I now had the chore of explaining things to Threnody, who had not been in a position to appreciate much of what had happened recently. I had to get things straight with her before the gnomes returned.

"Don't get excited," I murmured in my ear. It was a dirty ear; I really should have cleaned my head more often, especially after it had rolled in the dirt. "There has been an exchange of consciousness."

My eyes widened. My left arm jerked up before my face. My mouth opened.

"Don't scream!" I warned. "That's more trouble!"

She was smart enough to desist, but she took a while to get settled. "My arm," she whispered, horrified. "It's all big and hairy!"

"That's not all," I muttered. I explained the rest of it in terse whispers, bringing us up to date. "So now you must try to sing, using my voice," I concluded.

Once she accepted the reality of our exchange of bodies, she adapted readily. She didn't like it any better than I did, and had just as much trouble with the specialized male anatomy as I had with the female anatomy, but she was a clever and realistic woman. I realized that Magician Yang must have expected me to be nearest Pook or some other creature, perhaps a living tree, when the exchange spell was activated. Surely he would not have wanted me in the body of the woman he hoped to marry. Or *did* he hope to marry her? Maybe he would be satisfied to have her dead, regardless of the attitude of the common folk of Xanth. At any rate, Threnody and I were for the moment unified in objecting to the present situation.

"Gnomes are no good for us," she said. "They don't like to go on the surface by day, so have to hunt at night; they have spells to protect them from night creatures, or maybe it's just their bright torches that scare the beasts away. But they have an appetite for day-game, which they seldom have opportunity to assuage—and we are day-game." She looked down at my body, which was now clothed in only the merest tatters of her brown dress. "If I had known this was going to happen, I'd have let you get new trousers! Can this hunk of flesh survive being cooked and eaten?"

"I'm not sure," I said uncomfortably. "Swallowed whole by a dragon, sure; but spread among several stomachs— the more my body has to regenerate lost parts, the harder it is. Maybe if the bones were piled together—I think it's the bones that are the essence of me. But if they are kept separate—thrown away in different dumps—I don't think I'd be able to recover. I'm not like a worm, where each part becomes a new creature."

"That's what I thought. So if I get eaten by gnomes in this body, I'm done for—and my own body can't recover from simple death. There's no chance there. We've just got to avoid being eaten."

"I never much liked being eaten, anyway," I confessed.

"But how can we escape? Your body's a lot stronger than mine, but yours is pretty weak right now." She smiled with my brute, masculine face. "I'm in a position to know."

"After a recovery, my body needs a lot of food and rest," I explained. "It will be a couple of days before it's up to full snuff."

"And without a weapon or tool to fight with or pry us out of here, even your full strength won't do much good," she said. "We'll have to depend on my talent. My body can escape readily. But—"

"But mine can't," I finished for her. "And we need both bodies, until we can get switched back."

"I'm aware of the irony," she said, grimacing. "We've got to stick together and protect each other from further harm. But how can your body escape? Undoubtedly you, as a barbarian, have had prior experience with this sort of thing. Hairbreadth escapes and whatnot."

She gave me too much credit. Most of my life had been spent peacefully growing up in Fen Village. That was why I had had to go out on my own to fill my quota of adventure. I had drowned once, gotten zonked by the stare of a stray basilisk, and had my neck broken by a falling branch, but these were mere boyhood experiences, the kind any lad had. I had never been imprisoned and threatened with getting cooked, before this journey to central Xanth.

But I did know a way. "I could assume the form of a creature with strong teeth or cutting claws. Then I could cut you into chunks small enough to pass through these bars, and carry the chunks to the surface, one at a time. After that, I could put them together and wait for you to reconstitute."

She grimaced. "There are a squintillion problems with that! First, doesn't it hurt? And if you knocked me out first, wouldn't there be a lot of lost blood when you cut? And wouldn't it take so long—three hours—for you to change in my body and do the job that the gnomes will return and discover what we're up to? And if not, and you carry the chunks to the surface, what's to prevent some predator from consuming them up there, one at a time, while you're down here fetching another? And if all that can be overcome, how do you know your body will recover after that bad treatment, so soon after being hacked apart by the black sword? You hadn't recovered all the way from the stone-spell before, and I still feel a little stone in my toe."

I spread my small, pretty hands. "You're thinking better than I am, I guess. You're right; it wouldn't work. We can't escape on our own. But what else can we do?"

"I think you had the right idea before. We'll have to sing our way out."

"But can you sing well in my voice? I was never good at that sort of thing."

"Marvels can be done with harmony," she said. "It's one thing your weakened body can probably do as well as ever. Maybe we'd better practice."

"But the gnomes will hear!"

"And what if they do? They *want* us to sing, don't they? I can't think why they want song, but we'd better oblige them."

So we sang. Her body's voice was very good, even without the accompaniment of her lute, but I knew neither words nor tune, so could only ululate in the fashion I had done before. My body's voice was deep and rough, but Threnody knew the songs. It seemed impossible at first, but she knew what she was doing; that turned out to be an improvement on my situation and an important part of singing.

"I will teach you a song, so you can sing it properly," she said. "Then I will be the bass accompaniment. The secret is harmony and counterpoint; the two voices will complement each other and become more than they are separately. Let me see." She pondered briefly. "Let's start with a wordless one; you just learn the melody."

She made my voice sing the tune. As she got used to it, she made my voice perform better than it ever had sung before. It stopped barging about the basement and started marching in more disciplined fashion at ground level. I realized that my poor singing had been more a matter of attitude than ability; even the worst voice could sound halfway decent if properly managed. Then, with her voice, I was able to pick up the theme on a higher register and soon I could sing it. It was a sad but pretty thing that seemed appropriate for mourning a close friend's death or the tragedy of the human condition in general.

There was a tramping in the passage, and we broke off. Gnasty arrived, followed by several other gnomes. "See, Gnitwit," Gnasty said. "I told you they could sing."

Gnitwit gnodded. "So you did. But will the cowboys listen?"

"Why not try it and see? What do you think, Gnone-such?"

"Since the cowpokes infest our richest region," Gnone-such said, "anything's worth a try. If it doesn't work, we can always put them in the stew."

Gnitwit peered at me. "She looks delectable. Look at that thigh! I get first dibs on that!"

"Gno you don't!" Gnasty snapped, as I hastily tugged the hem of my skirt down to cover the exposed thigh. "I found them; I get first pick from the stew."

"Let's fatten them up so we can all feast," Gnonesuch suggested.

"Good gnotion!" Gnasty agreed.

They departed, and Threnody and I practiced some more harmony. We had extra incentive now! While I sang the tune I had learned, she used my voice to fill a deep underpinning, a sort of strumming that was nothing in itself but really sounded good when it lined up with what I was singing. We were a team!

There was more action in the passage. This time, the entrance was by gnomides, the gnome women, who were rather pretty little things. I have already remarked on how the human-related creatures seem to have better taste in women than in men, at least as far as appearances go. Structurally it's another matter, of course; legs that may look and taste delectable don't run as fast as those with muscles. I suppose there should be a reasonable compromise between appearance and performance; but of course, I was not the one to design the humanoid form.

The gnomides brought a pot of murky water and a bundle of cooked roots. The roots tasted awful and were threaded with undigestible strings, but we were both so hungry that we ate them without protest. At least there was plenty of the stuff, so that my body had the substance it needed for healing completely and strengthening.

The gnomides departed, and we had more time to ourselves. That's one thing prisoners have plenty of—time. We practiced our song some more, perfecting it, then rested. "The more you sleep, the faster my body will recover," I told her.

"I wonder whether you should practice changing form," she said. "We don't want the gnomes to know you can do it, but if the opportunity arises for a change, you do need to know how."

"I phased to smoke so I could bury the black sword in a stone," I said. "I just willed it, and it happened."

"Yes, that's the way. If you concentrate harder, it works faster, but you still can't do it in much under an hour. You were very smart to deal with the sword that way."

"I was desperate!" But I felt a feminine flush of pleasure at the compliment.

"The problem is, you can do only one kind of change at a time, and you have to complete that before you can begin another. You can't change size halfway, then change density halfway; the most you can do is change your mind and resolidify before you're done. So it's really quite limited—which is one reason I did not try to escape captivity till night. My body is vulnerable while it's in the process of change; it has to be undisturbed for things to work right."

"I know how it is," I said. "My body can't heal properly if it keeps getting messed up. But how does your body know when halfway is? I mean, couldn't you be shrinking to elf size, but stop at gnome size and decide that's where you were going anyway?"

My eyes widened in my handsome but smudged male face. "I never thought of that!" she exclaimed. "I always had an object in mind, like a mouse; first I'd change to mouse size and be so dense I'd almost sink through the ground. Then I'd diffuse back to normal density, at which point I'd be the size and mass of an imp. Then I'd change shape and be a complete mouse. I never was able to do it any other way—but I suppose it's possible."

"Just as it turned out to be possible for my voice to sing," I agreed. "What's this about super-density?"

"The mass of the body stays the same, unless that's what's being changed," she explained. "When I reduce my mass without changing size or form, I become ghost-like; then if I reduce my size commensurately, I become normally solid again. The mass of a mouse distributed through the volume of a woman is vaporous, but still there; when the size becomes that of a mouse, all is well."

"That's interesting," I said, not very interested. "But now you'd better sleep."

She agreed. My body settled back and in a moment was snoring. That startled me. Oh, I knew I snored sometimes, but hadn't realized it was that loud and vulgar. People at Fen Village had complained now and then, but I had believed they were joking.

I wasn't sleepy myself; this body was not busy recovering from decapitation and dismemberment, so was more alert. I decided to experiment cautiously with changing states. I had diffused before and returned to normality, so I knew I could handle that. What about shape? No, that would be too obvious, if the gnomes came back unexpectedly. Size? Yes, maybe I could do something with that. I would make myself larger—no, smaller, again to escape notice if observed. And I would stop wherever I chose, then decide what to do next. I wanted to know the limits of Threnody's talent. Our lives might depend on it.

I shrank for about a quarter of an hour, then checked the mark I had made on the wall. Yes, I was about three-quarters of my prior height. In an hour I could reduce to—to what, zero size? Microscopic? A microscope was a magic instrument used to see things too small to see; I could appear under that instrument and do a pantomime act, astonishing the Magician watching! Except that any larger creature could eat me; that thought changed my mind quickly.

I was denser; there was a different feel to my body, not comfortable. I was breathing more rapidly, as if my lungs were not taking in enough air. This made sense; they had to support the same mass, but they were smaller, so they had to work harder. How could Threnody have diminished to mouse size without suffocating? She must have diffused first, then shrunk, so she could breathe. I was also having a little trouble with my balance, because I was closer to the ground and had less time to correct my stance, as well as being overmassed for this size. I realized that even if density were kept constant, a person would not want to be the size of a mouse, for it would be hard to balance on two feet. The imps, of course, were used to it, and maybe had magic to keep them steady; but if I were the size of a mouse, I'd better also assume the form of a mouse. It was amazing how complex a simple thing like size-change became; no wonder Threnody hadn't been eager to launch into it. Now I decided to diffuse back to normal density so I wouldn't have to pant. Already I could see the limits of these changes. If I diffused too much, wind could blow me away or even apart; while if I became too solid, I could sink into the ground.

But wait—I wanted to find out whether I could stop here and do something else, or alternate one form of change with another. Threnody thought I couldn't—but again I reminded myself that I had thought I couldn't sing. I had shrunk some; better try diffusing.

I concentrated on diffusion, and in fifteen minutes I was breathing easier. So far so good; I had done a change in half an hour instead of two hours. What next?

Well, could this body change part of itself and not the rest? Threnody had been so sure of its limits—maybe she hadn't even tried new things.

I concentrated on my left hand, willing it to become a crab's pincer. I ignored the rest of the body, working on just that one thing.

And it worked! In just a few minutes that hand was a big green pincer. I tried it on my skin, but it wasn't a strong pincer; it had the form but not the power. No, this was not an easy way to convert the body into a natural weapon. Not without more time and practice. Still, this represented a breakthrough. Threnody's body had more talent than she had known. Because the focus of change was now narrow, it was relatively swift; she had required an hour per change because she insisted on doing the whole body, all the way. She had been limited in her thinking, and therefore in her talent.

But I'd better get back to normal, lest I be discovered. I tried to change size and claw simultaneously, but found

I could not; it had to be one or the other. Very well, claw first, then size.

It was easy. I changed the claw halfway to the hand, then switched to size-changing, switched again to density to catch up on my missing mass, and returned to finish the hand. I could only do one type of change at a time, but I could do whatever change I wanted, to whatever extent. I had, in effect, rendered Threnody's talent far more versatile.

Was that true for all people? I wondered. Could every person do much more than he believed, if he changed his belief? To what extent were all of us needlessly limited? The Mundanes refused to believe in magic and therefore could not practice it; *there* was a horrendous example!

But barbarians aren't much for philosophy. Maybe they could be, if they thought they could be? I got myself back to normal, then settled down and snoozed in and out. Threnody slept more solidly for several hours, waking when the gnomides brought more food. This time Gnasty was with them. "Prepare yourselves, chattel," he said gruffly. "Soon you will sing for the cowboys." He spun about and tramped off.

"Who or what are these cowboys?" I asked.

One of the gnomides glanced around to be sure Gnasty was out of hearing range. "They are bullheaded folk," she said.

"Well, so is Gnasty," I said.

She smiled, becoming more at ease. "No, you misunderstand, human woman. They—" She shrugged, at a loss to provide more detail.

"My name is—" I hesitated, but realized I had to go with my present body, lest there be considerable complications of understanding. "Threnody."

"Threnody," she repeated. "And I am Gnifty Gnomide."

"Gnice to know you, Gnifty," I said in my most feminine manner, while Threnody kept silent. And actually it *was* nice, for these gnomides were of quite a different personality from the gnomes. It served as a reminder that a person can not be said to know a species unless he knows both sexes of it. "What do I misunderstand about the cowboys? Do they herd cows or something?" Cows were mythical Mundane animals.

A titter rippled through the gnomides. "Of course not!" Gnifty said. "They are—their heads are—" She cast about for a better term, but found none. "Bulls," she finished.

"You mean their bodies are—like ours—but their heads—?"

"Yes!" she exclaimed, pleased at this success of communication. "They graze—"

"Graze?"

"On the moss of the rocks, where our men mine. And they get—they have horns—"

It was coming clear at last. "When the gnomes try to work, the cowboys want to graze, so they get ornery and interfere."

"Yes. And they are too big and strong to oppose, so we can't mine. But they're not aggressive, usually, and they like music—only we aren't good at music."

"Well, we'll sing for you," I said generously. "But suppose it doesn't work?"

"Oh, we don't like to think of that!" Gnifty said.

But an older gnomide, hardened to tougher stuff, managed to come up with the thought. "The pot."

"She's Gnaughty," Gnifty confided, embarrassed. "And she's Gnymph." She indicated the youngest gnomide, who was too shy to speak at all. As with human women, their shyness was inversely proportional to their age.

I knew better than to ask these little women to release us. They didn't have the key and they wouldn't dare defy their gruff men. As it was, they shied away from Threnody's side of the cell, afraid of the big, brute, male body despite the gate separating us. They took me for a woman, so were friendly with me. All women, I realized, shared a bond of awe and subservience, because of the roughness of men. How odd that I had never noticed this before assuming female aspect myself.

"Well, thank you so much for the food," I said. "My friend Jordan, there, has a big appetite. He was hurt;

that's why we came down here. We couldn't stay up there at night—not with all those monsters."

The gnomides shuddered. They were afraid of monsters too. That was why their kind lived safely underground.

"But why don't small monsters come in that open door in the tree?" I asked. "We came right down the stairs; we didn't know there were people here."

"There's an aversion spell on it," Gnifty explained. "Only our own kind can enter, or someone in such dire need that he overcomes the aversion."

"That was us," I said. "He was unconscious; I dragged him down."

"Our men have aversion spells on their hats," Gnifty continued. She was really quite talkative, now that the ice had been broken. "So that no big monsters come near, just creatures small enough to be hunted at night. When a dragon is near, they cry, 'Hang onto your hat!'"

"That makes sense," I agreed with maidenly agreement.

We finished eating, and the gnomides took away the refuse. Then the gnomes returned. "Move out!" Gnasty said as he unlocked the gate.

We were conducted to a deep region where the tunnels branched out in all directions. Apparently these ones had not been hollowed by the gnomes. They were larger and older, and their walls were covered by furry growths. In some sections, the walls had been chipped away by the miners, where they had delved for precious stones. The moss did not grow in the chipped sections. I could see why those who grazed would be annoyed. To them, perfectly good food was being destroyed. When two cultures interfaced, who was to say which one was right and which wrong? They merely had different viewpoints.

When I thought of it, that term "interface" was interesting. It derived from a spell in which the faces of two creatures were locked together or combined so that they interconnected. There had been a person whose talent was interfacing; she could lock any two faces together, however awkward it was for the participants. Later usage had been less specific, until now it meant the overlapping of any two things, including cultures—as in this case. I was fascinated by the way words came into the language; too bad I wasn't civilized! Words have always been very important to me, because we barbarians have only an oral tradition; without words, we would have no culture at all. Words have real power, and not just the magic ones. One has only to listen to a harpy swear to know that!

The gnomes slowed, becoming nervous. "They're near," Gnasty said. "I smell them. If only our aversion spells worked on them!"

Sure enough, there was a whiff of barnyard odor. Then we heard a kind of crunch, crunch—the sound of grazing and chewing—and every so often the burp of a wad of cud being brought up. Finally we came into a larger cavern, and there were the cowboys: true bullheaded men the size of my body.

They spied us. One snorted and pawed the floor of the cave with a bare foot. He was unclothed, but fairly furry all over so he didn't seem naked. He lowered his horns. Gnasty clapped his hand to his hat and backed off. This was really cowboy country.

"Sing!" Gnasty cried.

"Now look," I said reasonably. "Don't the cowboys have as much right to this cave as you do? After all, they're hungry, and this is where they graze."

"Gnitwit, go smoke up the pot," Gnasty said to his companion.

"We'll sing!" I exclaimed. The gnomes had a truly compelling argument! That was often the way of it, when reason met fanaticism.

So we sang, my pretty melody and Threnody's deep, resonating accompaniment. In this larger space it worked well; the sound sort of spread out and mellowed, and those bass notes reverberated while the high notes cut straight through to the ear. It was a nice effect, if I do say so myself.

And the cowboys responded. The aggressive bull un-aggressed and returned to his grazing. Beyond him was a cowgirl, with a body not unlike the one I was using. That one listened attentively, her ears cocked toward us.

"Move them down to the far side," Gnasty told us, gruffly pleased. "We want to work here."

So Threnody and I slowly walked to the far side of the cavern, and the cowfolk followed us, so as to be close to the song. Behind us, the gnomes unlimbered their picks and had at the wall, gouging out chunks of it, then using their mallets to smash apart the chunks. When they had reduced the rock to gravel, they sifted through it, searching for gems. They didn't find many, but of course such work is slow, as is anything worthwhile. I couldn't fault the industrious gnomes, but I was sorry to see the natural walls being torn down and the rubble accumulating. The gnomes were more civilized than the cowfolk, so naturally they had more destructive ways. Once the gnomes were through with a section, no one would have any use for it.

All we had was one song, but the cowfolk seemed satisfied with it. The cowgirl gradually came closer to me, avoiding Threnody, and I realized that she, like the gnomides, felt more comfortable with her own sex. Once again, the camaraderie of the gentle aspect prevailed.

I held out my hand to her, and she made so bold as to sniff it, then shied away, alarmed by her own boldness. These were basically shy folk, not looking for trouble; the bulls simply stood their ground when they had to. Maybe the aversion spell of the gnomes did work on the cowboys, but they became desperate when defending their diminishing pastures, so resisted it. My sympathy was with them. I seemed to have a lot of female sympathy now; maybe it derived from my present body, yet somehow I doubted it was any carryover from Threnody's personality.

But we were captives of the gnomes, and we didn't know much about the cowfolk, and my body had not yet recovered its full strength. We had to remain with the gnomes until we saw our way clear to escape.

We sang until we began to hoarsen, which was bad for pacifying cows, so we had to quit for the day. But the gnomes had done good mining during this period and were well satisfied. The gnomides carried several small diamonds; evidently they were the guardians of such stones.

The gnomes returned us to our cell and fed us well. I would have appreciated it more if I hadn't known they wanted us fat for the pot, at such time as our usefulness as singers ended. Once our effect on the cowboys diminished, or the gnomes completed their operations in cowfolk caves, we would be in hot water.

There didn't seem to be any gnomes near our cell this evening, but a barbarian never trusts appearances completely. They could have one of their number lurking in a nearby cell, listening to make sure we didn't make any secret escape plans. So I said nothing on this subject to Threnody. But as darkness closed at the ventilation shaft, I settled down next to her, put my face near hers—that is, near mine—and murmured: "They're going to cook us one of these days."

"Yes, we'll really go to pot," she agreed.

"So we must plan our escape. You'll be stronger tomorrow, but it will take one more day for full strength. Do you think we can wait that long?"

"I think so," she said. "That's a big cavern they're mining, and maybe not the only one. But let's plan it carefully now, just in case we have to try it tomorrow. I think the cowfolk will let us pass through their home passages—but we need to be sure there's a way to the surface from there."

I was propped on one elbow, so as to address her ear. My arm was getting uncomfortable, but I didn't want to move away and have to talk louder. "Uh, may I lean against you?" I asked.

"Sure," she said gruffly. "Here, put your head against my shoulder, and I'll hold you in place."

So I rested my head in the crook of her shoulder and neck, and she put her brawny arm around my body. One big hand fell rather familiarly across my bosom. "Uh, your hand—" I said.

"What?" She sounded annoyed. And she put both hands

on my shoulders, drew me in to my face, and kissed me on the mouth.

I wrenched away, brought up my own hand, and slapped her on the cheek, smartly. Then I scrambled out of her grasp.

"What did you do that for?" she demanded angrily. Even in the dark, I was aware of her big muscles tensing and I was uncomfortably conscious of the disparity in the powers of our bodies. She was not yet at full strength, but she could pick me up and throw me across the cell if she wanted to.

"You behave yourself, or I'll scream for the gnomes!" I said tersely.

"But all I was doing—" she began in a baffled voice.

"All you were doing was responding to your strong masculine passions! You think any available female is yours to—to—" I could not continue, appalled at the prospect.

"My masculine passions!" she retorted, outraged. Then she laughed ruefully. "You know, it's true; I've never felt stirrings like that before. I'm all—I—is that the way men react to women?"

"To pretty ones," I said guardedly.

"I never realized before how it was with men! How do you ever manage to control yourselves?"

"It isn't always easy," I admitted, grudgingly mollified. "That night when you lay against me, and breathed—"

She laughed again. "I know! Now I understand exactly how you felt. That dirt you said you have in your mind— I think some of that rubbed off on me, because—well, never mind. Oh, Jordan—you were a saint!"

"Saints are mythological Mundane creatures," I muttered, further mollified. But this experience had unsettled me, too; never before had I properly appreciated the woman's position.

"I apologize," Threnody said. "I got carried away."

"I accept your apology," I said graciously. And so we were reconciled. But we did not resume physical contact and we did not discuss our plans for escape that night.

* * *

Next day was much like the first. We ate, rehearsed another song, and sang it later for the cowfolk. This time three cowgirls approached. One was young, really a calf-child, with cute little horns. "Yooo nnize vvoook," she mooed as we paused between songs. We had found we didn't have to sing continuously; they would give us a few minutes for silence if it was obvious there would soon be more music.

I did a double take. Was she talking? It seemed so. The bovine lips and tongue were not well adapted for speech, but when I realized that the Z sound substituted for the S sound, and the V for the F, it made sense. "Thank you," I murmured. "You nice folk, too."

"Nnize zoongz," she said, pleased.

"Nice songs," I agreed, glancing to make sure the gnomes weren't paying attention. "Can all of you talk our language?"

She shook her head no. "Oonee mmeee. Mmiii zaa-lenz."

"Your talent," I agreed, understanding. I hadn't realized that nonhuman folk had magic talents, but of course, the cowfolk were mostly human. All except the heads. So it made sense that they should have souls and magic.

This was a very interesting development. Could we turn it to our advantage? We certainly needed an advantage!

We sang another song, to preserve appearances. Then I talked with the calfchild again. "What is your name?" I asked.

"Mmooola," she replied richly. "Hwaaz yoorz?" She had trouble with some consonants, but I could understand her increasingly well as I became attuned.

"Threnody," I said, feeling a twinge of guilt for this necessary deception. There was no way I could make these folk understand my real situation; and if I could, it would only frighten them away. I believe in good old-fashioned barbarian integrity, but there are times when it doesn't seem to apply.

"Zrennozee," she repeated carefully.

"You speak very well," I complimented her, and her

nostrils dilated with appreciation. I leaned forward confidentially. "Just between us girls—I have a secret."

Her beautiful bovine orbs brightened. All girls love secrets! Her furry ears twitched. "Zeekrez?"

"Yes. We are captives of the Gnobody Gnomes. Will you help us escape?"

Moola's nose wrinkled in perplexity. "Eezave?"

"Correct. Escape. The gnomes mean to cook us in a big pot when they're through with our singing."

"Vvigg vozz?"

"A *big*, big pot," I agreed. "We must escape—tomorrow. Will you help?"

The calf-brow creased and the ears twitched uncertainly. "Mmuuz aazg," she lowed, glancing at the largest bullhead, who was evidently in charge.

"Tomorrow," I repeated. Then we had to sing again, for the herd was getting restless.

That night we definitely had to make plans, so I trusted my valuable and delicate feminine body close to the brute hunk Threnody was using and discussed our escape. "I think all we have to do is walk into the midst of the cowfolk," I said. "The gnomes couldn't stop us. If Moola says it's okay."

"But can we trust them?" she asked with typically masculine suspicion. "What do they eat, besides moss?"

"Their mouths aren't suited for meat-eating," I said.

"Or for talking?"

"That's just Moola's talent." But I wasn't entirely easy, since I now inhabited what was surely a delectable carcass. "Anyway, what choice do we have? We don't want to wait for the gnomes to light a fire under the pot."

The notion of that smoking fire and boiling pot seemed to bother her as much as it did me. A pot is best left unsmoked. "We'd better trust them," she agreed. "They do seem like decent bovine folk."

"A better risk, anyway." I made ready to draw away, but she held me close.

"I'm sorry I killed you," she said.

We had been through that before. "Are you getting ready to make another pass at me?" I demanded, trying vainly to free myself from her grip.

"Of course not," she said insincerely. Then she laughed ruefully. "I never suspected what a difference a body makes," she said. "I mean, I have assumed many forms in the past; but always female."

"You could assume the male form, couldn't you?" I asked. "Maybe I should try it."

"It wouldn't work. My talent is form-changing, not—that. Maybe my body could look male, but inside, it would always be female."

That seemed reasonable. Yet now, in our exchanged bodies, she was assuming male attributes, and I female ones. Form did make a difference! Still, I definitely thought of myself as a male, and surely she remained female in outlook. Some questions have no easy answers, and I suspect the question of sexual outlook is about as uneasy as any.

We separated and slept. But perhaps we respected each other more than we had before.

Next day was as before, until we came to the cowfolk's cavern. About half the wall of it had been chipped away, so that there was much less grazing than previously. We sang the first song, and Moola approached. "Verzinanz zayz ogaa," she reported contentedly.

"Ferdinand says okay," I relayed to Threnody.

"Then let's get the hell on our way," she said gruffly. I don't know why males can't be more gracious about accepting favors, and I wish they would watch their rough language.

We got up and walked to the far end of the cave, where the main herd of the cowfolk was.

"Hey!" Gnasty Gnomad shouted, brandishing his pick. But two bullheads stood in the way, their horns lowered, and he could do nothing. "And we had the pot ready to smoke tonight!" he raged.

"Such a pity, creep," Threnody muttered without much sympathy. Males can be quite callous at times.

Moola skipped along ahead of us, showing the way. But neither of us escapees was completely sanguine about where this was leading.

Chapter 13. Knightmare

It led to a huge, barnlike cave, where motherly cows nursed small baby calves, and old bullheads chewed cud complacently. Standing in a Kingly stall was Ferdinand, a huge and noble bull of a man. Moola conducted us straight to him.

Moola had to translate, as we did not comprehend bovine language. The King, however, appeared to understand our speech well enough. Royal creatures do seem to place a premium on education, and at times that really helps.

"Greetings, your Majesty," Threnody said, making a formal bow. It was evident that the males dominated this herd, so she, as our apparent male, was expected to be the important person. I stifled my annoyance at this rank sexism for now; I'd give Threnody a piece of my mind later. "We are deeply grateful for your timely assistance in rescuing us from the gnomes."

The King mooed. Moola translated: "Zoze Mnovozzee Mnomz arr aa vaane!"

"Those Gnobody Gnomes are a pain," I repeated quietly for Threnody's benefit, as her masculine ear seemed to be less attuned to nuances. No wonder she couldn't sing as prettily as I could!

"They certainly are!" Threnody agreed. "They were going to smoke us in a pot."

The bullheaded King mooed again, and Moola said: "Nnoow yoo ghann zzingg vorr uz voreverr."

Oops! "Now you can sing—" I began, whispering.

"I heard!" Threnody snapped with insufferable masculine crudity. She raised my voice for the King. "Your

Majesty, we deeply appreciate what you have done for us. But we have business elsewhere. Perhaps there is some other service we can do for your good folk to show our gratitude."

"Mooo?" the King asked, disappointed.

"We can not stay here," Threnody said firmly. "This is no aspersion on your region or culture. It is just that we have a prior commitment. I am a King's daugh—a King's offspring, and the duties of my status—"

Regretfully, the King mooed again. He was not one to argue against the honoring of duties of royal status.

"The only other thing we need is more pasture," Moola translated in her fashion. I'm rendering it for the moment in our normal mode, though of course it wasn't. Actually, her accent was not bad, for a heifer, and I don't mean to disparage it; I'm sure we sounded as odd to the bovines. "But our deepest and best pastures are controlled by the Knights, and already we pay a terrible rental for the use of some of those caves."

"Nights?" Threnody asked. "They are very dark?"

"Knights," Moola said precisely, managing to convey a hard K sound at the beginning of the term. "We are bracketed above by the gnomes and below by the Knights. The Gnobody Gnomes and the Knock-Kneed Knights."

The story, as it emerged, was that terrible armored creatures called Knights allowed the cowfolk to graze in some nether pastures, but required the sacrifice of the finest bullocks and heifers each year. If the cowfolk refused to send their tribute, the Knights would cut off the pastures entirely. Now, with their upper pasture depleted by the ravages of the gnomes, the bovines would not have enough left to survive.

The annual ritual had started many years before, when the Knights had moved into the caves and proved to be too strong for the cowfolk. The invaders were from a far place called Kon-Krete, where everything was very hard. The bovines had tried to fight, but their horns were no match for the pikes of the Knights, and they had been driven relentlessly to the very fringe of their range, up against the gnomes. The Knights could have exterminated explained. "That would have taken an hour to complete. the cowfolk entirely, but preferred to save them for entertainment. So the tribute was not just for grazing; it was for the very survival of the bovine community. But it was a sporting thing, as the Knights liked sport. The sacrificial cowfolk were given swords and sent into the dread labyrinth to meet the Knight Tourney Champion. If they could run that gantlet and defeat him in battle, the tribute would be forgiven, and thereafter the bovines would be permitted to graze free. That gave them a genuine incentive to fight well—but so far none of them had prevailed, even though the bull and heifer were permitted to tackle the lone Knight together. The Knights' Champion had been too strong.

"But how do you know they would keep their word, if you ever won?" Threnody asked with male suspicion.

"Oh, the Knock-Kneed Knights always keep their word," Moola assured her. "They are creatures of chivalric honor. They believe that, without honor, they would be nothing at all. They are tough warriors and heartless creatures, but they would never dishonor their word."

I began to perceive a certain barbarian ethic here. Maybe we could come to terms with the Knights.

The only escapes from these caves were through the territories of the gnomes or Knights. So, if we did not wish to remain here, we would have to go one way or the other. If we really wanted to do the cowfolk a favor on our way out...

Threnody was doubtful, but I wasn't. "We ought to help these good folk," I said. "Not just because it's a way out, but because they are in genuine need. Besides, it sounds like a grand adventure."

"Grand adventure!" she exclaimed. "More like a nightmare! We could get killed!"

"I'd rather get killed in a good fight for justice than boiled ignominiously in a pot. Of course, the easy thing would be to stay here and sing for the bovines forever while they slowly starve."

"You retain some of those bold masculine notions," she muttered. "But I suppose we have little choice. You could change into a mouse and sneak out alone, but I can't—and anyway, I want my body back before you ruin it." She straightened my massive shoulders and addressed the King again. "Your Majesty, we have decided to take the place of your two sacrifices and go to battle with the Knights' Champion. Perhaps we shall defeat him and free you of your annual tribute; if not, at least two of your own folk shall be spared this year."

King Ferdinand made a bellow of pleased surprise. "Zhiz is aa heroig zhing yoo dzoo!" Moola translated. "Yoo arr aa graaze mmaann!"

"Aa graaze mmaann," Threnody agreed with irony. And privately to me: "You and your damned noble instincts!"

The sacrifice wasn't due until next month, but the King was sure the Knights would accept it early. We decided to go the next day.

First we had to prepare for the encounter. The cowfolk cooperated in fitting Threnody with a bullhead, so that she looked very much like the King himself. The bovines were fairly clever with their human hands and had fashioned likenesses of the heads of their heroes of the past, made from cloth, plaster, and paint. This particular maskhead was a representation of the Minotaur, a bygone hero who had gone to Mundania to seek his fortune. He was believed to have acquitted himself very well in labyrinth competition there, slaying many Mundanes. Naturally, things were better with fewer Mundanes. "Iv oonlee wee hadz hiz llighe aagenn," Moola said reverently. "Vudz wee arr zoo veesvull nnow."

"Too peaceful," I agreed. "Yet there is merit in that."

For my part, I used my body's talent. First I expanded my size to that of Threnody's body. *My* body, technically. Next I increased my density to make myself normal again. Then I changed my head to become that of a horned cow.

The cowfolk, watching this one-hour transformation, were amazed. So was Threnody. "You did it three times as fast as I do!" she exclaimed.

"I started to change to a giant twice as tall as you," I

I stopped when I was your height, so only ten minutes
had passed. Then I started to increase my mass eightfold,
but stopped after fifteen minutes, when it was only double. Finally I changed my head, leaving the rest of my
body alone, so that only took half an hour."

"But the whole body has to change!" she protested.

"No, it doesn't. If you change from human shape to
cowgirl shape, only the head changes. Otherwise you
couldn't assume some partly human forms, such as this
one or that of a harpy or centaur."

She shook her head. "I wouldn't believe it, but I just
saw you do it; you've learned more about my talent in
three days than I did in a lifetime!"

"Just lucky," I said smugly.

Her eyes narrowed. "I thought barbarians were sort
of stupid. You're smarter than—" She shrugged. "You're
really quite a—a person."

I shrugged. "I'm close to nature, that's all. Your talent
is a natural thing, your demon heritage."

"Natural!" she muttered with mixed emotions.

We had a supper of fresh moss, as that was all that
was available. It wasn't tasty by our standards, but it did
feed us. We slept in a chamber lined with old straw, which
was a precious substance here; the cowfolk were treating
us royally.

Next day we set out for the challenge. Moola had explained how to find the Knights, who would give us swords
if they accepted our status as Sacrifice. It was simply a
matter of walking to the lower level and mooing for attention. The Knights, like most arrogant conquerors, did
not bother to speak the subjects' language.

"Vaarr wwelll!" Moola said as we departed, a big, lovely
bovine tear in her brown eyes.

"Fare well, Moola," I replied, giving her a female hug.
I was now much bigger than she, but the sentiment was
the same. I had increased my size because I felt that would
give me a better chance in the action to come. Part of
what sets women at a disadvantage is their smaller size,
and that was one disadvantage this body did not have to
put up with.

We walked down the indicated route. The caves looked strange from my bovine eyes; I could see behind me as well as before me, but detail was not as clear as I liked. Very soon we were in the forbidden territory, so we started mooing to advertise our presence. Otherwise, we had been warned, we could be slaughtered casually as trespassers or as strays from the herd.

It wasn't long before a figure in metal armor appeared. It was large—as large as we were—and so completely covered that no flesh was visible. A forbidding apparition, indeed!

"Moo!" we mooed together.

The specter studied us, one gauntleted hand on the huge sword slung at its metal hip. Then it turned and walked away. Its armor did rattle some, but its knees did not actually knock. Nervously, we followed, presuming we had been accepted as the Sacrifice and would be permitted the privilege of Running the Gantlet.

Sure enough, we were brought to an arena. It wasn't really a labyrinth, or a gantlet, but rather an open area surrounded by a warren of low channels. As we stood in the center, more suits of armor filed in, taking seats on these low walls. In fact, I now saw that these were tiered benches, the ones behind set higher than those before, so that the Knights could all see clearly into the arena. Empty, it looked like a labyrinth; filled, it was an audience chamber.

In the center of the arena, beside us, was a ramp. It started level with the floor, fairly wide, and rose at a slight incline as it crossed the arena. Near the edge, the ramp curved and went back, still rising. Across the arena, it bent once more and had another straight run. By this time it was fairly high, so that a person would not want to fall from it.

At the uppermost end of the ramp, far overhead, was a metal gate—and beyond that was the light of day. That was the route to the surface! That was our escape! That distant spot of light looked wonderful. Below, the only illumination was by murky torches.

What was to prevent us from simply marching up that

ramp and out that gate? Well, the gate was closed and surely locked; we'd have to break through, which would be very difficult and perhaps impossible, or get the key to the lock. That key could be anywhere and certainly not where we could get it. The gate would open when the Knights chose to open it, not otherwise.

But why, then, make a ramp up to it? Was this a highway the Knights used themselves? Then why have it in the arena? Surely they did not form an audience every time one of their number went topside!

We were not kept waiting long. Once the theater was filled, a Knight walked to the base of the ramp. He faced us and drew out a chain with a large metal key on it. Then he walked up the ramp, swinging the key, tramping around each curve until he was high above the floor, approaching the gate. He used the key on the lock of the gate, and the gate swung open. Then he pulled the gate closed, locked it, and walked back down the ramp. No question about it; this was our escape route. We would have to earn that key.

As the Knight reached the base of the ramp, he looped the chain about his armored neck. Then he walked to the far wall. A door opened, and an armored horse emerged. The Knight went to this steed, mounted, and took up a long, sharp lance.

"But what about our swords?" Threnody asked nervously.

The Knight spurred his steed, who charged forward. The monstrous lance descended to point at us.

"I think the cowfolk got the wrong information about that!" I cried. I had kept a human tongue in my cowhead so I could talk readily.

"Or these honorable Knights have broken the agreement," Threnody said bitterly. "No wonder no cowboy has ever won this challenge!"

"But they're supposed to be nothing at all, without honor," I said. "Does this count as a breach of—"

We dived to either side as the mounted Knight charged through. The hooves of the steed barely missed us as it passed.

We scrambled to our feet as the Knight braked his steed, slowed, and turned. "We're lambs for the slaughter!" Threnody cried.

"You escape up the ramp while I distract him," I said, as the Knight started his next pass.

"No good without the key!" she cried.

The Knight charged again. That sent us both diving over the ramp. We had better sidewise maneuverability than the Knight did, but sooner or later that terrible lance would skewer one of us.

Again we scrambled as the Knight slowed and turned. "We've got to get rid of that lance!" I exclaimed.

"Sure! *How?*"

"I'll drop on him from above," I said. "You distract him so I can—"

The Knight thundered at us again. Threnody ran away to the side, while I raced up the ramp. With diverging targets, the Knight had to choose one, and he went after Threnody. She ran and dodged with the fleetness of desperation and a powerful body. The Knight swerved to pursue her, and I got the feeling that this was what the knightly audience really wanted—the sport of the hunt. We were not opponents, we were fleeing prey. One victim would have been too easy to dispatch, but two was more of a challenge, so they set it up that way. To help provide the illusion that the prey might escape.

I considered that as I ran upward, rounding the first turn. For sport, the Knight would not slaughter us right away; he would play with us, making us react, and perhaps be applauded by the audience for an artistic performance. That might give us more leeway. He might even withhold his killing stroke if the points were wrong, waiting for the chance for a better score.

"Threnody!" I called. "Take off your dress!" For my body, which she was using now, still was wearing the brown dress I had donned at Threnody's house. It was soiled and torn, but represented a fair quantity of material.

"Huh?" she called out as she cut back, causing the Knight to overshoot her position. No points for him on

that pass! My well-coordinated body was proving to be
a boon to her as she learned how to use it.

"Take it off!" I repeated, still running. I was now head
height; soon I'd be high enough to be above the Knight.
"Use it to bait him with!"

"I don't understand!" she cried, ducking out of the way
again.

There was no time for a detailed explanation. Maybe
the mask-helmet Threnody wore prevented her from hearing exactly what I was saying. I would have to make a
demonstration.

I struggled out of my own dress as I ran; it was tight
on me anyway, in my larger size, despite the tucks I had
let out to accommodate my girth. Theoretically, the dress
should have expanded with me, and maybe it had, but
somehow my extra mass bulged more in proportion. I saw
the helmeted heads of the Knights in the audience turn
to follow me. Oops—I hadn't thought of that! I wore
nothing under the dress and I was one big girl now. My
anatomy bobbled all over as I ran. I had tried to keep the
proportions the same, but realized belatedly that I should
have slimmed them down; mass does make a difference,
so that the giant has to have different proportions from
the normal person in order to carry his weight conveniently. Now that the dress was off, I was really hanging
out.

Well, that couldn't be helped. I had to show Threnody
what I meant. "Like this in front of him!" I cried, holding
the dress so it formed a swatch of gray to the side. "Make
him charge it instead of you!"

Now she understood. She ripped off her brown dress,
and I saw the visors of the audience swivel to follow her.
It seemed the Knights got a voyeuristic thrill from seeing
people disrobe; evidently they never got out of their armor. Not in public, anyway. Strange folk!

Threnody stood naked and held the dress to the side,
forming a cape of it. The Knight, who perhaps did not
see too well from the saddle with his visor closed, aimed
his lance at the dress. Of course the point slid through it,
brushing it aside, and Threnody did not have to dive out

of the way. Well, she still had to step clear of the horse, but this was an improvement.

"Get him to pass under me!" I cried, stopping at a suitable elevation on the ramp.

Threnody tried. She ran under—but the Knight passed to the side, so I couldn't drop on him. However, we seemed to have a viable program.

The Knight turned and came back—and this time he was on target. As he passed under me, I dropped on him, landing just in front of him on the horse. I could have sworn his visor slits widened as my bare anatomy came up against his faceplate. But my ample posterior was crushing down his arms and lance, interfering with his action. He could hardly have been pleased.

I grabbed the chain around his neck and ripped it off. I had the key! Then I realized that I had a pretty good position here and I tried to haul him off his horse with me. I squirmed around, attempting to pin his arms to his sides, but he turned out to be very strong, and I had only woman's muscles. His hands came up, letting go of the lance, and grasped me with horrible force. In a moment he heaved me from the horse.

I landed partly on my feet, but without balance, and sat down hard. I had a lot of padding in that region, but that landing smarted! It was as if I had been spanked by a giant.

However, I had a victory of sorts, for not only did I have the chain with the key, I had caused the Knight to drop his lance. Threnody was hurrying to pick it up.

"Go up and unlock the gate!" she cried. "I'll fend him off here!"

"You don't know how to use that thing," I pointed out. "He'll wipe you out with his sword!" Indeed, the Knight was already drawing his great blade. It was dusky black, and reminded me ominously of the evil sword Magician Yang had sent against me.

"But you don't have the muscle for this!" she responded. And she had a point; that lance was one heavy pole. I could see why the Knight was strong; he had to be, to carry his weapons.

Now the Knight charged us both, the terrible sword gleaming wickedly. We both wrestled with the lance, heaving it up—but we were at the end, and the point was at the other end, far distant, and by the time we managed to lift that point, the Knight was upon us. His sword slashed down and lopped off the point of the lance. Again we had to dive out of the way, ignominiously.

"We've got to stop splitting up this way!" Threnody gasped as we got up on either side of the fallen lance.

"We can still use this," I said, picking up the severed point, which was about half my body length. It was a sword of a sort. "You get the other part."

She picked it up, finding it more manageable now that it was shorter. The Knight had unwittingly done us a favor. He had helped arm us.

As the Knight charged this time, we attacked him from either side, swinging our sticks at him. He merely lifted his shield to fend me off on the left and slashed down at Threnody's arms on the right. She jerked back, but the sword cut off her left hand. It plopped to the floor, fingers curling spastically.

"Damn you!" she cried as the Knight turned for the next charge, a smear of blood on his blade. She jammed the stump of her wrist into her own side to stop the blood from spurting out, but already that flow was abating as my healing talent manifested. She stooped to pick up the fallen hand. Then, as the Knight advanced, she hurled that hand at his head.

The Knight was one tough fighter, but this startled him. The hand clutched at his visor, one finger poking into an eye-slit. It looked like a distorted spider trying to get inside the helmet. It couldn't get inside, of course. The Knight should have known the separated hand was harmless, but he reacted with remarkable vigor. He halted his steed and grabbed for the hand with his left gauntlet.

I took advantage of his distraction to leap up and spread my gray dress over the entire helmet. I clung, forming a hood of gray material, so that he was blinded. "Get his sword!" I cried.

But already that arm and sword were thrashing about,

and Threnody could not get close. So I grabbed for the sword arm myself. My leverage was bad, and when I let go of the hood, it started to slide off. The Knight got a glove up and shoved me violently away, so that I fell on my sore bare bottom again. The dress slid down. Now the Knight could see again and he retained his weapon.

However, Threnody saved the moment. Unable to get near the Knight, she went for the horse. She got her mouth close to an armored ear and yelled, "Booo!"

The horse spooked, naturally enough. It neighed and reared. The Knight fell off and clanked to the floor. Threnody scrambled to fling herself on the extended sword arm, pinning it to the floor, while I made a flying leap for the head.

My weight knocked the helmet from the armored body. It squirted out from under my feet and rolled across the floor. Simultaneously, the body went dead. Threnody was able to wrench the sword away from the abruptly flaccid gauntlet.

I peered into the neck of the armor—and there was nothing. I looked at the separated helmet. It, too, was empty!

There was nothing in this suit of armor. Nothing at all.

Threnody looked at me. "Empty armor?" she asked, bewildered. "But it fought us!"

"It fought without honor," I said. "We were unarmed. Without honor, the Knights are nothing at all."

"Then what about all the others, who permitted it?"

We looked out at the audience. Now each Knight there reached up a gauntlet to open his visor. Inside each helmet—was nothing.

"They're all empty!" I breathed. "The Knights are all bodiless!"

"No wonder they never removed their armor," Threnody said. "Without their armor—" She paused to look at me, realizing the significance of my statement about honor. "They're nothing!"

"Let's get out of here before they decide to do something dishonorable!" I said.

She looked around. "That horse," she said.

"What about it?"

"It looks familiar."

"It's buried in armor, just like the Knights," I protested. "It's probably empty too."

"No, its hooves show. It's a real horse."

I walked over to it. The armored horse stood still, waiting for its rider to return. I saw there were metal straps holding its armor together. I unbuckled one at the neck, so as to uncover the head.

Underneath was a real horsehead, no phantom. "What's a live horse doing in a place like this?" I asked.

Threnody, one-handed, removed a portion of the body armor. "It's a ghost horse!" she exclaimed.

Sure enough, there were the chains wrapped about the barrel. "A ghost horse, serving armored ghosts!" I said.

"We killed its master," she pointed out. "We're entitled to what the Knight had, anything of it we want. The spoils."

"We'll keep the sword," I said. "As for the horse— we can free it."

"Free *her*," Threnody said, unbuckling more armor. "She's a mare."

"A knight-mare," I said, realizing the manner in which this made sense. "Let's ride her up the ramp and out— and let her go on the surface."

"Agreed. We owe her that. We won the match when she spooked."

And Threnody had been the one to think of that ploy. I would remember that.

We got the rest of the armor off while the assembled Knights watched emptily, evincing no emotion. It seemed they did honor the rest of their deal. We had won; we were free. And there would be no more cowfolk sacrifices, and the grazing range would be expanded. We had done our part for the creatures who had helped us. That pleased me.

I mounted the ghost mare. "Don't forget my hand," I reminded Threnody.

She picked up the fallen hand and stuck it to her wrist, which had stopped bleeding and started to heal over. At first she placed it backward, but she corrected that immediately. "I'll walk," she decided. "I can't ride while holding this together."

"It won't take long to re-attach, but it will be weak for an hour or so," I advised her.

So I guided the mare up the ramp, carefully, while Threnody walked behind, holding my hand. The walk became slightly nervous business at the height, but the knight-mare was sure-footed, and we reached the gate without misstep. That was just as well. The assembled Knights watched us with their empty faces, still making no move to stop us.

"Those hollow men are eerie," Threnody muttered.

I dismounted and took the key to the lock. It worked, and the gate swung open. We moved through, then I returned to lock the gate behind us. I flung the key through, so that it dropped to the arena below; after all, it belonged to the Knights, and we had no intention of returning.

We stood in a pleasant, open forest of mixed types of trees—beeches, sandalwoods, and other shore types, which indicated there was a lake nearby. There were a number of fruit and nut trees. We could travel through this very comfortably.

"Well, ghost horse," I said. "You're on your own now."

The mare looked at me. She rattled her chains inquiringly.

"You're free," I said. "Go romp through the wilderness."

She just stood there and gazed at me from beneath long equine lashes. She had lovely dark eyes, even for a horse, though her coat was light.

"She doesn't understand," Threnody said, wiggling the fingers of her left hand, which was now firmly attached and improving rapidly. Then she removed her bovine mask.

"Nonsense!" I said. "Pook understands every word I say. I'm sure Peek does, too."

"Peek?"

"Look at her eyes!"

Indeed, the mare was peeking soulfully at us. Whoever says animals don't have souls is crazy.

"She's peeking," Threnody agreed. "Maybe she does

understand. But she may be tame. She could have been raised in captivity by the Knights; she's a knight-mare."

"You know, Pook could still be waiting for us among the artis-trees," I said, realizing. "Peek's a ghost mare. Do you think—?"

"You women are always matchmaking!" she said.

"And you men are always trying to avoid commitment!" I retorted. Then we both laughed, to the mare's confusion.

So we decided to take Peek back to the artis-forest to meet Pook. After that, it would be up to them. If Peek was nervous about going out alone, Pook could guide her.

I reduced myself to normal size, returned my head to human, and dissipated my extra mass. Peek watched all this with equine astonishment. Then we found a toga tree that enabled us to cover our immodesty with togas. I took a blue one, and Threnody a red one. Peek shook her head, knowing we had the colors reversed; even animals knew that blue was for boys and red for girls. I patted her neck. "It's complicated to explain," I said.

I rode Peek north, while Threnody walked; her big barbarian body could keep the pace much better than my feminine one could. Soon we reached the dead tree—and there was Pook, faithfully waiting. He gave a glad neigh as he spied us—then did a double take as he spied Peek.

I introduced them. "Pook, this is Peek. She helped us escape the underworld. Peek, this is Pook, my friend."

The two ghost horses sniffed noses cautiously. They rattled their chains, making a kind of music together. They decided they liked each other.

"If only it were that easy for human folk," Threnody said somewhat wistfully.

"If you two want to trot elsewhere, you're welcome," I told Pook. "Peek's not sure she's ready for the wilderness, but you can show her."

The two nickered at each other and decided to stay. "Does that mean we can both ride?" I asked, pleased. It turned out that it did.

So I took Pook and Threnody rode Peek, and we bore

south. In the evening we stopped and foraged and grazed, as the case might be. "Hey, look at this!" Threnody called.

I went over. It was a bush covered with bright disks of glass, each disk slightly curved. They were too small for mirrors. I picked a disk and held it to my right eye to see it better—and it jumped out of my hand and plunked itself against my eyeball. Startled, I stepped back, but the glass hadn't harmed me; it just covered the front of my eyeball so that I had to look through it. The surprising thing was that my vision seemed clearer through that eye than through the other. The focus was sharper and the colors better defined. "It's a vision-improver!" I exclaimed.

"Oh, I've heard of them," she said. "They're called contact lenses, because they make close contact. When your sight gets old and fuzzy, you wear a couple of these and they bring it up to snuff. We'll have to remember where this optical bush is; it's valuable."

I pried the lens off my eyeball. "I guess it's all right, but I don't need it."

Threnody peered over the bush. "What's that on the other side?" she asked.

I walked around the bush toward it, Threnody close on my heels. "Some sort of doll or figurine—"

The black doll flashed. And suddenly I was drifting out of my body, hovering and homing in on the brute, barbarian body beside me. I dropped into it, dizzy.

"The evil spell!" I cried with big, crude lips. "It was set here to intercept us—but we're already exchanged, so it just switched us back!"

Threnody patted herself, making sure. "So it did," she said, pleased. Then she looked at me. "Now we don't need each other any more."

I felt a sinking sensation. "You mean you're going to start running again?"

She considered. "You know, if I rode Peek, I could probably get home all right."

During our underground odyssey, I had tended to forget that we were enemies. Now I perceived the kind of trap this could be. I acted instantly, my barbarian reflexes

serving me well. "Pook! Peek!" I cried, running toward
the grazing horses. My big male muscles gave me more
speed than Threnody had now. "We've changed back!
Don't do anything Threnody says!"

Pook looked at me uncertainly, and it was evident that
Peek had no notion what I was talking about. "Remember
how we met," I said to Pook. "How you tried to scare
me at night, and I circled around you and you thought I
was still at my camp, and—"

Pook interrupted me with a neigh. He understood.

"Well, as long as we were in the wrong bodies, Threnody and I couldn't separate," I said. "We had to cooperate, just to survive. But now we're back in our own
bodies, and she can flee me. She wants to ride Peek back
to her home. Don't take us anywhere but south, toward
Castle Roogna. Can you tell Peek that, so she understands?"

Pook nodded. He would take care of it.

I relaxed. I had acted in time. I still did have my mission
to complete, after all.

Threnody came up behind me. "Well, you certainly
fixed that, barbarian!" she said severely. "You don't trust
me at all, do you!"

"Barbarians are ignorant, not stupid," I replied, stung.

It was getting dark now. She accompanied me to the
fern bed we had fashioned in the radiating branches of a
treehouse tree. "You will want to hold onto me again, to
be sure I don't flee in the night."

"I don't—"

"You can't afford to trust me, but I trust you." And
she curled up next to me, ready for sleep.

Somehow I didn't feel at ease, but I didn't seem to
have much choice in the matter, so I comported myself
for sleep.

This night was cooler than the others had been. "I've
gotten used to your larger mass," Threnody murmured.
"I'm cold in this little body."

"You can make it bigger," I reminded her.

"That takes too long."

"You can have my cloak," I offered, removing my red

toga and spreading it out. Now its color was wrong, as it was truly being used by a male; I'd fetch another in the morning.

"We'll share," she decided. She removed her own garment, arranged the two togas as blankets, and nestled right up next to me.

I lay stiffly awake for some time, wondering exactly how smart I was. Did I even *want* to deliver her to Castle Roogna now, so another man could marry her? Naturally I had no interest in her myself . . . or *did* I? Why did things have to be so complicated with human beings? Why couldn't we, as Threnody had remarked, just sniff noses, rattle chains, and be satisfied?

Yet if we were not what we were, creatures with at least the awareness of purpose and honor, what would we be? Empty knights in armor, seeming so strong on the outside, yet hollow inside? Who was I to deny the human condition, with all its problems of awareness?

"If I weren't on a mission, you wouldn't be safe a moment!" I muttered at her soft, warm, shapely, breathing, sleeping body.

"I know," she whispered, stretched electrically against me, and returned to sleep.

A pox on women!

Chapter 14. Idiocy

In the morning we donned new togas of the correct colors, foraged for more food, mounted, and rode south again. I knew we were getting reasonably close to Castle Roogna. I would be sorry to have this mission end. I hoped Threnody would never know how close she had come to diverting me from it. But if she had had occasion

to comprehend the male viewpoint, I had similarly experienced the female position. I knew her body well; I
had been in it, literally. I refused to take advantage of it.

Peek grew nervous as we progressed, and finally balked.
I was riding Pook, and we stopped beside her. "What's
the matter with her?" I asked, concerned. She was such
a nice horse, and had been quite docile till now.

Pook whinnied at her, then listened to her reply. He
tensed. "Some danger ahead?" I asked. "She knows this
region?"

"A monster?" Threnody asked. "I can change form
until she indicates that it matches whatever monster she's
thinking of. That way we can identify it precisely."

"At an hour a change?" I asked. "That could take forever!"

"Do you have a better way?"

"Yes." And I proceeded to name monsters for the
horses. Quickly we eliminated Dragon, Griffin, Sphinx,
Tarasque, Goblin, Callicantzari, Sea Monster, and Harpy.
I was beginning to fish for other notions, when Threnody
put in one.

"Basilisk," she said.

Peek nodded emphatically.

Further questioning turned up the news that it wasn't
just one basilisk, whose gaze would kill people; it was a
whole colony of them. This was, in fact, the Land of the
Basks, where cockatrices, henatrices, and chickatrices
congregated for regular staring tournaments. This was no
safe region for any other creature.

"But we have to pass it to reach Castle Roogna!" I
said. "Can we circle around the bask territory?"

It turned out that we couldn't; the mountains and sands
combined to make this the only feasible route south. But
there was a way to pass through it; at night the basks
slept, and if the two horses galloped through then, they
could clear the region by daybreak. Then it would be an
easy ride to Castle Roogna.

"Good," I said, relieved. "We'll rest here, then set off
at nightfall."

I set off foraging again, as this body liked to eat well.

I spied a spaghetti tree with the edible strands hanging down in tempting masses.

I grabbed a hank—and discovered hanging behind it a black eye-queue vine. "Oops," I said, drawing hastily away.

But of course, I couldn't escape it. The vine flashed—and suddenly I was so stupid I could hardly figure out what I was doing.

I stumbled back to the camp, dragging the hank of spaghetti strands behind me. "What's the matter, Jordan?" Threnody asked, perceiving that something was wrong.

"Duh," I replied.

"What?"

"Duh," I repeated firmly.

I was stupid, but she was not. "Those bad spells—you mentioned one for idiocy! Did that one strike?"

I nodded stupidly.

Had I been smarter, I could have anticipated her thought processes. But I was dull. In fact, I was about as unintelligent as a barbarian gets, which is pretty un.

"I think," she said slowly, "that, considering your condition, it is now too dangerous to proceed south through bask territory. One of those cocks or hens might wake up and wipe us all out. Don't you agree, Jordan?"

"Yuh," I said, happy to go along with superior reasoning.

Pook's ears flattened back. He was not stupid and he was not going to go along! Peek stood with him, following his lead.

"I think we should go north instead," Threnody continued carefully. "It is so much safer traveling a familiar route."

"Yuh," I agreed. It was a good thing she was still smart.

"Then we can go around to the north, and avoid both the basks and the sands, and reach Castle Roogna safely," she said. "This will take a little longer, but it's so much more certain. Don't you agree, Jordan?"

"Yuh," I agreed again. It was so nice of her to consult

me like this! Something nagged at my sodden brain, but I couldn't quite figure out what it was, so ignored it.

"We'll rest here tonight, and I'll take good care of you, and in the morning you'll just tell the horses to carry us north, won't you?" she asked persuasively.

"Yuh."

Pook looked ready to kick someone, maybe me. I couldn't think why.

"Because that business about going south no-matter-what doesn't apply any more, does it? You know better now."

"Yuh," I said, a little uncertainly.

She smiled. She was awfully pretty when she did that. "You've been struck by the idiocy spell, so I realize it's a little hard for you to figure out right now. But we'll sleep on it, and I'm sure you'll be satisfied by morning."

Pook snorted with absolute disgust and stomped away. I heard him neighing something to Peek. They were trying to figure out what to do. Evidently Pook didn't want to listen to what I would be telling him in the morning. Strange animal!

Then Threnody took me by the hand and led me to our niche for the night, and she was so lovely that I knew she must be right.

We settled down in that bower, and she arranged the togas over us as blankets, and crooned a lovely little melody, and got very close to me. She was all sleek and soft and warm, the shape of man's desire. "In fact, I have an even better idea," she murmured in my ear, her breath like a playful summer breezelet, ticklish and nice. "Let's go back to my house together."

"Huh?" I asked, perplexed.

"You don't really want to turn me over to some Magician at Castle Roogna, do you?" she urged convincingly.

I didn't follow all her reasoning, but her bare body was so smooth and special against mine, and I realized how nice it would be to do whatever she had in mind. Some things do not require a great deal of intelligence. "Nuh," I agreed.

She moved against me, and I hugged her to me, beginning to get a glimmer of what we could—

Then there was a fluttering in the forest, and something white showed. It came right up to us—a big, long-billed bird. In fact, it was a stork.

"A stork!" Threnody exclaimed, shaken. She drew away from me as if I had become a monster. "I hadn't thought of that!"

I reached for her again, but for some reason the sight of the stork had turned her off, and she shrank away from me. Women can be very funny about irrelevant things.

The stork landed beside us and closed its wings. "I'm looking for Jordan the Barbarian," it said.

"For *him*?" Threnody squeaked. "You birds never bring your bundles to *men*!" Then she turned thoughtful. "Though it might be a good thing if you did. After all, fair is fair."

The stork ignored her. Bureaucratic creatures seldom concern themselves with fairness. It turned to me. "Jordan?"

"Yuh," I answered.

"I am investigating a recent event. It seems that one of our number was lost during a mission, and we are uncertain whether his bundle was properly delivered. You have been implicated. Do you care to testify?"

Something about that last word sounded dirty to me. "To what?"

"To clarify what happened just north of the—wherever it was."

Oh. I was stupid, but I remembered the episode. "Ogre," I said.

The stork lifted a free feather and perused its lines closely. "Yes, that was an Oct-ogre delivery. What happened to the stork?"

"Dragon," I said. "Chomp. Injured wing—no fly more."

The bird used the tip of his bill to make a mark on the feather. "That corroborates what we concluded. What happened to the bundle?"

I concentrated, and some of my wit returned. "Delivered," I said.

The stork elevated one eyebrow. I hadn't realized before then that they had eyebrows. "*You* delivered it?"

"Yuh. Ogret."

He made another note on the feather. "Highly irregular!"

"I'll say!" Threnody put in. "Whoever heard of a man delivering a baby!"

"Had to be done," I said defensively.

The stork put away his feather. "To be sure. And what was the fate of the injured stork?"

"Eaten," I said.

The bird straightened up and half spread his wings. "You *what*?"

"Not me. 'Nother dragon."

"Oh." The stork relaxed, making another note. "Unable to fly, fell prey to dragon." He glanced up. "It is, after all, hazardous duty. We get flight pay. Just so long as the bundle was safely delivered."

"Yuh."

"Thank you. That will be all." The stork spread his wings, then paused. "It is our policy to reward those who render useful service. Would you like a—"

"No!" Threnody cried, alarmed.

The stork made another note. "Reward of lucky feather declined," he muttered, speaking to himself. Then he spread his wings again and took off.

"You cost me lucky feather!" I accused Threnody.

She ignored this. "You are on intimate terms with storks?" she demanded.

"Yuh." It was too complicated to explain in detail. "Now you." I reached for her.

She jerked away. "Don't you touch me!" she screeched.

"Huh?"

"Not while there are storks in the neighborhood!"

I didn't grasp her objection, but did grasp that she had changed her mind. Disappointed, I lay back. Women can be awfully hard to understand!

In the morning the horses were gone. Pook had left the bag with the remaining spells, so I knew he wasn't coming back. Stupid as I was, I still understood why: because he knew I was going to ask him and Peek to take us north. I couldn't figure out why it was so bad to go north, since Threnody had explained the reason so sensibly. But Pook wouldn't go that way, so he had left. Therefore we couldn't go north, either. He had been free to leave us anytime, but had chosen this time because of our irreconcilable difference of opinion about direction. I was really sorry to lose him, yet couldn't blame him. Sometimes the best thing a friend can do is to refuse to help a friend-gone-wrong. Not that I had gone wrong, but—well, anyway, it was too bad.

Then I had a notion. "Spells!" I exclaimed.

"But they don't work right," Threnody said, evidently nervous about another foul-up like the exchange of identities.

"Maybe help anyway," I said with foolish eagerness. I pawed through the mostly empty bag and fished out the little white skull. "Life!" I said.

"Life? You mean it—it restores someone who has died? You don't need that."

I wasn't smart, but my memory remained good. "Mixed up. This not life."

"Oh—you mean it has to be some other spell—one that may help us travel?"

"Yuh." Then, before I could become confused, I said: "Invoke."

The skull glowed—and expanded. A ridge appeared that circled around the staring face. This projected out until it formed a full-sized shield, while the face flattened into a picture of itself on the surface of that shield. The back of the skull became the apparatus by which the shield could be comfortably supported on the left arm.

"Say!" I exclaimed, pleased. "Nice shield!"

"If we had needed a shield," Threnody said curtly, "we could have taken the Knight's shield. How does this help us travel?"

But I remained delighted with this acquisition. I had never had a shield of my own before, because barbarians are too primitive to understand a shield's proper use.

However, my experiences with flame-shooting dragons and lance-bearing Knights had provided me with an inkling. Sometimes defense was a good thing, even for a barbarian. Or so I supposed, now that I was stupid.

I put the shield on my arm and postured with it, slicing the air with my sword. We now had two swords, since we had recovered my own from near the dead tree, as well as saving the Knight's. "Take that!" I exclaimed, striking at an imaginary foe. "And that!" Then I lifted the shield, as if warding off an enemy blow. "Nyaa! Nyaa! You can't get me!"

"Some toy!" Threnody muttered, disgusted. Women don't understand about war games. But they sure are fun for the young-of-brain.

In due course I settled down, and we came to grips with the problem of traveling. "I suppose we'll have to walk," Threnody said, unthrilled. "But it will take us a couple of days, and I'll be footsore. *Damn* those horses!"

"Yuh," I agreed amicably.

She focused on me. "You won't stay stupid forever," she said. "These spells wear off after a few days, don't they?"

"Yuh," I said. "Some do."

"A man does have his uses," she said to herself. "As long as I'm single, I'm vulnerable on one level or another. The only way to finish this nuisance for good is to marry an amiable man, not too bright . . ." Then she looked up, as if becoming aware of me. "Very well—I'll carry you. At least that will get us there."

"Huh?"

"I'll change into a dollarpede," she decided. "That's a hundred times the size of a centipede, but not vicious like the nickel or dimepedes, because it doesn't have any metal pincers. A dollarpede has no metal backbone, so it has been losing strength for decades. It's a helpless form, subject to the whims of whoever handles it; you'll have to protect me with your sword and shield."

"Helpless?"

"Dollarpedes just seem to keep getting devalued by everything else they encounter," she said. "Until finally they look as big as ever, but they're hardly worth anything at all. Maybe that's because they're made mostly of paper."

"Paper?" I was stupid, but even to me that sounded funny.

"Some of them have silver support," she said. "Those ones are stronger, but they're very rare. I'll become one of that kind."

"Yuh," I agreed, reassured.

Of course it took time. First she changed her form, after cautioning me to keep a sharp eye out for predators, as she was most vulnerable while changing. "Everybody grabs for dollarpedes!" Had I been smarter, I would have realized that that was the main reason she needed me right now. If she had been able to change safely when alone in the jungle, she could have deserted me and headed directly for home. So she had to take me along. My brain wasn't worth much now, but my body and sword and shield were. But of course she didn't tell me that; she told me she liked me and wanted my companionship. It's an old ploy women use on men. And I, being stupid, believed her.

Though even now I wonder what she could have meant by that remark about marrying an amiable, not-too-bright man. Certainly she didn't mean Magician Yin, and events were to prove that she didn't mean me. But as I have said, even when I have been smart, I haven't really understood women.

In an hour she was in the form of the dollarpede, with the mass of a person. Then she worked on her size, expanding up to a creature so large it could carry me—except that she was now too diffuse to support my weight, since her mass had not changed. In the third hour she increased her mass, until finally there she stood before me complete—a creature with fifty pairs of legs, dull green in hue on one side, gray on the other, with all sorts of print and numbers on it. The face was gray and looked a little like that of a sphinx, while the backside resembled a bird waxing amorous with a shield. Overall, the thing did seem sort of papery, with corrugations supporting each set of legs, but the silver backbone gave it strength to support me.

I mounted, and stacked the spell-bag and extra sword behind me. This was the strangest creature I had ridden—but of course, most of my prior experience had been with Pook. If this dollarpede could do the job, all right.

The creature started moving. This was interesting. First the number one set of legs stepped forward, quickly followed by the number two set, followed in turn by number three, and so on down the line in a ripple. There was a gentle sway as the ripple passed under me and proceeded to the tail. Then it bounced back and swayed me forward. It was a little like riding an ocean swell—which was an interesting thought, since I had never been to the ocean, swell or awful.

Threnody-dollarpede flowed over the irregularities in the landscape, picking up speed. Soon she was traveling as fast as a galloping ghost horse, and I was feeling seasick from all the swaying. But we were making excellent time!

Around noon a shadow descended. I looked up and saw a great bird circling. It was a roc and it looked hungry—and the dollarpede was about the right size for a snack. "Get under cover!" I cried, needing no special intelligence to recognize danger like this.

Threnody scooted for a nearby fallen tree, hoping to conceal herself under it. I dismounted, drew my sword, and held my shield firmly before me. I stood beside the fallen tree, facing out, while Threnody tried to get her length squeezed under it.

But it seemed that a dollarpede was very hard to hide from an alert predator. The roc quickly corrected course and descended. Phew! Those birds are huge! I keep forgetting how big they are, until I encounter another. The giant wings covered all the sky, and the monstrous talons came toward me like—like a roc's talons. There *isn't* anything else to compare them to!

I had fought a roc before and knew we were overmatched. But a barbarian warrior doesn't question the odds, he just fights on. Especially when he's stupid. So as that foot came at me, I held up my shield and swung with my sword.

My sword connected, cutting off the end of the claw. Blood gushed out, and a few seconds later, when the sensation reached the roc's head, there was an ear-dazzling squawk that shook the clouds in their orbits.

Now I had the roc's attention—and a baleful attention it was! The foot retreated, one claw snagging in a small palm-tree and ripping it out, fingers, toes, and all. The bird's head came down, the eyes peering at me. The beak pecked at me, and it was the size of the snout of a good-sized dragon. I was finished now!

But my shield came up and blocked the beak. I thought the impact of the beak against the shield would break my arm and knock me over and maybe drive the shield deep into the ground, but there was no recoil at all. Odd!

The roc squawked again, and such was the blast of air that the nearby saplings bent and their sap squirted out, and the fallen tree rolled a turn or two back, exposing the dollarpede. The roc peered at me again, straight down from above, and I knew I would be squished like a bug and perhaps spitted on bedrock below. There was fire in those little roc orbs!

My shield came up once more, and this time I knew I wasn't doing it. The thing was shifting itself, hauling my arm along with it! It stopped over my head, horizontal, blocking that plummeting beak.

The beak struck with a colossal clang—and I felt no shock. But the bird bounced off as if rejected by a stone mountain, its beak dented.

I was slow-witted, but now at last the truth managed to wedge itself through my brain—this was the magic of the shield! It was intended to combat the magic sword, but it wasn't smart enough to distinguish between types of attack, so it fended off whatever came at it. Self-powered, it absorbed the full thrust, transmitting no shock to me. As long as I held this shield, I could not be successfully attacked!

The big bird, its beak bashed, came to a similar conclusion. It backed off, spread its wings, and launched itself into the air. The downdraft flattened the nearby bushes and tore a branch from an acorn tree; the branch thudded into the ground and acorns peppered us like hailstones. But my shield protected me against those, too.

Threnody crawled out, somewhat bedraggled; her papery body did not stand up well to such high winds, and I dreaded to think what rain might do to it. She was unable to speak in this form, but I was sure she was pleased not to have been gobbled by the roc. I remounted, and we proceeded on north.

We stopped in midafternoon, back at the copse of artis-trees. Perhaps it was fitting that I brought the magic shield back here to where the magic sword had attacked me. Still, as my stupidity gradually abated—maybe my talent was healing my brain of this malady, too—I became increasingly uneasy about the direction of our travel. Castle Roogna, after all, was the opposite way.

It took Threnody three hours to change back to her normal form. First she went diffuse, then she sank to human size, and finally she changed to human shape. "I'm famished!" she exclaimed.

"Why not eat in dollarpede form?" I asked, concentrating so as to formulate my question properly, as it was hard to handle full sentences in my present state of mind. "Why so much trouble to change back?"

"My, you are improving!" she remarked, not entirely pleased. "You're not half as stupid as you were last night."

"I know," I agreed, dully satisfied. She certainly was pretty in this form. Had I been smarter, it might have occurred to me that, since she could control her form, she naturally made sure it was a good form. What woman, given the opportunity to make herself more attractive, would fail to exercise that power?

"I will answer your question," she said. "If I remained in dollarpede form and mass, I would have to feed that mass—and that would require a lot more food than my natural body does. Also, dollarpedes feed on things like Principal and Interest and Assets and Liabilities and Budgets; since there aren't any of those around here, this one would have to make do with bugs and moldy twigs and things, and I don't happen to like such food much. So I change back to human form so I can eat human food, which I do prefer."

I didn't know what an Asset was, but I could see why she wouldn't want to eat one. "But—"

"But how can a human meal feed the mass of a dollarpede? Because I only have to feed the form I'm in when eating. If I shrank to gnat size, I could feed myself on a gnat meal, then return to human size and not be hungry. But that would take three more hours, and I'd be vulnerable all the time. Any bird could come by and swallow me when I was in gnat form, and that would be the end of me. So I don't like to go to the small sizes, and my own form seems to be the best compromise."

All that was a bit more explanation than I could assimilate at my present level of intelligence; I merely smiled and nodded acquiescently. It was evident that Threnody did know what she was doing. Besides, why should I question such an excruciatingly beautiful woman? So what if she had used her talent to reshape herself? It was a lovely shaping.

She hardly had to work at fooling me; I was eager to fool myself!

So we foraged and ate, then removed ourselves from the immediate vicinity of the dead tree with the gnomes' entrance and made camp for the night. Once again Threnody cuddled up to me, after glancing around to make sure there was no stork nearby.

"Uh," I said, trying to organize my thought. "We should go south—"

"There is another reason to go north," she said quickly. It was almost as if she had expected me to remember my mission, and have a second thought about our direction of travel, as my intelligence increased. "You said the enemy spells have been placed along your route, so that when you go where you're going, you walk into them."

"Yes," I agreed. She had a good grasp of the situation.

"And most of those evil spells are a whole lot of trouble," she continued. "Like the black sword, and the personality exchange—I realize that was the good spell that hit us, but it was the same as the evil spell—and the idiocy."

"Yes."

"Well, if you don't go where you're going, you won't encounter the spells laid out along your route, will you?"

"Huh?"

"If we go to Castle Roogna, straight south, the next spell is sitting there somewhere in our path, waiting for you to meet it. Probably in the middle of the bask territory, so we'll *really* be in trouble. But if you don't go there, you won't walk into that spell. That makes this a better route, doesn't it?"

"Say, yes," I agreed, brightening. I was still too dull to figure out the predestination angle. "But how do we get to Castle Roogna, going north?"

She smiled in the dusk. "We go around the quicksand desert to the north, then turn south and proceed without further trouble."

"That's nice," I said, reassured.

"Still," she added, as if musingly, "it would be just as easy to turn west and return to my house. Then you and I could stay together forever."

It seemed to me that she had said something like that the night before, but we had been interrupted by the stork. Tonight I was a trifle smarter. "But what about my mission?" I asked.

"Let me show you how it can be with us," she said. "Then you can decide about the mission."

"Well, uh—" I said uncertainly, torn between loyalty and her beauty.

She wriggled, and her bare body came up against mine. She put her lovely face to mine for a kiss. The consciousness of my mission faded. I enfolded her in my arms and—

There was a noise.

Threnody stiffened. "Someone's near!" she whispered, alarmed.

I felt for my sword and shield in the darkness. In a moment I located the direction; the sound was in the area of the gnome-tree. "The Gnobody Gnomes," I whispered. "Out hunting."

"I've seen enough of them to last me a lifetime!" she said.

"I'll go out and slay them. With my sword and shield, in my own body, it will be easy."

"Don't be stupid. That won't—"

"But I *am* stupid!" I protested.

She chuckled. "So you are, at the moment. But trust me, Jordan; we don't need to attack the gnomes. They're only out foraging for food and supplies, not looking for us, and they're not such bad folk. If we kill the men, the gnomides will suffer. All we have to do is lie quiet, and they'll pass us by."

We lay quiet, though I wondered how folk who put strangers in the smoking pot could be considered "not bad," but I was not smart enough to figure that out. So I was still, and she was right; the gnomes moved on by and never knew we were there. But we had to bide some time, and in due course I fell asleep. Whatever it was that Threnody might have had in mind did not come to pass between us that night. The gnomes had saved me from— what?

In the morning we ate again, Threnody converted to the dollarpede form, and we moved north. In the afternoon we came to a huge chasm that neither of us remembered. That was odd, because it was far too big to be ignored. We stopped, and Threnody changed while I foraged and ate and made a hut from stray timbers. In the sky to the south, we saw huge shapes wheeling; we knew that the rocs were angry and were searching for us.

"We can't stay here and we can't go south again," Threnody said. "You fought valiantly to save me from the big bird yesterday, and I am duly grateful, but if a whole flock of them comes upon us, we'll be finished."

"But where can we go?" I asked, bewildered.

"I will assume another form, one that can traverse that chasm," she said. "I'll start early, so I'll be ready by dawn, and will carry you with me. Only—"

"Yuh?" I asked.

"I'm not certain which way to go."

I was yet smarter than before. "To the east, so then we can go south to Castle Roogna."

She sighed. "Yes, of course. But I don't want to go to Castle Roogna; I want to go home—which means turning west."

"Oh," I said, disappointed. "Well, good-bye, then."

She settled down next to me in our shelter. "Jordan, I need you with me; the episode of the roc shows that. You're powerful and brave and you're a good guy—even when you're stupid. And I think you need me with you, too, for my talent complements yours. We must travel together, and I don't want to have an argument about the direction at the brink of that chasm, with the rocs closing in on us."

"Yes," I agreed. I could see how that would be awkward. And she was so absolutely beautiful in the waning light that I could not take my eyes off her.

"But you want to go to Castle Roogna, and I want to go home. We have a fundamental conflict."

"I must complete my mission," I said, realizing that it had been an error to say good-bye to her; I couldn't let her go.

"Is there no way I can persuade you to come with me?" she asked.

But I was still stupid enough to hang onto my mission. "I must take you to Castle Roogna, or die in the attempt," I said. "Like the stork, I must deliver."

"Even though you can be with me forever, possessing all that I have to offer, if you come with me now?" she asked, nudging closer. "Even though you will lose me to Magician Yin if you take me to Castle Roogna, and the castle itself will fall?"

I felt miserable and every bit as stupid as I was. "Yes."

"You are too damn incorruptible for your own good, barbarian!"

"Yes."

She turned her face away for a moment. Then she turned back. "*You* are the man I want to marry, Jordan, not Magician Yin! You are bold and strong and honest and nice, while he is more devious than you can grasp. Please, please, come with me!"

Now she had spoken openly of marriage between us. Temptation took me like the wind from a storm. She was all that I ever wanted in a woman—or so I thought at the time—yet I could not see my way clear to do what she asked. I was no thief—not even of love. I did not answer.

"I will show you!" she said, almost savagely. She half-way flung herself on me, and hugged me to her, and kissed me and stroked me. I had occupied her body, and knew the difference in attitude between man and woman, but now she was as aggressive as a man.

And I, like the idiot I was, did not think to ask why, or to reflect on the unnaturalness of her attitude. Scarcely any woman flings herself on a man she doesn't plan to marry. But because I was stupid, and she had timed her effort with that stupidity in mind, I lacked the proper suspicion. I was overwhelmed by her urgency. I reacted as she intended me to and I knew that I loved her, absolutely and eternally, whatever else might come.

Greater folly has no man than this.

Early in the morning, before dawn, she woke me. "Jordan, I must begin my change," she said. "I love you. Do you love me?"

I was smarter than I had been—but that no longer mattered. "Yes," I said.

"Will you come with me?"

My heart felt as if it were cracking in two. "No."

"There is no way I can turn you from the course you have set?"

"No."

She sighed. "Then I must go with you, though it be disaster for us both."

So I had won. Why did I feel so miserable?

She proceeded to change, stage by stage, and three hours later, as dawn peeked shyly into the gloomy chasm, she was ready. She had become a giant snail, with a shell the size of a small house.

I climbed up on the shell, keeping the shield and the

two swords tied to me, and took firm hold of the corrugations. The bag with the few remaining spells dangled from my waist. Nothing could dislodge me—I hoped.

The snail crawled forward toward the chasm. It quested along the lip until it found a rounded part, then slid over that and down onto the face of the cliff itself.

Now I had to hold on tight! The depth of the chasm yawned beneath us awesomely; if I fell, I would be smashed to death on the rock below—and this time had no ghost horse to scrape up the pieces. If Threnody's sticky undersurface became unstuck, she, too, would fall—with no hope at all of revival. I could understand why she did not want any arguments about direction at this stage. I became nervous.

But her surface held, and we slid slowly down into the chasm and east along its face. If she had decided to turn about and go west, I could not have stopped her, but she had agreed to go east and she was doing it. I knew now that I had never had any chance to bring this creature to Castle Roogna without her acquiescence. She had used love to persuade me to go her way; instead it had persuaded her to go my way. Or so I believed then, in my idiocy.

I heard a noise and looked down. Far below, I saw a huge, six-legged dragon pacing us, evidently hoping we would fall. It was so eager for our flesh that puffs of steam drifted up from it.

Then I heard another noise and looked up—and saw a little roc. The big birds had found us at last!

The roc swooped down, and I knew doom was upon us, for even a little roc is a giant creature. I hated being helpless before this predator; I felt the way I had when I occupied Threnody's body and faced the griffin.

Something nagged the slow molasses of my brain. Didn't griffins and rocs have something in common? Some weakness, or at least some kind of finickiness? How had I stopped the griffin?

Desperation once again lent me a stupid kind of genius. "Yuck!" I cried, making a grotesque face. Rocs were big, but their eyesight and hearing were excellent. "This snail tastes awful. Gunky! Putrid! It's just a shell full of pus!"

It was a little roc; did it understand what I was saying? Would it be fooled? A mature one might be too canny, but . . .

The roc veered off, the wind from its wings almost tearing us off the wall. We clung, sliding down helplessly—and the bird departed. My ploy had worked! Some snails did taste bad, so maybe the roc had been ready to believe. Actually, those birds, being roc-headed, weren't the smartest creatures in Xanth. But a young roc surely tried eating anything that moved, at first, so had many bad experiences and would be eager to avoid more of them. Maybe this one *had* once gulped a shell full of pus.

Threnody managed to skid to a halt on the wall, then continued her slow slide to the east, and in due course she crossed over the lip of the chasm and onto level land. The quicksand was behind; now we could safely proceed south.

I let go of the shell, but my arms were locked into position from the long clutch and had to be unkinked joint by joint. Threnody was so tired she just slumped in her shell. But we had made it.

Ahead, had I but known, was the cruel lie.

Chapter 15. Cruel Lie

After a while Threnody changed back to her human form, looking somewhat wasted. I fetched her food and water, and she kissed me, and we rested there a time, just appreciating each other's company.

"A shell full of pus?" she asked wryly.

"Well, it worked," I said, embarrassed.

"I would never have forgiven you if it hadn't worked," she said. "Well, let's get moving again."

"But you are tired. Let me carry you, now. Change to something small."

She smiled. "I'll simply diffuse; that will take less time."

She did so. When she was smoky-thin, looking indeed like the demoness she derived from, she put her vaporous arms around me, and I marched south, carrying her along with me without effort. When a passing wyvern thought to take a bite of us, Threnody simply floated up and breathed, "Booo!" and the poor creature took off as if it had seen a ghost. I wasn't worried anyway; my sword and shield and stupidity—the "Three S's," as Threnody put it—made me practically invulnerable to attack. But it was true that our two talents complemented each other, making safe travel possible and easy. We were a good team.

We made excellent progress that day and camped for the night not far from Castle Roogna. Threnody densified, resuming her natural and lovely solidity, and embraced me. "This may be our last night together, Jordan," she said soberly.

"We must tell Magician Yin what we feel," I said. "Maybe he won't want to marry you then. Some men are very choosy about winning a lady's love for themselves."

"That thought had crossed my mind," she confessed. "When you deliver me there, Yin will win, and be the next King of Xanth, and surely he will be good for the land. But if he rejects me, and sends me away, the castle will not fall, and I can be yours. But—"

"But?" I asked. The plan seemed quite feasible to me.

"But there is also Yang," she said reluctantly. "Yang is evil. He cares nothing for anything decent, including the fact that I now belong to another man; he might choose to take me for that reason."

"But you don't want to go with Yang!" I protested.

"Jordan, I may not have much choice." She kissed me again, lingeringly. "You have seen the power of his spells. No ordinary person can stand against the power of a Magician, good or evil; that's why a Magician is always King.

If you bring me near Castle Roogna, but not all the way there, then Yang will win and be King, and he, more than Yin, may want the aspect of legitimacy conferred by marriage to the daughter of the prior King. Sometimes the least worthy folk crave legitimacy the most. I will no longer be able to threaten to throw myself into the—the—whatever; I will not be able to escape." She took me by the hand and gazed into my eyes. "But whatever happens, Jordan, remember that I love you."

"And I love you!" I said.

Then she began singing, in her low, sad way, and her voice was so eerily beautiful that it brought tears to my eyes. As I listened to her, it seemed that some terrible tragedy was in the offing. But I was too dull to grasp what that could be, or to wonder how she could know what was to come.

"I'm sorry I did not let you bring your lute," I told her.

She paused to put her fair hand on mine. "I forgive you, Jordan." There were tears in her eyes, too.

In the morning we set out for Castle Roogna on foot, as we were. It was not that far, and Threnody wanted there to be no doubt about her identity so that there could be no misunderstanding as to the success of my mission. We held hands, and it was a sad rather than a joyous occasion. But what could I do? A good barbarian always completes his mission.

We saw the highest spire of the old castle, poking above the trees to the south. Threnody paused to kiss me. "I love you, Jordan," she said again. I, total fool, believed her. Yet even now, seeing it in the picture of the tapestry, I find it hard to believe that she could have been false; everything about her signaled the sorrow of love about to be lost. Almost, I wish—but of course, I am not now the idiot I was then. Experience has been an exceedingly cruel teacher.

We came to the ring of gnarled old trees surrounding the castle. They still didn't like me. Branches descended to bar our progress. I drew my sword. "I told you before,

trees, that I'd lop off any branch opposing me," I said.
"I have to deliver this object to the castle, and that I shall
do. Now clear the way!"

But this time they did not yield the right of way. Angry,
I hacked at the branches, making good my threat, and
the afflicted trees groaned woodenly with the pain and
dripped colored sap, but still would not give over. They
were stupidly loyal to their perceived cause, as was I.

"They know," Threnody said. "They remember the
curse of my return. They don't care who is to be King of
Xanth; they merely protect the castle from ruin. Jordan,
believe me, only tragedy can come of this delivery."

"I promised to deliver you, and I will," I grunted, hacking away.

She shook her head with resignation. "If only your
loyalty were rightly fixed, what a hero you would be!"

I didn't know what she meant by that, so I ignored it.
Forcing a way through the trees took time, but I was
barbarianishly determined, and I cleared a channel through
the resistant forest. We emerged to the inner orchard,
with its marvelous array of fruits and nuts.

I was hungry after my exertion, so I reached for a big
red apple—and it jerked away. I blinked, then reached
for another—and it, too, avoided me.

"Now this is pushing it!" I snapped, not so dull as not
to realize I was being snubbed. "I'm going to have some
fruit, or do some cutting here!" I walked around the tree,
stalking the evasive fruit.

A cherry dropped near me from a neighboring cherry
tree. The thing exploded as it touched the ground, blasting
dirt at my legs. I jumped away—and almost collided with
a pineapple tree. "Look out!" Threnody cried.

A pineapple dropped, but I managed to reach out and
catch it and hurl it away before it detonated. The explosion shook the orchard, and fruits dropped all around us.
Several more cherries went off around me, but my shield
alertly blocked off the shrapnel of juice and cherry pits.
"They know," Threnody repeated.

I shook my sword at the cherry tree, but dared not try
to chop it down, because the cherries would have blown

me to bits. In Mundania it may be possible to chop down cherry trees, but not in Xanth. And as for pineapples— I have heard, but naturally do not believe, that they don't even grow on trees in Mundania; they supposedly grow directly from the ground, one pineapple to a plant. Ludicrous! Next thing we'll be expected to believe is that Mundane cherries and pineapples don't explode.

We went on to the plain surrounding the castle. There stood a truly motley assembly: dozens of zombies. Dirt sifted from their sodden shoulders, showing that they had recently disinterred themselves. Gobbets of rotten flesh festooned their spindly bones. Each skull stared out with maggoty sockets.

"The zombies rise when Castle Roogna is threatened," Threnody said. "They know that the moment I set foot in the castle, it will fall. I remember, when I was a girl, a rogue dragon came, and the zombies marched against it. The creature was covered with slime and rot before it gave up the attempt. Are you sure you want to—"

"I have a mission," I said sullenly. I may have mentioned the oinkheadedness of barbarians, particularly stupid ones. I drew my sword and held my magic shield high and marched into the awful throng.

The zombies were no cowards; I'll say that for them! They threw themselves on me as if not caring for their own lives at all. My shield moved about, fending them off, and my sword hacked off arms, legs, and heads with abandon. Pieces of zombie soon littered the landscape. Threnody had to use the almost empty bag of spells to shield herself from flying rot; for some reason, she didn't seem to like getting it in her hair or down her front or in her slippers. Women do tend to be fussy at times. Finally the last of the zombies had been cut to grotesque pieces, and the way was clear to the castle.

I took Threnody by the hand and led her onward. She remained reluctant, but did not resist.

We came to the moat. The drawbridge was up, and the moat monsters were on full alert, in contrast to their prior attitude. Well, I had fought monsters before.

I needed to get that drawbridge lowered so Threnody

could cross. I wasn't going to drag her through the moat!
Then she would be at Castle Roogna, and my mission
would be successfully accomplished, despite all Yang's
machinations. Then, and only then, could I relax. Perhaps
I would recover Threnody; perhaps not. Either way, it
would be done.

"Wait here," I told her. Then I jumped down into the
moat. Naturally the nearest monster pounced on me, its
huge fangs spearing for my head.

My shield hefted up to intercept the strike, and the
fangs clamped down onto it. There the monster's maw
froze, two fangs projecting down inside the shield, drip-
ping saliva, while the eyes of the monster stared at me,
startled. I lifted my trusty sword and brought the blade
down, cutting off the end of the snout, including the fangs.
The monster gave a squeal of pain and jerked back, blood
and spittle flying. I suspect it was none too pleased. Mon-
ster-fighting can be a messy business at times.

"Look, monster," I said. "I've got a job to do, same
as you do. I'm crossing this moat and letting down the
drawbridge. I'm a barbarian warrior, none too smart at
the moment, and cutting up monsters is my profession.
Either you can let me operate in peace, or you can get
yourself hacked to pieces. It's your choice."

And I waded on across the clogged waterway without
waiting for the monster's response. That's the way you
have to deal with monsters—firmly and fairly.

The monster considered. It was an old one, long past
its prime, unable to mount the savagery of its youth, and
I'd given it a painful wound. It probably hadn't gulped
down a maiden in years. By the time it decided to attack
again, I was across.

I climbed to the drawbridge mechanism. No one was
there; this castle no longer had human guards, which was
part of its problem. There was only so much that trees
and zombies and monsters could do, without competent
human support. Modern battle is an integrated matter,
each aspect dependent on the others. Had the human
element been present, I would not have been able to storm
Castle Roogna, an edifice that had withstood attack for

four hundred years. When Magician Yin became King, surely he would upgrade the defenses, assuming the castle was still standing. I cranked the chain and lowered the bridge until it fell into place with a heavy thunk.

I walked out on it. "Now you can cross," I called to Threnody.

She approached reluctantly, and I went to meet her. Just this short distance across the moat, and it would be done.

"Maybe it will count if I don't actually get off the bridge and touch the castle itself," Threnody said. "If my father the King sees that you have completed your mission."

"Maybe so," I agreed. I really didn't want Castle Roogna to fall.

Threnody paused, picking up something at the edge of the planking. "What's this?" she asked. "It looks like—"

I reached for it. It was a small black ball. As I took it in my hand, I saw its other side. There were two squarish sockets and a grinning set of teeth.

"That's the black skull!" I exclaimed, trying to throw it away.

Too late. The evil skull flashed—and I fell dead.

"Jordan!" Threnody cried as I dropped from the edge of the bridge to the ground beyond the moat. She tried to catch me, but there was nothing she could do for me; I was already deceased. There was the counterspell in the bag, but we didn't know which one that was, and only I could invoke it—and as a dead man, I couldn't even do that. The evil spell had operated much more rapidly than it was supposed to.

A figure appeared across the moat, at the castle gate. It was Magician Yin. "So you have come to me at last, Princess Threnody," he said. "The barbarian has done good service."

She stood frozen for a moment, staring at him. "The mission is not yet complete," she said.

"But you can step right across and make it complete," Yin pointed out.

"And Castle Roogna will fall," she said disdainfully.

"But your father wishes this union to be," Yin reminded her. "We can build another castle."

"Not like this one!"

"Come, lovely woman," Yin pleaded. "The ignorant barbarian has given his life to bring you this far. Would you cause that sacrifice to be in vain?"

"Pah!" Threnody exclaimed. "I am demon-spawned; I have no conscience. All I want is to spare the castle where I grew up, the one place where I was happy. Now I shall live my own life. You would not let me do that, once you have power, Magician Yin."

"Ah—so the maiden plans to run away with the barbarian when he revives."

Had I been alive then, I would have been startled by that; I had thought Yin did not know about my talent. But of course Magicians tend to know more than they let on; it's part of their power.

"Hardly, Magician! This oaf lives only to complete his mission—to bring me to you, Yin. I tried to seduce him away from that, but the fool would not be swayed. Only by being rid of him can I be rid of you."

"But you will never be rid of him, Princess, since he can not be killed. That was my little ace in the hole against Yang's machinations. So you might as well cross the moat and marry me."

"I shall be rid of him—and you!" she exclaimed. "I know how to keep the barbarian dead!" And she took my sword and struck at my body. The magic shield tried to lift itself to block the attack, but its spell was no longer new, and I was dead, so it couldn't do much. In a moment she hacked off my shield arm, and the shield was finished.

Then she hacked off my other limbs, and my head, and cut my torso into two chunks. I looked like a dismembered zombie, except that there was a good deal more blood spread about. "This moron will never bother me again!" she gasped, spearing my staring head on the point and carrying it into the orchard.

Yin stood, watching her go. "Then you are determined not to let the barbarian's mission be complete?" he called after her.

"Absolutely!" she called back as she disappeared among the fruit trees.

Time passed. Then she returned to spear another chunk of my body. "And you refuse to cross over and marry me?" Yin asked, as if this were a routine matter.

"You got it, Magician," she agreed, hauling the second chunk away in a different direction.

When she returned again, Yin asked: "Despite the wishes of your dying father?"

"If my father knew the truth, he would repent those wishes." She marched away in a new direction with the third chunk.

Next time she appeared, Yin asked: "Don't you know that if I am not King, my evil brother will be King instead?"

"Of course I know it!" she exclaimed. "What care I for your politics?" She took the fourth part of me away in a new direction.

When she returned yet again, Yin said: "Don't you realize that if you do not marry me, you must marry Magician Yang?"

"Maybe Yang won't want me. But if he does, he won't make me live at Castle Roogna," she said, spearing a fifth chunk and toting it away.

Soon she was back again, for the next-to-the-last chunk. "What do you care for Magician Yang?" Yin demanded.

Threnody paused in her labor. "Well, if you want it straight, I *am* demon-spawn. I prefer evil to good—and Yang is evil." She hauled the chunk away.

"That isn't what you told the barbarian," Yin said when she returned for the final chunk.

"I told the barbarian I was a liar. That much was true." She carried away the seventh piece of me.

When she returned, Yin tried yet once more. "The barbarian is finished, but you could still cross over to me. I ask you, daughter of the King, one last time—"

"Oh, stop this charade!" she exclaimed, picking up my magic shield and dumping it into the moat. Then she tossed my sword in after it. "Do you think I don't know your secret?"

"Secret, Princess?"

"That Yin is merely the white-magic side, and Yang the black-magic side, of the same person. You are not contesting to see which Magician shall be King; you are deciding which facet of your personality will dominate. Since that decision turns out to be mine to make, I am choosing—and I choose Yang. Come to me, you evil creature, for I shall not come to you! The price of me is to turn your back forever on Castle Roogna."

"Then so I shall!" Yin said. He turned about, his cloak flaring—and as he turned, his color changed, and he became the black-robed Yang. He strode across the drawbridge and took Threnody's hand. "You have done well, evil creature!" he told her. "Even to seducing the barbarian, for you know I could not touch a pristine woman."

"Only Yin could do that," she agreed, kissing him. "The placement of that last spell was beautiful. The oaf never suspected the drawbridge itself!"

"Thank you. You realize, of course, that I was testing you? I feared you might actually have some feeling for that barbarian, though I know what a consummate actress you are. So I arranged to—"

"I do have some feeling for him," she said. "Contempt! He was a fool even before your idiocy spell hit him. And there was another stroke of genius—mixing up Yin's spells! Even so, it was uncomfortably close, for the barbarian was the most oinkheadedly determined fool I've ever seen."

"A close contest is more tantalizing," Yang said. "I knew I would win; but for the sake of appearances, I preferred the outcome to seem in doubt."

"Well, Evil Magician, you will be King now. So take me away from here and do what you will with me."

"I *am* King now. Your father died yesterday."

Threnody stiffened. If she had cared for anything at all, it was for her father. "Then I could have killed the barbarian last night, and my father would not have known! Why did you torture me like that?"

"It is my nature," Yang said. "As it is yours. Together, we have betrayed all that is decent in Xanth."

She smiled. "Why, so we have!"

"And now we shall neglect the interests of Xanth completely, letting Castle Roogna go to ruin in its own fashion. I shall devote myself to crafting spells of every type, and who knows what mischief they may do in the course of future centuries as they are discovered, while you—"

"While I will assume whatever strange forms you wish, for your sinister pleasure," Threnody finished.

Together, they walked away from the castle, their cruel lie complete at last.

Of course, I was dead, so I was no longer much concerned with this. But my ghost was present at the spot where I had died, and my ghost was appalled at this evidence of the betrayal of myself and Xanth that Threnody had wrought. All the time she had been collaborating with the Evil Magician, plotting to—

But the Evil Magician and the Good Magician were one and the same! And Threnody had known this! And chosen the Evil aspect to go with! All the while playing up to me, the ignorant barbarian fool! When I had not failed to bring her back to Castle Roogna, she had had to come into the open about it. Why had I been so blind?

Why, indeed! They had chosen me for this very quality! If my course for the mission had been predestined, so had my course before it, bringing me to Castle Roogna at precisely the time they needed such a fool. How could a mere barbarian comprehend the intricacies of civilized treachery? Perhaps King Gromden, a good man, had suspected and tried to tell me, but his illness had prevented him. That very illness might have been sent by a spell from one of the aspirants to the throne, since Yin-Yang had free access to Castle Roogna. It would have been better had I never entered the picture, for I had been the unwitting tool of their treachery. I, as much as Threnody, was responsible for the demise of Castle Roogna as the center of the human government of Xanth, and for the centuries of the decline that followed. How great was my guilt!

But it was done, and I was helpless to undo it. All I could do was watch.

A few hours after my death, Pook and Peek arrived on the scene. Pook came and sniffed the mostly empty bag of spells Threnody had dropped on the bank of the moat and forgotten. He knew I had been there and that I had been betrayed by the cruelest of lies. He had tried to warn me, to discourage me; he had refused to aid me in my folly. But I had pursued it anyway, bewitched by foolish love, and met my ordained fate. Now Pook could do nothing; he didn't know where evil Threnody had buried my pieces, and lacked the means to dig them up besides. Nobody knew but her, and she would never tell. Truly, she had sealed my fate!

Disconsolately, Pook picked up the limp bag of spells with his teeth, craned his head around to tuck it in amidst his chains so that he could carry it as a memento, then departed. Peek went with him, sharing his melancholy with her beautiful, moist brown eyes. She was an animal; she did not deceive or betray her companion the way a human woman could.

And so I was dead and dead I remained. Evil Threnody had seen to that! My ghost moved into Castle Roogna, as that was the only building within range, and ghosts do prefer a structure to haunt. I met the other ghosts there and learned their sad stories. One was Millie the Maid, who had been killed by a jealous rival for the Magician she loved. The others each had his or her life history, as tragic or ironic as mine. Oh, we shared common heritage of folly and grief, we ghosts of the castle! And so we remained over the centuries, while the castle stood idle.

For Magician Yang, the evil aspect of the man, indeed cared nothing for Castle Roogna or the welfare of Xanth. He moved back to his home village and made his nefarious spells, for that was his chief entertainment. In truth, most of his spells were neutral, for there is no real good or evil in a given spell. Only in its actual use does it become good or evil. All the spells and enchanted objects in Xanth date from his reign, including the magic weapons of the Castle Roogna arsenal, made before he left. Some of those spells, like the forget-spell on the Gap Chasm, date from before his time, yet he made them, too; I don't know how that was arranged. He was a great Magician, but an evil man. Those spells proliferated, and Xanth declined, because the spells were not used in any organized service of man. They were just scattered about the kingdom, whimsically, to do what mischief they might in ignorant hands. We ghosts had news of outside events only occasionally, when some traveling spook or wraith passed through; we ourselves were unable to leave the castle premises. So this is sketchy. But in the course of centuries, we did catch up on the major items.

Eventually Magician Yang died—but the next King of Xanth did not return to Castle Roogna to reign. It seemed it had become fashionable for Kings to remain in their home villages. There was no longer a centralized government in Xanth. The Mundane Waves washed freely over Xanth. It was the dark age—all because of Threnody's cruel lie. She had sought to preserve Castle Roogna from falling, whatever the cost, but it had fallen anyway, figuratively—and who is to say that was not the real nature of the curse?

Yet perhaps she was not directly to blame for the evil times that came to all Xanth, for the tides of men are slow and subtle, and answer to no isolated influences. Maybe Xanth was doomed, anyway, and would have suffered some other calamity if not this one. Threnody had not chosen to be cursed, or even to be delivered by the stork. Maybe it had really started with the demoness who had humiliated King Gromden and succeeded in her mischief beyond her most infernal expectations.

Still, this does not excuse me. I, utter fool, had helped Threnody to do it—by trusting her when I knew she was untrustworthy and loving her when I should have known that the spawn of a demon could not truly love in return, whatever she might say. She had done to me what her mother had done to her father, and together, they had ruined more lives than anyone can know. My pain was all the greater because I *had* loved her, however foolishly. Now it was hate—but still my emotion for her, whether positive or negative, dominated my tenuous existence as a ghost. I had been a fool in life; I remained a fool in death. But what was to be expected of a barbarian lout?

One thing came to bother me increasingly in my spirit existence—Elsie, the girl I had left behind in Fen Village. I had promised to return to her when my adventure was done—and after I had learned the folly of loving demon-spawn, I would have been glad to settle down with a decent girl. But I could not; I was dead. If I had known more of the true situation with Magician Yin-Yang and Threnody, I would have set her on the drawbridge, said, "Here you are; cross or not, as you see fit," and departed for home, to be with Elsie, a genuinely decent young woman who would never have betrayed me. But I hadn't known, so I had died, and now could not know how Elsie fared. Was she waiting for me throughout her life, for a promise never to be fulfilled? How cruel a lie had I told *her*? In this I perceived a certain justice to my own fate. I had been served as I had served another person. I had perhaps ruined a fine girl and now I was ruined myself. The two griefs merged and fused in my being; as time passed, I tended to forget the more recent horror in favor of the earlier one, perhaps because the guilt of all Xanth was not associated there.

Yet it was not all bad for me, and perhaps not for Xanth. With the decline of human power, the several creature kingdoms strengthened, and mankind had to learn to deal with animals as equals. Centaurs in particular had been treated mainly as beasts of burden and laborers; now they formed an island kingdom of their own and became quite civilized. I like to think that the elven tribes prospered and that Bluebell's descendants exist today, because of the diminished interference of human folk.

The other ghosts of the castle were decent sorts, very supportive; they had been through their fatal experiences and understood exactly how that felt. They regarded themselves as keepers of the castle, preserving it for that day when a King would return to rule Xanth properly and usher in a new golden age of man. Castle Roogna itself had a spirit; it kept itself whole, and its ambience extended out through the surrounding orchards and trees. Now I understood why the trees had fought me; they had known that my presence meant doom to the castle, whichever way my mission turned out.

As a ghost, I ranged the whole region, apologizing to every tree and zombie I had injured with my sword, and to the old moat monster, too. "I'm very sorry, and I won't do it again," I promised. But that was empty; I *couldn't* do it again. Still, they accepted my penitence, knowing the ignorance and frailties of the mortal condition, and I became one with the castle. An empty promise is still a promise; I have tried in whatever way I can to help Castle Roogna, and perhaps I succeeded when the King Mare needed help to save it from occupation by the evil Horseman. That can hardly make up for the evil I did originally, but it's a beginning.

In a couple of years a new ghost appeared. She was Renee, whom you have met. She was bewildered by her abrupt death, though it had been suicide. People who die by their own hands often don't realize quite what they are getting into. She had come to the deserted castle to end her misery and had not expected to retain awareness in this form. She had suffered an unhappy marriage, not being able to marry her true love, and had finally taken this way out. She reminded me poignantly of Elsie, though I ardently hoped I had *not* driven Elsie into such a situation by my defection.

I had been the youngest ghost, in terms of the period of my spirit's existence; now Renee was. I was glad to help her and show her the ghostly ropes, and she was very appreciative. This helped me forget my own distress, and I trust it helped her, too. It is a truth of death as well as of life that the surest amelioration of one's own misery is to be obtained by helping another person.

In time—much time, for the emotions of ghosts are as diffuse as their physical essences—this relationship evolved into love. Now Threnody was but a distant memory; Renee was the one I existed for. In death I had found my life's partner, and I knew she felt the same—though it was too late for us even before we met.

Eventually King Trent came to Castle Roogna and brought the monarchy back to its rightful seat. Once again Xanth flourished, and the dark age was behind. We are now some thirty years into the new age, and man prospers, but we ghosts remain. For our stories are not yet finished, and perhaps will never be.

Chapter 16. Caustic Truth

"And that," Jordan the Ghost concluded, "is my story, sad as it may be. I was an ignorant barbarian fool and I paid the price. Yet today I have happiness of a sort, for I have seen the dark age of Xanth end at last and I love Renee. And now I have the memory of my living history, thanks to the crewel lye you used to clarify the tapestry. I thank you, little Princess, though not all of my memories are pleasant."

Ivy considered. She had found the ghost's tale to be more of a narrative than anticipated, with some aspects that were a trifle awkward for a girl of five to comprehend. It had granted her the wish she had made on a starfish: to know the origin of the forget-spell on the Gap. A certain mystery remained about that, since that spell had been applied to the Gap long before Magician Yin-Yang lived, but still, it was an answer. Now she wondered what the big deal was about summoning the stork; wasn't it just a matter of kissing? Her parents tended to get evasive when her questions about such points became too pointed, and she had the suspicion that Jordan would be no more candid. Still, it was worth a try. "Some things have changed," she said.

"Oh?"

"We live in modern times. Storks no longer deliver babies directly to the mothers."

"They don't?" Jordan asked as if amused. That was an annoying trait adults had. "I must be out of touch."

"Yes. Today the storks deposit the bundles under cabbage leaves. Probably it saves them time. If you had done that with the ogret, you wouldn't have had to worry about the ogre and ogress."

"That must be why the storks changed it," Jordan agreed.

"That's where my mother found dumb Dolph, my piddling baby brother."

"That's no way to speak of him," Jordan said.

"Well, he *is* piddling," she insisted stoutly. "They have to keep a diaper on him all the time, and keep changing it. I'm sure it's more trouble than he's worth."

"There is that," the ghost agreed.

Now came the clincher. "I don't quite understand this business about summoning storks anyway," Ivy said petulantly. "Exactly how is that done?"

"Um, I forget," Jordan said awkwardly.

"Well, let's zero in on one of those scenes in the tapestry and enlarge the detail. That should refresh your memory." Ivy was very practical about satisfying her curiosity.

"I'm sure that's not necessary," Jordan said quickly. "It's a very dull business."

"How do you know, if you don't remember?"

"Well, I just remember that it probably wouldn't interest you. Children don't do it, you see." But the ghost had turned a shade or two whiter than he had been.

There was no question about it; Jordan was part of the Adult Conspiracy. There was some secret here that all grown-ups wanted to keep from all children. "Let's go back to the beginning," Ivy said. "Where you and Elsie—"

"Ah, Elsie," the ghost said sadly. "I'd like to know how she survived."

"Uh, yes," Ivy agreed, curious about that, too. So when the tapestry zeroed in on Elsie, just after Jordan had left her, she followed the woman forward instead of backward. Ivy, like Jordan, had her weaknesses; curiosity tended to overcome her common sense. What *had* happened to Elsie?

As it turned out, Elsie did not grieve long. A handsome farmer began paying attention to her the moment Jordan left; as time passed, without Jordan's return, her interest turned to the farmer. In due course she married him, and the stork delivered a baby, but the lights were always out when the couple set about signaling the stork, so Ivy still was unenlightened.

"That's a relief!" Jordan exclaimed.

"What?" Ivy demanded irately.

"To learn that I didn't ruin Elsie after all," the ghost said. "Now I don't have to feel guilty any more. She was better off without me. I was just a passing fling for her, as she was for me."

"Oh." Now Ivy's full attention returned to Jordan. "Your magic talent—could you revive today, if your bones were put back together?"

The ghost considered. "I don't know. It's been a long time—and anyway, I don't know where my parts are buried, so they can't be put together."

"I know where they are," a faint voice said behind him.

Jordan turned. "Oh—Renee! I didn't know you were there!"

The female ghost took better form. Ivy could see that she must have been very pretty in her life. "I—looked for them, and the trees showed me," Renee said.

"Why did you do that?" Jordan asked, perplexed.

"Because I love you."

Jordan was abashed. "I never thought to look for *your* bones! I must not love you as much as you love me!"

"It's all right," Renee said comfortingly. "I am not as lovable as you are, Jordan."

Ivy pounced on the information. "Take me to Jordan's bones!" she exclaimed. "I'm going to put them together, so he can live again!"

"But it might not work," Jordan protested.

"Nonsense!" Ivy said with the certainty only a child

her age could muster. "You can do it if you try." She
turned to Renee. "Show me!"

Obediently, Renee led the way out of the castle and
across the moat and into the orchard. "The head is here,
under the roots of this skullery tree." She indicated the
tree, which was hung with pots and kettles and other
kitchen utensils. Indeed, there did seem to be skull de-
signs on the utensils. This location was obvious, now that
attention had been called to it.

"We'll have to dig it out," Ivy said, eying the firm turf
beneath the tree.

The two ghosts spread their foggy hands. "We are unable to affect material things," Jordan said. "I could not
even invoke the pictures of the tapestry myself; only a
living, solid creature can do that, and not all of them."

Ivy looked at her cute little hands. She considered the
trouble she would be in if she got them and her dress
messed up. "I'll get help," she decided.

"Help?" Jordan asked. "Any adult is likely to ask awkward questions."

"Don't I know it! That's the one thing adults are really
good at." She glanced at the ghost. "Except maybe barbarians."

"Thank you," Jordan said wryly.

"Perhaps the little dragon—" Renee murmured.

Ivy brightened. She put two fingers into her mouth and
made a piercing whistle.

There was a stir from the far side of the castle. In a
moment Stanley came steaming along. He whomped up
to Ivy expectantly.

Ivy pointed to the ground. "There is a skull under here.
Sniff!"

Stanley sniffed. In a moment he located it. He indicated
the spot with a jet of steam.

"Dig it out—carefully," Ivy ordered.

Stanley was glad to cooperate. He steamed the ground,
making it soft, then dug with his front claws. Soon he
sniffed again, steamed the dirt sodden, and used his teeth
to dig out the dirty skull.

"Oh, you're so *good* at that!" Ivy exclaimed, stretching

her arms around Stanley's neck for a hug. She had perfected the technique of female flattery by watching her mother handle her father. It certainly worked on Stanley; he blushed bright green with pleasure.

Soon they steamed the skull clean and white, and Ivy carried it to the next location. Renee showed them to a shoe-tree, with boys' and men's shoes in every stage of growth. Sure enough, down under the roots, its foot nestled in a buried hiking shoe, was one of Jordan's skeletal legs. Stanley dug it out carefully and steamed it clean.

This growing mass of bones was getting complicated for Ivy to carry, so they made a cache of bones under a parasol tree, out of sight of the castle. Ivy didn't want any adult telling her no! Adults were all too prone to say no, apparently for no reason other than sinister pleasure in uttering the syllable.

The other leg was under a female shoe-tree, wearing a ragged lady-slipper; no one would have thought to look for it there! Stanley was enjoying this; he liked finding things, though he was a little miffed about not being allowed to chew up the bones after he found them. But he was willing to settle for Ivy's hugs instead. "Males have always been fools about that sort of thing," Jordan muttered reminiscently.

The arms were beneath separate arms-trees, nestled among the old rusted swords, maces, and spears that had been dropped unharvested in bygone years. One hand still held the sword recovered from the Knight, which remained stainlessly shiny. "Odd that she should have taken the trouble to put that sword in my hand," Jordan mused. "As if I died fighting. Why should she bother?" Jordan's own sword, of course, had been used by the evil Threnody to bury the chunks of him; there was no telling where that was now, if it hadn't rusted away entirely. It had been a good sword, but not *that* good.

The upper section of the torso was buried beneath a chest-nut tree. The skeletal rib cage was packed in a chest: another retrospectively obvious location. Threnody had evidently taken a lot of care in hiding each piece in a region so fitting that no one would think of it. "She must have been afraid that if any piece of me were found, someone would realize where the others were," Jordan said, shuddering at the mute malice of the demon-spawn's mischief.

One section remained, and this was beneath a huge, thick ash tree. "She planted my posterior 'neath the grass of an ash!" the ghost lamented.

"A fat ash," Ivy agreed, contemplating the girth of the tree.

Stanley sneezed as he sniffed out the precise location, for the fine ashes beneath the tree tickled his snoot. Then he dug down through the stratified layers of ash until he could get a tooth on the skeletal rump.

At last Jordan's entire skeleton was heaped beneath the parasol. Ivy arranged the pieces in order, so that the figure lay complete on the ground. "Now what?" she asked. "Does it just start walking, like one of the skeletons of the gourd?"

"After four hundred years, as I said, I'm not sure," Jordan replied cautiously. "I've never been dead that long before."

"Here, I brought some healing 'lixer," Ivy said. She took out a bottle and sprinkled it over the bones. Still, nothing happened.

"You see, since all my flesh is gone—" Jordan began.

"Nonsense! All it takes is concentration." And Ivy concentrated.

Ivy, though a child, was a full Sorceress, with power that rivaled that of any Magician in Xanth. When she focused it, remarkable things tended to happen, such as dragons turning tame and thyme accelerating. Now she intensified Jordan's talent of recovery, which had already been boosted by the healing elixir—which itself was intensified by her talent. Jordan had no flesh to heal; only the most enduring part of him remained. It seemed like a lost cause. Yet even four hundred years could not stand against Ivy's power. Few folk ever had occasion to perceive the full extent of the magic of a Magician or Sorceress, for usually the ramifications were subtle. This was an exception.

The effect was gratifying. The bones began to knit. The leg bone connected to the thigh bone, and the arm bone connected to the shoulder bone, and the shoulder bone connected to the neck bone. All the bones connected, and soon the skeleton was intact.

Now tendons sprouted from the bones, stringing them together in a new way. Flesh formed on the surfaces, like mildew growing, surrounding the bones and tendons, thickening, turning red. Muscles developed, and organs. The skeleton became a cadaverous body. Probably the bones were becoming hollow, for Jordan's healing talent did not generate flesh from nothing; it was taken from the existing substance. But in due course, a layer of skin formed and the starving figure lay complete, the thinnest man in Xanth.

"It has to eat," Jordan the Ghost said. "It's too thin to support life, so it's still a dead man."

"Then why doesn't it eat?" Ivy asked.

"Dead men don't eat. It's still too weak."

Ivy went to a nearby breadfruit tree, plucked a loaf of bread, and took out a slice. She held this to the figure's almost lipless mouth.

"That did it!" Jordan exclaimed. He floated through the air toward the figure as if drawn by some vacuum. The figure inhaled—and the ghost was sucked into the mouth.

"Good-bye, Jordan!" Renee cried faintly, sounding sad for this parting. And of course it was a parting, for he was departing the world of ghosts.

Now the body was breathing. The mouth opened slightly, and Ivy poked in the bite of bread. The mouth closed, and the jaws slowly chewed. At first it seemed almost too much for the teeth to bite through the soft bread, but soon the motions strengthened as the nourishment entered the body.

She fed him several pieces, and then some fruits, and gradually the body became more animated. The sunken eyes opened, and one arm twitched. Finally that hand was able to lift and grasp a piece of bread and move it to the mouth. Jordan was feeding himself!

But time was passing, and Ivy had to return to the castle for supper, lest the grown-ups get suspicious. "Stanley—guard!" she ordered the little dragon, indicating the strengthening body. She plucked assorted additional fruits and dumped them down in a pile for the body to eat. Then she went into the Castle Roogna, where she got caught up in all the make-work adults foisted off on children, such as eating greens, brushing her teeth, looking at picture books, and going to bed. She couldn't get away to see to the important business. Angry, she kicked at the monster under the bed, but it was smart enough to skulk just out of reach.

First thing in the morning, she returned to the orchard. Jordan was gone—but Stanley came frisking up and led her to the former ghost. Jordan the man was now on his feet and picking fruit for himself. He was still very thin, but the healing elixir and his healing talent, as enhanced by Ivy's own talent, had restored him remarkably. He was now the shadow of his former barbarian self, tall and broad-shouldered and hank-haired and big-footed, the very outline of the model of a handsome man. He was walking from tree to tree, taking all the fruit he could reach and cramming it into his mouth, still ravenous.

Ivy clapped her hands with childish glee. "Jordan, you're really alive!" she cried. Of course he had been alive the evening before, but so thin and weak that she really didn't think of it the same way.

"Mph sre m," he agreed through a mouthful of fruitcake from one of the garden's valuable crossbreed trees. "Vut—"

"But what?"

He swallowed, clearing his mouth somewhat so he could speak more clearly. "But Renee isn't."

Ivy looked around, spying the female ghost, who hovered at the fringe of vision. "That's right. I guess you miss her now."

"I am glad for Jordan," Renee said faintly. "He will be able to finish his real life. I will fade away."

"No!" Jordan cried, clearing the rest of his mouthful. "I love you, Renee. I don't want life if it means I must lose you! I'll become a ghost again!" He glanced back toward the parasol tree, where the Knight's sword still lay. He took a step toward it.

"Don't you dare!" Ivy said severely. "I went to a lot of trouble to get you back alive! We'll just have to make Renee alive, too."

"No, that is not necessary," Renee protested. "Jordan deserves to live; I don't."

"But *how*?" Jordan asked Ivy, interested.

Ivy pondered. It was an awkward question, the very type that adults favored. "I'd better ask Hugo."

"Hugo?"

"My friend at Magician Humfrey's castle. Hugo's very smart."

"That's not what I've heard," Jordan said.

"Well, he's always smart when I'm with him."

Jordan had just experienced a demonstration of her power and began to understand. If she thought Hugo was smart, Hugo would be smart—for her. "Humfrey's castle—isn't that where Millie went? I remember when she left us thirty years ago."

"Thirty-one years," Renee said. Evidently she was good at figures, having a good one herself. Naturally these ghosts had known Millie the Ghost before she was restored to life.

"Millie—you mean Lacuna's mom?" Ivy asked. "She lives in the Zombie Castle. Humfrey's castle is east."

"Yes, but that's still a long way away. It would take a long time to go there, even if you used the gourd again."

"We'll use the mirror, silly! Come on!" And Ivy headed toward the castle at a brisk skip.

"But if the adults see me, they'll ask questions," Jordan pointed out.

That made Ivy pause. It was a big nuisance when people asked questions. She was coming to understand why Magician Humfrey discouraged it. "Okay. You stay here and eat. And find something to wear."

"Oops," Jordan said, realizing that his clothing had not revived with him. It seemed he had been so hungry that he hadn't paid attention to other details.

Ivy returned to the castle and went straight to the magic mirror. "Mirror, mirror, on the wall, who's the cutest of them all?" she asked rhetorically.

"You are, you ravishing little snippet!" the mirror replied, showing the image of a kiss. It was a game they played. As Magician Humfrey aged, he had gotten to tinkering with things he had not had time for in his senior years and had fixed the various inoperative mirrors, so that now intercastle communications were excellent. Ivy's talent hadn't hurt, either; the mirror responded especially well to her attention.

Ivy made a grab for the kiss, but it danced away, back beyond the glassy surface where she couldn't get it. This mirror was a tease. "And who's the smartest of them all?"

"Now that depends," the mirror began.

"Oh, just give me Hugo."

"I thought you were working up to that," the mirror grumped. It flickered, and then Hugo came on.

"Hugo, I need some advice," Ivy said. "You're real smart, aren't you?"

"I am now," he agreed warily. He had been through this before.

"How can we bring a ghost back to life?"

"That's easy. Use a reanimation spell."

Ivy considered. "The only one of those I know of was taken away by a ghost horse four hundred years ago."

Hugo shook his head. "Ivy, you've said some foolish things in your day, but this is worse yet. How could you have lost such a spell four hundred years ago? You didn't exist then."

"Just tell me how to bring back that ghost horse," Ivy said evenly.

"I'll have to ask my father. He's a brat now, but he likes to show off his information." Hugo disappeared from the mirror, which played innocuous music and ran color patterns during the interim. Soon he returned. "He says, quote, you idiot, all you have to do is rattle some chains, unquote."

"Okay. Tell the brat thanks." Ivy dashed down to the arsenal, found the heaviest chain she could carry, shook the bones out of it, and dragged it out to the orchard. The moat monster spooked as she hauled it across the draw-bridge, for it made a loud noise on the wooden planks.

Panting from the effort, she brought the chain to Jordan, who had already filled out some more. Apparently Ivy's presence had accelerated his healing again. "Rattle this!" she told him.

Perplexed, he obeyed. He took the chain and shook it. The rattling noise filled the orchard, causing the trees to avert their leaves.

In a moment there was a distant answering rattle. "Pook!" Jordan cried, surprised and pleased. "I'd know that sound anywhere!"

Indeed it was the ghost horse, who was eternal as long as he wore his chains and avoided getting killed. Pook galloped up, gave a startled neigh when he saw Jordan, and practically knocked him down in greeting. "Yes, I'm alive again!" Jordan said. "Did you miss me?"

Pook shrugged. Then he turned and neighed. There was an answering neigh—and in a moment Peek, the female ghost horse, trotted up. Trailing her was a little colt, wearing cute little chains.

"I guess you found a way to pass the time," Jordan remarked. "But four hundred years—just when did the stork deliver that colt?"

"Ooo, nice!" Ivy exclaimed, fascinated by the little ghost horse. The feeling seemed mutual.

"Of course, these things do take time," Jordan decided. "When you're a ghost. I've had some experience that way myself. That colt could be a century old." And Pook nodded.

"I'll call you Puck!" Ivy told the ghost colt, patting his pretty little mane.

Jordan checked Pook's chains. There were the tattered remains of the bag of spells. He pulled it free, and two unused white spells dropped out: a shield and a stone. "One of these must be the reanimation spell," he exclaimed. "And the other—" He paused to tally them up in his mind. "The monster-banishing-spell."

"But which is which?" Ivy asked.

"We'll just have to try them both. But first we have to find Renee's bones."

"No," Renee said timidly. "I really don't deserve—"

"Either you join me in life, or I'll rejoin you in death." And Jordan's barbarian jaw was set so hard it was evident he meant it.

"You don't understand," Renee demurred. "You wouldn't like me alive. I never intended to live again."

"Well, I never intended to die for four hundred years," Jordan retorted. "That was the mischief of Threnody's cruel lie, may she be forever damned! But now I'm glad I did, because that's how I met you. I love you; I'll either live with you or die with you."

"Come on, Renee," Ivy said persuasively. She loved a good romance, even if there were aspects of it she had been unable to fathom yet. "Don't be shy. I know my father will make a place for you at Castle Roogna—"

"No! Never!" the ghost cried.

"But after all, you've been here for centuries!"

"That's different. Ghosts don't count. I could never stay, in life," Renee protested, wringing her diaphanous hands.

"Then we can live somewhere else," Jordan said. "Anywhere you want. Just so long as we're together. You want that, don't you?"

"Oh, yes! But—"

"Then it's decided," Ivy said decisively. "Show us your bones."

Reluctantly, Renee led them to one more site—a sophis-tree. This looked like a solid, regular tree, but on closer examination, it turned out to be a clever deception—an animal masquerading as a tree by standing on its thick tail and spreading its limbs out, covered with bits of green to emulate branches and leaves. Obviously it was an intruder in the orchard, a weed-creature, but the effort was so ingenious that no one had noticed for centuries, until now. Ivy decided to pretend not to notice; if the creature tried that hard and long to look and act like a tree, it deserved to succeed. After all, it wasn't doing any harm.

Stanley sniffed out the bones and dug them up. They were very shapely bones; obviously Renee had been a beautiful woman, so her appearance wasn't the reason for her reluctance to reanimate. That was fine, for, as Jordan continued to pluck and eat fruit, he was filling out into a muscular and handsome man. Ivy just knew they would make a lovely couple and she was thrilled to be able to reunite them in life. She liked the ghosts of Castle Roogna and would be sorry to lose these two as ghosts— but life was even better.

Jordan reached into the bag and brought out the little white stone and shield. "These stand for life and monster-banishment," he said. "But there's no way to tell which is which, short of invoking one. I'll just have to guess. At least neither one will hurt anyone."

"But—" Renee protested. "I really think you shouldn't—"

Jordan held up the white stone. "Invoke!" he said.

There was a flash from the stone—and a pop behind them. They glanced around. "Stanley's gone!" Ivy cried, appalled.

Jordan looked abashed. "I forgot he was a monster," he said. "He was so helpful during the night. But I guess a little monster is still a monster."

"But where is he?" Ivy demanded, peering around the orchard.

"Don't worry—I'm sure he's all right," Jordan said. "He must have been sent to wherever monsters live when they're not monstering. I mean, when I ran into the black monster-summoning-spell, it was a pretty healthy tarasque that appeared, and this spell is just the reverse. I'm sure Stanley will find his way home."

"He'd better!" Ivy said, poking out her lower lip. "Or I'll give him holy whatfor!"

Jordan held up the little white shield. "This has to be it, by elimination. Invoke!"

Renee's bones quivered. Then the ghost was drawn to them—and as she settled onto the pattern of bones, her ghostly outline clarified, thickened, and became solid. In a moment she was a bare, beautiful woman with flowing black hair.

Jordan stared at her, stumbling back as if struck. "Threnody!" he cried.

"Who?" Ivy asked, bewildered.

The woman got to her feet. She had gone through none of the agonizing stages of restoration that Jordan had; this spell had been quick and strong. She gazed sadly at Jordan. "I tried to dissuade you, barbarian," she said. "I warned you that you wouldn't like me alive."

"You—you substituted your bones for Renee's!" Jordan cried. "You tricked me into reviving you instead of the one I love!" Behind him, Pook snorted agreement. Pook had never liked Threnody.

"Now how could a dead person change bones with another?" Threnody asked with the same air of regret. "I was always Renee—THreneeDY. I just simplified my name, so you wouldn't know."

It was obviously true. "You deceived me—even in death!" Jordan said. "Even as a ghost!"

"Even as a ghost," she agreed, walking to a clothing tree and making tasteful selections from it. Ivy had never seen a better-formed woman, not excepting her mother Irene. Even as a female child, Ivy could appreciate how such a figure could dazzle a man's mind. Threnody spoke again. "That was the cruelest lie of all."

Jordan's prospective joy had changed abruptly to bewildered horror. "But—*why*? You had gotten what you wanted! Why torture me even in death?"

She sighed. "I don't suppose you could believe that I have always loved you?"

Jordan's big fist clenched so hard the knuckle cracked. "Don't give me any more of your lies! For once in your foul life, tell the simple truth! *Why?*"

She nodded as if she had expected this. "No more lies, Jordan. I'll just do you the favor of getting out of your life. You're alive now; you can make a new life for yourself. I'm sure any decent and lovely maiden would be glad to comfort a handsome barbarian like you. You certainly don't need anything from demon-spawn." She completed

her dressing and walked out of the orchard, away from
the castle.

Jordan's hurt bafflement turned to outrage. "Oh, no,
you don't! You can't destroy my love twice over and just
walk away! I promised to deliver you to Castle Roogna,
and now I will! King Dor will decide what to do with
you!" And he ran after her, grabbed her by her slender
waist, and picked her up. He had not yet recovered his
full mass and strength, but he was already a powerful
man.

"Stop that!" Threnody cried. "Put me down! I can't
go to Castle Roogna!"

"We'll see about that!" he gritted. "There's no Evil
Magician now to kill me on the way. Once my mission is
done, I'm through with you—but not before!"

She kicked and fought, but he carried her through the
orchard toward the castle, while Ivy and the three ghost
horses followed. Pook snorted approval; this was at least
a fitting conclusion to Jordan's mission. Threnody would
at last pay the penalty for her many treacheries.

But as they approached the drawbridge, there was dust
rising from the zombie graveyard to the side. The zombies
were dragging themselves out of their graves, trying to
protect the castle. But they were too slow. Jordan reached
the bridge first and started boldly across it, despite the
woman's struggles.

Castle Roogna began to shake. There were cries from
within it as startled people reacted. Still Jordan marched
forward. The moat monster forged through the water toward them, but it, too, was too late. All the castle's defenses had been caught off guard by this sudden
occurrence.

The shaking got worse. The water of the moat rippled.
A stone fell from a turret and crashed to the ground.

"The castle's falling, you idiot!" Threnody screamed.
"It will kill everyone!"

Jordan stopped, amazed. "It really is!" he exclaimed.
"I thought that was just a threat!"

Threnody managed to squirm out of his grasp and get
back on her feet. "You never did know the truth from a

lie!" she said and ran back across the bridge. "You were always a fool!" She brushed past Ivy and the horses, tears on her cheeks. No one tried to stop her.

The shuddering diminished as Threnody got away from the castle. The threat was easing. The disinterred zombies paused, and so did the moat monster, watching her depart.

"She sure didn't lie about that part," Ivy said, shaken by more than the castle. "But I don't understand. Why did she pretend to be Renee?"

"To trick me into reanimating her!" Jordan said bitterly. "I would never have done it if I'd known she was the evil Threnody."

"But Renee told you not to do it," Ivy pointed out.

"She knew I'd do it anyway."

"But when she came here to die, four hundred years ago, you had no spell. She thought you were dead to stay, didn't she? Why did she choose to become a ghost—or if not a ghost, why did she come here to die?"

Jordan shook his head, bewildered. "I guess I can't make sense of it at all. If she had had any change of heart, she could have dug up my bones herself; she knew where they were. But she's demon-spawn; I never truly understood her nature. Her mother destroyed her father, and she destroyed me. Now she's taken Renee from me, and left me not only desolate but branded as big a fool as a ghost as I was in life. The cruelty of her lies just goes on and on!" And he sat on the edge of the bridge and put his head in his hands.

Pook approached from one side, not knowing how to comfort the man who had loved so unwisely, and even the moat monster looked sad. The tragedy of Jordan's first life had seemed to be beyond redemption, yet he had redeemed it in death—only to have it eclipsed by the tragedy of his second life.

Ivy had some idea how he felt. After all, she had just lost Stanley Steamer. But somehow it didn't make enough sense to satisfy her. "I'm going to ask Hugo," she announced.

Jordan did not answer. He just sat silently, gazing into the water of the moat, his new life turned to ashes.

Ivy had been grounded for getting into some perfectly innocent trouble on the way to the North Village several days ago. This time, she knew, the trouble was not innocent. Lives had been restored—and ruined. Castle Roogna had nearly fallen. What explanation could Hugo offer that would make any of this right? But she had to ask.

She left the little group on the drawbridge, returned to the castle, and hurried through the halls. No one noticed her; they were all too upset about the mysterious shaking of the castle. Once they realized what her part in this had been—she quailed before a mental picture of the giant flying hairbrush she had encountered at the Good Magician's castle. Yet that could hardly be the worst of it. What would the other ghosts say to her after what she had done to two of their number?

She reached the mirror and called Hugo again. "You're the only one smart enough to figure this out, Hugo," she said tearfully when his face appeared in the glass. "I'm in a big awful lot of trouble!"

"But I'm not smart!" he protested, none too eager to get involved in her trouble. It took no genius to know that what Ivy considered little trouble was big trouble to anyone else, and what she called big trouble was apt to be downright dangerous.

"Yes, you are!" she insisted. Hugo was stuck for it; he changed his mind for a smarter one.

Ivy told him what had happened, and Hugo listened intelligently. "Why, the answer is obvious," he said as she concluded; he explained it to her.

Ivy brightened phenomenally. "That's it!" she exclaimed happily. "That solves everything! Oh, thank you, Hugo!" And she dashed out of the still-confused castle.

She returned to Jordan, who remained seated forlornly on the bridge, in the gloomy company of the ghost horses, the moat monster, and a stray zombie. "I know why!" she cried.

"Because she hated me and wanted to humiliate me yet again," Jordan mumbled.

"No! Because she truly loved you, Jordan!"

Jordan looked up. "Some love!" he growled.

"Now listen, you dumb barbarian," Ivy told him severely. "You don't know a thing about women!"

"On target," he agreed morosely.

"Threnody knew about Yin and Yang, right? That they were just different sides of the same Magician?"

"She had to know," he said lugubriously.

"So she knew that all the evil that was in Yang was in Yin, too, only it didn't show. Because the whole man is the sum of his parts. If she married Yin, she was marrying Yang, too—and Castle Roogna would fall before she even got to Yin, since she had to return there in order for him to win. And since they were the same Magician, she knew that all those bad spells that were trying to kill you were really from Yin as well as Yang; in fact, maybe Yin mixed up the white spells himself, to be quite sure you'd be killed, without King Gromden knowing why. Because that Magician liked his evil side better, but had to do the contest to get Good King Gromden's approval. So the contest really was fixed, with no way Yin could win. Threnody knew that."

"Yes," Jordan agreed, seeing it. "And she helped them get rid of me. Was that love?"

"Yes! Because she knew Yin-Yang would kill you all the way dead if he realized she loved you. And he was a Magician, a strong one, and he was going to be King no matter how the contest turned out, so no one could stop him. He would burn your body to ashes and scatter them in the sea, or seal them in stones, or something, so there'd be no chance at all for you ever to recover. And because she loved you, she had to pretend she hated you, because he was already suspicious and probably would have killed you anyway; there was a lot of evil in him."

Jordan nodded, becoming interested. "Yin-Yang was evil; surely he had nothing good for me in mind. I was just a tool for his ambition, to be used and thrown away. Even without Threnody, he would have had to get rid of me so no one would know how he cheated. But Threnody didn't have to—to make me love her, then kill me herself!"

"She didn't, not exactly," Ivy said. "She didn't know you before you came for her, and then she tried to kill you, but gradually, as she got to know you, she got to love you, too. She told the truth when she said she loved you. She had never loved any man other than her father before, but you proved to her she was, after all, human. Then she really had to kill you!"

"Huh?" Even the ghost horses and the moat monster and the zombie looked perplexed at this.

Ivy realized that Hugo's clear explanation was getting a bit garbled in translation. She concentrated her mind and tried again. "Actually, it was Yang's evil death-spell that killed you. Then Threnody knew he'd finish the job if she didn't act quickly. So she cut up your body and hid the pieces very carefully to be sure she could find them again. She knew she could bring you back to life—after the Magician had forgotten about you. That's why she told that cruel lie—to save you from real death! She was lying to the Magician when she said she hated you. She told you the truth when she said she loved you."

"I don't know—" Jordan began doubtfully.

"Remember when you were in Threnody's body, holding the evil sword, and you couldn't tell Pook the truth?" Ivy asked. "You lied—to fool the sword, not Pook! Well, Threnody was in a similar situation, because Yin-Yang was more dangerous than that black sword ever had been."

Jordan brightened, then dulled again. "But she never did bring me back."

"Because Yang remained suspicious. Evil people are like that; it's the good people who are too trusting. Yang must have watched her all the time. Renee told you how unhappy her marriage was! It must have been truly terrible—because she really hated the Magician and had to pretend she loved him. Finally she couldn't take it any more. She realized he would never give her a chance to return to you. Not while he lived. Not before she was an old hag. She could do nothing about him, because his Magician's power was much more than hers could ever be, and also, he was the King. The moment she made any motion to dig up your bones, he would have known, and destroyed you both in terrible fashion. So she joined you the only way she could—in death. She loved you enough to die for you. She hadn't known about the ghosts at Castle Roogna."

"Yes..." Jordan said, wishing he could believe. "But why didn't she tell me then?"

"Two reasons. Yin-Yang knew she was dead, but didn't know she had become a ghost; only people with horrendously unresolved problems become ghosts. But when she said anything about her identity, the Magician would recognize her and know it wasn't over and take steps to finish it, if only by digging up your bones and burning them. She couldn't risk that! So, to protect you as a ghost, she lied to you again."

"But Yin-Yang didn't live forever!" Jordan protested. "After he died, she could have told me!"

"No. You hated Threnody for what you thought she had done to you. You would have thought it was just another lie. You were coming to love Renee; if she told you, all that she could expect was that you would hate her—as you did when her identity was revealed just now. She loved you and just wanted your love in return; her name didn't matter to her. So she loved you as Renee, and you loved her, and that was enough. Until you messed it up by returning her to life. And then she couldn't tell you, for the same reason, because you wouldn't listen, so she just went away, heartbroken, and I guess she'll turn herself into a skunk-cabbage or something and wilt away."

"But Renee helped me find my bones!"

"Because she wanted what was best for you, and life was best. If it hadn't been for her, you wouldn't have died before, so she helped give that life back to you. She felt she owed it to you, to make up for the way she had ruined a fine man. She didn't know you would bring her back, too, and didn't know how to handle it. She had expected you to return to life, slowly forget about her, and find someone new. Then she would have done the right thing at last and made up for her cruel lies."

Jordan considered that. "But she really didn't try very hard to convince me."

"What use?" Ivy asked. "Your mind was closed. And she's a proud woman. She wasn't going to beg. She never begged in her life; she just did what she had to. So when you rejected her—"

Jordan was stricken. "True, true! I have wronged her!"

"Well, you didn't know. You're sort of proud, too. But now it's all right. You can go to her!"

Jordan seemed awed. "All that she's done—she did for love of me! Even her cruelest lies! I was too ready to believe in her guilt!"

"Well, so was I," Ivy said. "Until Hugo explained it all to me. But of course, I'm only five years old; I don't understand about romance."

"All those centuries!" Jordan lamented. "What Renee told me is true; she was miserable because she could not marry her true love—who was me! I must beg her forgiveness!" He got up and hurried in the direction Threnody had gone.

Pook started to follow, then decided not to; some scenes were better without audiences. "I guess she'll forgive him," Ivy said with satisfaction. "She can change her form; she can change her mind, too." She looked around. "Oh, I've just got to hug somebody! You!" And she hugged Puck, the little ghost horse. "And you." She hugged Pook, and Peek, and even the nose of the moat monster. "But not you," she decided, encountering the zombie.

She looked toward the orchard; did she see two figures merging behind the trees? She realized that she would not see Jordan again after this day, for Threnody would never enter the castle alive. Not with her curse. She might be demon-spawned, but she had love and conscience and surely a soul, and she didn't want the castle to fall. The happy couple would have to go elsewhere, and that meant Pook and his family would go, too. Ivy knew she would be very sad about that when she got over her present happiness.

"I suppose I'd better tell my folks about why we've lost two ghosts and a dragon and why the castle shook," she said to herself. She didn't relish the prospect, but it was best to get it over with early.

She went inside. Things had settled down somewhat now. Her mother was sitting pensively, while Baby Dolph was fussing in his crib. "What's the matter, Mom?" Ivy asked, willing to postpone the inevitable a little longer.

"He's so restless," Irene said. "I don't know what's the matter. I thought it was because of the earthquake tremor, but that's past now. I'm at my wit's end!"

Ivy studied her little brother. She had resented him from slightly before the moment he arrived at the cabbage, but had never really looked at him. He was an ugly thing, sort of bald and fat and toothless and drooly, and she couldn't see why anyone would want to pay so much attention to him. But the story of Jordan the Ghost and Threnody the Demon-Spawned was fresh in her mind, and she had just had a lesson in prejudice. If Jordan had been ready to believe the truth instead of the cruel lie told to save him—

Suddenly Dolph reminded her of Threnody. It was a completely incongruous impression on the physical side, yet a profound one emotionally. Why did her helpless, roly-poly baby brother remind her of that beautiful woman?

Well, there was one way to find out. Ivy moved closer to the crib and concentrated, enhancing the baby's qualities. "What's his talent?" she asked.

"We don't know, dear," Irene said. "Sometimes it takes years to discover a person's magic talent, and there's no guarantee it will be worthwhile." Irene was really worried about that, Ivy saw. She didn't want any child of hers to have a poor talent.

"He's trying to do his magic," Ivy declared, trusting her little-girl intuition. "But he can't quite do it yet, so he's frustrated." Ivy was something of an expert on frustration.

Irene smiled, not taking her seriously. Adults could be especially annoying that way. "Whatever you say, dear."

Ivy continued her concentration, knowing that something was bound to show. It always did when she willed it so. She was sure there was some reason Dolph reminded her of Threnody, and sure she could make this apparent if she just intensified it enough.

Suddenly there was a wolf cub in the crib. "Say, look at that!" Ivy exclaimed, pleased.

Irene looked—and screamed.

In a moment Daddy King Dor and half the personnel of the castle were in the room. They were all edgy because of the earthquake—maybe it should be left at that?—but it was too late. Startled by the scream, Dolph had changed back into a baby. "Aw, you missed it," Ivy said petulantly. "Dolph's a changer."

Irene calmed down enough to pay attention. "A what?"

"Like Threnody. Only he's fast. He does it in an instant, not an hour. He—"

"Who?"

"Threnody. That's a long story." Ivy looked again at the baby, who was now peacefully sleeping, satisfied with his effort. Dolph no longer looked as disgusting. "Maybe Dolph has demon blood in him."

"Not from *my* side of the family!" Irene snapped.

"I wonder if he can diffuse?" Ivy mused.

"Instant form-changing?" King Dor asked. "If he's a werewolf, that's one thing, a minor talent. If he can change instantly to any form, that's another."

"Oh, sure, it's any form," Ivy said with certainty. "He just needs a little help to get it started. He's only a baby, you know."

Dor picked her up. "I hadn't realized that," he said with a straight face, teasing her in the nice way daddies had. "I thought perhaps he was an adult, like you."

"Oh, shut up, Daddy," she said, kissing him on the cheek.

Irene exchanged a glance with her daughter. "Any form? Changing himself? That's Magician-caliber talent!"

"At least," Ivy agreed. She had discovered it, so now it was to her credit, and the greater the talent was, the better.

After that the discussion became animated, and Ivy was left out of it. But she didn't mind that, either. She could handle a few more days of neglect, until the matter of the ghosts blew over. It might be interesting having a brother who could become any creature in an instant. She could show him how to reach the high cookie jar by changing into a snail and crawling up the wall, so they would never starve between meals. Or how to become a little dragon, and breathe fire to toast marshmallows and give people hotfoots. The possibilities were endless!

Yes, life was bound to get more interesting soon.

Author's Note

In the last Xanth novel, *Dragon on a Pedestal*, I used a number of puns contributed by fans, listing the credits at the end, and suggested that this was punnishment enough. But before that novel was published, fans had sent many more puns. Some sent whole pages of them—a veritable Pundora's Box. I used about fifty of those suggestions and give due credit here. But this resulted in such a concentration of puns in the first chapter that the publisher suffered pundigestion. You see, I have many young readers, who write to me in much greater numbers than the older ones do, but they are really not the largest audience for Xanth. Despite appearances, Xanth is intended mostly for adults, which may be why the kids like it. The question was whether that plethora of puns would alienate more people than it pleased. So—that chapter was deleted, because it isn't good form to annoy more readers than strictly necessary, even in Xanth. The present version of the novel begins with what was originally Chapter 2.

But for those of you who can't live without knowing what was in it, here is a summary of the missing chapter. On the eve of her baby brother's arrival, Ivy went to visit her Grandfather Trent, along with Grundy and Stanley. She got them all into enormous mischief, but the timely arrival of a package from her pun-pal Rapunzel helped them survive it, along with Tangleman, who is a tangle tree transformed into a man.

Now, though most of these puns have been deleted, I'm leaving their credits as originally listed so you folk who sent them in will know they really were there. This may seem peculiar—but what did you expect from Xanth? And those of you who remain out there, bursting with puns—stifle them, because there's only so much of this nonsense anyone can take. By the time *Lye* burns into print, I should have completed the following Xanth novel, and plans are inchoate beyond that, so any puns you might send are apt to be wasted anyway.

Are you ready? Here are the credits, real and potential, for *Lye*, and if there is some overlap, it is because a given pun may have been suggested by more than one person. David Branson suggested deadstock, pun-pal, crab-grass, fris-bees, demon-stration (which I modified for my own sinister purpose), baseball bat, the night mare being out of her gourd, air waves, outcry, and worry wart. Andrea DeSimone and Laura T. Maberry collaborated to suggest sound of mind, shadow of a doubt, clinging vines, cat o' nine tails, scaredy cat, dumb bells, screaming meanies, copperhead snake, snake-eyes, and kitty hawk. Martin Musick suggested the dark lantern, kitty hawk, headstone, bear witness, and worry wart. As you can see, I used three of his in a bunch, and there's a reason. I had a request from a fan who was organizing a Dungeons and Dragons type game using a Xanth setting: could I provide some challenges for entry into the Good Magician's castle that hadn't already been published, since all the game-players had read all the Xanths already? So I listed the ones used in *Dragon*, which had not yet been published, and then sat down and made notes for the equivalent scene in *Lye*, which novel I hadn't even started. I have never-failing inspiration, which makes me virtually unique among writers, but this was a strain. So I checked Mr. Musick's list of about ten notions, selected three, and built my scene around them; then I sent off the information to the fan and later wrote that scene when I came to it in the novel. I hope they had a successful D&D game; I never heard. Most fan-puns I include as a courtesy; in this case, they were a real help.

But back to work here. Greg Burns suggested the gold fish, silver fish, hedge hog, hem lock, horsetail, horse chestnut, honey comb, and golden rod. Dave Schwartz had the living room; David Miles the seeing-eye dogwood tree; Katherine A. Lowe the bum steer; and Bryce Cockson suggested the catch-your-breath. Karen Vinyard suggested that a girl be turned into a tree to be a companion for Justin Tree; I thought it was a good idea, but didn't manage to fit it in this time. Diane Le Roux inquired why Justin Tree didn't become a man again in the Time of No Magic, so that is explained here. She also asked a number of awkward questions about the centaurs' aging rate—obviously it is the same as the rate for human beings, contrary to what Bink believed in Xanth 1—and how come the Siren could look at the Gorgon in Xanth 2 and not in Xanth 6? Well, I think that when the Gorgon was young, she only stoned male creatures, but when she matured, so did her talent, so she stoned everyone. After all, we don't want any sexism here; everyone should suffer alike. And other awkward questions that, um—look, Diane, I'm awfully busy at the moment, trying to type a manuscript, so if you'll just go on to the next author in line and ask him or her some awkward questions instead, that's a good girl . . .

Michael Saul, also focusing on the Gorgon, asks how Dor could see her wink, in Xanth 3, when her face was invisible. Ah, Michael, see that line over there that Diane is standing in? Just take your place behind her, and don't shove. (And I think I'd better wrap this up and get out of here before those fans reach the head of that next line and spring those questions on that next author. I wonder who he is? Let's see, if it's alphabetical . . . that must be Poul Anderson of the Society for Creative Anachronisms—you know, the folk who dress up in armor and authentic medieval swords. Yes, I'd definitely better get out of here!) (Then again, maybe I should shunt those fans to the author on the other side. That looks like Isaac Asimov, whose *Foundation's Edge* is, at this writing, just about to blast Xanth 7 off the bestseller lists. But his line is so long that my fans will never reach the head of it. Well, now...)

Terry Cook suggested that King Trent turn a tangle tree into a person. Keith Helgason suggested both Ivy's talent and Dolph's talent, after I had worked them out myself, but before the novels were published; evidently great minds work in similar ways. Richard Ralls suggested the leather-strip body armor for the warrior; that's not a pun but a useful device. Penny Jacob suggested the dirty mind, after analyzing her father's nature. Charles Cohen suggested that I include elves in Xanth, and it did seem to be about time for them. Chris McVetta described the contact lens bush. Ginger Gibson suggested Xantha Claus. I regret I was not imaginative enough to fit him in here, but what do you expect from someone named Pier Xanthony? And perhaps I should catch up on an overdue credit: I borrowed the name of a fan in Estonia, Martin Roogna, to use for Castle Roogna, way back when. Mr. Roogna says he's not sure he has ancestry quite like that, but who knows?

So much for the credits; let me ramble on just a bit more before I meander off to my next novel. Xanth has been quite successful as a series, making all the bestseller lists. It seems that ninety-nine percent of its readers love it; the other one percent review it, accusing me of things like reveling in sexism and execrable puns. However, *Patchen Review* did say: "Hostility from serious reviewers to Anthony is out of all proportion; perhaps it stems more from jealousy than lit crit." I do work hard at what I do; a storm came up and splattered water through the cracks in my study while I was typing *Lye*, so I had to prop an umbrella over my desk to keep the page dry, rather than interrupt my schedule. That happened to be the scene in which Jordan is recovering from getting stoned. No, I never get stoned myself, pun or no pun, and that's no lie; I don't believe in zonking out my mind for anything short of a medical emergency.

I've been writing about fifty letters a month, mostly answering Xanth fan mail, and that interferes with my paying writing, so I'd like to cut it down. Let me address here some of the questions my fans commonly ask me, so you won't have to write to inquire. Such as:

What other books are similar to Xanth? Well, none, really; I seem to have the execrable pun fantasy market to myself. But though I have not read Asprin's Myth series, I have met the author and understand his puns are almost as bad as mine, so you might try his *Myth Conceptions* or others and see for yourself. There's also quite a bit of humor in Adams' *Hitchhiker's Guide* series. If you like candy landscapes and are truly young at heart— in the four- to eight-year-old range, I'd say—try Gruelle's *Raggedy Ann* series. Moving up from there, Baum's *Oz* books are good, and Alexander's *Chronicles of Prydain*. Eddings' *Belgariad* seems closest in tone and competence to Xanth, but without the puns; you should like it. Then there is Hambly's *Darwath* trilogy, and McCaffrey's *Pern* series. My daughter Cheryl also recommends the *Doctor Who* books; I don't, but Cheryl is thirteen and I'm forty-nine, so she may know better than I do. After that you're ready for the hard stuff; you can safely sample anything put out by this publisher, and proceed with caution to the offerings of other publishers. Along the way, do try the *Elfquest* comics by the Pini couple; there seems to be a fair overlap in readers between Xanth and the Elves, and these are not cheap or inferior offerings.

Why don't I write more novels featuring Dor and Irene as teenagers, or King Trent, or Bink, or the centaurs, etc.? Every fan seems to have his favorite character and would like to see a series of novels centering on that one, forever unchanging. I refuse to do this, because in Xanth, as in Mundania, life is not a static thing. It keeps moving into new territory. I'm not a formula writer; I like each story to be different and original within the limits of the larger framework. So new characters constantly appear, and old ones gracefully fade out. That's just the way it has to be, folks. Xanth has a few constants, such as the geography, the puns, the magic, and the struggle to get into the Good Magician's castle; usually there is a serious romance, and the conception, organization, and literacy are better than the critics choose to perceive. Beyond that, anything can happen.

"Dear Mr. Anthony, I'm 13 years old and I want to become a writer..." This is a direct quote from a letter I received today, as I was typing this Author's Note, and it is typical of a number of requests I receive. A high percentage of my fans want to be writers, so they ask me for advice. That's sensible, and I'm not disparaging this approach, but it's a hellish thing to answer. I'll try to digest it into a nutshell. First, catch your rabbit. That is, read a lot, become familiar with your subject, learn your syntax and spelling, and LEARN TO TYPE. Editors are a peculiar breed; they don't know how to read a hand-written manuscript. Go to the library and read a good book on the subject of writing, such as one by Jack Wood-ford, and pay attention to what it says. Then write, re-write, re-rewrite, and revise until it's the best you can do. Get a copy of *Writer's Market* or similar, find several good prospects, and ship your manuscript to the one that appeals to you most. In the genres of fantasy and science fiction, Del Rey Books will consider your manuscript.

Good luck, you fool; the odds are still a hundred to one against you. It took me eight years of trying to make my first sale, and I was twenty-eight years old at the time. If you are better than I am, you may do it faster. If your interest is easy money, be advised that the average writer's earnings from writing put him somewhere below the poverty level; even if you are successful, you will probably be lean and hungry. (Now do you see why I don't like to answer this question? I really don't like reducing thirteen-year-old girls to tears, and no part of this is a joke.) Oh, sure—*I'm* not starving, any more. But I got lucky. You can count on the fingers of one foot the contemporary fantasy writers who are more successful than I am. But it did take time and luck.

This leads into my most important advice: make sure

you have some other source of money while you're trying to write, such as a working spouse, so that you *don't* starve. My wife worked for several years before and after I made my first sale; otherwise I could not have done it. Even so, it was a narrow squeak. Talent, if you have it, is only one of a number of requirements for eventual success; you have to be ready to absorb a fair amount of grief along the way.

Another typical question: will I autograph thirty-five copies of my books if they are sent to me? Sigh; I'd really rather not. Even one book is a chore to handle and reship and costs me more in working time than the book is worth. I prefer to have my readers understand what I'm saying, rather than to dote on a confounded signature scrawl. I'll sign copies at conventions (lots of luck; as a rule, I don't attend conventions) and bookstores; otherwise, please leave me alone.

Will I dedicate a book to a fan? No; There are simply too many fans. But I am dedicating this paragraph to Alan Carpenter and his sister Karen.

And finally: Will there be another Xanth novel, and what's it all about? Yes, there will be; more puns are already piling in for it, the pesky things. It's titled *Golem in the Gears*, and it's about Grundy the Golem, who rides the monster under the bed on his quest to find the little lost dragon for Ivy, and how he finds true love and laughter with the lovely, lonely, long-locked Rapunzel, the distant descendant of Jordan the Barbarian and Bluebell Elf. Stop! Stop! I'll never get the thing written if sanity doesn't return soon!

About the Author

Piers Anthony lives near the North Village of Xanth. He and his wife, Carol, recently arranged to buy part of the Gap Chasm, but hostile magic intervened, and long-forgotten mundane reversion clauses interfered with all but a fragment of it. His daughter Penny still rides the night mare, but his daughter Cheryl now associates with elves instead of ogres.

Crewel Lye is the eighth Xanth novel smuggled into Mundania. The first one, *A Spell for Chameleon*, won the August Derleth Fantasy Award as the best novel for the year 1977. The fifth, sixth, and seventh Xanth novels made the *New York Times* bestseller list, the last also peaking at number one on both the B. Dalton and Waldenbooks bestseller lists. Of course no one in Xanth pays attention to such things, but Mundania is a strange place.